THE JUDGE'S LIST

JOHN
GRISHAM

=====

THE
JUDGE'S
LIST

RANDOM HOUSE
LARGE PRINT

Copyright © 2021 by Belfry Holdings, Inc.

Published in the United States of America by Random House Large Print in association with Doubleday, a division of Penguin Random House LLC, New York.

Cover photograph: person © Christoph Hetzmannseder / Moment / Getty; landscape © Captureworx / Millennium Images, U.K.
Cover design by John Fontana

The Library of Congress has established a Cataloging-in-Publication record for this title.

ISBN: 978-0-593-16853-0

www.penguinrandomhouse.com/large-print-format-books

FIRST LARGE PRINT EDITION

Printed in the United States of America

10 9 8 7 6 5 4 3 2 1

This Large Print edition published in accord with the standards of the N.A.V.H.

THE JUDGE'S LIST

1

The call came through the office landline, through a system that was at least twenty years old and had fought off all technological advances. It was taken by a tattooed receptionist named Felicity, a new girl who would be gone before she fully understood the phones. They were all leaving, it seemed, especially the clerical help. Turnover was ridiculous. Morale was low. The Board on Judicial Conduct had just seen its budget chopped for the fourth straight year by a legislature that hardly knew it existed.

Felicity managed to route the call down the hall to the cluttered desk of Lacy Stoltz. "There's a call on line three," she announced.

"Who is it?" Lacy asked.

"She wouldn't say."

There were so many ways to respond. At that moment, though, Lacy was bored, and she did not wish to waste the emotional energy necessary to properly chastise the kid and set her straight. Routines and protocols were crumbling. Office discipline was waning as BJC spiraled into a leaderless mess.

As a veteran, **the** veteran, it was important to set an example. "Thanks," she said and punched the blinking light. "Lacy Stoltz."

"Good afternoon, Ms. Stoltz. Do you have a moment?"

Female, educated, no hint of an accent, mid-forties, give or take three years. Lacy always played the voice game. "And to whom do I have the pleasure?"

"My name is Margie for now, but I use other ones."

Lacy was amused and almost chuckled. "Well, at least you're up front about it. It normally takes me some time to work through the aliases."

Anonymous callers were routine. People with gripes about judges were always cautious and hesitant to come forward and take on the system. Almost all feared retaliation from the powers on high.

Margie said, "I'd like to talk to you, somewhere private."

"My office is private, if you'd like."

"Oh no," she snapped, apparently frightened at the thought. "That won't work. You know the Siler Building, next door?"

"Of course," Lacy said as she stood and looked out her window at the Siler Building, one of several nondescript government addresses in downtown Tallahassee.

Margie said, "There's a coffee bar on the ground floor. Can we meet there?"

"I suppose. When?"

"Now. I'm on my second latte."

"Slow down. Give me a few minutes. And you'll recognize me?"

"Yes. You're on the website. I'm in the rear, left side."

Lacy's office was indeed private. The one to her left was empty, vacated by an ex-colleague who'd moved on to a bigger agency. Across the hall an office had been converted into a makeshift storage closet. She walked toward Felicity and ducked into the office of Darren Trope, a two-year man already prowling for another job.

"You busy?" she asked as she interrupted whatever he was doing.

"Not really." It didn't matter what he was or was not doing. If Lacy needed anything, Darren belonged to her.

"Need a favor. I'm stepping over to Siler to meet a stranger who just admitted that she is using a fake name."

"Oh, I love the cloak-and-dagger. Sure beats sitting here reading about some judge who made lewd comments to a witness."

"How lewd?"

"Pretty graphic."

"Any photos, videos?"

"Not yet."

"Let me know if you get them. So, mind stepping over in fifteen minutes and taking a picture?"

"Sure. No problem. No idea who she is?"

"None whatsoever."

Lacy left the building, took her time walking around the block, enjoyed a moment of cool air, and strolled into the lobby of the Siler Building. It was almost 4:00 p.m. and there were no other customers drinking coffee at that hour. Margie was at a small table in the rear, to the left. She waved quickly as though someone might notice and she didn't want to get caught. Lacy smiled and walked toward her.

African American, mid-forties, professional, attractive, educated, slacks and heels and dressed nicer than Lacy, though around BJC these days any and all attire was allowed. The old boss wanted coats and ties and hated jeans, but he had retired two years ago and took most of the rules with him.

Lacy passed the counter where the barista was loafing with both elbows stuck on the Formica, hands cradling her pink phone that had her thoroughly fascinated. She did not look up, never thought about greeting a customer, and Lacy decided to pass on more caffeine anyway.

Without standing, Margie stuck out a hand and said, "Nice to meet you. Would you like some coffee?"

Lacy smiled, shook her hand, and sat across the square table. "No thanks. And it's Margie, right?"

"For now."

"Okay, we're off to a bad start. Why are you using an alias?"

"My story will take hours to tell and I'm not sure you want to hear it."

"Then why bother?"

"Please, Ms. Stoltz."

"Lacy."

"Please, Lacy. You have no idea the emotional trauma I've been through trying to get to this point in my life. I'm a wreck right now, okay?"

She seemed fine, though a bit on edge. Perhaps it was the second latte. Her eyes darted right and left. They were pretty and surrounded by large purple frames. The lenses were probably not needed. The glasses were part of the outfit, a subtle disguise.

Lacy said, "I'm not sure what to say. Why don't you start talking and maybe we'll get somewhere?"

"I've read about you." She reached down into a backpack and deftly pulled out a file. "The Indian casino case, not long ago. You caught a judge skimming and put her away. One reporter described it as the largest bribery scandal in the history of American jurisprudence." The file was two inches thick and gave every impression of being immaculately organized.

Lacy noted the use of the word "jurisprudence." Odd for a layperson.

"It was a big case," she said, feigning modesty.

Margie smiled and said, "Big? You broke up a crime syndicate, nailed the judge, and sent a bunch of people to prison. All are still there, I believe."

"True, but it was far from a one-girl takedown. The FBI was heavily involved. It was a complicated case and some people were killed."

"Including your colleague, Mr. Hugo Hatch."

"Yes, including Hugo. Curious. Why all of this research about me?"

Margie folded her hands and rested them on top of the file, which she had not opened. Her index fingers were shaking slightly. She looked at the entrance and glanced around again, though no one had entered, no one had left, no one had moved, not even the barista who was lost in the clouds. She took a sip from her straw. If it really was her second latte, it had barely been touched. She had used the word "trauma." Admitted to being a "wreck." Lacy realized the woman was frightened.

Margie said, "Oh, I'm not sure it's research. Just some stuff off the Internet. Everything's out there, you know."

Lacy smiled and tried to be patient. "I'm not sure we're getting anywhere."

"Your job is to investigate judges who are accused of wrongdoing, right?"

"That's correct."

"And you've been doing it for how long?"

"I'm sorry. Why is this relevant?"

"Please."

"Twelve years." Giving that number was like admitting defeat. It sounded so long.

"How do you get involved in a case?" Margie asked, bouncing around.

Lacy took a deep breath and reminded herself to be patient. People with complaints who got this far were often rattled. She smiled and said, "Well, typically a person with a complaint against a judge will contact us and we'll have a meeting. If the gripe appears to have some merit, then the person will file a formal complaint, which we keep locked up for forty-five days while we take a look. We call it an assessment. Nine times out of ten that's as far as it gets and the complaint is dismissed. If we find possible wrongdoing, then we notify the judge and he or she has thirty days to respond. Usually, everybody lawyers up. We investigate, have hearings, bring in witnesses, the works."

As she spoke, Darren strolled in alone, disturbed the barista by ordering decaf, waited on it while ignoring the two women, then took it to a table on the other side of the room where he opened a laptop and began what appeared to be some serious work. Without giving the slightest hint, he aimed the laptop's camera at Lacy's back and Margie's face, zoomed in for a close shot, and began filming. He took a video and some still shots.

If Margie noticed him it was not apparent.

She listened intently to Lacy and asked, "How often is a judge removed from office?"

Again, why is this relevant? "Not very often, fortunately. We have jurisdiction over one thousand judges and the vast majority are honest, hardworking professionals. Most of the complaints we see are just not that serious. Disgruntled litigants who didn't get what they wanted. A lot of divorce cases. A lot of lawyers mad because they lost. We stay busy, but for the most part the conflicts are resolved."

She made the job sound boring, and, after twelve years, it rather felt that way.

Margie listened carefully, her fingertips tapping the file. She took a deep breath and asked, "The person who files the complaint, is he or she always identified?"

Lacy thought for a second and said, "Eventually, yes. It's quite rare for the complaining party to remain anonymous."

"Why?"

"Because the complainant usually knows the facts of the case and needs to testify against the judge. It's hard to nail a judge when the people he ticked off are afraid to come forward. Are you afraid?"

The very word seemed to frighten her. "Yes, you could say that," she admitted.

Lacy frowned and appeared bored. "Look, let's cut to the chase here. How serious is the behavior that you're talking about?"

Margie closed her eyes and managed to say, "Murder."

She immediately opened them and glanced around to see if anyone had overheard. There was no one close enough to hear anything except Lacy, who absorbed this with the hard-boiled skepticism she had developed after so many years on the job. She reminded herself again to be patient. When she looked at Margie's eyes again they were wet.

Lacy leaned in a bit closer and softly asked, "Are you suggesting that one of our sitting judges has committed a murder?"

Margie bit her lip and shook her head. "I know he has."

"May I ask how you know this?"

"My father was one of his victims."

Lacy inhaled this and glanced around herself. "Victims? As in more than one?"

"Yes. I believe my father was his second victim. I'm not sure which number, but I'm certain of his guilt."

"Interesting."

"That's an understatement. How many complaints have you had about judges killing people?"

"Well, none."

"Exactly. In the history of America, how many judges have been convicted of murder while on the bench?"

"I've never heard of one."

"Exactly. Zero. So don't dismiss this as something 'interesting.'"

"Didn't mean to offend."

Across the way, Darren finished his important business and left. Neither woman acknowledged his departure.

Margie said, "No offense taken. I'm not going any further in this coffee bar. I have a lot of information that I would like to share with you and no one else, but not here."

Lacy had encountered her share of nuts and unbalanced souls with boxes and paper sacks filled with documents that clearly proved that some sleazeball up on the bench was thoroughly corrupt. Almost always, after a few minutes of face-to-face interaction, she could reach her verdict and began making plans to route the complaint to the dismissal drawer. Over the years she had learned to read people, though with many of the wackos that came her way a quick evaluation wasn't much of a challenge.

Margie, or whoever, was neither a nut nor a

wacko, nor an unbalanced soul. She was onto something and she was frightened.

Lacy said, "Okay. Where do we go next?"

"What is next?"

"Look, you contacted me. Do you want to talk or not? I don't play games and I don't have time to pry information out of you or any other person who wants to complain about a judge. I waste a lot of time cajoling information out of people who call me in the first place. I go down a dead-end trail once a month. Are you talking or not?"

Margie was crying again and wiping her cheeks. Lacy studied her with as much compassion as possible, but she was also willing to leave the table and never come back.

However, she was intrigued by the idea of murder. Part of her daily grind around BJC was suffering through the mundane and frivolous gripes of unhappy people with small problems and little to lose. A murder by a sitting judge seemed too sensational to believe.

Finally, Margie said, "I have a room at the Ramada on East Gaines. We could meet there after hours. But you have to come alone."

Lacy nodded as if she'd anticipated this. "With precautions. We have a rule that prohibits me from conducting an initial meeting with a complaining party off premises and alone. I would have to bring another investigator, one of my colleagues."

"Like Mr. Trope over there?" Margie asked, nodding at Darren's empty chair.

Lacy slowly turned around to see what in the world she was talking about as she tried desperately to think of a response.

Margie continued, "It's your website, okay? Smiling faces of all staff." From her briefcase she removed an 8×10 color photo of herself and slid it across the table. "Here, with best wishes, a current color mug of myself that's far better than the ones Mr. Trope just stole."

"What are you talking about?"

"I'm sure he's already run my pic through your facial recognition software and he's found nothing. I'm in nobody's data bank."

"What are you talking about?" Margie was dead-on but Lacy was rattled and not ready to come clean.

"Oh, I think you know. You come alone or you'll never see me again. You're the most experienced investigator in your office and at this moment your boss is only a temp. You can probably do whatever you want."

"I wish it were that easy."

"Let's call it an after-work drink, that's all. We'll meet in the bar and if it goes well we can go upstairs to my room and talk with even more privacy."

"I cannot go to your room. It's against our procedures. If a complaint is filed and it becomes necessary to meet in private, then I can do so. Someone has to know where I am, at least initially."

"Fair enough. What time?"

"How about six?"

"I'll be in the back corner, right-hand side, and I'll be alone, same as you. No wires, recorders, secret cameras, no colleagues pretending to drink as they film away. And say hello to Darren. Maybe one day I'll have the pleasure. Deal?"

"Deal."

"Okay. You can go now."

As Lacy walked around the block and drifted back to her office, she had to admit that she could not remember ever getting her butt so thoroughly kicked at the first interview.

She slid the color photo across Darren's desk and said, "Nice work. Busted big-time. She knows our names, ranks, and serial numbers. She gave me this photo and said it was far better than the ones you were taking with your laptop."

Darren held the photo and said, "Well, she's right."

"Any idea who she is?"

"Nope. I've run her face through our laundry and got nothing. Which, as you know, means little."

"Means she has not been arrested in Florida in the past six years. Can you punch it through the FBI?"

"Probably not. They require a reason, and since

I know nothing I can't give them one. Can I ask an obvious question?"

"Please do."

"BJC is an investigative agency, right?"

"Supposed to be."

"Then why do we post our photos and bios on a rather stupid website?"

"Ask the boss."

"We don't have a boss. We have a career paper-pusher who'll be gone before we miss her."

"Probably. Look, Darren, we've had this conversation a dozen times. We don't want our lovely faces on any BJC page. That's why I haven't updated mine in five years. I still look thirty-four."

"I'd say thirty-one, but then I'm biased."

"Thank you."

"I guess there's no real harm. It's not like we're going after murderers and drug dealers."

"Right."

"So what's her complaint, whoever she is?"

"Don't know yet. Thanks for the backup."

"A lot of good it did."

2

The Ramada lounge covered one large corner of the hotel's soaring glass atrium. By six, its chrome bar was crowded with well-dressed lobbyists trolling for attractive secretaries from the agencies, and most of the tables were taken. The Florida legislature was in session five blocks away at the Capitol, and all the downtown lounges were busy with important people talking politics and angling for money and sex.

Lacy entered, got her share of looks from the male crowd, and walked toward the right rear where she found Margie alone at a small table in a corner with a glass of water in front of her. "Thanks for coming," she said as Lacy took a seat.

"Sure. You know this place?"

"No. First time. Pretty popular, huh?"

"This time of the year, yes. Things settle down when the carnival is over."

"The carnival?"

"The legislative session. January through March. Lock the liquor cabinet. Hide the women and children. You know the routine."

"I'm sorry."

"I take it you don't live here."

"No, I don't."

A harried waitress rushed to a stop and asked if they wanted something to drink as she frowned at the glass of water. Her message was pretty clear: Hey gals, we're busy and I can give your table to somebody who'll pay for booze.

"A glass of pinot grigio," Lacy said.

"Same," Margie quickly agreed, and the waitress was gone.

Lacy glanced right and left to make sure whatever they said could not be overheard. It could not. The tables were spaced far enough apart, and a steady roar emanated from the bar and drowned out everything else.

Lacy said, "Okay. So you don't live here and I don't know your real name. I'd say we're off to a slow start, which I'm accustomed to. However, as I think I told you, I waste a lot of time with people who contact me then clam up when it's time to tell their stories."

"What would you like to know first?"

"How about your name?"

"I can do that."

"Great."

"But I'd like to know what you'll do with my name. Do you open a file? Is it a digital file or an old-fashioned pen-on-paper file? If it's digital where is it stored? Who else will know my name?"

Lacy swallowed hard and studied her eyes. Margie could not hold the stare and glanced away.

Lacy asked, "You're nervous and act as though you're being followed."

"I'm not being followed, Lacy, but everything leaves a trail."

"A trail for someone else to follow. Is this someone the judge you suspect of murder? Help me here, Margie. Give me something."

"Everything leaves a trail."

"You've said that."

The waitress hustled by, pausing just long enough to set down two glasses of wine and a bowl of nuts.

Margie appeared not to notice the wine but Lacy took a sip. She said, "So, we're still stuck on the name thing. I'll write it down somewhere and keep it off our network, initially."

Margie nodded and became someone else. "Jeri Crosby, age forty-six, professor of political science at the University of South Alabama in Mobile. One marriage, one divorce, one child, a daughter."

"Thank you. And you believe your father was murdered by a judge who's now on the bench. Correct?"

"Yes, a Florida judge."

"That narrows it down to about a thousand."

"A circuit judge in the Twenty-Second District."

"Impressive. Now we're down to about forty. When do I get the name of your suspect?"

"Real soon. Can we slow down a bit? Right now it doesn't take much to rattle me."

"You haven't touched your wine. It might help."

Jeri took a sip and a deep breath and said, "I'm guessing you're around forty years old."

"Almost. Thirty-nine, so I'll turn forty soon enough. Traumatic?"

"Well, sort of, I guess. But life goes on. So, twenty-two years ago you were still in high school, right?"

"I suppose. Why is this relevant?"

"Relax, Lacy, I'm talking now, okay? We're getting somewhere. You were just a kid and you probably never read about the murder of Bryan Burke, a retired professor of law."

"Never heard of it. Your father?"

"Yes."

"I'm sorry."

"Thanks. For almost thirty years my father taught at Stetson Law School in Gulfport, Florida. In the Tampa area."

"I'm familiar with the school."

"He retired at the age of sixty, for family reasons, and returned to his hometown in South Carolina. I have a thorough file on my father which I'll give you at some point. He was quite a man.

Needless to say, his murder rocked our world and, frankly, I'm still reeling. Losing a parent too young is bad enough, but when it's murder, and an unsolved murder, it's even more devastating. Twenty-two years later the case is even colder and the police have all but given up. Once we realized that they were getting nowhere, I vowed to try everything to find his killer."

"The police gave up?"

She drank some wine. "Over time, yes. The file is still open and I talk to them occasionally. I'm not knocking the cops, you understand? They did the best they could under the circumstances, but it was a perfect murder. All of them are."

Lacy drank some wine. "A perfect murder?"

"Yes. No witnesses. No forensics, or least none that can be traced to the killer. No apparent motive."

Lacy almost asked: **And so what am I supposed to do?**

But she took another sip and said, "I'm not sure the Board on Judicial Conduct is equipped to investigate an old murder case in South Carolina."

"I'm not asking for that. Your jurisdiction is over Florida judges who might be involved in wrong-doing, right?"

"Right."

"And that includes murder?"

"I suppose, but we've never been involved in that. That's heavier work for the state boys, maybe the FBI."

"The state boys have tried. The FBI has no interest for two reasons. First, there is no federal issue. Second, there is no evidence linking the murders, thus the FBI doesn't know, no one knows but me I guess, that we're dealing with a potential serial killer."

"You've contacted the FBI?"

"Years ago. As the family of the victim we were desperate for help. Got nowhere."

Lacy drank some more wine. "Okay, you're making me nervous, so let's walk through this real slow. You believe a sitting judge murdered your father twenty-two years ago. Was that judge on the bench when the murder occurred?"

"No. He was elected in 2004."

Lacy absorbed this and looked around. What appeared to be a lobbyist was now sitting at the next table, gawking at her with a sort of leering vulgarity that was not uncommon around the Capitol. She glared at him until he looked away, then leaned in closer. "I'd feel more comfortable if we could talk somewhere else. This place is getting crowded."

Jeri said, "I have a small conference room on the first floor. I promise it's safe and secure. If I try to assault you, you can scream and get away."

"I'm sure it's okay."

Jeri paid for the wine and they left the bar and the atrium and rode the escalator up one flight to the business mezzanine, where Jeri unlocked a small conference room, one of many. On the table were several files.

The women settled on opposite sides of the table, the files within reaching distance and nothing in front of them. No laptops. No legal pads. Both cell phones were still in their purses. Jeri was visibly more relaxed than in the bar, and began with "So, let's talk off the record, with no notes. None for now anyway. My father, Bryan Burke, retired from Stetson in 1990. He'd taught there for almost thirty years and was a legend, a beloved professor. He and my mother decided to return home to Gaffney, South Carolina, the small town where they grew up. They had lots of family in the area and there's some land that had been handed down. They built this beautiful little cottage in the woods and planted a garden. My mother's mother lived on the property and they took care of her. All in all, it was a pleasant retirement. They were set financially, in pretty good health, active in a country church. Dad read a lot, wrote articles for legal magazines, kept up with old friends, made some new ones around town. Then, he was murdered."

She reached to retrieve a file, a blue one, letter-sized, about an inch thick, same as the others. She slid it across the table as she said, "This is a collection of articles about my father, his career, and his death. Some dug up by hand, some pulled from the Internet, but none of the file is stored online."

Lacy didn't open the file.

Jeri continued, "Behind the yellow tab there is a crime scene photo of my father. I've seen it several times and prefer not to see it again. Have a look."

Lacy opened to the tab and frowned at the enlarged color photo. The deceased was lying in some weeds with a small rope around his neck, pulled tightly and cutting into his skin. The rope appeared to be nylon, blue in color, and stained with dried blood. At the back of the neck it was secured with a thick knot.

Lacy closed the file and whispered, "I'm so sorry."

"It's weird. After twenty-two years, you learn to deal with the pain and place it in a box where it tends to stay if you work hard enough. But it's always easy to drop your guard and allow the memories to come back. Right now I'm okay, Lacy. Right now I'm real good because I'm talking to you and doing something about it. You have no idea how many hours I've spent pushing myself to get here. This is so hard, so terrifying."

"Perhaps if we talked about the crime."

She took a deep breath. "Sure. Dad liked to take long walks through the woods behind his cottage. Mom often went along but she struggled with arthritis. One lovely spring morning in 1992 he kissed her goodbye, grabbed his walking stick, and headed down the trail. The autopsy revealed death by asphyxiation, but there was also a head wound.

It wasn't hard to speculate that he encountered someone who hit him in the head, knocked him out, then finished him off with the nylon rope. He was dragged off the trail and left in a ravine, where they found him late in the afternoon. The crime scene revealed nothing—no blunt instrument, no shoe or boot prints—the ground was dry. No signs of a struggle, no stray hairs or fabrics left behind. Nothing. The rope has been analyzed by crime labs and gives no clue. There's a description of it in the file. The cottage isn't far from town but it's still somewhat isolated, and there were no witnesses, nothing out of the ordinary. No car or truck with out-of-state tags. No strangers lurking around. There are many different places to park and hide and sneak into the area, then leave without a trace. Nothing has come to the surface in twenty-two years, Lacy. It's a very cold case. We have accepted the harsh reality that the crime will never be solved."

"We?"

"Yes, well, but it's more like a one-cowboy rodeo. My mother died two years after my father. She never recovered and kinda went off the deep end. I have an older brother in California and he hung in for a few years before losing interest. He got tired of the police reporting no progress. We talk occasionally but rarely mention Dad. So, I'm on my own. It's lonely out here."

"Sounds awful. It also seems a long way from

the crime scene in South Carolina to a courthouse in the Florida Panhandle. What's the connection?"

"There's not much, honestly. Just a lot of speculation."

"You haven't come this far with nothing but speculation. What about motive?"

"Motive is all I have."

"Do you plan to share it with me?"

"Hang on, Lacy. You have no idea. I can't believe I'm sitting here accusing someone of murder, without proof."

"You're not accusing anyone, Jeri. You have a potential suspect, otherwise you wouldn't be here. You tell me his name and I tell no one. Not until you authorize it, okay? Understood?"

"Yes."

"Now, back to motive."

"Motive has consumed me since the beginning. I've found no one in my father's world who disliked him. He was an academic who drew a nice salary and saved his money. He never invested in deals or land or anything like that. In fact, he was disdainful of developers and speculators. He had a couple of colleagues, other law professors, who lost money in the stock market and condos and other schemes, and he had little sympathy for them. He had no business interests, no partners, no joint ventures, stuff that generally creates conflict and enemies. He hated debt and paid his bills on time. He was faithful to his wife and family, as far as we knew. If you knew Bryan Burke you would have found it impossible to believe that he would be unfaithful to his wife. He was treated fairly by his employers, Stetson, and admired by his students. Four times in thirty years at Stetson he was voted Outstanding Professor of Law. He routinely passed up a promotion to the dean's office because he considered teaching the highest calling and he wanted to be in the classroom. He wasn't perfect, Lacy, but he was pretty damned close to it."

"I wish I had known him."

"He was a charming, sweet man with no known enemies. It wasn't a robbery, because his wallet was in the house and nothing was missing from his body. It certainly wasn't an accident. So, the police have been baffled from the beginning."

"But."

"But. There could be more. It's a long shot but it's all I have. I'm thirsty. You?"

Lacy shook her head. Jeri walked to a credenza, poured ice water from a pitcher, and returned to her seat. She took a deep breath and continued. "As I've said, my father loved the classroom. He loved to lecture. To him it was a performance, and he was the only actor onstage. He loved being in full command of his surroundings, his material, and, especially, his students. There's a room on the second floor of the law school that was his domain for decades. There's a plaque there now and it's named for him. It's a mini lecture hall with eighty seats in a half moon, and every performance was sold out. His lectures on constitutional law were captivating, challenging, often funny. He had a great sense of humor. Every student wanted Professor Burke—he hated being called Dr. Burke—for constitutional law, and those who didn't make the cut often audited the class and sat through his lectures. It was not unusual for visiting professors, deans, alumni, and former students to squeeze in for a seat, often in folding chairs in the rear or down the aisles. The president of the university, himself a lawyer, was a frequent visitor. You get the picture?"

"I do, and I can't imagine it. I can recall, with horror, my con law course."

"That seems to be the norm. The eighty students, all first year, who were lucky enough to get in, knew that he could be tough. He expected them to be prepared and ready to express themselves."

Her eyes moistened again as she remembered her father. Lacy smiled and nodded and tried to encourage her.

"Dad loved to lecture, and he also loved the Socratic method of teaching, where he would select a student at random and ask him or her to brief a case for the benefit of the class. If the student made a mistake, or couldn't hold her ground, then the discussion often became contentious. Over the years I've talked to many of his former students, and while all still express admiration, they still shudder at the thought of trying to argue con law with Professor Burke. He was feared, but in the end greatly admired. And every former student was shocked by his murder. Who could possibly want to kill Professor Burke?"

"You've talked to former students?"

"Yes. Under the guise of collecting anecdotes about my father for a possible book. I've been doing this for years. The book will never be written but it's a great way to initiate a conversation. Just say you're working on a book and people start talking. I have at least two dozen photographs sent by his former students. Dad at graduation. Dad drinking a beer at a student softball game. Dad on the bench during moot court. All little slices of college life. They loved him."

"I'm sure you have a file."

"Of course. Not here, but I'm happy to show it to you."

"Maybe later. We were talking about motive."

"Yes. Well, many years ago I was talking to a lawyer in Orlando who studied under my father, and he told me an interesting story. There was a kid in his class who was rank and file, nothing special. My father called on him in class one day to discuss a case involving the Fourth Amendment, searches and seizures. The kid was prepared but believed something contrary to what my father was saying, and so they had a pretty good row.

My father loved it when students became passion-
ate and fought back. But this student made some
comments that were a bit extreme and out of line,
and he was somewhat cocky in the way he ban-
tered with Professor Burke, who managed to wrap
things up with a laugh. The next class, the student probably figured that he was off the hook for
a while, and came in unprepared. Dad called on
him again. Trying to wing it was an unpardonable
sin, and the student flamed out in a big way. Two
days later, Professor Burke called on this student
for the third time. He was prepared and ready to
fight. Back and forth they went as Dad slowly
boxed him into a corner. It's not wise to argue
with any professor who's taught the same material for years, but this guy was arrogant and sure
of himself. The knockout punch was a one-liner
that destroyed the student's position and brought
down the house. He was humiliated and he totally
lost it. He cursed, flung a notebook, snatched his
backpack and stomped out of the classroom, the
door almost shattering behind him.

"With perfect timing, my father said, 'I'm not
sure he's cut out for jury trials.'

"The classroom exploded with laughter, so loud
the student could not have missed it. He dropped
the class and began a counterattack. He complained to the dean and the president. He considered himself a laughingstock and eventually
withdrew from the law school. He wrote letters to

alumni, politicians, other professors, some really bizarre behavior. He wrote letters to my father. They were remarkably well written but rambling and not really threatening. The last letter was sent from a private mental health facility near Fort Lauderdale and written in longhand on its stationery. In it he claimed to be suffering from a nervous breakdown caused entirely by my father."

She paused and took a drink of water.

Lacy waited, then said, "That's it? Motive is a disgruntled law student?"

"Yes, but it's far more complicated than that."

"Let's hope so. What happened to him?"

"He got his head together and finished law school at Miami. Now he's a judge. Look, I know you're skeptical, and with good reason, but he is the only possible suspect in the world."

"Why is it more complicated?"

Jeri took a long look at the files at the end of the table. There were five of them, all an inch thick, each a different color. Lacy followed her gaze, finally caught her drift, and asked, "And those are five more victims of the same killer?"

"If I didn't think so I wouldn't be here."

"I'm sure there is a connection."

"There are two. One is the method. All six were hit in the head and then asphyxiated with the identical type of nylon rope. Each ligature was grated into the skin of the neck and tied off by the same knot and left behind, sort of like a calling card. And all six had a bad history with our judge."

"A bad history?"

"He knew them well. And he stalked them for years."

Lacy caught her breath, swallowed hard, and felt a clutching fear in her stomach. Her mouth was suddenly dry, but she managed to say, "Don't tell me his name. I'm not sure I'm ready for it."

There was a long gap in the conversation as both women gazed at the walls. Lacy finally said, "Look, I've heard enough for one day. Let me stew on this and I'll give you a call."

Jeri smiled and nodded and was suddenly subdued. They swapped phone numbers and said their goodbyes. Lacy hurried through the lobby and couldn't wait to get in her car.

3

Her apartment was a chic, ultra-modern unit in a newly renovated warehouse not far from the Florida State campus. She lived alone, at least most of the time, with Frankie, her obnoxious French bulldog. The dog was always waiting at the door, turning flips to urinate in the flower beds, regardless of the hour. Lacy let him outside for a pee, then poured a glass of wine, fell onto the sofa, and stared out the large plate glass window.

It was early March, the days were getting longer but they were still too short. She had grown up in the Midwest and did not miss the cold dark winters with too much snow and too little sunshine. She loved the Panhandle with its mild winters, real seasons, and long warm spring days. In two weeks the clock would change, the days would lengthen, and the college town would get even livelier with backyard cookouts, pool parties, rooftop cocktails, and outdoor dining. And that was for the adults. The students would live in the sun, head for the beach, and work on their tans.

Six murders.

After twelve years of investigating judges, Lacy considered herself immune from shock. She was also calloused and jaded enough to have serious doubts about Jeri's story, much the same way she doubted every complaint that landed on her desk.

But Jeri Crosby wasn't lying.

Her theories might be wrong; her hunches off-base; her fears unfounded. But she believed that her father was murdered by a sitting judge.

Lacy had left their meeting at the Ramada with nothing. The one file she opened had been left on the table for Jeri to deal with. Curiosity settled in. She checked her phone and saw two missed calls from Allie Pacheco, her boyfriend. He was out of town and she would chat with him later. She fetched her laptop and began searching.

The Twenty-Second Judicial District encompassed three counties in the far northwest corner of the state. Among the 400,000 or so people who lived in the Twenty-Second were forty-one circuit judges, elected by that same population. In her twelve years at BJC, Lacy could remember only two or three minor cases from the Twenty-Second.

Of the forty-one judges, fifteen had been elected in 2004, the year Jeri said her suspect took the bench. Of those fifteen, only one finished law school at the University of Miami.

In less than ten minutes, Lacy had the name of Ross Bannick.

He was forty-nine, a native of Pensacola, undergrad at the University of Florida, no mention of a wife or family. Scant bio on the judicial district's website. His photo portrayed a rather handsome guy with dark eyes, strong chin, and lots of salt-and-pepper hair. Lacy found him quite attractive and wondered why he wasn't married. Maybe he was divorced. She dug some more without getting too deep and found little about Judge Bannick. Evidently, he had managed to avoid controversy during his two-and-a-half terms on the bench. She went to her BJC files and found no complaint filed against him. In Florida, lawyers were expected to submit an annual review of the judges they encountered, anonymously of course. For the past five years, Bannick had received a stellar A+ rating from the bar. The comments were glowing: prompt, punctual, prepared, courteous, professional, witty, compassionate, bright, an "intimidating intellect." Only two other judges in the Twenty-Second received such high marks.

She kept digging and finally found some dirt. It was a newspaper article from the **Pensacola Ledger,** dated April 18, 2000. A local lawyer,

Ross Bannick, age thirty-five, was seeking his first political office and trying to unseat an old judge in the Twenty-Second. Controversy arose when one of Bannick's clients, a real estate developer, proposed a water park on some prime property near a Pensacola beach. The park was strongly opposed by seemingly everyone, and in the midst of the lawsuits and related brouhaha it was revealed that lawyer Bannick owned a 10 percent stake in the venture. The facts were not that clear, but it was alleged that he tried to hide his involvement. His opponent seized the moment and ran ads that proved fatal. The election returns, from a later edition of the paper, showed a landslide defeat for Bannick. Though it was impossible to determine with such scant evidence, it looked as though he had done nothing wrong. Nonetheless, he was beaten badly by the incumbent.

Lacy dug some more and found the election coverage from 2004. There was a photo of the old judge, who appeared to be at least ninety, and two stories about his declining health. Bannick ran a slick campaign and the controversy from four years earlier was apparently forgotten. He won his race by a thousand votes. His opponent died three months later.

Lacy realized she was hungry and pulled a left-over quiche out of the fridge. Allie had been gone for three nights and she had not been cooking.

She poured more wine and sat at her kitchen table, pecking away. In 2008, Bannick was unopposed for reelection. Sitting circuit judges rarely faced serious opposition in Florida, or any other state for that matter, and he seemed to be set for a long career on the bench.

Her phone pinged and she jumped. Lost in another world, she had even forgotten about the quiche. Caller unknown.

"Got his name yet?" Jeri asked.

Lacy smiled and replied, "It wasn't difficult. Miami Law, elected in 2004 in the Twenty-Second. That narrowed it down to one."

"Nice-looking guy, huh?"

"Yes. Why is he not married?"

"Don't get any ideas."

"I wasn't."

"He has a problem with women, part of his long history."

Lacy took a deep breath. "Okay. I don't suppose you've met him?"

"Oh no. Wouldn't go near him. He has security cameras everywhere—his courtroom, office, home."

"That's weird."

"Weird doesn't touch it."

"Are you in the car?"

"I'm driving to Pensacola, maybe on to Mobile. I don't suppose you could meet me tomorrow."

"Where?"

"Pensacola."

"That's three hours from here."

"Tell me about it."

"And what would be the purpose of our meeting?"

"I have only one purpose in life, Lacy, and you know what it is."

"I have a busy day."

"They're all busy, aren't they?"

"Afraid so."

"Okay. Then please put me on the calendar and let me know when we can meet there."

"Sure. I'll take a look."

There was a long gap in the conversation, so long that Lacy finally asked, "Are you there?"

"Yes. Sorry. I tend to drift. Have you found much online?"

"Some. Several stories about his elections, all from the **Ledger.**"

"How about the one from 2000 about the land deal, in bed with the crooked developer, the one that cost him the election?"

"Yes. I've read that one."

"I have all of them in a file, whenever you want to take it."

"Okay, we'll see."

"That reporter was a guy named Danny Cleveland, originally from up north somewhere. He spent about six years with the **Ledger,** then moved around some. The newspaper in Little Rock, Arkansas, was his last stop."

"Last stop?"

"Yes. They found him in his apartment. Asphyxiation. Same rope, same unusual knot. Sailors call it the double clove hitch, pretty rare. Another unsolved mystery, another very cold case."

Lacy struggled to respond and noticed that her left hand was shaking.

"Are you still there?" Jeri asked.

"I think so. When was—"

"Two thousand nine. Not a trace of evidence left behind. Look, Lacy, we're talking too much on the phone. I prefer face-to-face. Let me know when we can meet again." She abruptly ended the call.

Her romance with Allie Pacheco was now into its third year and, in her opinion, was stalling. He was thirty-eight years old and, though he denied it, even in therapy, he was still scarred from a terrible first marriage eleven years earlier. It had lasted four miserable months and, mercifully, ended without a pregnancy.

The biggest obstacle to a more serious arrangement was a fact that was becoming more and more obvious: both enjoyed the freedom of living alone. Since high school, Lacy had not lived with a man in the house and she wasn't keen on having one around. She had loved her father but remembered him as a domineering, chauvinistic sort who treated his wife like a maid. Her mother, always subservient, excused his behavior and whispered over and over, "It's just his generation."

It was a lame excuse and one Lacy vowed to never accept. Allie was indeed different. He was kind, thoughtful, funny, and, for the most part, attentive to her. He was also an FBI special agent who these days was spending most of his time in south Florida chasing narco-traffickers. When things were slow, which was rare, he was assigned to counterterrorism. There was even talk of him being transferred. After eight years as a special agent with no shortage of commendations, he was always on the block to be shipped out. At least, in Lacy's opinion.

He kept a toothbrush and a shaving kit in her spare bathroom, along with some sweats and casual stuff in a closet, enough to sleep over whenever he wanted. She, on the other hand, maintained a presence in his small apartment fifteen minutes away. Pajamas, old sneakers, older jeans, a toothbrush, and some fashion magazines on the coffee table. Neither was the jealous type, but each had quietly marked their territory in the other's place.

Lacy would have been shocked to learn that Allie slept around. He just wasn't the type. Nor was she. Their challenge, with his travel and their demanding schedules, was keeping each other satisfied. It was taking more and more effort, and that was because, as a close girlfriend said, "You're approaching middle age." Lacy had been appalled at that term and for the next month chased Allie from her condo to his apartment and back, until both were exhausted and called time-out.

He checked in at seven thirty and they chatted for a moment. He was "on surveillance," whatever that meant, and couldn't say much. She knew he was somewhere around Miami. They both said "I love you" and rang off.

As a seasoned agent whose career meant everything, Allie was the consummate professional, and as such said little about his work, to Lacy anyway. To those he hardly knew he would not even give the name of his employer. If pressed, his standard reply was "Security." He pronounced the word with such authority that further questions were cut off. His friends were other agents. There were times, though, maybe after a drink or two, that he lowered his guard a bit and talked, in generic terms, about his work. It was often dangerous and he, like most agents, lived for the adrenaline rush.

By comparison, her cases were the same mundane complaints about judges drinking too much, taking gifts from law firms, dragging their feet, showing partiality, and getting involved in local politics.

Six murders would certainly liven up her caseload.

She sent an email to her boss with the message that she had decided to take a personal day tomorrow and would not be in the office. The handbook gave her four PDs a year, with no questions asked. She rarely took one, and even had three left over from the previous year.

Lacy called Jeri and made arrangements to meet at one o'clock the next day in Pensacola.

4

But for Frankie, her PD would have begun with sleeping in, something she could only dream of. The dog was making noises before sunrise and needed to go outside. Afterward, Lacy stretched out on the sofa and tried to nap, but Frankie decided it was time for breakfast. So Lacy sipped her coffee and watched the day slowly arrive.

Her thoughts were a mix of excitement over the meeting with Jeri and the usual angst over her career. In seven months she would turn forty, a reality that saddened her. She was enjoying her life but it was slipping by, with no real plans to marry. She had never longed for children of her own and had already decided it wouldn't happen. And she was fine with that. All her friends had children, some even teenagers, and she was thankful she wasn't burdened with those challenges. She could not imagine finding the patience to raise kids in the age of cell phones, drugs, casual sex, social media, and everything else on the Internet.

She had joined BJC twelve years earlier. She should have left years ago, like virtually all the colleagues she had known. BJC was a nice place to begin a career but a dead end for any serious lawyer. Her best friend from law school was a partner in a mega-firm in Washington, but it was an all-consuming lifestyle that she wanted no part of. Their friendship required work, and Lacy often asked herself if it was worth it. Her other girlfriends from back then had drifted away, all scattered around the country, all consumed with busy lives at their desks, and, when time allowed, at home with their families.

Lacy wasn't sure where to look, or what she wanted, so she had hung around BJC for too long and now worried that she had missed better opportunities. Her biggest case, her pinnacle, was behind her. Three years earlier she had led an investigation that took down a circuit judge in the largest judicial bribery scandal in Florida history. She had caught the judge in bed with a crime syndicate that was skimming millions from an Indian casino. The criminals were now locked away in federal prisons with years to serve.

The case was sensational, and for a brief period of time gave BJC its finest hour. Most of her colleagues quickly parlayed the success into better jobs. The legislature, however, showed its gratitude with another round of budget cuts.

Her pinnacle had cost her dearly. She had been severely injured in a staged auto accident near the casino. She spent weeks in a hospital and months in physical therapy. Her injuries had healed but the aches and stiffness were still there. Hugo Hatch, her friend, colleague, and passenger, had been killed at the scene. His widow filed a wrongful death suit and Lacy pursued her own case for damages. The litigation looked promising, a nice settlement was all but guaranteed, but it was dragging on, as do most civil lawsuits.

She found it impossible not to think about the settlement. A pile of money was almost on the table, funds that were being aggregated by the government forfeiture of dirty assets. But the issues, both criminal and civil, were complicated. There was no shortage of aggrieved people, and their hungry lawyers, clamoring for the cash.

Her case was not yet set for trial, and she had been assured from the beginning that it would never happen. Her lawyer was confident the defendants were horrified at the prospect of facing a jury and trying to explain away the intricate planning of a deliberate crash that killed Hugo and injured her. Settlement negotiations should commence any day now, and the opening round would be in excess of "seven figures."

Turning forty might be traumatic, but doing so with a fortified bank account would take some of the sting out of it. She had a decent salary, some money inherited from her mother, no debts, and plenty of savings. The settlement would push her over the edge and allow her to walk away. To where, she wasn't sure, but it was certainly fun to think about. Her days at BJC were numbered, and that in itself made her smile. It was almost time for a new career, and the fact that she didn't have a clue as to where she might go was actually exhilarating.

In the meantime, though, she had a few files to close, a few judges to investigate. Normally, she began each day with a pep talk to force herself back to the office, but not today. She was intrigued by Jeri Crosby and her fantastic story about a murderous judge. She had doubts about its veracity, but was curious enough to take the next step. What if it were true? What if Lacy Stoltz topped off her stellar career with another pinnacle? Another glorious moment that solved half a dozen cold cases and captured headlines. She told herself to stop dreaming and get on with the day.

She took a quick shower, spent a few minutes with her hair and makeup, threw on some jeans and sneakers, put down food and water for Frankie, and left her apartment. At the first intersection, she eased through a yield sign, one that always reminded her of her car crash. It was odd how certain landmarks triggered certain memories, and each morning she looked at the sign and flashed back. The memory was gone in an instant, until the next day. Three years after the nightmare, she was still cautious behind the wheel, always yielding, never exceeding the limit.

At the western edge of town, away from the Capitol and the campus, she pulled into an old shopping center, parked, and at 8:05 entered Bonnie's Big Breakfast, a local hangout with no students, no lobbyists. As always, it was crowded with salesmen and cops. She picked up a news-paper and found a seat at the counter, not far from the kitchen window where the waitresses chirped at the cooks, who snapped back their own colorful comments. The menu offered a poached egg on avocado toast that was legendary, and Lacy treated herself to it at least once a month. As she waited, she checked her email and texts and was pleased that all the important messages could be put off for twenty-four hours. She sent a note to Darren with the news that she would not be in.

He replied quickly and asked if she was quitting.

Such was the mood around BJC these days. Those still hanging around were suspected of planning their escapes.

At 9:30, Lacy was on Interstate 10 going west. It was March 4, a Tuesday, and each week on that day at about that hour she expected a call from her older brother and only sibling, Gunther. He lived in Atlanta where he was a player in the real estate development business. Regardless of the market, he was always upbeat and on the verge of another major deal, conversations that Lacy had grown weary of but had no choice but to endure. He worried about her and usually hinted that she should shuck her job and come make some big bucks with him. She always politely declined. Gunther lived on a tightrope and seemed to relish borrowing from one bank to pay another, always one step ahead of the bankruptcy lawyers. The last career she could imagine was building more strip malls in the Atlanta suburbs. Another recurring nightmare was having Gunther for a boss.

They had always been close, but seven months earlier their mother had died suddenly and the loss made them even closer. And, Lacy suspected, so had her pending lawsuit. Gunther believed she was due millions and had developed the irritating habit of tossing around investment advice for his kid sister. She was not looking forward to the day when he needed a loan. Gunther lived in a world of debt and would promise the moon to secure more of it.

"Hey Sis," he said cheerfully. "How's it going down there?"

"I'm fine, Gunther. And you?"

"Got the tiger by the tail. How's Allie? How's your love life?"

"Pretty dull. He's out of town a lot these days. And yours?"

"Not much to report." Recently divorced, he chased women with the same enthusiasm as he did banks, and she really didn't want to hear about it. After two failed marriages she had encouraged him to be more selective, advice he routinely ignored.

"You sound like you're in the car," he said.

"I'm driving to Pensacola to chase down a witness. Nothing exciting."

"You always say that. Are you still looking for another job?"

"I never said I was looking for another job. I said that I'm getting a bit bored with the one I have."

"There's more action up here, kid."

"So you've said. I don't suppose you've talked to Aunt Trudy lately."

"Not if I can help it, you know?"

Trudy was their mother's sister, a real busybody who was working too hard to keep the family together. She was grieving over her sister's sudden death and wanted to share her misery with her niece and nephew.

"She called two days ago, sounded awful," Lacy said.

"She always sounds awful. That's why I can't talk to her. Strange, isn't it? We barely spoke to the woman until Mom died, and now she really wants to be pals."

"She's struggling, Gunther. Give her a break."

"Who's not struggling these days? Oops. Look, got another call. It's a banker who wants to throw some money at me. Gotta go. Will call later. Love you, Sis."

"You too."

Most of their Tuesday chats ended abruptly when he was besieged with other, more important calls. Lacy was relieved, because he usually asked about her lawsuit. She called Darren at the office just to say hello and reassure him that she would indeed be back tomorrow. She called Allie and left a voicemail. She turned off her phone and turned on the stereo. **Adele Live in London.**

5

Thanks to GPS, she found the Brookleaf Cemetery in an old section of Pensacola and parked in the empty lot. Just ahead was a square, bunker-like building that could only be a mausoleum, and beyond it were acres and acres of tombstones and monuments. It was a slow day for burials and there was only one other car.

She was ten minutes early and punched in Jeri's number. She answered with "Are you in the copper-colored Subaru?"

"I am. Where are you?"

"I'm in the cemetery. Go through the main gate and past the old graves."

Lacy walked along a paved trail lined with weathered monuments and family tombs, the last stops for the prominent from other centuries. With time the tombs lost their significance and yielded to elaborate headstones. Quick looks to both sides dated burials to mere decades ago. The trail turned to the left, and Jeri Crosby appeared from behind one of the few trees left standing.

"Hello, Lacy," she said with a smile.

"Hello, Jeri. Why are we meeting in a cemetery?"

"Thought you might ask. I could say it's privacy, a change of scenery, other reasons."

"Let's pursue the other reasons."

"Sure." She nodded and said, "This way." They walked past hundreds of headstones and could see thousands in the distance. On a slight incline far away, a crew of gravediggers labored under a purple canopy. Another casket was on the way. "Here," Jeri said as she stepped off the trail and wound her way around a row of graves. She stopped and nodded silently at the final resting place of the Leawood family. Father, infant daughter, and son Thad, who was born in 1950 and died in 1991.

After staring at the single headstone for a moment or so, Lacy was about to start asking questions when Jeri said, "Thad was a local boy, grew up around here, went off to college, came back, got a job as a social worker. Never married. He was an Eagle Scout and loved scouting, loved working with kids. Coached youth baseball, taught kids in church, that sort of stuff. Lived alone in a small apartment not far from here. In his mid-twenties he became scoutmaster of Troop 722, one of the oldest troops in the area. He treated it like a full-time job and seemed to love every minute of it.

Many of his former scouts still remember him fondly. Others, not so much. Around 1990, he abruptly quit and left the area amid allegations of abuse and molestation. It became a scandal and the police opened an investigation, but nothing came of it because the victims backed away. Can't really blame them. Who would want the attention? After he left town, things settled down and the alleged victims went silent. The police lost interest. After he died, the case was closed."

"He died young," Lacy observed and waited for more.

"He did. He lived in Birmingham for a while, then drifted here and there. They found him in Signal Mountain, a small town outside of Chattanooga. He was living in a cheap apartment and driving a forklift in a warehouse. Went out for a jog one evening and never came back. Some kids found his body in the woods. The same rope around his neck. A nasty blow to the head, then asphyxiation. As far as I can tell, he was the first, but who knows?"

"I'm sure you have a file."

"Oh yes. There were stories in the Chattanooga paper, and the **Ledger** covered it down here. A short obit. The family brought him back for a simple ceremony. And here he is. Seen enough?"

"I guess."

"Let's walk."

They followed the trail back to their cars. Jeri

said, "Get in and I'll drive. It's a brief tour. Have you had lunch?"

"No. I'm not hungry."

They got in Jeri's white Toyota Camry and drove away. She was extremely cautious and nervously checked her rearview mirror. Lacy finally said, "You act as though someone is following you."

"That's the way I live, Lacy. We're on his turf now."

"You can't be serious."

"Dead serious. For twenty years I've stalked the killer and at times I think he's stalking me. He's back there, somewhere, and he's smarter than I am."

"But he's not following you?"

"I can't be certain."

"You don't know for sure?"

"I don't think so."

Lacy bit her tongue and let it go.

A few blocks away Jeri turned onto a wider street and nodded at a church. "That's the Westburg Methodist Church, one of the largest in town. In the basement there is a large fellowship room, and that's where Troop 722 has met forever."

"Can I assume that Ross Bannick was a member of the troop?"

"Yes."

They drove past the church and weaved through several streets. Lacy bit her tongue to suppress a flood of questions. It was apparent that Jeri was telling the story at her own pace. She turned onto Hemlock, a lovely shaded street with pre-war homes, all well preserved with narrow drives and flower beds around the porches. Jeri pointed and said, "That blue one up there on the left, that's where the Bannick family lived. Ross grew up there and, as you can tell, he could walk to school and church, and Boy Scouts. His parents are dead and his sister got the house. She's a good bit older. He inherited some land next door in Chavez County, and that's where he lives. Alone. Never married."

They drove past the house. Lacy finally asked, "Was his family prominent?"

"His father was a beloved pediatrician who died at the age of sixty-one. His mother was an eccentric artist who went nuts and died in an institution. The family was fairly well known back then. They were members of the Episcopal church just around the corner. Evidently it was a nice, cozy little neighborhood."

"Any allegations that he was molested by Thad Leawood?"

"None. And no evidence of it. As I said yesterday, Lacy, I have no evidence. Only assumptions based on unfounded theories."

Lacy almost said something sarcastic but let it go. They turned onto a wider street and drove for a few minutes with no conversation. Jeri turned and the streets were narrower, the houses smaller, the lawns not as well manicured. She pointed to her right and said, "Up there, the white frame house with the brown pickup. That's where the Leawoods lived. Thad grew up there. He was fifteen years older than Ross."

They drove past the house. Lacy asked, "Who lives there now?"

"Don't know. It's not important. All the Leawoods are gone."

Jeri turned at an intersection, then zigzagged away from the residential areas. They were on a busy highway headed north. Finally, Lacy asked, "So how much longer is the tour?"

"We're getting there."

"Okay. As we drive around, mind if I ask some questions?"

"Sure. Anything."

"The crime scene, up in Signal Mountain, and the investigation. What do you know?"

"Almost nothing. The killing was in an area that was popular with joggers and walkers, but there were no witnesses. According to the autopsy, the time of death was between seven and eight p.m., on a warm day in October. Leawood punched the clock at the warehouse at five-oh-five, the usual time, and left. He lived alone and kept to himself, very few friends. A neighbor saw him jog away from his apartment around six thirty, and as far as the police know, that was the last he was seen. He lived at the edge of town, not far from where the walking trail begins."

The traffic thinned as they left the sprawl of Pensacola. A sign read: CULLMAN, 8 MILES.

Lacy said, "I take it we're going to Cullman."

"Yes. We'll cross into Chavez County in about two miles."

"Can't wait."

"Be patient, Lacy. This is not easy for me. You're the only person I've confided in and you have to trust me."

"Back to the crime scene."

"Yes, back to the crime scene. The police found nothing. No hairs or fabrics, no blunt instrument, nothing but the nylon rope around his neck, tied off with the same knot, a double clove hitch."

"And it was the same type of nylon rope?"

"Yes. Identical to the others."

A sign informed them that they were now in Chavez County. Lacy asked, "We're dropping in on Judge Bannick?"

"No we are not."

They turned onto a four-lane highway and began passing the sprawl of Cullman: fast-food restaurants, travel motels, shopping centers.

Lacy asked, "So, what did the police do?"

"The usual. They dug around, went door to door, talked to other joggers and walkers, and coworkers, found a friend or two. Searched his apartment, nothing was missing, so they ruled out robbery as a motive. They did their best but got nowhere."

"And this was 1991?"

"Yes. A very cold case with no clues."

Lacy was learning patience and took deep breaths between questions. "I'm sure you have all of this in a file."

"I do."

"How do you gather this information from the police? They are notoriously protective of their files."

"Freedom of Information requests. They'll comply to some degree, but you're right, they'll never give you everything. All they have to do is claim it's an ongoing investigation and slam the door. However, with the old cases they sometimes relax a little. That, plus I go talk to them."

"Doesn't that leave a trail?"

"It could."

They turned off the highway onto an exit ramp and followed a sign pointing toward the historic downtown. "Ever been to Cullman?" Jeri asked.

"I don't think so. I checked last night, and BJC has not had a case here in the past twenty years. Several in Pensacola, but things have been quiet in Chavez County."

"How many counties do you cover?"

"Too many. We have four investigators in the Tallahassee office and three in Fort Lauderdale. That's seven for sixty-seven counties, one thousand judges, six hundred courtrooms."

"Is that enough?"

"For the most part. Thankfully, the vast majority of our judges behave, with only a few bad apples."

"Well, you've got one here."

Lacy did not respond. They were on an extended section of Main Street. Jeri turned off of it, turned again, and paused at an intersection. Across the road was an entrance to a gated community. Behind the gate were modern homes and condos with small neat lawns.

Jeri said, "Dr. Bannick bought this land raw forty years ago and it was a good investment. Ross lives in there, and this is as close as we'll get. There are a lot of surveillance cameras."

"I'm close enough," Lacy said, and wanted to ask about the benefits of knowing where he lived. But she held her tongue. As they drove away she said, "Let's get back to the local police up there. How do you talk to them without worrying about leaving a trail?"

Jeri chuckled and offered a smile, a rare one. "I've created a fictional world, Lacy, and in it I am many characters. A freelance journalist, a crime reporter, a private investigator, even a novelist, all with different names and addresses. In this case, I posed as a crime reporter from Memphis, working on a long story about cold cases in Tennessee. Gave the chief my business card, even a phone number and email. Short skirts and a lot of charm can work wonders. They're all men, you know, the weaker sex. After a few friendly chats they open up, somewhat."

"How many phones do you have?"

"Oh, I don't know. At least half a dozen."

Lacy shook her head in disbelief.

"Plus, you have to remember that this case is all but forgotten. It's considered 'cold' for a reason. Once the police realized they had nothing to work with, they lost interest in a hurry. The victim was not from their town and had no family to poke around and pressure them. The crime seemed thoroughly random and impossible to solve. In some of these cold cases the cops even welcome a fresh set of eyes digging through the file."

They were back on Main Street, in the historic section. A stately Grecian courthouse came into view, in the very center of the town. The square around it was busy with shops and offices.

"That's where he works," Jeri said, looking at the courthouse. "We won't go in."

"I've seen enough."

"There are cameras everywhere."

"Do you really think Bannick would recognize you? I mean, come on. You've never met the man and he has no idea who you are or what you're after, right?"

"Right, but why take the chance? Actually, I walked in one time, years ago. It was the first day of a term and the courthouse was crawling with

people, over a hundred prospective jurors summoned for duty. I stayed in the crowd and had
a look around. His courtroom is on the second
floor, his office just down the hall. It was really
weird, almost overwhelming, just being in the
same place as the man who killed my father."

Lacy was struck by the certainty of her words.
With no proof, no evidence, she was convinced
Bannick was a murderer. And she, Lacy, was expected to get involved and somehow find truth
and justice.

They circled the square and left downtown. Jeri
said, "I need some coffee. You?"

"Sure. Is the tour over?"

"Yes, but we have much more to talk about."

6

At the edge of town they stopped at a chain restaurant and went inside. At two thirty the place was empty and they chose a booth in a corner, far away from the deserted bar. Jeri carried a large bag, too big for a purse. Lacy assumed it contained files. They ordered coffee and sipped ice water while they waited.

Lacy said, "On more than one occasion you've described Thad Leawood as the first. Who was the second?"

"Well, I don't know how many victims there are, so I can't be certain Thad was the first. My project has uncovered six, so far. Thad was 1991, and I think my father was number two, the following year."

"Okay. And you don't want me to take notes."

"Not yet."

"Danny Cleveland, the reporter, was 2009. So was he the third?"

"I don't think so."

Lacy exhaled in exasperation. "Forgive me, Jeri, but I'm pulling teeth here. I'm getting frustrated again."

"Be patient. Number three, on my list anyway, was a girl he knew in law school."

"A girl?"

"Yes."

"And why did he kill her?"

The coffee arrived and they went silent. Jeri mixed in cream and took her time. She glanced around casually and said, "Let's deal with that one later. We've talked about three. That's enough for now."

"Sure. But just curious—do you have more proof in the other three than you have for the first ones?"

"Not really. I have motive and I have method. That's all. But I'm convinced they're all linked to Bannick."

"Got that. He's been on the bench for ten years. Do you suspect him in any case after he became a judge? In other words, is he still at it?"

"Oh yes. His last one was two years ago, a retired lawyer living in the Keys. A former big firm guy they found strangled on his fishing boat."

"I remember that. Kronkite, or something like that?"

"Kronke, Perry Kronke, eighty-one years old when he caught his last fish."

"It was a sensational case."

"Well, at least for Miami. Down there they have more murdered lawyers per capita than any other place. Quite a distinction, huh?"

"Drug trafficking."

"Of course."

"And the connection to Bannick?"

"He was an intern in Kronke's firm in the summer of 1989, then he got stiffed when there was no job offer. Evidently it really pissed him off, because he waited two decades to get revenge. He has remarkable patience, Lacy."

It took Lacy a moment to absorb this. She sipped her coffee and looked out the window.

Jeri leaned in and said, "In my opinion, as a pseudo expert in serial killers now, it was his biggest mistake, so far. He murdered an old lawyer with many friends and who once had a fine reputation. Two of his victims were men of stature—my father and Kronke."

"And their murders were twenty years apart."

"Yes, that's his MO, Lacy. It's unusual but not unheard of for sociopaths."

"I'm sorry but I'm not up on the lingo here. I deal with judges who are mentally sound, for the most part, and screw up when they ignore cases or mix personal business with their judicial duties."

Jeri smiled knowingly and sipped her coffee. Another glance around, then, "A psychopath has a severe mental disorder and antisocial behavior. A sociopath is a psychopath on steroids. Not exactly medical definitions but close enough."

"I'll just listen and you keep talking."

"My theory is that Bannick keeps a list of people who have harmed or slighted him. It could be something as trivial as a law professor who embarrassed him, and it could be something as devastating as a scoutmaster who sexually abused him. He was probably okay until he was raped as a child. It's hard to imagine what that would do to a kid. That's why he has always struggled with women."

Again, her certainty was disarming, yet astonishing. She had been chasing Bannick for so long, his guilt had become a hard fact.

She continued, "I've read a hundred books about serial killers. From the gossipy tabloids to the academic treatises. Virtually none of them want to get caught, but yet they want someone out there—the police, the victims' families, the press—to know they are at work. Many are brilliant, some are incredibly stupid. They run the gamut. Some kill for decades and are never caught, others go crazy and do their work in a hurry. These usually make mistakes. Some have a clear motive, others kill at random."

"But they're usually caught, right?"

"Hard to say. This country averages fifteen thousand murders a year. One-third are never solved. That's five thousand this year, last year, the year before. Since 1960, over two hundred thousand. There are so many unsolved murders that it's impossible to say this victim or that victim died at the hands of a serial killer. Most experts believe that's one of the reasons they leave behind clues. They want someone to know they're out there. They thrive on the fear and terror. As I said, they don't want to get caught, but they want someone to know."

"So no one, not even the FBI, knows how many serial killers are loose?"

"No one. And some of the more famous were never identified. They never caught Jack the Ripper."

Lacy couldn't suppress a laugh. "Forgive me, but I find it hard to believe that I'm sitting here in Podunk, Florida, having a pleasant cup of coffee and talking about Jack the Ripper."

"Please don't laugh, Lacy. I know it's bizarre but it's all true."

"What do you expect me to do?"

"Just believe me, Lacy. You have to believe me."

Lacy stopped smiling and drank some more coffee. After a long pause, in which neither made eye contact, she said, "Okay, I'm still listening. Using your theory, are you saying that Bannick wants to get caught?"

"Oh no. He's too careful, too smart, too patient. Plus he has too much to lose. Most serial killers, same as other killers, are misfits from the fringes of society. Bannick has status, a rewarding career, probably some old family money. He's a sick man but he puts up a good front. Church, country club, stuff like that. He's active in the local bar, president of a historical society, even fancies himself as an actor with a county thespian group. I've seen two of his performances, just dreadful."

"You watched him onstage?"

"Yes. The crowds were small, for good reason, but the theaters were dark. It wasn't risky."

"He doesn't sound antisocial."

"As I said, he puts up a good front. No one would ever suspect him. He's even seen around the Pensacola area with a blonde on his arm. He uses several, probably pays them, but I don't know that."

"How do you know about the blondes?"

"Social media. For example, the local chapter of the American Cancer Society holds an annual gala, black tie and all. His father, the pediatrician, died of cancer, so Bannick is involved. It's a big gala and they raise a lot of money. Everything gets posted online. Not much is private anymore, Lacy."

"But he doesn't post anything."

"Nothing. No social media presence at all. But you'd be surprised what you can dig up when you live online like I do."

"But you said everything leaves a trail."

"Yes, but casual browsing is hard to track. And I take precautions."

Another long pause as Lacy struggled for the next question. Jeri waited nervously, as if the next

revelation might frighten away her new confi-
dante. The waitress breezed by with a pot of coffee
and refilled their cups.

Lacy ignored hers and said, "A question. You
said that most serial killers want someone to
know that they're out there, or whatever. Same
for Bannick?"

"Oh yes. There's an old saying among FBI investigators that 'sooner or later a man will sign
his name.' I got that from a book, maybe even a
novel. I can't remember. I've read so much."

"The rope?"

"The rope. He always uses a three-eighths-inch
nylon cord, marine grade, double twin-braided,
light duty. A length about thirty inches long,
wrapped twice around the neck so hard that the
skin is always cut, and secured with a double clove
hitch knot, probably learned in the Boy Scouts.
I have crime scene photos from every murder
but Kronke's."

"Isn't that careless?"

"It could be, but then who's really investigating? There are six murders in six different juris-
dictions, six different states, over a twenty-year
period. None of the six police departments have
compared notes with the others. They just don't
work that way, and he knows it."

"And only one in Florida?"

"Yes, Mr. Kronke. Two years ago."

"And where was that?"

"The town of Marathon, in the Keys."

"So why can't you go to the police down there and show them your files, give them your theory?"

"That's a good question. That may happen, Lacy. I might be forced to do so, but I have my doubts. What do you think the police will do? Chase down five cold cases from five other states? I doubt it. You can't forget that I have no proof yet, nothing concrete to give the police, and for the most part they've stopped digging."

Lacy sipped her coffee and nodded along, unconvinced.

Jeri said, "And there is a much more important reason I can't go barging in with scant evidence. It's terrifying, actually."

"You're afraid of him."

"Damned right I am. He's too smart to commit a murder and leave it alone. For twenty years I've operated under the assumption that he's back there, watching, still covering his tracks."

"And you want me to get involved?"

"You have to, Lacy. There's no one else."

"I don't believe that."

"Do you believe me?"

"I don't know, Jeri. I really don't know. I'm sorry, but this is not sinking in yet."

"If we don't stop him, he'll kill again."

Lacy absorbed this and was rattled by the casual use of the pronoun "we." She pushed her coffee cup away and said, "Jeri, I've had enough for one day. I need to digest this, sleep on it, try to get my bearings."

"I get it, Lacy. And you have to understand that it's lonely out here. For many years now I've lived with this. It has consumed my life and at times pushed me to the edge. I've spent hours in therapy and still have a long way to go. It caused my divorce and almost ruined my career. But I can't quit. My father won't allow it. I can't believe I'm here now, finally at the point of telling someone, a person I trust."

"I haven't earned your trust."

"But you have it anyway. There's no one else. I need a friend, Lacy. Please don't abandon me."

"It's not a question of abandoning you. The biggest issue is what am I supposed to do? We don't investigate murders, Jeri. That's for the state boys or maybe even the FBI. We're just not equipped for work like this."

"But you can help me, Lacy. You can listen to me, hold my hand. You can investigate on some level. The BJC has subpoena powers. In the casino case, you took down a crooked judge and an entire criminal gang."

"With a lot of help from others, primarily the FBI. I'm not sure you understand how we work, Jeri. We don't get involved in allegations of wrongdoing until someone files a complaint. Nothing happens until then."

"Is the complaint anonymous?"

"Initially, yes. Later, no. After the complaint is filed we have forty-five days to investigate the allegations."

"Does the judge know about your investigation?"

"That depends. Most of the time the judge knows he or she has a problem. The complaining party has made it known they're unhappy and have issues. Some of these disputes have dragged on for months, even years. But, it's not uncommon for the judge to get blindsided. If we decide the allegations have merit, which is rare, we file a formal notice with the judge."

"And at that point he'll know my name?"

"That's usually how it works. I can't remember a case where the complaining party remained completely anonymous."

"But it could be done, right?"

"I'll have to talk to the director, my boss."

"That scares me, Lacy. My dream is to nail the man who killed my father. My other dream is to keep my name off his list. It's too dangerous."

Lacy glanced at her watch and shoved her cup away another inch or two. She exhaled and said, "Look, I've had a lot for one day and I have a long drive. Let's take a break."

"Sure, but you have to promise me complete confidentiality, Lacy. Understood?"

"Okay, but I have to discuss this with my boss."

"Can he be trusted?"

"It's a she and the answer is yes. This is delicate

work, as you might guess. We're dealing with the reputations of elected judges and we understand discretion. No one will know anything until they have to know. Fair enough?"

"I guess. But you have to keep me in the loop."

The twenty-minute drive back to the cemetery was subdued. To keep things light, Lacy asked about Jeri's daughter, Denise, a graduate student at the University of Michigan. No, she did not remember her grandfather and knew little about his murder. Jeri was intrigued by Lacy's life as an attractive single woman who had never married, but that conversation fizzled. Lacy was accustomed to such curiosity and had no patience with it. Her dear late mother had hounded her for years about growing old alone and childless, and Lacy was adept in deflecting the nosiness.

At the cemetery, Jeri handed her a cloth shopping bag and said, "Here are some files, just some preliminary stuff. There's a lot more."

"For the first three, I presume?"

"Yes. My father, Thad Leawood, and Danny Cleveland. We can discuss the others later."

The bag was heavy enough already and Lacy wasn't sure she wanted to take possession. She couldn't wait to get in her car, lock the door, and drive away. They said their goodbyes, promised to talk soon and so on, and left the cemetery.

Halfway to Tallahassee, Lacy's phone buzzed with a call from Allie. He would be in late and wanted a pizza and wine by the fire. She had not seen him in four days and suddenly missed him. She smiled at the idea of cuddling up with a seasoned FBI agent and talking about something other than their work.

7

Darren Trope bounced into her office bright and early Wednesday morning and began with "Well, well, how was the PD? Do something exciting?"

"Not really."

"Did you miss us?"

"No, sorry," Lacy replied with a smile. She was about to reach for a file, one of about a dozen stacked neatly in a rack at the corner of her desk. A judge down in Gilchrist County was irritating both lawyers and litigants alike with his inability to set cases for trials. Alcohol was rumored to be involved. Lacy had reluctantly decided the allegations had merit and was preparing to notify His Honor that he was under investigation.

"Sleep late? A long fancy lunch somewhere with our FBI boy?"

"They're called personal days for a reason."

"Well, you didn't miss anything around here."

"I'm sure of that."

"I'm going out for some decent coffee. Want anything?"

"Sure, the usual."

Darren's coffee runs were taking longer and longer. He had been at BJC for two years and showing all the usual signs of being bored with a stalled career. He left, she closed the door behind him, and tried to concentrate on another drunk judge. An hour passed with little progress and she finally shoved the file aside.

Maddy Reese was her most trusted colleague around the office. She had been there for four years and, among the four lawyers, was now second in seniority, far behind Lacy. She tapped on the door as she walked through it and said, "Got a minute?"

The last director had imposed an open-door policy that had led to a freewheeling culture in which privacy was almost impossible and work was routinely interrupted. But he was gone now, and though most office doors were closed, old habits were hard to break.

"Sure," Lacy said. "What's up?"

"Cleo wants you to review the Handy matter, thinks we should get involved."

Cleo was Cleopatra, the secret nickname of the current director, an ambitious woman who had managed to alienate the entire office in a matter of weeks.

"Not Handy again," Lacy said in frustration.

"Oh yes. Seems he keeps overturning zoning ordinances in favor of a certain developer, who just happens to be a friend of his nephew."

"This is Florida. That's not uncommon."

"Well, the adjoining landowners are upset and they've hired lawyers. Another complaint was filed against him last week and things do look rather suspicious. I know how much you love zoning cases."

"I live for them. Bring me the file and I'll take a look."

"Thanks. And Cleo is calling a staff meeting for two this afternoon."

"I thought we suffered through those on Monday mornings."

"We do. But Cleo is making her own rules."

Maddy left without closing the door, and Lacy looked at the screen on her desktop. She scrolled through the usual lineup of emails she could either ignore or postpone, and stopped at one from Jeri Crosby.

Can we talk? I'll call you. Number is 776-145-0088. Your phone won't recognize it.

Lacy stared at the email for a long time as she tried to think of ways to avoid a response. She wondered which of the half-dozen cell phones Jeri was using. Hers buzzed and the number appeared.

"Hello, Jeri," she said as she walked to the door to close it.

"Thanks for yesterday, Lacy, you have no idea what that meant to me. I slept last night for the first time in forever."

Well, I'm glad **you** did. Even with Allie's warm body next to her, she'd had trouble shutting out the events of the day. "That's nice, Jeri. Yesterday was quite interesting."

"To say the least. So, what's up?"

The question threw her as she suddenly realized that her new friend might feel the need to call every day for updates. "What do you mean?"

"Well, what do you think? What's next?"

"I haven't thought about it," she lied. "A day out of the office and I'm still trying to catch up."

"Sure, and I don't mean to bother. Forgive me, but I'm so relieved that you're on the case now. You have no idea how lonely this has been."

"I'm not sure there is a case, Jeri."

"Of course there is. Did you look through the files?"

"No, I haven't got there yet, Jeri. I'm busy with other stuff right now."

"I see. Look, we need to meet again and cover the other victims. I know it's a lot for you to digest so soon, but, I dare say nothing on your desk could possibly be as important as Bannick."

True. Everything in the office paled in comparison to allegations of murder against a judge.

"Jeri, I can't just drop everything else and open a new case. Any involvement on my part must be approved by the director. Didn't I explain this?"

"I guess." Brushing it aside, she continued, "I'm in class today and tomorrow, but what about Saturday? I'll make the drive over and we can meet somewhere private."

"I thought about this driving home yesterday, for three hours, and I still don't see how we have any jurisdiction. We're just not equipped to investigate a murder, singular or plural."

"Your friend Hugo Hatch was murdered, in a staged car wreck, and I believe there was another murder in the casino case. Right, Lacy? You were involved in that one up to your ears." Her tone was becoming aggressive, but there was still a fragility in her voice.

Calmly, Lacy replied, "We talked about that and I explained that there were real detectives in that case, even the FBI."

"But you made it happen, Lacy. Without you, the crimes would not have been solved."

"Jeri, what am I supposed to do? Go to Signal Mountain, Tennessee, and Little Rock, Arkansas, and Marathon, Florida, and dig through old police files and somehow find evidence that isn't there? The police, the pros, couldn't find it. You've been trying for twenty years. There is simply not enough proof."

"Six dead people, all killed the same identical way,

and all six had a connection to Bannick. And you think that's not enough? Come on, Lacy. You can't let me down here. I'm at my wit's end. If you turn your back on me, then where am I supposed to go?"

Anywhere. Just please go away.

Lacy exhaled and told herself to be patient. "I understand, Jeri. Look, I'm busy right now. Let's talk later."

If she heard this she didn't acknowledge it. "I've checked around, Lacy. Every state has a different way to deal with judicial complaints, but almost every state allows an aggrieved party to initiate an investigation in some anonymous way. I'm sure it can be done in Florida."

"Are you willing to sign a complaint?"

"Maybe, but we need to talk some more. It seems possible to do it with an alias or something. Don't you think?"

"I'm not sure right now, Jeri. Please, let's talk tomorrow."

As soon as she managed to end the call, Darren finally arrived with her almond latte, almost an hour after he had left to fetch it. She thanked him, and when it appeared as though he wanted to loiter and share the break, she said she needed to make a call. At noon, she eased from her office, left the building, walked five blocks to meet Allie for lunch.

—

BJC's secret weapon was a badly aging woman named Sadelle, a career paralegal who decades earlier had given up on the bar exam. She had once smoked three packs a day, many of them around the office, and had been unable to quit until she was diagnosed with terminal lung cancer. Suddenly motivated, she had laid down her smokes and made preparations for the end. Seven years later, she was still on the job and working more hours than anyone else. BJC was her life, and she not only knew everything but remembered most of it as well. She was the archive, the search engine, the expert on the many ways judges could screw up their careers.

After the staff meeting, Lacy sent her an email with some questions. Fifteen minutes later, Sadelle rolled into her office in her motorized chair, an oxygen tube attached to her nose. Though her voice was strained, scratchy, at times almost desperate, she nonetheless enjoyed talking, often far too much.

She said, "We've done this before. I can think of three cases in the past forty years in which the aggrieved party was too spooked to sign on. Perhaps the biggest one involved a judge down around Tampa who discovered cocaine. He was thoroughly seduced by the drug and it became a real problem. Because of his position he found it difficult to buy the stuff." She paused for a second to take on oxygen. "Anyway, his problems were solved when a drug dealer appeared in his court on charges. He got friendly with the guy, gave him a light sentence, and eventually got in bed with his pusher, who was in with a major trafficker. With a steady supply guaranteed, the judge really went off the deep end and things deteriorated. He couldn't do his job, couldn't sit on the bench for more than fifteen minutes without calling a recess for a quick snort. The lawyers were whispering but, as usual, didn't want to squeal. A court reporter was watching closely and knew the dirt. She contacted us, terrified, of course, because the gang had some nasty boys. She eventually filed a Jane Doe complaint and we went in with subpoenas, the works. She even funneled documents and we had plenty of proof. We were preparing to bring in the Feds when the judge agreed to step down, so he was never indicted." Her face contorted as she sucked in more oxygen.

"What happened to him?"

"Killed himself. They called it an accidental overdose, but it looked suspicious. Saturated with coke. I guess he went out the way he wanted."

"When was this?"

"Not sure of the exact date, but it was before your time."

"What happened to the court reporter?"

"Nothing. We protected her identity and no one ever knew. So, yes, it can be done."

"What about the other two cases?"

"Either Jane or John. Not sure, but I can find them. As I recall, both were dismissed after the initial assessment, so there wasn't much to the allegations." Another pause to reload. Then she asked, "What kinda case you got?"

"Murder."

"Wow, that could be fun. I can't remember one of those, other than the casino case. Does it have merit?"

"I don't know. That's the challenge right now. Trying to determine what might be the truth."

"An allegation of murder against a sitting judge."

"Yes. Maybe."

"I like it. Don't hesitate to keep me in the loop."

"Thanks, Sadelle."

"Don't mention it."

Sadelle filled her scarred lungs, put the chair in reverse, and scooted away.

8

The painter's name was Lanny Verno. Late on a Friday afternoon the previous October, he was on a ladder in the den of an unfinished home, one of several dozen packed together on an unpaved street in a sprawling new subdivision just outside the city limits of Biloxi. He was touching up the trim at the edge of a twelve-foot ceiling, a gallon bucket of white paint in one hand, a two-inch brush in the other. He was alone; his coworker had already left for the day, the week, and the bar. Lanny glanced at his watch and shook his head. Still working past five on a Friday. A radio in the kitchen played the latest country hits.

He was eager to get to the bar too, for a rowdy night of beer drinking, and he would have already been there but for the promise of a check. His contractor was to deliver one by quitting time, and Lanny was growing irritated as the minutes passed.

The front door was open, but the music drowned out the sound of a truck door closing in the driveway.

A man appeared in the den and greeted him with a friendly hello. "Name's Butler, county inspector."

"Come on in," Verno said with hardly a look. The home was a construction site with steady foot traffic.

"Workin' mighty late," Butler drawled.

"Yeah, ready for a beer."

"Anybody else here?"

"Nope, just me and I'm on the way out." Verno glanced down again and noticed that the inspector had on disposable shoe covers, a soft blue in color. Odd, he thought for a second. Both hands were covered with matching disposable gloves. The guy must be some kind of germ nut. The right hand held a clipboard.

Butler said, "Remind me where the fuse box is."

Verno nodded, said, "At the end of the hall." He dipped his brush into the bucket and kept painting.

Butler left the den, walked down the hall, checked all three bedrooms and the two baths, and hurried to the kitchen. He glanced out the dining room window and saw no one. His pickup was parked in the drive behind what could only be a painter's truck. He returned to the den and without a word shoved over the ladder. Verno yelled as he tumbled and crashed against the fireplace hearth, his head landing hard on the brick. Stunned, he tried to scramble and get his feet under him, but it was too late.

From his right pants pocket, Butler pulled out an eight-inch steel rod with a twelve-ounce lead ball on the tip. He affectionately called it Leddie. He flicked it like an expert and the telescopic rod doubled, then tripled in length. He karate-kicked Verno in the ribs and heard them crunch. Verno shrieked in pain, and before he could make another sound the lead ball landed squarely at the back of his cranium, shattering it like a raw eggshell. For practical purposes, he was all but dead. If left alone his body would rapidly shut down and his heart would beat slower and slower until the ten-minute mark, when he stopped breathing. But Butler couldn't wait that long. From his left pants pocket he pulled out a short length of rope—⅜-inch nylon, double twin-braided, marine grade, bright blue and white in color. Quickly, he wrapped it twice around Verno's neck, then rammed his knee into the spinal cord between his shoulder blades and yanked both ends of the rope savagely, snapping back his neck until the top vertebrae began popping.

In his final seconds, Verno grunted one last time and tried to move, as if his body instinctively fought to save itself. He was not a small man and in his younger days had been known to brawl, but with a rope cutting into his throat and his skull fractured, his body had lost all strength. The knee in his back kept him pinned while the monster tried to decapitate him. His last thought may have been one of amazement, at the power and strength of the guy with the goofy shoe covers.

Butler learned years ago that the fight belonged to the fittest. In those crucial seconds, strength and quickness were everything. For thirty years he had pumped iron, practiced karate and tae kwon do, not for his health and not to impress women, but for the surprise attacks.

After two minutes of strangulation, Verno went limp. Butler pulled even tighter, then looped the ends together like a veteran sailor and secured the rope in place with a perfect double clove hitch. He stood, careful to avoid the spattered blood, and allowed himself a few seconds to admire his work. The blood bothered him. There was too much of it and he loathed a messy crime scene. His surgical gloves were covered and there were some small flecks on his work khakis. He should have worn black pants. What was he thinking?

Otherwise, he rather admired the scene. The body was facedown, arms and legs at odd angles. Blood was slowly spreading from the corpse and contrasting nicely with the new pine flooring. The white paint had splattered across the hearth and against a wall, even reaching so far as a window.

The ladder on its side was a nice touch. At first glance, the next person on the scene might think Verno had taken a bad fall and struck his head. A step closer, though, and the rope would tell another story.

Checklist: perimeter, phone, photo, blood, footprints. He glanced through a window and saw nothing moving in the street. He went to the kitchen and rinsed the gloves on his hands, then wiped everything carefully with a paper towel he crammed into a pocket. He closed the two back doors and locked them. Verno's phone was on the counter next to his radio. Butler turned down the radio so he could hear and stuck the phone in his rear pocket. He picked up his clipboard and walked to the foyer where he stopped and breathed deeply. Don't waste a second but never hurry.

He was about to reach for the knob to the front door when he heard the engine of a truck. Then a door slammed. He ducked into the dining room and glanced out the window. "Oh shit."

It was an oversized Ram truck parked at the curb, with DUNWOODY CUSTOM HOMES painted on the driver's door. Its driver was walking across the front yard, holding an envelope. Average height and weight, about fifty years old, with a slight limp. He would enter and immediately see Verno's body in the den to his left. From that moment on, he would be aware of nothing else.

The killer calmly moved into position, ready with his weapon.

A husky voice called out, "Verno, where are you?" Steps, a pause, then "Lanny, you okay?" He took three steps into the den before the lead ball shattered the back of his skull. He fell hard, almost landing on Verno, and was too stunned, too wounded to look behind him. Butler hit him again and again, each blow splintering his cranium and spraying blood across the room.

Butler hadn't brought enough rope for two strangulations, and besides, Dunwoody didn't deserve one. Only the special people got the rope. Dunwoody groaned and thrashed as his mortal wounds shut down his organs. He turned his head and looked at Butler, his eyes red and glazed and seeing nothing. He tried to say something but only grunted again. Finally, he fell hard on his chest and stopped moving altogether. Butler waited patiently and watched him breathe. When he stopped, Butler took his cell phone out of a small pocket of his jacket and added it to his growing collection.

Suddenly, he felt like he had been there for an hour. He checked the street again, eased out the front door, and locked it behind him—all three doors were locked now, which might stall them for a few minutes—and climbed into his truck. Cap down, sunglasses on, though the day had been cloudy. He backed into the street and drove slowly away, just another inspector closing out a busy week.

He parked in a shopping center, far away from the stores and their cameras. He removed the surgical gloves and shoe covers and put them in a bag. He placed the two stolen phones on the seat where he could see and hear them. He tapped one and the name MIKE DUNWOODY flashed on the screen. He tapped the other and saw the name LANNY VERNO. He was not about to get caught with the phones and would lose them in short order. He sat for a long time and collected his thoughts.

Verno had it coming. His name had been on the list for a long time as he drifted from one town to the next, from one bad romance to another, living from paycheck to paycheck. If he had not been such a shiftless and sorry bastard, his life might have been worth something. His early demise could have been avoided. He had signed his death warrant years earlier when he physically threatened the man who called himself Butler.

Dunwoody's mistake was simply bad timing. He had never met Butler and certainly didn't deserve such a violent end. Collateral damage, as they say in the military, but at that moment Butler didn't like what he had done. He didn't kill innocent people. Dunwoody was probably a decent man with a family and a company, maybe even went to church and played with his grandchildren.

Dunwoody's phone blinked and hummed at two minutes after seven. "Marsha" was calling. No voicemail. She waited six minutes and called again.

Probably his wife, thought Butler. Really sad and all, but he had almost no capacity for sympathy, or remorse.

Collateral damage. It had not happened before, but he was proud of the way he handled it.

Mike Dunwoody had stopped drinking years earlier, and his Friday nights in the bars were now history. Marsha wasn't worried about a relapse, though she still had vivid memories of the pub-crawling days with his buddies, almost all of whom worked in construction. In her last call that afternoon she had been specific: Stop by the grocery and get a pound of pasta and fresh garlic. She was making spaghetti and their daughter was coming over. He thought he would be home around six, after he dropped off some checks in the subdivision. With a dozen subs building eight houses, he lived on the phone, and if he didn't take a call it usually meant he was on another line. If he missed a call, especially one from his wife, he returned it almost immediately.

At 7:31, Marsha called his cell for the third time. Butler looked at the screen and almost felt pity, but that lasted for only a second.

She called her son and asked him to drive to
the subdivision and look for his father.

No one was calling Verno.

Butler was driving on county roads and heading north, away from the coast. He figured that by
now the bodies had been discovered and the cops
knew the phones were missing. It was time to get
rid of them. He found the town of Neely, population 400, and drove through it. He had been
there before, scouting. The only business that appeared to be open on a Friday night was a café
on one end of the settlement. The post office was on
the other end with an ancient blue drop box outside, next to a gravel drive. Butler parked in front
of the tiny building, got out and walked to the
door, opened it, went inside to the cramped lobby
and saw a wall of small square rentals. Seeing
no cameras inside or out, he left the building and
casually dropped a 5×8 padded envelope in the
drop box.

Dale Black was the elected sheriff of Harrison
County. He had finished dinner with his wife
and was leashing his dog for their nightly post-
meal walk through the neighborhood. His wife
was already outside, waiting, checking her phone.
His buzzed and he wanted to cuss. It was the

dispatcher, and any call at eight o'clock on a Friday night was not good news.

Twenty minutes later, he turned in to the new development and was met with an impressive display of emergency lights. He parked and hustled to the scene. A deputy, Mancuso, met him at the curb. The sheriff looked at a truck and said, "That's Mike Dunwoody's truck."

"Damned sure is."

"Where's Mike?"

"Inside. One of the two."

"Dead?"

"Oh yes. Cracked skull, I'd say." Mancuso nodded across the street to another truck. "You know his kid Joey?"

"Sure."

"That's him over there. He came out looking for his dad, saw his truck, went to the house but the doors were locked. He got a flashlight and looked through the front window over there, saw the two bodies on the floor. He did not go charging in but had the good sense to call us."

"I'm sure he's a mess."

"And then some."

They walked up the drive toward the house, passing other deputies and first responders, all waiting for something to do. Mancuso said, "I kicked the kitchen door in, got inside, took a look, but kept everybody else out till now."

"Nice work."

They entered the house through the kitchen and flipped on every light switch. They stopped at the entrance to the den and tried to absorb the ghastly crime scene. Two lifeless bodies, faces down, heads covered in blood, dark red pools around them, paint splattered, the ladder on its side.

"Have you touched anything?" Black asked.

"Nothing."

"I assume that's Mike," Black said, nodding.

"Yes."

"And the painter?"

"Got no idea."

"Looks like he has a wallet. Get it."

In the wallet, they found a Mississippi driver's license issued to one Lanny L. Verno, address in Gulfport. The sheriff and the deputy stared at the scene for a few minutes, saying nothing, until Mancuso asked, "Got any knee-jerk reactions?"

"You mean, theories about what happened?"

"Something like that. Joey said his dad was in the subdivision wrapping up the week, paying his subs."

Black scratched his chin and said, "So, Verno here got jumped, knocked off his ladder by somebody who really didn't like him. Cracked his skull, then finished him off with the rope. Then Mike showed up at the wrong time and had to be neutralized. Two killings. The first was well planned and done for a reason. The second was not planned and done to cover up the first. You agree?"

"I got nothing else."

"More than likely the work of someone who knows what he's doing."

"He brought the rope."

"I say we call in the state boys. There's no hurry. Let's protect the scene and let them worry about the forensics."

"Good idea."

He had never returned to the scene. He had read countless stories, some fictional, others supposedly true, about killers who got a thrill by going back. And he had never planned to do so, but the moment suddenly seemed right. He had made no mistakes. No one had a clue. His gray pickup looked like a thousand others in the area. Its fake Mississippi license plates seemed perfectly authentic. And if for any reason things appeared threatening, he could always abort and leave the state.

He took his time and zigzagged back to the subdivision. He saw lights before he got to the street. It was blocked by squad cars. As he drove past he nodded at the cop and glanced beyond him. A thousand red and blue lights lit up the street. Something really bad must have happened down there.

He drove on, with a slight rush, but certainly no thrill.

—

Just before 10:00 p.m., Sheriff Black and Chief Deputy Mancuso approached the town of Neely. In the rear seat was Nic, a twenty-year-old college kid who hung around the police station as the department's part-time techie. He was staring at his iPad and giving directions.

"We're getting close," he said. "Take a right. It appears to be at the post office."

"The post office?" Mancuso said. "Why would he drop off a stolen cell phone at a post office?"

"Because he had to get rid of it," Black said.

"Why not throw it in the river?"

"I don't know. You'll have to ask him."

"Real close now," Nic said. "Right here."

Black pulled into the gravel lot and all three stared at the dark and deserted Neely Post Office. Nic fiddled with his iPad and said, "It's actually right over there, in that blue drop box."

"Of course," Mancuso said. "Makes perfect sense."

Black asked, "Who's the damned postmaster around here?"

"Who'd want to be?" asked Mancuso.

Nic pecked away and said, "Herschel Dereford. Here's his number."

Herschel was sleeping peacefully in his small home five miles out from Neely when he answered the emergency call from a Sheriff Black. It took a few minutes for things to register, and Herschel was at first reluctant to get involved. He said he didn't have the authority, under federal guidelines, to open "his" drop box and allow local authorities to pick through "his" mail.

Sheriff Black pressed harder and said that two men had been murdered that evening, not far away, and they were in pursuit of the killer. An iPhone tracking app had led them to Neely, to "his" post office, and, well, it was crucial to get their hands on the phone immediately. This frightened Herschel enough to agree. He showed up fifteen minutes later but was not happy to be called out. He mumbled something about violations of federal law as he rattled his keys. He explained that he collected the mail every afternoon at precisely 5:00 p.m. when he closed the post office. A truck from Hattiesburg picked it up. Since it was now pushing 11:00 p.m., he expected no other mail to be in the box.

Sheriff Black said to Nic, "Get your phone and film this. Everything."

Herschel turned a key and the front door of the box swung open. From inside he removed a square aluminum box, which he sat on the ground. It had no top. Inside was a single mailer. Mancuso covered it with a flashlight.

Herschel said, "I told you there wouldn't be much."

Sheriff Black said, "Let's go real slow here. Okay, I'm going to take my cell phone and call Mike Dunwoody's number. Understood?"

The rest of them nodded as they stared at the small package. After a few seconds it began emitting a ringing noise.

Sheriff Black ended the call. He took his time and said, "Now, I'll call Lanny Verno's number, the one given to us by his girlfriend." He tapped the number, waited, and from the envelope came the chorus of "On the Road Again" by Willie Nelson. Just as the girlfriend said.

With Nic filming with his iPhone and Mancuso holding his flashlight, and with Herschel not sure what to do next, if anything, the sheriff calmly explained, "Now, we called both numbers, and it's safe to assume both cell phones are in the mailer, about five-by-eight, here in the drop box." He reached into a pocket of his windbreaker and pulled out a pair of surgical gloves. Nic filmed it all. Black said, "Now I'm going to retrieve the package, the mailer, but we will not open it here. The prudent thing to do is to give it to the state crime lab and let their experts analyze things."

He reached down, gently took the envelope, pulled it up for all to see, and for Nic to film, then turned it over. There was an address label on the flip side, and printed in a weird font was: **Cherry McGraw, 114 Fairway #72, Biloxi, MS 39503.**

He exhaled, mumbled an "Oh shit!" and almost dropped the envelope.

"Who is it, boss?" Mancuso asked.

"That's my daughter's address."

His daughter was upset but unharmed. She had been married less than a year and lived near her parents. Her husband had been raised in the country, was an avid hunter, and owned a nice collection of guns. He assured the sheriff that they were safe and taking no chances.

A deputy was dispatched to sit in the sheriff's driveway. Mrs. Black promised her husband that she was safe.

Halfway back to the crime scene, Nic in the rear seat finally said, "I don't think he intended to mail the phones to your daughter."

Sheriff Black did not suffer fools, was otherwise preoccupied anyway, and not eager to hear theories from a college kid who could pass for a fourteen-year-old. "Okay," he said.

"He knew we'd find the phones, plain and simple. There are about ten different ways to find a lost cell phone and he knew we'd track 'em down. According to the postmaster, the late Friday mail is not picked up until Monday after 5:00 p.m. There's no way the package would sit there for seventy-two hours without being found. He had to know that."

"So why address the envelope to my daughter?"

"I don't know. Probably because he's a psychopath who's smart as hell. Many of them are."

Mancuso said, "He's just having a little fun, huh?"

"Ha, ha."

The sheriff was not in the mood for conversation. There were too many conflicting thoughts, unanswered questions, and frightening scenarios.

9

The nickname of "Cleopatra" had followed her from the Tourism Council, a much larger state agency where she had worked for a few years as a staff attorney. Before that, there had been brief stints in state offices that dealt in such matters as mental health, air quality, and beach erosion. It would never be known who tagged her as "Cleopatra," and it wasn't clear, at least to those laboring at the Board on Judicial Conduct, if Charlotte was even aware what her underlings called her. It stuck because it fit, or because Elizabeth Taylor's version was somewhat similar. Pitch-black hair, straight and long with obnoxious bangs that tickled her thick eyebrows and must have required constant care; layers of foundation that strove to fill the cracks and wrinkles the Botox couldn't get to; and enough liner and mascara to doll up a dozen hookers in Vegas. A decade or two earlier, Charlotte might have had a chance at being pretty, but the years of constant work and misguided improvements had robbed her of all possibilities. Any lawyer whose reputation and gossip dwelled on her bad makeup and tight clothing as opposed to her legal skills was doomed to toil in the netherworld of the profession.

She had other physical problems. She liked skirts that were too short that revealed thighs that were too thick. Outside the office she wore six-inch dagger-like heels that would make a stripper blush. They were abnormal and painful to wear, and for that reason she went barefoot at her desk. She had no sense of fashion, which was okay around BJC, where slumming had become the trend. Charlotte's problem was that she fancied herself a real trendsetter. No one was following.

Lacy was wary from day one, for two reasons. The first was that Cleo had a reputation as a climber who was always on the prowl for a bigger job, something that was hardly unusual among the agencies. The second was related to the first, but far more problematic. Cleo didn't like women with law degrees and viewed them all as threats. She knew that most hiring was done by men, and since her entire career was predicated on the next move, she had no time for the girls.

"We may have a serious problem," Lacy said.

Cleo frowned, though the wrinkles in her forehead were well hidden by the bangs. "Okay. Let's have it."

It was late on Thursday and most of the others were already gone. The door to Cleo's large office was closed. "I'm expecting a complaint, one filed with an alias, and one that will be difficult to handle. I'm not sure what to do."

"The judge?"

"Unidentified as of now. Circuit court, ten years on the bench."

"Are you going to make me beg for the dirt?"

Cleo fancied herself a tough cookie, a no-nonsense lawyer with little time for small talk or bullshit. Just give her the facts, because she could damned sure handle them.

"The alleged wrongdoing is murder."

The bangs dangled slightly. "By a sitting judge?"

"I just said that." Lacy was not an abrupt person, but she entered into every conversation with Cleo with her guard up, her tongue ready to fight back, even to strike first.

"Yes you did. When was the alleged murder?"

"Well, there have been several. Alleged. The last was about two years ago, in Florida."

"Several?"

"Yes, several. The complainant thinks there may be as many as six, over the past two decades."

"Do you believe him?"

"I didn't say it was a him. And I don't know what I believe right now. But, I do believe that she or he is near the point of filing a complaint with this office."

Cleo stood, much shorter without those heels, and walked to the window behind her desk. From there she had a splendid view of two other state office buildings. She spoke to the glass: "Well, the obvious question is why not go to the police? I'm sure you've asked that, right?"

"It is indeed obvious and it was my first question. His or her reply was that the police cannot be trusted, not at this point. No one can be trusted. And it's obvious that there isn't enough evidence to prove anything."

"Then what does he or she have?"

"Some rather compelling coincidental proof. The murders took place over a twenty-year period and in several different states. All are unsolved and quite cold. At some point during the judge's life, he crossed paths with each of his victims. And, he has his own method of murder. All of the killings are virtually the same."

"Interesting, to a point. May I ask another obvious question?"

"You're the boss."

"Thank you. If these cases are indeed cold, and the local cops have given up, then how in hell are we supposed to determine that one of our judges is the killer?"

"That's the obvious question, all right. I don't have an answer."

"If you ask me, she sounds like a nut, which, I guess, is about par for the course around here."

"Clients or staff?"

"Complaining parties. We don't have clients."

"Right. The law says we have no choice but to investigate the allegations once a complaint is filed. What do you suggest we do?"

Cleo slid into her executive swivel and looked much taller. "I'm not sure what we will do, but I can promise you what we will not do. This office is not equipped to investigate a murder. If she files a complaint, we will have no choice but to refer it to the Florida state police. It's that simple."

Lacy gave a fake smile and said, "Sounds good to me. But I doubt if we'll see the complaint."

"Let's hope not."

The initial strategy was to inform Jeri by email, and try to avoid any possible histrionics. Lacy sent a terse business-like note that read: Margie. After meeting with our director, I am sorry to inform you that the complaint you suggested will not be handled by our office. If it is filed, it will be referred to the state police.

Within seconds her cell phone rang with an un-identified caller. Normally she would have ignored it but she figured it was Jeri, who began pleasantly,

"You can't go to the state police. The statute says it's up to you to investigate the allegations."

"Hello, Jeri. So how are you today?"

"Miserable, now, anyway. I can't believe this. I'm willing to stick my neck out and file a complaint, but the BJC doesn't have the balls to investigate. You're willing to just sit by and push papers around your desk while this guy literally gets away with murder and keeps on killing."

"I thought you didn't like phones."

"I don't. But this one can't be traced. What am I supposed to do now, Lacy? Pack up twenty years of hard work and go home, pretend like nothing ever happened? Allow my father's killer to go free? Help me here, Lacy."

"It's not my decision, Jeri, I promise."

"Did you recommend that BJC investigate?"

"There's nothing to investigate, not until a formal complaint is filed."

"So why bother if you're just going to run to the police? I can't believe this, Lacy. I really thought you had more guts than this. I'm stunned."

"I'm sorry, Jeri, but there are some cases we're just not equipped to handle."

"That's not what the statute says. The law directs the BJC to assess every complaint that's filed against any judge. There is absolutely no language that says BJC can dump the complaint on the police until after its assessment. You want me to send you a copy of the statute?"

"No, that won't be necessary. I didn't make the decision, Jeri. That's why we have bosses."

"Okay, I'll send the statute to your boss. What's her name? I saw her on the website."

"Don't do that. She knows the statutes."

"Doesn't sound like it. What am I supposed to do now, Lacy? Just forget about Bannick? I've spent the last twenty years."

"I'm sorry, Jeri."

"No you're not. I was planning to drive over Saturday and meet with you in private, lay out everything from the six murders. Give me some guidance here, Lacy."

"I'm out of town this weekend, Jeri. I'm sorry."

"How convenient." After a long pause, she rang off with "Think about this, Lacy. What are you going to do when he kills again? Huh? At some point you and your little BJC become complicit."

Her line went dead.

10

With discipline on the wane, Fridays were quiet around the office. Friday afternoons were tomb-like, as the higher-ups left for long lunches and never returned, and the dwindling hourly staff sneaked off as soon as Cleo closed her door. No one really worried, because Sadelle would work until dark and handle any stray phone calls.

Lacy left before lunch with no plans to return. She went home, changed into shorts, threw a few clothes in a bag, hid a key for Rachel, her new neighbor who was also her dog sitter, and just before 1:00 p.m. hopped in the car with her boyfriend and raced away in the general direction of Rosemary Beach, two and a half hours west along the Gulf Coast. The temperature was pushing eighty and there were no clouds anywhere. She had no laptop, no files, no paperwork of any kind, and, as per their agreement, Allie was similarly un-armed. All evidence of his profession was left in his apartment. Only cell phones were permitted.

The obvious goal of the weekend was to get out of town, leave work behind, go play in the sun and work on their tans. The real reason was far more serious. They were both approaching forty and uncertain about their future, either alone or together. They had been a couple for over two years and had passed through the initial phases of the romance—the dating, the sex, the sleepovers, the trips, the introductions to families, the decla-rations to friends that they were indeed a pair, the unspoken commitment to faithfulness. There was no hint that either wanted to end the relationship; in fact, both seemed content to keep it on course.

What bothered Lacy, and she wasn't sure if it also bothered Allie, was the uncertainty of the fu-ture. Where would they be in five years? She had serious doubts of continuing much longer at BJC. Allie's frustration with the FBI was growing. He thrived in his work and was proud of what he did, but the seventy-hour weeks were taking a toll. If he worked less, could they spend more time to-gether? And if so, could that lead to a closeness? Could that enable them to finally decide if they loved each other? They tossed the L-word around, almost playfully at times, but neither seemed fully committed to it. They had avoided it for the first year and still used it reluctantly.

Lacy's fear was that she would never truly love him, but the romance would plod along conveniently from one stage to the next until there was nothing left but a wedding. And then, at the age of forty or even forty-plus, she would not be able to walk away. She would marry a man she adored but didn't really love. Or did she?

Half her girlfriends were telling her to ditch the guy after two years. The other half were advising her to snag him before he got away.

The weekend was supposed to answer their most serious questions, though she had read enough trashy novels and watched enough romantic comedies to know that the big summit, the grand romantic getaway, seldom worked. Crumbling marriages were rarely saved by a few days at the beach, nor did struggling love affairs gain traction and find clear definition.

She suspected they would have some fun in the sun as they avoided the future and simply kept kicking the can down the road.

"Something's bugging you," he said as he drove with his left hand and rubbed her knee with his right.

It was too early in the weekend to plunge into the serious stuff, so she did a quick pivot and replied, "We have this case that's keeping me awake at night."

"You don't normally stress over your cases."

"They don't normally involve murder."

He looked at her with a smile and said, "Do tell."

"I can't tell, okay. Like yours, my cases are strictly confidential. However, I could probably get the story across if we stick to hypotheticals."

"I'm all ears."

"So, there's a judge, a hypothetical one, let's say he's about fifty, been on the bench for about ten years, and he's a sociopath. Follow?"

"Of course. Most of them are, right?"

"Come on. I'm serious."

"Okay. We studied those in training at Quantico. The BAU—Behavioral Analysis Unit. Part of our standard routine. But that was a long time ago and I've yet to run across one in my work. My specialty is cold-blooded murderers who traffic cocaine and neo-Nazis who mail bombs. Keep going."

"This is all speculation and none of it can be proven, at least not now. According to my witness, also unnamed and too terrified to show her face, the judge has murdered at least six people over the past twenty years. Six kills in six different states. He knew all six victims, had issues with each, of course, and he patiently stalked them until the right moment. All were killed the same way—strangulation with the same type of rope, same method. His signature. Perfect crime scenes, no forensics, nothing but the rope around the neck."

"All cold cases?"

"Ice cold. The police have nothing. No witnesses, no prints, no fibers, no boot marks, no blood, no motive. Nothing at all."

"If he knew them, then there must be a motive."

"You're such a brilliant FBI agent."

"Thanks. Pretty obvious though."

"Yes. The motives vary. Some seem serious, others trivial. I don't know all of them."

"He thinks they're serious."

"He does."

Allie took his right hand off her knee and scratched his chin with it. After a moment he asked, "And this one is on your desk, right?"

"No. The witness has yet to file a formal complaint against the judge. She's too frightened. And Cleopatra told me yesterday that BJC will not get involved in a murder investigation."

"So what happens next?"

"Nothing, I guess. If there's no complaint there's nothing for us to do. The judge remains untouched and goes about his business, even if it includes murder."

"You sound like you believe this witness."

"I do. I've struggled with it since Monday, the day I met her, and I've reached the point where I believe her."

"Why can't she go to the police with her suspect?"

"Several reasons. One, she's frightened and convinced that the killer will find out and add her name to his list. Perhaps the biggest hesitation is that the police have no reason to believe her. The cops in small-town South Carolina don't have time to worry about a cold case in south Florida. The cops in Little Rock don't have time for a similar killing near Chattanooga, one with no forensics."

Allie nodded as he thought. "That's four. Where are the other two?"

"She hasn't told me yet."

"Who was murdered in Little Rock?"

"A newspaper reporter."

"And why was his name on the list?"

"We're getting away from the hypothetical, Agent Pacheco. I can't give you any more details."

"Fair enough. Have you discussed the FBI with her?"

"Yes, briefly, and as of now she has no interest. She's convinced it's too dangerous and she also has strong doubts about its willingness to get involved. Why would the FBI get excited about a string of murders they have no chance of solving?"

"She might be surprised at what we can do."

Lacy thought about this for a few miles as they listened to the radio and zipped through traffic. Allie was a compulsive speeder and when he got nailed by radar, at least twice a year, he loved to pull out his badge and wink at the trooper. He boasted of never getting a ticket.

Lacy asked, "How would that work? Say the witness wanted to lay everything on the table in front of the FBI."

Allie shrugged and said, "I don't know, but I can find out."

"Not yet. I have to go real slow with this witness. She's damaged."

"Damaged?"

"Yes, her father was victim number two."

"Wow. This gets better." His most obnoxious habit, to date, was chewing his fingernails, and only the left ones. The ones on the right were never attacked. When he began chewing he was thoroughly engrossed in something and she could almost hear his brain churning away.

After a few miles he said, frowning at the windshield, "This is pretty intense. Hypothetically, let's say you're in the room with the police—us, locals, state, doesn't matter—and you say, 'Here's your killer.' Name, rank, serial number, address. And here are his six victims, all strangled over the past twenty-plus years, and—"

"And there's no way to prove it."

"And there's no way to prove it. Unless."

"Unless what?"

"Unless you find evidence from the killer himself."

"That would require a warrant, wouldn't it? A document that would be impossible to obtain without probable cause. There's no cause whatsoever, only some wild speculation."

"I thought you said you believe her."

"I think I do."

"You're not convinced."

"Not all the time. You have to admit, it's far-fetched."

"Indeed it is. I've never heard of anything like it. But then, as you know, I chase a different class of criminal."

"A warrant is unlikely. Plus, he's probably paranoid and too smart to get caught."

"What do you know about him?"

"Nothing. He's just a hypothetical."

"Come on. We've gone this far."

"Single, never married, probably lives alone. Security cameras everywhere. A respected judge who gets out enough to appear socially acceptable. Highly regarded by colleagues and lawyers. And voters. You're the profiler, what else do you want?"

"I'm not a profiler. Again, that's a different section."

"Got it. So if you took the six murders and didn't mention the suspect, and presented them to the top FBI profilers, what would they say?"

"I have no idea."

"But could you ask someone, you know, sort of off the record?"

"Why bother? You already know the killer."

Their favorite hotel was the Lonely Dunes, a quaint little boutique getaway with forty rooms, all facing the water and just inches from the sand.

They checked in, left their bags unpacked in their room, and hurried to the pool where they found a shaded table and ordered lunch and a bottle of cold wine. A young couple cavorted at the far end of the pool; something was happening just under the surface. Beyond the patio the Gulf shimmered in a brilliant blue as the sun beat down upon it.

When their drinks were half gone, Allie's cell phone vibrated on the table. Lacy said, "What's that?"

"Sorry."

"I thought we agreed no phones at lunch. I left mine in the room."

Allie grabbed his and said, "It's the guy I mentioned. He knows a couple of the profilers."

"No. Let it ring. I've said too much and I don't want to talk about the case."

The phone eventually stopped vibrating. Allie put it in his pocket as if he would never touch it again. The crab salads were served and the waiter poured more wine. As if on cue, the clouds rolled in and the sun disappeared.

"Chance of scattered showers," Allie said. "As I recall from my weather app, which is still on my phone, which is tucked away in my pocket and untouchable."

"Ignore it. If it rains it rains. We're not going anywhere. A question."

"Sure."

"It's almost three on a Friday afternoon. Does your boss know where you are?"

"Not exactly, but he knows I'm off with my girlfriend for the weekend. And Cleopatra?"

"I don't care. And she doesn't either. She'll be gone in a few months."

"And you, Lacy? How much longer will you be there?"

"Oh, that's the great question, isn't it? I've stayed too long in a dead-end job and now it's past time to leave. But where do I go?"

"It's not a dead end. You enjoy your work and it's important."

"Perhaps. Maybe occasionally. But it's not exactly heavy lifting anymore. I'm bored with it and I probably say that to you too often."

"It's just me here. You can tell me anything."

"My deepest, darkest secrets?"

"Please. I'd love to hear them."

"But you wouldn't tell me, Allie. You're not wired that way. You're too much of an agent to drop your guard."

"What do you want to know?"

She smiled at him and sipped her wine. "Okay. Where will you be one year from now?"

He frowned and looked away. "That's a punch in the gut." A sip of his own wine. "I don't know, really. I've been with the Bureau for eight years and love it. I always figured I'd be a lifer, that I'd chase the bad guys until they put me in an office at the age of fifty and kicked me out the door at fifty-seven, the mandatory. But, I'm not so sure now. What I do is often thrilling and rarely boring, but it's definitely a younger man's job. I look at the guys who are pushing fifty and they're burning out. Fifty is not that old, Lacy. I'm not sure I'll be a career guy."

"You've thought about leaving?"

"Yes." It was tough to admit and she doubted he had ever said so before. He sniffed his wine, drank some, and said, "And, there's something else. I've been in Tallahassee for five years and it's time for a change. There are more and more hints of transfers. It's part of the business, something we all expect."

"You're getting transferred?"

"I didn't say that. But there might be some pressure over the next few months."

Lacy was stunned and tried hard not to show it. After a moment she was surprised by how unsettling it was. The thought of not being with Allie was, well, inconceivable. She managed to ask, calmly, "Where would you go?"

He casually glanced around, the way savvy agents learn to do, saw no one even remotely interested in them, and said, "This is on the quiet. The director is organizing a national task force on hate groups and I've been invited to sort of try out for the team. I have not said yes or no, and if I said yes there's no guarantee that I would be chosen. But it's a prestigious group of elite agents."

"Okay. Where would you be assigned?"

"Either Kansas City or Portland. But it's all preliminary."

"Are you tired of Florida?"

"No. I'm tired of lost weekends chasing cartels. I'm tired of living in a cheap apartment and not being sure about the future."

"I can't handle a long-distance romance, Allie. I prefer to have you close by."

"Well, as of now, I have no plans to leave. It's just a possibility. Can we talk about you?"

"I'm an open book."

"Anything but. The same question: Where will you be one year from now?"

She drank some wine. The waiter brushed by, stopped long enough to top off both glasses, and disappeared. She shook her head and said, "I really don't know. I doubt I'll be at BJC, but I've been telling myself that for several years now. I'm not sure I have the guts to quit and leave the job security."

"You have a law degree."

"Yes, but I'm almost forty and I have no speciality, something that law firms prefer. If I hung out my shingle and started drafting wills I'd starve to death. I've never written one. My only option is to do what most government lawyers do and scramble up the food chain for a bigger salary. I'm thinking of something different, Allie. Maybe a midlife crisis at the age of forty. Any interest?"

"A joint crisis?"

"Sort of. More like a partnership. Look, both of us have doubts about our futures. We're forty years old, give or take, still single, no kids, and we can afford to take a chance, do something stupid, fall flat and pick ourselves up."

There it was. Finally on the table. She took a deep breath, couldn't believe she had gone so far, and watched his eyes carefully. They were curious and surprised. He said, "There were a couple of important words in there. The first I heard was 'afford.' I'm in no position to stop working at my age and launch myself into a crisis."

"What was the second word?"

"'Stupid.'"

"Just a figure of speech. As a general rule, neither of us do stupid things."

The waiter appeared with a tray and began clearing the table. When he grabbed the empty wine bottle he asked, "Another?" Both shook their heads.

They charged the lunch to their room, which was $200 a night, off-season, and when they checked out on Sunday they would split the bill. They tried to split everything. Both earned around $70,000 a year. Hardly retirement money, but then no one had mentioned retirement.

They left the pool and walked to the edge of the ocean where they realized the water was too cold even for a quick plunge. Arm in arm, they strolled along the beach, drifting aimlessly like the waves.

"I have a confession," he said.

"You never confess."

"Okay, try me. For about a year I've been sav-ing money to buy you a ring."

She stopped cold as they disentangled and looked at each other.

"And? What happened to it?"

"I haven't bought one because I'm not sure you'll take it."

"Are you sure you want to offer it?"

He hesitated, for too long, and finally said, "That's what we have to decide, right, Lacy? Where are we going?"

She crossed her arms and tapped her lips with an index finger. "You want to take a break, Allie?"

"A break?"

"Yes, some time off. From me."

"Not really. Do you?"

"No. I kinda like having you around."

They smiled, then hugged, then continued along the beach. With nothing resolved.

11

The email arrived at 9:40 on Sunday night, when Jeri was alone, as always in her townhouse preparing her week's lectures and debating whether to watch a television show. The address was one of several permanent ones she maintained, heavily encrypted and seldom used. Only four people had access to it, and no one could follow it. The man on the other end was someone she had never met, would indeed never have reason to, and she did not know his real name. When she paid him, always in cash, she sent the money inside a thin paperback in a little package through the mail to a post office box in Camden, Maine, to a vague outfit called KL Data.

Nor did he know her name. Online, her handle was "LuLu," and that was all he wanted or needed. As in, Hello LuLu. Got a nibble on something of possible interest.??

LuLu? She smiled and shook her head in slight bewilderment at the number of facades she had built around herself in the past twenty years. Aliases, temporary post office boxes, facial disguises, impenetrable email addresses with two-factor identification, a bag of cell phones and cheap burners.

In her solitary world she referred to him as KL, and having no idea what those initials meant, she had tagged him as Kenny Lee. According to a reference years ago, Kenny Lee had a background in law enforcement but she had no idea how that career came to an end. She knew he had lost a brother in an unsolved murder, a cold case that haunted him and drove him to his present calling. "Well hello, Kenny Lee," she mumbled.

She replied: How many hours?

Less than three.

Okay.

She had never heard his voice and had no idea if he was eighty or forty. They had been involved in whatever their relationship could be called for almost ten years. She said to herself, "Let's see what you have, Kenny Lee."

His rate was $200 an hour and she could not afford any surprises. He was a freelance investigator, a lone gunman who worked for no one and anyone who was willing to pay his rate. He worked for the families of victims, small-town cops in dozens of states, the FBI, investigative journalists, novelists, and Hollywood producers. For those seeking data on violent crime, he was the source. He seldom left his basement and lived online digging, trolling, gathering, reporting, and selling his data. He absorbed murder statistics from all fifty states and probably spent more time in the FBI's violent crime clearinghouse than anyone inside or outside the Bureau.

When the issue was murder, and especially unsolved murder, Kenny Lee was the man. Above the table, he ran his little business through a Bangor lawyer who handled his contracts and wire transfers of fees. All of his business was word of mouth, and quiet words at that. KL did not advertise and could say no to anyone. Under the table, he used aliases and coded emails and took his fees in cash, anything to protect the identity of his clients and the killers they were stalking.

An hour later, Jeri was sitting in the dark, waiting, asking herself what she would do if KL had another victim. He wasn't always right. No one could be. Ten months earlier, KL had appeared from the clouds and reported on a strangulation in Kentucky that at first looked promising. Jeri paid him for four hours of work, then spent two months digging before she hit a dead end, a rather abrupt one, when the police arrested a man who confessed.

KL had sent a note and said too bad, those are the breaks. He followed thousands of cases around the country, and many of them were old and would never be solved.

Each year in the United States there were about three hundred murders officially categorized as suffocation/strangulation/asphyxiation. Half involved a lunge for the throat to end a domestic disagreement, and those were usually solved in short order.

The rest involved strangulation, the act of wrapping something violently around the neck, with the murderer routinely leaving behind the ligature. Electrical cords, belts, bandanas, baling wire, chains, bootlaces, coat hangers, and ropes and cords of many makes and varieties. The same type of nylon rope used to kill her father was used all the time. It was readily available in stores and online.

Most of the murders in the second category were never solved.

Her laptop pinged, and she opened it and went through her authentication protocols and typed in her passcodes. It was Kenny Lee:

Five months ago, in Biloxi, Mississippi, Harrison County, victim name of Lanny Verno was found strangled. No crime scene photos yet but maybe soon. Description of ligature sounds close. 3/8 inch nylon rope tied off with the same knot to keep pressure on. Severe head wound, probably before death. Deceased was 37 years old and working as a house painter, killed on the job, no witnesses. However, a complication. The police think a witness appeared at the wrong time and met the same fate, minus the rope. Severe head wounds. Police believe second victim had stopped by to give Verno a check—it was Friday afternoon and Verno was expecting a check—and the second murder was not planned. The Verno murder was definitely planned. No crime scene evidence, other than the rope. No blood samples from anyone other than the two victims. No fibers, no prints, no forensics, and no witnesses. Another clean site—too clean. Active investigation with little word to the press. File is being tightly sealed—thus no photos, no autopsy reports. As you well know, these always take time.

KL paused to give Jeri time to respond. She shook her head in frustration as she remembered her often futile efforts to go through police files that had been gathering dust for years. As was always the case, the fewer clues the investigators had, the more zealous their protection of their files.

They didn't want anyone to know of their paltry progress.

She wrote: What do you know about the rope and the knot?

Method and motive. The first was in plain sight for the detectives to ponder and the lab technicians to analyze. The second, though, could take weeks and months to track down.

KL replied: I have the report filed by the state crime lab with the FBI clearinghouse. The rope is described as nylon, green in color, 3/8 inch, a 30 inch section, tied and secured in place and left behind, obviously. There is no mention of a knot, tourniquet, ratchet, or any device to hold the rope in place. No photos were attached to the report. The crime is obviously unsolved, the investigation is open and in full swing, so most of the relevant details are being guarded by the police. Standard procedure. The old stonewall.

Jeri walked to her kitchen and took a diet soda from the fridge. She popped the top, took a drink, and returned to the sofa and her laptop. She wrote: Okay, I'm in. Send what you have. Thanks.

My pleasure. In fifteen minutes.

Driving along the Gulf Coast on Interstate 10, Mobile was only an hour from Biloxi, but the two towns were in different states, different worlds.

Mobile's **Press-Register** had few readers next door, and Biloxi's **Sun Herald** had even fewer subscribers in Alabama.

Jeri was not surprised that the Mobile press had not covered a double murder sixty miles away. She opened her laptop, turned on her security VPN, and began searching. On Saturday, October 19, the front page of the **Sun Herald** was covered with breaking news of the twin homicides. Mike Dunwoody was a well-known builder around Biloxi and along the Gulf Coast. There was a photo of Mike taken from his company's website. He left behind his wife, Marsha, two children, and three grandchildren. His funeral arrangements were incomplete when the story was published.

Of Lanny Verno, much less was known. He lived in a trailer park somewhere near Biloxi. A neighbor said he had been there for a couple years. His live-in girlfriend came and went. One of his employees said Lanny was from somewhere in Georgia but had lived all over the place.

In the days that followed, the **Sun Herald** worked hard to keep the story fresh. The police were incredibly quiet and offered almost nothing. No one in the Dunwoody family would venture a word. The funeral was at a large church and drew a crowd. Reporters were kept away by deputies, at the request of the family. A distant cousin of

Verno's showed up to reluctantly claim the body and take it back to Georgia. He cursed a reporter. A week after the murders, Sheriff Black held a press conference and divulged absolutely nothing new. A reporter asked if any portable phones were retrieved from the bodies, and this drew a firm "No comment."

"But isn't it true that two cell phones were recovered from a postal box in the town of Neely?"

The sheriff looked like someone had just revealed the killer's name, but managed to recover with a stern "No comment."

Virtually every other question was met with the same response.

The lack of cooperation by the sheriff fueled gossip that something big was coming down, that perhaps they were so tight-lipped because they were closing in on the killer and didn't want to spook him.

Nothing happened, though, and the days dragged into weeks and months. The Dunwoody family posted a reward of $25,000 for any information about the murders. This attracted a rash of calls from nuts who knew nothing.

The Verno family was never heard from.

At midnight, Jeri was drinking strong coffee and preparing for another sleepless night at the computer. KL sent his summary along with a copy of the official violent crime report the Mississippi state police had filed with the FBI.

She had been down this road many times and did not look forward to opening another file.

12

BJC was governed by a five-person Board of Directors, all retired judges and lawyers who had found favor, or something along those lines, with the Governor. The big donors and heavy hitters were awarded appointments far more prestigious than BJC—college boards and gaming commissions and such, gigs with nice budgets and perks that allowed the chosen ones to travel and rub elbows with the powerful; whereas BJC board members got meals, rooms, and fifty cents a mile. They met six times a year—three in Tallahassee and three in Fort Lauderdale—to review cases, hold hearings, and occasionally reprimand judges. Removal from office was rare. Since the BJC's creation in 1968, only three judges had been kicked off the bench.

Four of the five board members gathered late Monday morning for a scheduled meeting. The fifth seat was vacant and the Governor was too busy to fill it. His last two invitations had been declined by his chosen appointees, so he said screw it. Meetings were held in a borrowed conference room at the Supreme Court because the BJC suite was too depressing to take over for the day.

The first item on their agenda was a ten o'clock appointment with the director, a private, one-hour recap of the agency's caseload, finances, personnel, and so on. It had become an unpleasant ritual because Charlotte Baskin had one foot out the door and everyone knew it.

After going through the motions with her, the members were scheduled to take up the docket of pending cases.

Lacy was thankful she had nothing on the docket and would not appear before the board. Her Monday began like most others and required the usual pep talk to herself about hustling to the office and, as the senior investigator, arriving with lots of smiles and encouragement and excitement about serving the taxpayers. But the pep talk didn't work, primarily because she was still mentally at the beach and by the pool. She and Allie had enjoyed three long lunches, with wine, and plenty of naps and sex and long walks along the water's edge. At some point they had agreed that they should forget the future for the time being and simply live in the moment. Worry about the important stuff later.

Once she was away from him, though, she began to ask herself the question that had nagged her since Friday: If he gave me a ring, what would I do with it?

The answer was elusive.

At 9:48 another email arrived, again from Jeri. There had been at least five over the weekend, all ignored until now. Lacy had put off the difficult conversation long enough. She had learned long ago that procrastination only made the task more unpleasant. On her cell phone, she punched one number. No answer. No voicemail. She tried another one. Same result. She was quickly losing patience with the cloak-and-dagger as she punched the last number she had for Jeri.

"Hi, Lacy," came the pleasant but tired voice. "Where have you been?"

And how is that any of your business? She swallowed hard, took a deep breath, and replied, "Good morning, Jeri. I trust this line is secure."

"Of course. Sorry for the inconvenience."

"Yes. You've called and emailed all weekend, I see."

"Yes, we need to talk, Lacy."

"We're talking now, on Monday. I thought I explained to you that I do not work on weekends and I asked you not to call or email me. Right?"

"Yes, you're right, and I'm sorry, but this is really important."

"I know it is, Jeri, and I have some bad news. I met again with my boss and presented the allegations, and she was adamant. We will not get involved in a murder investigation. Period. As I have already told you several times, we are not equipped or trained for that kind of work."

A pause. One that would be brief because, Lacy knew Jeri was not accustomed to taking no. Then she said, "But I have the right to file a complaint. I've memorized the statute. I can do so anonymously. And by law the BJC is required to spend forty-five days assessing the allegations. Right, Lacy?"

"Yes, that's the statute."

"Then I'll file a complaint."

"And my boss says we will immediately refer it to the state police for investigation."

Lacy waited for a sharp rebuke, one that Jeri had no doubt worked on. She waited and waited and finally realized the call was over. Jeri had abruptly ended it and walked away.

Lacy was not naive enough to think they would never speak again. Maybe, though, Jeri would simply go away for a while. They had met only a week before.

And maybe the killings would stop.

—

Half an hour later, Jeri was back. She began with "I'm not sure, Lacy, but there could be two more dead bodies. Numbers seven and eight. I'm digging for confirmation and I could be wrong. I certainly hope so. Regardless, he will not stop."

"Confirmation? I didn't know you had confirmed the others."

"I have, in my mind at least. My theory may be based on coincidental evidence, but you have to admit it's overwhelming."

"I'm not sure it's overwhelming but it's certainly insufficient to start an investigation. I'll say it again, Jeri, we are not getting involved."

"Is it your decision or your interim director's?"

"What difference does it make? We're not getting involved."

"Would you if you had the authority?"

"Goodbye, Jeri."

"Fine, Lacy, but from this point on the blood will be on your hands."

"That strikes me as an overreaction."

Jeri mumbled incoherently as if trying to hide her words. After a few seconds she said, "He's killing more these days, Lacy, almost one victim per year. This is not unusual for serial killers, the smart ones anyway. They start slow, find some success, hone their skills, lose their reluctance and fear, and convince themselves they are too clever. That's when they start making mistakes."

"What kind of mistakes?"

"I'm not going to discuss this on the phone."

"You called me."

"Right, and I'm not sure why." Her line went dead again.

Felicity suddenly appeared at her desk without making a sound and handed over a telephone message, an old-fashioned pink slip. "Better call this guy," she said. "He was pretty rude."

"Thanks," Lacy said, taking the message and looking at her receptionist as if she could leave now. "Please close the door on the way out."

Earl Hatley was the current chairman of the BJC. He was a former judge, a nice gentleman, and one of the few members Lacy had met over the years who actually cared about improving the judiciary. He must have been holding his phone because he answered immediately. He asked if she could drop whatever she was doing and hustle over to the Supreme Court building for an urgent meeting.

Fifteen minutes later, Lacy walked into a small conference room and was greeted by the four. Earl asked her to have a seat and pointed to a chair at the end of the table. He said, "I'll skip the preliminaries, Lacy, because we're running behind schedule, and we have a more pressing matter."

She showed them both palms and said, "I'm all ears."

"We met with Charlotte Baskin first thing this morning and she handed in her resignation. She's gone, moving out today. It was a mutual parting. She was a bad fit, as I'm sure you were very much aware, and we were getting complaints. So, once again, we have no executive director."

"Am I still employed?" Lacy asked, not the least bit perturbed.

"Oh, yes. You can't leave, Lacy."

"Thanks."

"As you well know, Charlotte was the fourth ED in the past two years. I've heard that morale is quite low."

"What morale? Everybody is looking for another job. We sit over there, year in, year out, waiting for the ax to fall. What do you expect? It's hard to remain enthusiastic when our meager budget gets cut every year."

"We understand this. It's not our fault. We're on the same team."

"I know who's at fault and I'm not blaming you. But it's hard to do our work with weak leadership, sometimes no leadership, and fading support from the legislature. The Governor couldn't care less what we do."

Judith Taylor said, "I'm meeting with Senator Fowinkle next week. He's chair of finance, as you know, and his staff thinks we can get some more money."

Lacy smiled and nodded as if she were truly grateful. She'd heard it all before.

Earl said, "Here's our plan, Lacy. You're the

senior investigator and the star of the organization. You are respected, even admired, by your colleagues. We're asking you to become the interim director until we can find a permanent one."

"No thanks."

"That was quick."

"Well, so was your request. I've been here for twelve years and know my way around. The big office is the worst one."

"It's just temporary."

"Everything is temporary these days."

"You're not thinking about leaving, are you?"

"We all think about it. Who can blame us? As state employees, the law says we get the same raises as everyone else, if the legislature is feeling generous. So when they cut our budget, we have no choice but to cut everything but salaries. Staff, equipment, travel, you name it."

The four looked at each other in defeat. The situation seemed hopeless and at that moment all four could walk out the door, resign, go home, and let someone else worry about judicial complaints.

But Judith gamely hung on and said, "Help us here, Lacy. Take the job for six months. You can stabilize the agency and give us some time to shore up the budget. You'll be the boss and have complete authority. We have confidence in you."

Earl added quickly, "A ton of confidence, Lacy. You are by far the most experienced."

Judith said, "The salary is not bad."

"It's not about money," Lacy said. The salary was $95,000 a year, a nice improvement over her current $70,000. She had never really thought about the director's salary, at least not in a covetous way. But it was indeed a substantial raise.

Earl said, "You can restructure the place any way you want. Hire or fire, we don't care. But the ship is sinking and we need stability."

Lacy asked, "How do you plan to shore up the budget, as you say? This year the legislature cut it again, down to one-point-nine million. Four years ago BJC got two-point-three million. Peanuts compared to a sixty-billion-dollar state government, but we were created by the same legislature and given our orders."

Judith smiled and said, "We're tired of the cuts too, Lacy, and we're going after the legislature. Let us worry about that. You run the agency and we'll find the money."

Lacy's judgment was suddenly clouded with thoughts of Jeri Crosby. What if her suspicions were true? What if the killings continued? As director, interim or not, Lacy would have the authority to do whatever she wanted with Jeri's complaint.

And she thought about the money, the not insignificant raise. She rather liked the idea of restructuring the office, getting rid of some dead weight and finding younger talent. She thought of her weekend with Allie and the reality that they had not made any progress in planning their

future, so a dramatic change in scenery was unlikely, at least anytime soon.

The four smiled at her and waited, as if desperate for the right answer. Lacy kept her frown and
said, "Give me twenty-four hours."

13

In stalking Ross Bannick, she had learned to work with one crucial assumption: he was a killer with great patience. He had waited five years to kill her father, nine to kill the reporter, twenty-two to kill Kronke, and approximately fourteen to kill his scoutmaster. Finding the point at which his path crossed with that of Lanny Verno, if it happened at all, would require the usual painstaking and dogged digging through a mountain of public records that stretched back for years, even decades.

She was a tenured professor who lectured three days a week and kept somewhat regular office hours. The book she was writing was years past due. She managed to work just enough to satisfy her dean and her students, but she was far too occupied with crime to excel as a teacher like her father. She was divorced and attractive but had no time to even think about romance. Her daughter was doing fine with her graduate studies at Michigan, and they chatted or emailed every other day. Jeri had almost no other diversions from her real calling, her pursuit. She worked hours each night and early into the mornings chasing leads, pursuing wild theories, hitting dead-ends, and burning enormous amounts of time. "I'm wasting my life," she said over and over in her loneliness.

Jeri guessed that, as an itinerant house painter, Verno didn't bother to vote, but nonetheless she dug through the registration records for Chavez, Escambia, and Santa Rosa Counties. She found two Lanny L. Vernos. One was too old, the other was dead. Vehicle registration found another one, but he was still alive.

The online locators, both the free and the pricey, found five Lanny Vernos in the Florida Panhandle. The obvious problem was that Jeri had no idea, and no way to know, when her Lanny Verno had ever lived in the area, and, if so, when he moved on. He was definitely not living there when he was murdered. According to the bare-bones police report Kenny Lee obtained from the FBI clearinghouse, Verno's female companion said they had "been together" for less than two years and lived in a trailer near Biloxi.

If he had a history with women then perhaps he had been through divorce court. Jeri spent hours online digging through those Florida records and found nothing helpful. If he had children scattered around then maybe he'd had support problems, but the court records yielded nothing. As a veteran sleuth with over twenty years of experience, she knew how precarious family and youth court records were. So much of the useful information was sealed for privacy reasons.

If he had spent his life as a house painter, then the odds were decent that he'd been in trouble with the police.

There were no felony convictions for Lanny Verno, at least not in Florida, and he had been involved in no civil litigation. Fortunately, though, the Pensacola City police department had digitized its records a decade earlier, and in the process had memorialized thirty years' worth of arrests and old court dockets somewhere deep in the cloud. At two thirty in the morning, as she sipped another diet cola, no caffeine, she found a simple entry for the arrest of one Lanny L. Verno in April of 2001. The alleged crime was attempted assault with a weapon. He posted $500 bond and bailed out. She began cross-checking the arrest with the court docket and found another entry. On June 11, 2001, Verno was found not guilty in Pensacola city court. Case dismissed.

At that time, Ross Bannick was thirty-six years

old and had been practicing law in the area for ten years.

Could it be the crossing of their paths? Was that where it happened?

It was a long shot, but in Jeri's world so was everything else.

She chose a private detective from Mobile, one who would claim to be from Atlanta, or anywhere else for that matter. The sparse remnants of Verno's family had buried him near Atlanta, according to an Internet posting from a low-end burial service.

She hated to pay private detectives but often had no choice. Almost all police investigators were middle-aged white guys who frowned on women digging through old crimes, especially women of color. Theirs was a man's business, and the whiter the better. Most of her spare cash went to private eyes who looked and talked remarkably like the cops they dealt with.

His name was Rollie Tabor, ex-cop, $150 an hour, no-nonsense, and able to live with her fiction. He'd done it before and she liked his work. He drove to Pensacola, went to the police department, and shot enough bull with the desk jockeys to get himself sent to a warehouse several blocks away where all the old stuff was stored. Primarily evidence—court exhibits, rape kits, thousands of confiscated weapons of every variety—but also unclaimed goods, and rows and rows of tall cabinets filled with too many retired files to count. An ancient clerk in a faded police uniform met him at the front counter and asked what he wanted.

"Name's Dunlap, Jeff Dunlap," Tabor said. As the clerk scribbled on a log sheet, Tabor studied his name badge. Sergeant Mack Faldo. He'd been there at least fifty years and could not remember when he stopped caring.

"Got an ID?" Faldo grunted.

Tabor had an impressive collection of IDs. He pulled out his wallet and removed a Georgia driver's license for Jeff Dunlap, who, as a real person, lived quietly and unsuspectingly in the town of Conyers, just outside of Atlanta. If the sergeant bothered to check, which he never thought about doing, he would find a real person at a real address and immediately lose whatever interest he had. But Faldo was too jaded to even glance at the card and then glance at Dunlap to compare. He grunted again, "Gotta make a copy."

He walked over to an ancient Xerox, took his time, and walked back with the license.

"Now, what can I do for you?" he asked, as if doing anything would upset his day.

"Looking for a court file from about fifteen years ago. Guy named Lanny Verno got himself arrested but got off in city court. He was murdered a few months back over in Biloxi and his family has hired me to dig through his past. He lived here for a spell and may have left behind a kid or two. Sort of a drifter."

Tabor handed over a sheet of paper printed from a computer with the name of Lanny L. Verno, his Social Security number, his date of birth, and date of death. It was nothing official but Faldo took it. "When, exactly?"

"June 2001."

Faldo's eyelids half closed, as if he might begin a nap right then, and he nodded toward a door. "Meet me over there."

Through the door, Tabor followed the old man into a cavernous room with more filing cabinets. Each drawer was labeled with months and years. Into 2001, Faldo stopped, reached up, yanked open and removed an entire drawer. He mumbled, "June 2001." He carried it to a long table covered with dust and clutter and said, "Here it is. Have fun."

Tabor looked around and asked, "Isn't this stuff online now?"

"Not all of it. These are the files for the cases that were dismissed, for whatever reason. If there was a conviction, then those files are supposed to be in the archives. These files here, Mr. Dunlap, need to be burned."

"Got it."

Faldo was tired when he came to work and

exhausted by now. He said, "No unauthorized photos. You need copies, bring it to me. A dollar a page."

"Thanks."

"Don't mention it." Faldo walked away, leaving Dunlap alone with a million worthless files.

There were at least a hundred in the drawer on the table, neatly arranged by date. In a matter of minutes, Tabor found June 12, flipped through it alphabetically, and pulled out a file for Lanny L. Verno.

Clipped inside were several sheets of paper. The first was labeled INCIDENT REPORT and an Officer N. Ozment had typed: Victim [name redacted] came to the station, said he had an altercation earlier that day in his garage with Verno, said there was a dispute over payment for services, said Verno threatened him and even pulled out a handgun; after that things settled down and Verno left. There were no witnesses. Victim [name redacted] swore the warrant, charging attempted assault.

Someone had obviously covered the name of the alleged victim with a thick black marker.

Page 2 was an ARREST REPORT with a mug shot of Verno at the city jail, and it included his address, phone number, Social Security number, and listed him as self-employed. His criminal record had only one DUI.

Page 3 was a copy of the $500 bond agreement with AAA Bail.

Page 4 was labeled: COURT ABSTRACT. But the entire page was blank.

Tabor spent the next few minutes flipping through other files in the drawer and studying the Court Abstracts. Each was a standard form that, when filled in, gave a concise summary of what happened in court, with the names of the judge, prosecutor, defendant, defense lawyer (if any), complaining party, victim, and witnesses and exhibits. He found a completed Court Abstract for each of the other files. Shoplifting, simple assault, unleashed dogs, public drunkenness, public profanity, public lewdness, harassment, and so on. The drawer was filled with all manner of allegations—none, evidently, that were proven in court.

A sign warned: NO UNAUTHORIZED PHOTOS OR COPIES.

He asked himself who, other than himself and his client, could possibly want copies or photos, authorized or not.

He took the file back to the front counter and disturbed Faldo again. "Can I get this file copied? Four pages."

Faldo almost smiled as he got up and lumbered over. "A dollar apiece," he said as he took the file. Tabor watched as he methodically unclipped the four sheets, copied them, clipped them back just so, and returned them to the counter. The investigator offered a $5 bill but Faldo would have none of it.

"Only credit cards," he said.

"I don't use 'em," Tabor said. "Gave 'em up in a bankruptcy years ago."

This really upset Faldo's world and he frowned as if hit with irritable bowels. "No cash, sorry." The four copied sheets were lying on the counter, unneeded and unwanted by anyone else in the world.

Tabor dropped the $5 bill, picked up the copies, and asked, "Shall I put the file back?"

"Nope. I got it. That's my job."

And what a crucial job it was. "Thanks."

"Don't mention it."

In his car, Tabor called Jeri but got her voicemail. He went to a coffee shop, and as he killed time he took photos of the four sheets of paper and sent them to her. After his third cup, she finally called. He described what he had found and what the other files looked like. It was obvious that Verno's had been doctored.

"This officer, N. Ozment, is he still around?" she asked.

"No. I've already checked."

"And no other names in the file? Just Verno and Ozment?"

"That's all."

"Well, that makes the next step easier. See if you can find Mr. N. Ozment."

—

Jeri was in her office on campus, her door open so any student could pop in for a chat, but she was alone as she crunched on a light salad and sipped a diet soda. Eating was difficult with her stomach flipping the way it always did when someone she was paying $150 an hour was on the job with no idea how long the job might take. There was also the excitement of finding paperwork that had been tampered with. She reminded herself that she did not yet know if the Lanny Verno she was tracking in Pensacola was also the one who had been murdered in Biloxi, and she admitted that the odds were long. There were ninety-eight Lanny Vernos in the country.

However, the facts might be tilting in her favor. As an esteemed member of the judiciary, Judge Bannick would certainly have easy access to old court files and evidence. He would be respected by the police. As an elected official, he would need their support every four years. He would be able to come and go through their many protocols and procedures.

Lanny Verno, a house painter, pulling a gun on Ross Bannick, a hotshot lawyer, thirteen years ago? And winning the case?

As always, she scanned several newspapers as she ate lunch. Same for breakfast and dinner. She found an interesting item in the **Tallahassee Democrat.** At the bottom of page 6 in the State section there was a recap of government news. The last item was a less than urgent announcement that Lacy Stoltz had been appointed as the interim director of the Board on Judicial Conduct, replacing Charlotte Baskin, who had been nominated by the Governor to run the Gaming Commission.

14

Clawing her way up the ladder, and moving from office to office, Cleo had learned to pack lightly and never fill the drawers or decorate the walls. Without a word to anyone, though the gossip was raging, she packed her things and left the building. The gossip did not follow her but instead turned to Lacy and the welcome rumor that she was taking over.

The following morning, she called everyone together in the workroom adjacent to the director's rather depressing office and confirmed that she would be the acting, and quite interim, director for the near future. The news thrilled her colleagues and the staff, and there were plenty of smiles for the first time in months. She rattled off a few changes in office rules: (1) work from home as much as you want as long as the work gets done; (2) Friday afternoons off in the summer, as long as someone answered the phone; (3) no staff meetings unless absolutely necessary; (4) a mutual coffee fund to buy better stuff; (5) forget the open-door policy; (6) an extra week of vacation, unofficially. She promised to seek more funding while lowering the stress levels. She would keep her old office because she had never liked the big one and did not want to be associated with it.

She was congratulated by everyone and finally made her way back to her desk where a florist had just delivered a beautiful arrangement. The note was from Allie, with love and admiration. Felicity handed her a phone message. Jeri Crosby was calling with best wishes on the big promotion.

Tabor picked up the scent by casually stopping at a police substation in east Pensacola and asking an older cop behind the desk if he knew where Officer Ozment was these days.

"Norris?" the sergeant asked.

Since Tabor had only the initial "N" for the first name, he glanced at a blank notepad, frowned, and replied, "That's him. Norris Ozment."

"What's he done now?"

"Nothing bad. His uncle died in Duval County and left him a check. I'm working for the estate lawyers."

"I see. Norris quit five, maybe six years ago,

went into private security. Last I heard, he was down the coast working at a resort."

Tabor scribbled nothing legible on his notepad. "Remember which one?"

Another cop rumbled in and the sergeant asked him, "Say, Ted, you remember which hotel hired Norris?"

Ted took a bite of a donut and pondered the heavy question. "Down on Seagrove Beach, wasn't it? The Pelican Point?"

"That's it," the sergeant chimed in. "Got a nice gig at the Pelican Point. Not sure if he's still there."

"Thanks a lot, guys," Tabor said with a smile.

"Just leave the check here," the sergeant said and everyone howled. Such a comedian.

Tabor left town on Highway 98 and went east as it snaked along the coast. He called the Pelican Point and confirmed that Norris Ozment was still working there, though he was too busy to answer his landline. His cell number could not be passed out. Tabor arrived at the hotel, found him in the lobby, and turned on the charm. He stuck to his ruse of being a security officer from the Atlanta area, hired by the family of a deceased gentleman to track down some potential offspring. "Five minutes is all I need," he said with a friendly grin.

The lobby was empty, the resort half-full. Ozment could manage to spare a few minutes. They sat at a table in the grill and ordered coffee.

Tabor said, "It's about a case you had in Pensacola back in 2001."

"You gotta be kidding, right? I can't even tell you what I did last week."

"Neither can I. It was city court."

"Even worse."

Tabor pulled out a folded copy of the arrest report and slid it across. "This might help."

Ozment read what he had written in another lifetime, shrugged, said, "Vaguely rings a bell. Why is the name blacked out?"

"Don't know. Good question. Verno was murdered five months ago over in Biloxi. His family has hired me. Nothing from this old case rings a bell?"

"Not right off the bat. Look, I was in city court every day, a real grind. That's one reason I quit. Got tired of the lawyers and judges."

"Do you remember a lawyer named Ross Bannick?"

"Sure. I knew most of the locals. He later got elected judge. I think he's still there."

"Any chance he could be the other guy here, the alleged victim?"

Ozment stared again at the arrest report and finally smiled. "That's it. You're right. I remember now. This guy Verno painted Bannick's house in town, and he claimed Bannick wouldn't pay him all the money. Bannick claimed the work wasn't finished. They squared off one day and Bannick claimed Verno pulled a gun. Verno denied it. If I recall, the judge dismissed the case because there was no other proof. One's word against the other."

"You're sure."

"Yeah, I remember it now. It was pretty unusual to have a lawyer involved in a case, as the victim. I didn't testify because I didn't see anything. I remember Bannick being really pissed because he was a lawyer and he thought the judge should've seen things his way."

"You seen Bannick since then?"

"Sure. After he got elected to the circuit court, I saw him all the time. But I've been gone for years now. Haven't missed it for a minute."

"No word from him since you left the force?"

"No reason to."

"Thanks. I may need to call you later."

"Anytime."

As they talked, Ozment's staff ran the tag numbers on the investigator's car. It was a rental. His story barely stuck together. If Ozment had shown any more interest, he would have tracked down Jeff Dunlap. But an old city court case was of no interest.

As Tabor drove away in his rental, he called his client.

Jeri felt dizzy and her knees were weak. She reclined on the sofa in her cluttered condo, closed her eyes, and made herself breathe deeply. Eight dead people in seven different states. Seven victims of the same type of strangulation, all unlucky enough to have bumped into Ross Bannick along the way.

The cops in Biloxi would never find Norris Ozment, and they would never know of the courtroom altercation between Lanny Verno and Bannick. They would dig deep enough to know that Verno's criminal record was only a DUI in Florida, and they would dismiss that as nothing. Verno was, after all, the victim, not the killer, and they were not too concerned with his past. The case was already cold, the investigation at a dead end.

The killer had stalked his prey for almost thirteen years. He was far ahead of the police.

Breathe deep, she told herself. You can't solve all the murders. You just need one.

15

In addition to the substantial increase in salary, which she was happy to accept, and the larger office, which she was even happier to decline, her promotion offered little in the way of perks. One, though, was a state-owned vehicle, a late model Impala with low mileage. Not too many years earlier, all of the investigators drove state cars and never worried about their travel expenses. Budget cuts had changed things.

Lacy had decided that Darren Trope would become her wingman, and as such he would do a lot of the driving. He would soon learn of the mysterious witness and her breathtaking accusations, though he would not know her real identity, at least not in the near future.

Darren parked in the half-empty lot of a hotel beside Interstate 10 a few miles west of Tallahassee.

Lacy said, "The contact will watch us enter the hotel, so the contact knows you are here."

"The contact?"

"Sorry, but that's as far as I can go right now."

"I love it. All this intrigue."

"You have no idea what you're getting into. Just hang out in the lobby or the café."

"Where are you meeting this contact?"

"A room on the third floor."

"And you feel safe?"

"Sure, plus I have you downstairs ready to come to my rescue. Got your gun?"

"Forgot it."

"What kind of agent are you?"

"I don't know. I thought I was just a lowly investigator working for minimum wage."

"I'll get you a raise. If I'm not back in an hour, then assume I've been kidnapped and probably tortured."

"And then I do what?"

"Run."

"You got it. So look, Lacy, what exactly is the purpose of this little rendezvous?"

"Right. What are we doing here? I expect the contact will hand me a formal complaint against a circuit court judge, and in the complaint there will be allegations that the judge has committed murder while on the bench. Perhaps more than once. I have tried numerous times to send the contact away, preferably to the FBI or some other crime-fighting outfit, but the contact is adamant and frightened. The investigation, whatever it looks like, will begin with us. And where it ends, I have no idea."

"And you know this contact pretty well?"

"No. We met two weeks ago. In the coffee shop, ground floor of Siler. You took her photo."

"Oh, so that's the woman?"

"Yep."

"Do you believe her?"

"I think so. I go back and forth. It's an outrageous accusation, but the contact presents some pretty strong circumstantial evidence. No real proof, mind you, but enough suspicion to make things interesting."

"This is awesome, Lacy. You gotta let me in on the investigation. I love this cloak-and-dagger stuff."

"You're in, Darren. You and Sadelle. That's the team. Got it? Just the three of us. And you have to promise you will not ask for the real identity of the contact."

He sealed his lips and said, "Promise."

"Let's go."

There was a café on the far left side of the lobby behind the registration desk. Darren peeled off without a word as Lacy walked to the elevators. She rode alone to the third floor, found the right room, and pushed the doorbell.

Jeri opened the door without a smile, without a word. She nodded toward the room behind her, and Lacy stepped in slowly, glancing around. It was a small room with only one bed.

"Thanks for coming," Jeri said. "Have a seat." There was one chair next to the television.

"Are you okay?" Lacy asked.

"I'm a wreck, a total disaster." Gone were the stylish clothes and fake designer frames. Jeri was garbed in an old black jogging suit and scruffy sneakers. She wore no makeup and looked years older. "Sit down, please."

Lacy sat in the chair and Jeri sat on the edge of the bed. She pointed to some papers on the desk. "There's the complaint, Lacy. I kept it short, used the name of Betty Roe. I have your word that no one else will ever know my real name?"

"I can't promise that, Jeri. We've been through this. I can guarantee that no one at BJC will know who you are, but beyond that there are no promises."

"Beyond that? What is beyond that, Lacy?"

"We now have forty-five days to investigate your complaint. If we find evidence to support your allegations, then we'll have no choice but to go to the police or FBI. We can't arrest this judge for murder, Jeri. We've had that discussion. We can remove him from the bench, but by then losing his job will be the least of his worries."

"You have to protect me at all times."

"We'll do our job, that's all I can promise. At BJC, your name will be known to no one."

"I prefer to stay off his list, Lacy."

"Well, so do I."

Jeri stuck her hands in her pockets and rocked forward, and then back, lost in another world. After a long, awkward pause she said, "He's killing again, Lacy, not that he ever stopped."

"You said there might be another one."

"There is. Five months ago he killed a man named Lanny Verno in Biloxi, Mississippi. Same method, same rope. I found out why. Me, Lacy, not the police, but me. I found Verno's trail in Pensacola thirteen years ago. I searched for the intersection, the crossing of the paths, and found it, but not the police. They have no clue."

"They also have no idea about Bannick," Lacy said. "What happened?"

"An old dispute over some remodeling in Bannick's house. Looks like Verno pulled a gun, should've pulled the trigger. Bannick was just a lawyer then, not a judge, and he took him to court on assault charges. Lost. Verno walked, and I guess he walked himself right onto Bannick's list. Thirteen years he waited, can you believe that, Lacy?"

"No."

"He's killing more frequently, which is not unusual. Every serial killer is different and there are certainly no rules to the game. But it's not unusual for them to speed up and then slow down." She rocked slowly back and forth, staring ahead, trance-like.

She said, "He's also taking chances, making mistakes. He almost got caught with Verno when some poor guy showed up at the wrong time, wrong place. Bannick cracked his skull, killed him, but didn't use a rope. It's reserved for chosen ones."

Lacy again marveled at the certainty with which she described things she had never seen and certainly couldn't prove. It was frustrating how convincing she was. Lacy asked, "And the crime scene?"

"We don't know much about it because it's an active investigation and the police are sitting on everything. The second guy was a local builder with lots of friends and the police are taking heat. But, as always, it appears as though Bannick left nothing behind."

"Six and two make eight."

"That we know about, Lacy. There could be others."

Lacy reached over and picked up the complaint but didn't read it. "What's in here?"

Jeri stopped rocking and rubbed her eyes as if sleepy. "Only three murders. The last three. Lanny Verno and Mike Dunwoody last year, and Perry Kronke from two years ago. Kronke's case is down in the Keys, the big-firm lawyer who supposedly withheld a job offer when Bannick was finishing law school."

"And why these cases?"

"Verno because it's easy to prove his connection to Pensacola. He once lived there and I tracked him down. Easy once we show the police how to do it. It involves old dockets buried in digital bins and old files stacked away in warehouses. Stuff I found, Lacy. Spoon-feed this stuff to the cops and maybe they can put together a case."

"They'll need evidence for that, Jeri. Not mere coincidences."

"True. But they've never heard the name of Ross Bannick. Once you tell them, once you connect the dots for them, then they can barge in with subpoenas."

"And Kronke? Why him?"

"It's the only Florida case and it involved travel. It takes ten hours to drive from Pensacola to Marathon, so Bannick probably didn't do it in one day. Hotels, gas purchases, maybe he took a flight. Lots of records along the way. You should be able to track his movements before and after the murder. Look at his court dockets, see when he was on the bench, that sort of stuff. Basic detective work."

"We're not detectives, Jeri."

"Well, you're investigators, aren't you?"

"Sort of."

Jeri stood and stretched and walked to the window. Looking through it she asked, "Who was the guy you brought with you?"

"Darren, a colleague from work."

"Why bring him?"

"Because that's the way I want to operate, Jeri. I'm the boss now and I'll make the rules."

"Yes, but can I trust you?"

"If you don't trust me, then take the complaint to the police. That's where it should be anyway. I've never asked for this case."

Jeri suddenly covered her eyes with her hands and cried for a moment. Lacy was stunned by the sudden emotion and felt guilty for not being more compassionate. She was dealing with a fragile woman.

Lacy handed her tissues from the bathroom and waited for the moment to pass. When Jeri finished wiping her face she said, "I'm sorry, Lacy. I'm a mess and I'm not sure how much longer I can go on. I never thought I could make it to this point."

"It's okay, Jeri. I promise I'll do what I can, and I promise to protect your name."

"Thank you."

Lacy glanced at her watch and realized that she had been there for only eighteen minutes. Jeri had traveled four hours from Mobile. There was no sign of coffee, water, pastries, anything related to breakfast.

Lacy said, "I need coffee. Would you like some?"

"Sure. Thanks."

Lacy texted Darren and ordered two large cups to go. She would meet him downstairs at the elevators in ten minutes. As she put her phone away she said, "Wait a minute. You included Verno because he once lived in Pensacola and that's where he ran into Bannick, right?"

"That's right."

"But he's not the only one from Pensacola. The first one, the scoutmaster, Thad Leawood, grew up in town, not far from Bannick. Murdered in 1991, right?"

"Correct as to the year."

"And you think he was the first?"

"I hope so, but I don't really know. No one does but Bannick."

"And the reporter, Danny Cleveland, wrote for the **Pensacola Ledger** and lived there about fifteen years ago. Found dead in his apartment in Little Rock in 2009."

"You've done your homework."

Lacy left the room shaking her head. She got the coffee from Darren and was back in minutes. Jeri ignored hers on the credenza. After a long sip, Lacy walked to the door and back and said, "In the first round of files, the stuff you gave me initially, there are two women among his victims. But you don't say much about them. Can you tell me more?"

"Sure. When he was an undergrad at Florida, he knew a girl named Eileen Nickleberry. He was a frat boy, she was in a sorority, and they partied in the same circles. They were at a social one night in the Pike house on campus and everybody was drinking. A lot of booze, pot, casual sex. Bannick and Eileen went to his room and, evidently, he couldn't perform. She laughed at him, had a big mouth, told others, and he was humiliated. He became the butt of a lot of jokes around the frat house. That was around 1985. Some thirteen years later Eileen was murdered near Wilmington, North Carolina."

Lacy listened in disbelief.

Jeri continued, "The other girl was Ashley Barasso. They were in law school together at Miami, that much is certain. She was murdered by strangulation, same rope, six years after they graduated. I know less about her than any of his other victims."

"Where was she murdered?"

"Columbus, Georgia. Married with two small children."

"That's awful."

"They're all awful, Lacy."

"Of course they are."

"You see, my theory is that Bannick has a real problem with sex. Probably goes back to the abuse when he was eleven or twelve at the hands of Thad Leawood. He probably didn't get the help and support he needed. That's not unusual with kids. Anyway, he has never recovered from it. He murdered Eileen because she laughed at him. I don't know what happened between him and Ashley Barasso and will probably never find out. But they were at the law school together, the same class, so it's safe to assume that they knew one another."

"When they were murdered were they sexually molested?"

"No, he's too smart for that. At a crime scene the most important piece of evidence is the corpse. It can and usually does reveal so much. Bannick, though, is careful and leaves behind only the rope and the blow to the head. His motive is always revenge, except for Mike Dunwoody. Poor guy just timed things badly."

"Okay, okay. Please allow me to say something that's pretty obvious here. You're an African American woman."

"True."

"And I'm guessing that in 1985 or so the fraternity life at the University of Florida was basically all-white."

"Indeed."

"And you've never been a student there?"

"Never."

"So, how did you manage to get the story about Bannick and Eileen? It's all hearsay and third-hand and urban legend, all remembered and told by a bunch of drunk rich kids. Right?"

"For the most part, yes."

"So?"

Jeri reached for a large, well-worn briefcase, snapped it open, and pulled out a book. She handed it to Lacy who took it and stared at it.

"Who's Jill Monroe?"

"Me. It's a book I self-published, one of several, all with different pseudonyms, all by me. The publisher is a low-end vanity press out West. It's basically unreadable and not intended to be really read by anyone. It's part of the disguise, Lacy, part of the fiction that is my life."

"What's in the book?"

"True crime, stuff I pulled off the Internet, all stolen but not copyrighted."

"I'm listening."

"I use these to get attention and establish credibility. I show up claiming to be a veteran writer of true crime and police stories. Freelance, of course, always freelance. I say I'm working on a book about cold cases involving young women who were strangled. In this case, I checked the listings of fraternities and sororities at UF and finally put together the puzzle. None of Eileen's old friends would talk. It took months, even years, but I finally found a frat brother with a big mouth. Met him in a bar in St. Pete and he claimed to have known Eileen, said lots of boys did. Said he had not talked to Bannick in years, but, after a few drinks, he told me the story about his bad night with Eileen. Said Bannick was really humiliated."

Lacy paced a bit as she tried to absorb it. "Okay, but how did you hear of Eileen's death in the first place?"

"I have a source. A mad scientist. An ex-cop

who collects and studies more crime stats than anybody on the planet. There are only about three hundred murders by strangulation each year. All are reported in various ways to the FBI's clearinghouse on violent crime. My source studies the cold cases, looks for patterns and similarities. He found Eileen Nickleberry ten years ago and passed it on. He found the Lanny Verno case and passed it on. He doesn't know about Bannick and he has no idea what I do with the info. He thinks I'm a crime writer of some variety."

"Does he agree with your theory? A serial killer?"

"He's not paid to agree or disagree and we never discuss it. He's paid to sift through the rubble and alert me if something looks suspicious."

"Just curious. Where is this guy?"

"I don't know. He uses different names and addresses, like me. We've never met, never chatted on the phone, never will. He promises complete anonymity."

"How do you pay him? If you don't mind."

"Hard cash to a post office box in Maine."

Lacy was overwhelmed and sat down. She sipped her coffee and breathed deeply. It dawned on her how much Jeri had learned and collected in the past twenty-plus years.

As if reading her mind, Jeri said, "I know this is a lot." From a pocket she removed a thumb drive and handed it over. "It's all there, over six hundred pages of research, news articles, police files, everything I've found that might be useful. And probably a lot of stuff that's not."

Lacy took the thumb drive and stuck it in a pocket.

Jeri said, "It's encrypted. I'll text you the key."

"Why is it encrypted?"

"Because my whole life is encrypted, Lacy. Everything we do leaves a trail."

"And you think he's back there somewhere, on the trail?"

"I don't know, but I limit my exposure."

"Okay, along these same lines, what are the chances Bannick knows someone is on to him? You're talking about eight murders, Jeri. That's a lot of territory you've covered."

"Don't you think I know that? Eight murders in twenty-two years, and counting. I've talked to hundreds of people, most of whom were of no use. Sure, there's a chance someone from his college days told him that a stranger was asking around, but I never use my real name. And, yes, a cop in Little Rock or Signal Mountain or Wilmington might let it slip that a private investigator was sniffing around an old murder file, but there's no way to link me to it. I'm too careful."

"Then why are you so worried?"

"Because he's so smart, and so patient, and because it would not surprise me if he goes back."

Lacy waited, then asked, "Back where?"

"Back to the crime scenes. Ted Bundy did that,

you know, and other killers did too. Bannick's not that careless, but he might monitor the police, see what's happening with the old files, ask if anyone has come around lately."

"But how?"

"The Internet. He could easily hack the police files and monitor things. Also private investigators, Lacy. You pay them enough and they'll do the work for you and keep quiet."

Lacy's phone buzzed and she looked at it. Darren was checking in. "Things okay up there?" he asked.

"Yeah, ten minutes." She put her phone down and looked at Jeri, who was wiping her face again and rocking.

Lacy said, "Well, Jeri, consider your complaint filed and the clock ticking."

"Do I get updates?"

"How often?"

"Daily?"

"No. I'll let you know when and if we make any progress."

"You have to make progress, Lacy, you have to stop him. I can't do anything else. I'm done, okay. I'm physically, emotionally, and financially wiped out and I've reached the end. I can't believe I've finally made it here and I cannot go on."

"I'll keep in touch, I promise."

"Thanks, Lacy. Please be careful."

16

Saturday, March 22, was a warm beautiful day, and Darren Trope, single and twenty-eight, wasn't keen to spend it indoors at the office. He had arrived in Tallahassee ten years earlier as a freshman, studied business and law for eight glorious years, and had no current plans to get too far away from the campus and all of its related activities. He was, however, infatuated with Lacy Stoltz, his new boss, and when she said meet her at the office at 10:00 a.m. Saturday, and bring designer coffees, Darren arrived ten minutes early. He also brought a standard coffee for Sadelle, the third member of their "task force." Being the youngest, Darren was in charge of technology, along with coffee.

Lacy told the rest of the staff that the office was off-limits Saturday morning, not that she was too worried about seeing a crowd. For a team that routinely skipped out at noon Friday, there was little chance of anyone pulling overtime over the weekend. Nine o'clock Monday morning would arrive soon enough.

They gathered in the conference room next to the director's office. Because Darren had driven his boss to meet "The Contact" the previous Wednesday, he knew a few of the details and was eager to learn more. Sadelle, ashen, pale, sick, and as ghost-like as she had been for the past seven years, sat at the table in her motorized chair and savored her oxygen.

Lacy handed each a copy of Betty Roe's complaint, and they read it in silence. Sadelle inhaled mightily and said, "So this is the murder complaint you mentioned."

"This is it."

"And Betty Roe is our mystery girl?"

"She is."

"Why may I ask are we getting involved? Looks like it belongs with the boys who carry guns."

"I tried to dissuade the witness from filing the complaint, but I couldn't stop her. She's terrified of going to the police because she is afraid of Ross Bannick. She is convinced she might become another one of his targets."

Sadelle gave Darren a look of uncertainty, then both returned to the complaint. When they finished, they contemplated the allegations and there was a long silence. Finally, Darren said to Lacy,

"You used the word 'targets.' As if there might be more to the story."

Lacy smiled and said, "There are eight dead bodies. The three you have in this complaint, plus five others. According to Betty's theory, the killings began in 1991 and have continued, at least until Verno five months ago. Betty believes Bannick is still at it and might be getting careless."

"She's an expert on serial killers?" Darren asked.

"Well, I'm not sure how one becomes an expert in such matters, but she knows a lot. She's been stalking—her word, not mine—Bannick for over twenty years."

"And what got her started?"

"He murdered her father, victim number two, 1992."

Another long silence as Darren and Sadelle stared at the conference table.

"Is she credible?" Sadelle asked.

"At times, yes. Quite. She believes that Bannick kills out of revenge and keeps a list of potential victims. She sees him as methodical, patient, and brilliant."

"What's his rap sheet with us?" Darren asked.

"A near perfect record on the bench, no complaints at all. High ratings from the bar."

Sadelle took in oxygen and said, "Revenge would mean that he knew all of his victims, right?"

"That's correct."

Darren began chuckling and when both women

stared at him he said, "Sorry, but I can't help but think of the other four files on my desk right now. One involves a ninety-year-old judge who can't make it to court anymore. May be on life support. Another has a judge speaking before a Rotary Club and commenting on a pending case."

"We get the picture, Darren," Lacy said. "We've all handled those cases."

"I know, I'm sorry. It's just that now we're supposed to solve eight murders."

"No. The complaint covers only three."

Sadelle looked at her copy of the complaint again and said, "Okay, the first two here. Lanny Verno and Mike Dunwoody. What was Bannick's connection, or alleged connection, to those two?"

"No connection to Dunwoody. He just showed up at the crime scene not long after Verno went down. Verno and Bannick had a spat in Pensacola city court some thirteen years ago. Verno won. Got his name on the blacklist."

"Why did Betty choose to include this case?"

"It's active, ongoing, with two dead bodies at the same scene. Maybe the cops in Mississippi know something."

"And the other, Perry Kronke?"

"It's an active case and the only one in Florida. Betty claims the police down in Marathon have no leads. Bannick knows what he's doing and leaves nothing behind, nothing but the rope around the neck."

"All eight were strangled?" Darren asked.

"Not Dunwoody. The other seven were choked with the same type of rope. Tied and secured with the same weird sailor's knot."

"What was Kronke's connection?"

"How'd he make the list?"

"Whatever."

"Bannick finished law school at the University of Miami. He clerked for a big firm there and met Kronke, a senior partner. Betty believes the firm yanked a job offer at the last minute and Bannick got stiffed. Must've really upset him."

"He waited twenty-one years?" Sadelle asked.

"That's what Betty thinks."

"And they found him in his fishing boat with a rope around his neck?"

"Yes, according to a preliminary police report. As I said, the case is still active, even though it's now two years old with no leads, and the police are guarding the file."

All three sipped their coffee and tried to arrange their thoughts. After a while, Lacy said, "We have forty-five days to assess, to do something. Who has an idea?"

Sadelle wheezed and said, "I think it's time for me to retire."

This got a laugh from the other two, though she was not known for her humor. Her colleagues at BJC fully expected her to die before she retired.

Lacy said, "Your letter of resignation is hereby rejected. You gotta stick with me on this one. Darren?"

"I don't know. These murders are being investigated by homicide detectives who are trained and experienced. And they're not finding any clues? They have no suspects? What the hell are **we** supposed to do? I'm seduced by the idea of such exciting work, but this is for someone else."

Lacy listened and nodded. Sadelle said, "I'm sure you have a plan."

"Yes. Betty is afraid to deal with the police because she wants to remain anonymous. So, she's using us to go to the police. She knows we have limited jurisdiction, limited resources, limited everything. She also knows that the law requires us to investigate every complaint, so we can't just kick the can. I say we do it quietly, safely, careful not to tip our hand to Bannick, and after about thirty days we reevaluate. At that time we'll probably dump it on the state police."

"Now we're talking," Darren said. "If Bannick is a serial killer, and I have doubts, then let the real cops chase him."

"Sadelle?"

"Just keep me off his list."

17

The following Tuesday, two-thirds of the task force left Tallahassee at 8:00 a.m. for the five-hour drive to Biloxi. Darren, the wingman, drove while Lacy, the boss, read reports, made phone calls, and in general acted the way any interim director of BJC would act. She was quickly learning that managing people was an unpleasant part of her job.

During a lull, Darren, waiting to pounce, said, "So, I'm reading up on serial killers these days. Who holds the American record for kills?"

"Kills?"

"Kills. Dead bodies. That's what the cops say."

"Gee, I don't know. Didn't that Gacy guy kill a few dozen in Chicago?"

"John Wayne Gacy killed thirty-two, or at least that's all he could remember. Buried 'em under his house in the suburbs. Forensics found the remains of twenty-eight, so the cops believed his confession. He said he tossed a few in the river but he wasn't sure how many."

"Ted Bundy?"

"Bundy officially confessed to thirty but he kept changing his stories. Before he was fried in the electric chair, here in our beloved state, by the way, he spent a lot of time with investigators from all over the country, primarily out West, where he was from. He had a brilliant mind but he simply couldn't remember all of his victims. It is widely believed that he killed as many as one hundred young women, but it has been impossible to confirm. He often killed several in one day and even abducted his victims from the same location. He gets my vote as the sickest of a very sick bunch."

"And he holds the record?"

"No, not for confirmed kills. A guy named Samuel Little confessed to ninety murders and was active until ten years ago. The authorities are still investigating and so far have confirmed about sixty."

"You're getting into this, aren't you?"

"It's fascinating. Ever hear of the Green River Killer?"

"I think so."

"Confessed to seventy, convicted of forty-nine. Almost all sex workers in the Seattle area."

"What's your point?"

"I didn't say I have one. What's fascinating

is that none of these guys killed the same way. I've yet to find a single one who did it for twenty years and killed only those he knew. They're all deranged sociopaths, some are brilliant, most are not, but none, so far, in my vast research, are even remotely similar to Bannick. Someone who kills only for revenge and keeps a list."

"We don't know if he keeps a list."

"Call it what you want, okay? He keeps the names of those who've crossed him and stalks them for years. That appears to be highly unusual."

Lacy sighed, shook her head, and said, "I still can't believe this. We're talking about a popular elected judge as if we know for a fact that he's killed several people. Murdered them in cold blood."

"You're not convinced?"

"I still don't know. Are you?"

"I think so. If Betty Roe has her facts straight, and if Bannick did indeed know the first seven victims, then it can't be just coincidental."

Lacy's phone buzzed and she took the call.

Dale Black, the Harrison County sheriff, was waiting when they arrived promptly at 2:00 p.m. He led them down a hallway to a small multi-purpose room with a table in the rear, and he introduced them to Detective Napier who was in charge of the investigation. Quick introductions were made and they sat around the table.

The sheriff began the conversation with "So, we've checked you out online and know something about your work. You're not really criminal investigators, right?"

Lacy smiled, because she knew that when she dealt with men her age or older her charming smile normally got her what she wanted, or something close to it. And if she didn't get what she wanted she could always count on disarming the men and neutralizing their attitudes. She said, "That's right. We're lawyers and we review complaints filed against judges."

Napier liked her smile and offered one of his own, one with considerably less appeal. "In Florida, right?" he asked.

"Yes, we're out of Tallahassee and work for the state."

Darren had been told to remain silent and take notes, and he was complying on all fronts.

Napier asked, "Well, then, the obvious question is why are you interested in this double murder?"

"That is obvious, isn't it? We're fishing, okay? We've just been handed a complaint against a judge, in an unrelated case, and through our initial work we've come across some information on Lanny Verno. You do know that he once lived in Florida, right?"

Napier's smile vanished and he glanced at his boss. "I think so," he mumbled as he whipped open a thick file. He licked his thumb, flipped some pages, and said, "Yep, got a DUI over there a few years ago."

"Do you have any record of him living in the Pensacola area around 2001?"

Napier frowned, kept flipping, searching now. He finally shook his head, no.

Very pleasantly, Lacy said, "We know he lived there around 2000 and worked as a painter and remodeler. This might be useful to you."

Napier closed the file and managed another grin. "His girlfriend, the one he was living with, said he moved into this area a few years ago, but she has proven to be unreliable, to say the least."

"And his family is from the Atlanta area?" Lacy asked. It was a question but her tone left no doubt that she knew the answer.

"How'd you know that?"

"We found his obituary, if you could call it that."

Napier said, "We've had little contact with his family. Quite a bit, though, with the Dunwoodys."

Lacy offered another smile and asked, "Is it fair for me to ask if you have a suspect?"

Napier frowned at the sheriff, who returned the scowl. Before they could say no, Lacy said, "I'm not asking for the name of a suspect, I'm just curious as to whether you have any solid leads."

Sheriff Black blurted, "There are no suspects."

"Do **you** have one?" Napier asked.

"Maybe," Lacy said without a smile. Both cops

exhaled loudly, as if suddenly relieved of a burden. Darren would say later that he caught them glancing at each other as if they wanted to pounce on her single word: "Maybe."

Lacy asked, "What can you tell us about the crime scene?"

Napier shrugged as if this might be difficult. Black said, "Okay, what are the rules here? You're not law enforcement, you're not even from this state. How confidential is this little chat? If we talk details they stay here, right?"

"Of course. We're not policemen but we do occasionally deal with criminal behavior, so we understand confidentiality. We have nothing to gain by repeating any of this. You have my word."

Black said, "The crime scene revealed nothing. No prints, fibers, hairs, nothing. The only blood belonged to the two victims. No signs of resistance or a struggle. Verno was strangled but also had a severe head wound. Dunwoody's skull was splintered."

"And the rope?"

"The rope?"

"The rope around Verno's neck."

Napier was about to respond when Black stopped him. "Wait. Can you describe the rope?" he asked Lacy.

"Probably. A thirty-inch piece of three-eighths nylon, double twin braid, marine grade, either blue and white or green and white."

She paused and watched as both faces registered disbelief. Then, "Secured at the base of the skull with a double clove hitch knot."

Both cops recovered quickly and regained their poker faces. Napier said, "I take it you know our man from somewhere else."

"Possibly. Can we take a look at the photos?"

Lacy had no idea of their frustration. For five months now, every lead had gone nowhere. Every Crime Stopper's tip had done nothing but waste more time. Every new theory had eventually petered out. Verno's murder was so carefully planned that there had to be a reason for it, but motive eluded them. Little was known of his unremarkable past. On the other hand, they were convinced that Dunwoody had simply picked the wrong spot. They knew everything about him and nothing suggested a motive.

Could Lacy and the BJC be their first break?

They spent half an hour poring over the gruesome crime scene photos. Sheriff Black had important meetings elsewhere but they were suddenly canceled.

When Lacy and Darren, still silent, had seen enough, they packed their briefcases and got ready to leave.

The sheriff asked, "So, when do we talk about this suspect of yours?"

Lacy smiled and replied, "Not now. We see this meeting as the first of several. We want a good working relationship with you, one built on trust. Give us some time, let us do our investigation, and we'll be back."

"Fair enough. There is one other bit of evidence here that might be helpful. It's not in the file because we've been sitting on it since the murders. It seems as though our man may have made a mistake. We know what he was driving."

"Helpful? Sounds pretty crucial."

"Perhaps. You saw the photos of the two cell phones he took from his victims. He drove about an hour north of here to the small town of Neely, Mississippi. He put them in an envelope, a five-by-eight-inch padded mailer, and addressed it to my daughter in Biloxi. He dropped the package into a standard blue box outside the post office."

Napier pulled out another photo, one of the mailer with the address.

The sheriff continued. "We tracked down the cell phones within hours and found them in the box in Neely. They're still at the state crime lab but so far have given us nothing."

He looked at Napier, who took the handoff. "Someone saw him stop at the post office. It was about seven p.m. on that Friday night, roughly two hours after the murders. There was no traffic in Neely because there never is, but a neighbor saw a pickup truck stop at the post office. A man walked to the box and dropped in the package, the only one deposited after five p.m. on that

Friday. Not much mail in Neely either. The neighbor thought it was odd that anyone would choose that time to drop off some mail. He was on his porch a good ways off and he cannot identify the driver. But the truck was a gray Chevrolet, fairly late model, with Mississippi tags."

"And you're certain it was the killer?" Lacy asked, a very nonprofessional question.

"No. We're certain it was the man who dropped off the cell phones. Probably the killer but we're not sure."

"Right. Why would he drive up there to ditch the phones?"

Napier shrugged and smiled. Black said, "Now you're playing his game. I think he was just having some fun with us, and especially with me. He had to know that we'd find the cell phones in a matter of hours and that they wouldn't be mailed to my daughter."

Napier added, "Or maybe he wanted to be seen driving a vehicle with Mississippi tags because he's not from Mississippi. He's pretty clever, isn't he?"

"Extremely."

"And he's done this before?" asked the sheriff.

"We believe so."

"And he's not from Mississippi, is he?"

"We think not."

18

Jeri was not prepared for the next phase of her life. For over twenty years she had been driven by the dream of finding and confronting her father's murderer. Identifying him was difficult enough, and she had done so only with a determination and perseverance that often surprised herself. Accusing him was another matter. Pointing the finger at Ross Bannick was a terrifying act, not because she was afraid of being wrong, but because she feared the man himself.

But she had done it. She had filed her complaint with an official agency, one established by law to investigate wayward judges, and now it was up to the Board on Judicial Conduct to go after Bannick. She wasn't sure what to expect from Lacy Stoltz and her BJC, but the case was now on her desk. If all went as planned, Lacy would put in motion the apprehension and prosecution of a man Jeri could never stop thinking about.

In the days following her last meeting with Lacy, Jeri found it impossible to prepare lectures, or do research for her book, or see what few friends she had. She did see her therapist twice and complained of feeling depressed, lonely, of little value. She fought the temptation to jump back online and dig through old crimes. She often stared at her phone and waited for a call from Lacy, and she fought the urge to email her every hour.

On day ten, Lacy called and they chatted for a few minutes. Not surprisingly, she had nothing to report. She and her team were getting organized, reviewing the file, making plans, and so on. Jeri ended the call abruptly and went for a walk.

Thirty-five days to go and apparently nothing was happening, at least not around the offices of the BJC.

According to the records of the Chavez County tax office, Ross Bannick purchased a used, light gray, 2009 model Chevrolet half-ton pickup in May of 2012 and owned it for two years before selling it the previous November, one month after the murders of Verno and Dunwoody. His buyer was a used car dealer named Udell, who flipped it to a man named Robert Trager, the present owner. Darren drove to Pensacola and found Mr. Trager, who explained that he no longer had the truck. On New Year's Eve, a drunk driver ran a stop sign and crashed into him, totaling the truck. He had settled with State Farm under his uninsured motorist coverage, sold the truck for scrap, and felt lucky to be alive. As they sipped iced tea on the front porch, Mrs. Trager found a photo of Robert and his grandson holding fishing rods and posing beside the gray pickup. With his smartphone, Darren took a picture of the photo and sent it to Detective Napier in Biloxi, who eventually made the trip to Neely and showed it to the only eyewitness.

In his email to Lacy, Napier said, curtly: **The witness says it looks "very similar" to the one he saw. This narrows it down to about five thousand gray Chevrolet pickups in this state. Good luck.**

Further digging revealed that Bannick was quite the truck trader. In the previous fifteen years, he had bought and sold at least eight used pickups of various makes, models, and colors.

Why would a judge need so many trucks?

He was currently driving a 2013 Ford Explorer, leased from a local dealer.

On Monday, March 31, the thirteenth day into the assessment period commenced by the filing of the complaint, Lacy and Darren flew from Tallahassee to Miami where they rented a car and drove south through the Keys to the town of Marathon, population 9,000. Two years earlier, a retired lawyer named Perry Kronke had been found dead, beaten and strangled in his fishing boat as it drifted in shallow water near the Great White Heron preserve. His skull had been shattered, there was blood everywhere, the cause of death was asphyxiation caused by a length of nylon rope pulled around his neck so violently that the skin ripped. There were no witnesses, no suspicious characters, no suspects, no forensics. The case was still considered active and few details had been released.

Jeri's go-to man, Kenny Lee, had been unable to obtain crime scene photos from the FBI\ clearinghouse.

The Marathon police department was the domain of Chief Turnbull, a snowbird from Michigan who had never gone back home. He was also the homicide detective, among other duties. He greeted Lacy and Darren warmly but with suspicion, and, like Sheriff Black in Biloxi, cleared the air immediately by establishing that the two were not cops.

"We don't pretend to be," Lacy said with a megawatt smile. "We investigate complaints against judges, and with a thousand of them in this state that keeps us very busy."

Nervous laughter all around. Gotta get those crooked judges.

"So, why are you interested in the Kronke case?" Turnbull asked.

Darren had once again been told to keep quiet. His boss would do the talking, all of it. They had rehearsed their fiction and both thought it sounded plausible. She said, "Just some routine stuff, really. We're digging through a new complaint filed against a judge in Miami and we've run across some possible criminal activity by the late Mr. Kronke. Did you by chance know him before he was murdered?"

"No. He lived out at Grassy Key. Are you familiar with this area?"

"No."

"It's a swanky retirement enclave on a bay north of here. The residents tend to stick to themselves. Out of my price range."

"The murder was two years ago. Do you have any suspects?"

The chief actually laughed, as though the idea of a decent lead was so far-fetched it was humorous. He collected himself quickly and said, "I'm not sure I should answer that question, as bold as it is. Where are you going with this?"

"We're just doing our jobs, Chief Turnbull."

"How confidential is this conversation?"

"Totally. We have nothing to gain by repeating any of this. We work for the State of Florida and it's our job to investigate allegations of wrongdoing, same as you."

The chief pondered this for a moment, his nervous eyes darting from one to the other. He finally took a deep breath, relaxed, and said, "Yes, early on, we had a suspect, or at least we thought we were on the trail. We've always assumed that the killer was in a boat. He found Mr. Kronke alone, fishing for red drum, something he did all the time. There were several fish he'd caught in the cooler. His wife said he'd left home around seven that morning and was expecting a pleasant day on the water. We went to every marina within fifty miles of here and checked the records for boat rentals." He paused long enough to pull reading glasses out of a shirt pocket and open a file. He scanned it quickly, found his number. "There were twenty-seven boats rented that morning, all, of course, to fishermen. The murder was August the fifth, red drum season, you understand?"

"Of course." Lacy had never heard of a red drum and wasn't sure what one was.

"We checked all twenty-seven names. Took us a while, but hey, that's our job. One guy was a convicted felon, served some time in a federal pen for assaulting an FBI agent, pretty nasty dude. We got excited and spent some time with him. But he eventually checked out."

Lacy doubted if Ross Bannick was careless enough to rent a boat in the vicinity at about the same time he murdered Perry Kronke, after stalking him for over twenty years, but she feigned deep interest. After spending fifteen minutes with Chief Turnbull and seeing his operation, she was not impressed.

"Did you ask the state police for help?" she asked.

"Of course. Right off the bat. They're the pros, you know. They did the autopsy, forensics, most of the preliminary investigation. We worked side by side, a joint effort in all aspects. Great guys. I like them."

That's nice. "Could we take a look at the file?" she asked sweetly.

Thick wrinkles broke out across his forehead. He yanked off his readers and chewed on a stem, glaring at her as if she had asked about his wife's sex life. "Why?" he demanded.

"There might be something about this case that's relevant to our investigation."

"I don't get it. Murder here, crooked judge there. What's the connection?"

"We don't know, Chief Turnbull, we're just digging, the way you often do. Just good police work."

"I can't release the file. Sorry. Get a court order or something and I'll be happy to help, but without one, no go."

"Fair enough." She shrugged as if to give up. There was nothing else to talk about. "Thanks for your time."

"Don't mention it."

"We'll be back with a court order."

"Great."

"One last question, though, if you don't mind."

"Try me."

"The rope used by the killer—is it in the evidence file?"

"You bet. We have it."

"And you're familiar with it?"

"Of course. It's the murder weapon."

"Can you describe it?"

"Sure, but I won't. Come back with your court order."

"I'll bet it's nylon, about thirty inches in length, double twin braid, marine grade, either blue and white or green and white in color."

The wrinkles broke out again as his jaw dropped. He rocked back in his chair and clasped his hands together behind his head. "Well, I'll be damned."

"Close enough?" Lacy asked.

"Yes. Close enough. You've seen this guy's work before, I take it."

"Maybe. Maybe we have a suspect. I can't talk about him now but maybe next week or next month. We're on the same team, Chief."

"What do you want?"

"I want to see the file, all of it. And everything is confidential."

Turnbull bounced to his feet and said, "Follow me."

—

Two hours later, they parked at a marina and followed Turnbull, their new buddy, down a dock to a thirty-foot patrol boat with the word POLICE painted boldly on both sides. The captain was an old cop in official shorts, and he welcomed them aboard as if they were headed for a luxury cruise. Lacy and Darren sat knee-to-knee on a bench starboard side and enjoyed the ride over the smooth water. Turnbull stood next to the captain and they chatted in indecipherable cop-speak. Fifteen minutes into the trip the boat decelerated and floated almost to a stop.

Turnbull walked to the front and pointed at the water. "Somewhere right around here is where they found him. As you can see, it's pretty remote."

Lacy and Darren stood and took in the surroundings, endlss water in all directions. The nearest shore was a mile away and dotted with homes that were barely visible. There was no other watercraft to be seen.

"Who found him?" Lacy asked.

"Coast Guard. His wife got worried when he didn't show and she made some calls. We found his truck and trailer at the marina and figured he was still on the water. We called the Coast Guard and began searching."

"Not a bad place for a murder," mused Darren, practically his first words of the day.

Turnbull grunted and said, "Damned near perfect, if you ask me."

——

He owned the boat, had bought it a year earlier as the master plan came together. It wasn't a
particularly nice one, not nearly as fancy as the
one owned by the target, but he wasn't trying to
impress. To avoid a trailer and parking and all
that hassle, he rented a slip at a marina south of
Marathon. Ownership would negate the need to
rent. He would sell it later, as well as the small
condo near the harbor, both, hopefully, at a profit.
Established in the area, and knowing no one, he
fished the waters, something he came to enjoy,
and he stalked his target, something he lived for.
The paperwork—the bill of sale for the boat, the
local bank account, the land records, the fishing
license, property taxes, the fuel receipts—was
all easily forged. State and local paperwork were
child's play for a man with a hundred bank accounts, a man who bought and sold things with
fake names just for the fun of it.

He bumped into Kronke on the dock one day
and got close enough to say hello. The ass did not
reply. Back in the day he was known to be a prick.
Things hadn't changed. Staying away from that
law firm had been a blessing.

On the day, he watched Kronke unload his
boat, buy some fuel, arrange his rods and lures,
and eventually speed away from the dock, too fast

and leaving a wake. What an ass. He followed him at a distance, one that grew because Kronke's engines were bigger. When Kronke found his spot, stopped and began casting, he backed away even more and watched him with binoculars. Two months earlier he had drifted in close and used the artifice of engine trouble to seek help. Kronke, ever the prick, left him stranded a mile from shore.

On the day, with Kronke busy with his red drum, he navigated straight to the bigger boat. Realizing he was getting too close, Kronke froze and glared at him as if he were an idiot.

"Hey, I'm taking on water," he yelled, idling closer.

Kronke shrugged as if to say, **That's your problem.** He laid down his rod.

When the boats touched hard, Kronke growled, "What the hell!"

His final words. He was eighty-one years old, fit for his age, but still a step or two slower.

Quickly, the killer looped his rope over a cleat, jumped onto Kronke's boat, whipped out Leddie, flicked it twice, and smacked the lead ball into the side of Kronke's head, crunching his skull. He loved the sound. He hit him again, though it was unnecessary. He pulled out the nylon rope, wrapped it twice around his neck, put his knee at the top of his spinal cord, and yanked hard enough to tear skin.

> Dear Mr. Bannick:
> We enjoyed your term as a clerk this
> past summer. We were impressed with
> your work and had every intention
> of offering you an associate's position
> beginning next fall. However, as you may
> have heard, our firm has just merged
> with Reed & Gabbanoff, a global giant
> based in London. This is causing a major
> shift in personnel. Unfortunately, we are
> not in the position of hiring all of last
> summer's interns.
> We wish you a very bright future.
> Sincerely,
> H. Perry Kronke,
> Managing Partner

As he pulled tighter and tighter he kept saying, "And here's to your very bright future, H. Perry."

Twenty-three years had passed and the rejection still hurt. The sting was still there. Every other summer intern was offered a job. The merger never happened. Someone, no doubt another cutthroat intern, had started the rumor that Bannick didn't like girls, didn't date them.

He tied off the rope with a double clove hitch, and for a few seconds admired his work. He glanced around and saw the nearest boat half a mile away, going for the open water. He grabbed the rope to his boat and pulled it closer, then he eased into the water and went under, washing off any blood that may have splattered.

"And here's to your very bright future, H. Perry."

A year later he sold both the boat and the condo at modest profits. Both transactions were done in the name of Robert West, one of thirty-four in the state.

He loved the alias game.

19

From her extensive reading about serial killers, Jeri knew that almost none of them stopped until they were caught or killed, either by the police or by themselves, or otherwise forced into retirement by age or perhaps prison. The demons that drove them were relentless and cruel and could never be exorcised. They could be neutralized by death or incarceration, but nothing else. The few killers who attempted to come to grips with their carnage did so from a prison cell.

According to her timeline, Bannick had once gone eleven years without killing. He murdered Eileen Nickleberry near Wilmington in 1998, then waited until 2009 to catch the reporter, Danny Cleveland, alone in his apartment in Little Rock. Since then he had killed three more times. His pace was quickening, which was not unusual.

She reminded herself that her timeline was

essentially worthless, because she had no real idea how many victims were out there. Could there be bodies still unfound? Some killers hid them, then forgot years later where all of them were buried. Other killers, like Bannick, wanted the victims found, and with clues. As an amateur profiler, Jeri believed Bannick wanted someone—the police, the press, the families—to know the killings were related. But why? It was probably his warped ego, a desire for acknowledgment that he was smarter than the police. He took such great pride in his methods that it would be a shame not to be admired, even if by strangers from a distance. It was likely that he wanted his work to become legendary.

She had never believed that Bannick wanted to get caught. He had status, prestige, popularity, money, education—far more going for him than the average serial killer, if there was such a thing. But he loved the gamesmanship. He was a sociopath who killed for revenge, but he thrived on the planning and execution, and the perfection of his crimes.

Eight murders, at least in her book, in seven states, over twenty-two years. He was only forty-nine years old and probably in his prime as a killer. Each murder gave him even more confidence, more thrills. A veteran now, he probably believed that he could never be caught. Who else was on his list?

The paper was standard copy, plain white, 8.5×11, purchased a year earlier at a Staples in

Dallas. The envelope was just as plain and untraceable. The word processor was an ancient Olivetti, one of the first generation with a small screen and little memory, circa 1985. She had bought it second- or third-hand in an antiques warehouse in Montgomery.

Wearing disposable plastic gloves, she carefully placed several sheets of copy paper in the tray and opened the screen and stared at it for a long time. The knot twisted in her stomach and she couldn't keep going. Finally, she managed to type slowly, awkwardly, one key at a time:

Judge Bannick: The Florida Board on Judicial Conduct is investigating your recent activities, re Verno, Dunwoody, Kronke. Could there be others? I think so.

Typically she ate little, and was surprised when her stomach flipped, and she raced to the bathroom where she vomited and retched until her chest and back ached. Moving around gingerly, she drank some water and eventually made it back to her desk. She stared at what she had written, a note she had composed a thousand times in her mind, words she had uttered and practiced again and again.

How would he react? Receiving the anonymous letter would be catastrophic, devastating, life-altering, terrifying. Or at least she hoped so. He was too cool and cold-blooded to panic, but his world would never be the same. His world would be rocked, and he and his demons would drive themselves even crazier now that someone was on his trail. There was no one he could tell, no one to confide in, no one to run to.

She wanted to rock his world. She wanted Bannick to watch every step, look over his shoulder, jump at every noise, study every stranger. She wanted him to stay awake at night, listening to every sound and trembling in fear, the way she had lived for so long.

She thought of Lacy and again debated the strategy of exposing her. Jeri had convinced herself that Bannick was too smart to do anything stupid. Plus, Lacy was a tough girl who could take care of herself. At some point soon Jeri would warn her.

She printed the note on a sheet of the copy paper and put it in the envelope. Typing his name gave her another chill. **R. Bannick, 825 Eastman Lane, Cullman, Florida, 32533.**

The stamp was generic and applied without saliva. She was sweating and lay down on the sofa for a long time.

The next note was also on white copy paper, but from a different manufacturer. She typed:

Now that I know who you are
I send greetings from my grave
So long ago and so far
From that night with you and Dave

You stalked and waited all those years
To find me in a place unseen
And act out all your anger and fears
On a girl you knew as Eileen

Unsteady as she was, she managed to laugh out loud at the image of Bannick reading her poem. She laughed at his horror, his disbelief, and his rage that a victim had caught up with him.

On Saturday, Jeri left Mobile and drove an hour to Pensacola. In a suburban shopping center, she found a blue postal box sitting between a drop-off for FedEx and one for UPS. The nearest security camera was far away, over the door of a coffee shop. Wearing gloves and staying in her car, she placed the first letter into the slot. It would be postmarked Monday at the Pensacola distribution center and delivered to the box beside the front door of Bannick's home no later than the following Tuesday.

Two hours later she pulled off the expressway at Greenville, Alabama, and dropped off her poem at the city post office. It would be collected Monday and trucked to Montgomery where it would be postmarked and sent back south to Pensacola. Bannick should have it by the following Wednesday, Thursday at the latest.

She took the backroads home to Mobile and enjoyed the drive. She listened to jazz on Sirius and kept checking her smile in the mirror. The first two of her letters had been mailed. She had found the courage to confront the killer, or at least set in motion his endgame. The hunting phase was over, and for that she was elated. Now she moved into the next phase, still unnamed. Her work was not over, by any means, but the heavy lifting had been done, all twenty-two years of it.

Now Lacy had the case, and she would eventually bring in the state police, maybe the FBI. And Bannick would never know who stalked him.

Late that night she was reading a novel, sipping her second glass of wine, and fighting the temptation to go online and dig more. Her phone pinged with an email arriving on one of her secure accounts. It was KL, or Kenny Lee, and he asked if she was awake. She was suddenly weary of sleuthing and just wanted to be left alone, but he was an old friend, one she would never meet.

She wrote back: Hey there. How's life?

Living the dream. Got a new death-by-rope
out of Missouri, case is four months old,
looks similar.

As always, Jeri grimaced at the news of another murder, and, as always, she jumped to the conclusion that it was Bannick. But she'd had enough and didn't want to spend more money and waste more energy. How similar?

No photos yet, no description of the rope. But no suspects and nothing from the scene.

She reminded herself that three hundred people a year were murdered by strangulation and about 60 percent of those cases were eventually solved. That left 120 cold cases, far too many to blame on one man.

Let me sleep on it. In other words, don't start your clock at $200 an hour. Kenny Lee had led her to four of Bannick's victims and she had paid him enough.

Sweet dreams.

Still snowing up there? She mailed him cash payments to a post office box in Camden, Maine. She assumed he lived somewhere around there.

As we speak. What's your body count now?

Eight. Seven by the rope and Dunwoody.

It's time for help. Gotta stop this guy. I have contacts.

So do I. Things are moving.

Okay.

20

The task force gathered in its workroom late Monday morning and compared notes. Twenty days into the assessment period and they had little to show for their efforts. Lacy recounted for Sadelle's benefit their trip to Marathon, but the poor lady was either half asleep or stoned from her pain meds.

Darren, though, had some interesting news. Sipping his high-end coffee, he said, "So I had a chat with a Mr. Larry Toscano, partner in the Miami firm of Paine & Steinholtz, which has descended all these many years from Paine & Grubber, the old firm where Bannick spent the summer of 1989 as an intern. Toscano at first was reluctant to get involved, but when I explained that the BJC does possess subpoena powers in certain cases and that, if necessary, we would raid their offices and start snatching files, which of course is

a joke with our limited staff, but anyway the bluff
worked and Toscano fell in line. He found the records in short order and confirmed that Bannick
did indeed work there the summer before his last
year of law school. He said the kid's file was clean
and he did good work, got high marks from his
supervisor and such, but was not offered an associate's position. I pressed Toscano for more details and he had to go back to the file. Seems as
if there were twenty-seven interns that summer,
from a variety of law schools, and that everyone
but Bannick received an offer of employment.
Twenty-one accepted. I asked why Bannick got
stiffed if his file was clean and, of course, Toscano
had no clue. At the time, Perry Kronke was one of
two managing partners and was in charge of their
summer intern program. Toscano said there is a
copy of a letter in the file from Kronke to Bannick
in which no job was offered. He sent me a copy
of the entire file, again after I mentioned a subpoena. There's not much to it, but it does prove
what we already knew—that their paths crossed
in 1989."

Sadelle sucked in some air and growled, "And
tell me again. How did Betty Roe know about
this connection?"

Lacy said, "She says in her complaint that she
found a former partner of the big firm, a guy same
age as Bannick, and he was in the intern class of
1989. Thus he knew Bannick well, maybe still

does for all we know. Says he really wanted the job and took the rejection hard."

Sadelle said, "Added it to his list. Take a name now, kick an ass years later."

"Something like that. Twenty-plus years."

"Sure hope I haven't done anything to upset him. But I'm more than half dead anyway."

"Enough of that."

"You'll outlive all of us," Darren said.

"Wanna bet?"

"How do I collect if I win?"

"Good point."

Lacy closed the file and looked at her task force. "So, folks, where exactly are we now? We know that Bannick knew two of the victims, which was alleged by Betty in her complaint. As I've said, she has given me documentation, off the record so far, of five more murders involving five more victims who had the misfortune of angering Judge Bannick somewhere along the way. Thankfully, we don't have to worry about those."

"Why don't we just go to the state police?" Sadelle asked.

"Because they're already on the case, have been from the Kronke murder. We saw the file, hundreds of pages."

"Thousands," Darren said.

"Okay, thousands. They talked to dozens of people who knew Kronke in and around Marathon. Nothing. They checked every boat rental record, every fuel purchase, every new fishing license. Nothing. They talked to his former law partners in Miami. Nothing. And former clients. Nothing. His family. Nothing. They've done a thorough job of digging into the victim's past and present, and they have come up with exactly nothing. Not a decent lead anywhere. They've done their work, have nothing to show for it, and so it's just sitting there, another cold case waiting on a miracle."

Darren said, "I'm flying back down to Miami on Wednesday to meet with the state investigators. I've talked to them several times on the phone and they seem willing to at least indulge us. I'm sure I'll see the same file we saw in Marathon, but you never know. Maybe they know something that Chief Turnbull doesn't."

Sadelle wheezed and said, "So, why not tell them about Bannick? If we know the killer's name, or at least we have a sworn complaint alleging he did it, why not hand that information over to the investigators?"

She arched her shoulders and braced for another intake. Her machine hummed a bit louder as she strained. "I mean, look, Lacy, we're just spinning our wheels here. There's really not much for us to do. The real cops have billion-dollar budgets, everything from bloodhounds to helicopters and satellites, and they can't solve the crimes. How are we supposed to? I say we punt this thing over to the state police and let them go after him."

Darren said, "That's where it's headed."

Lacy said, "Maybe so, but I promised Betty we wouldn't involve the police until she approves."

"That's not how we operate, Lacy," Sadelle said. "Once the complaint is filed it becomes our jurisdiction. The complaining party is not allowed to dictate how we proceed. You know that."

"I do, but thanks for the lecture."

"Don't mention it."

"She's using us, Lacy," Darren said. "Just like we discussed last week. Betty wants to hide behind us and get the police involved. So, that's our next step."

"We'll see. Go to Miami, meet with the state boys, and give us a report next Monday."

That afternoon, Lacy left early and drove across town to a complex filled with two-story office buildings. The suite owned by R. Buford Furr was quiet, plush, well appointed, and spoke of a successful lawyer. There were no other clients waiting in the reception area and a handsome young intern was answering the phone. At precisely four, he escorted Lacy back to a sprawling war room where Buford did battle with the world. He hugged her warmly as if they had been friends for years and showed her to a sofa that probably cost more than her car.

Furr was one of the top trial lawyers in Florida

and had many large verdicts to brag about. Which he did, with framed newspaper headlines and photos on his walls. All lawyers knew of him, and when Lacy had decided to sue over the staged car wreck that injured her and killed Hugo Hatch, her former colleague, she really had no choice.

Verna Hatch, Hugo's widow, hired him first and they filed a wrongful death action seeking $10 million. A week later, Furr sued on Lacy's behalf. The lawsuits had been stymied by an unusual obstacle—an abundance of cash. The crime syndicate that had skimmed millions from an Indian casino had buried its loot around the world. The Feds were still finding it, and the fact that there was so much of it was attracting an astonishing number of aggrieved parties. And their lawyers. The state and federal court dockets were loaded with claims.

The most serious impediment to a resolution was a huge and complicated federal lawsuit involving the conflicting claims of the Native Americans who owned the casino. Until that mess was settled, no one really knew how much cash would be left for the other aggrieved parties, including Lacy and Verna Hatch.

Furr walked her through the latest developments in the asset forfeiture proceedings and other litigation. He frowned when he said, "Lacy, I'm afraid they want to take your deposition."

"I don't want to go through that," she said. "We've talked about this."

"I know. One problem is that the attorneys appointed by the court to hand out the money are working by the hour, at very good rates, and they're in no hurry to wrap things up."

"Gee. I've never heard that before."

Furr laughed and said, "We're not talking about small-town Tallahassee rates. These guys are billing eight hundred bucks an hour. We'll be lucky if there's anything left."

"Can't you complain to the judges?"

"There are lots of complaints. Everything is contentious right now."

Lacy thought for a moment as Furr watched her. "A depo won't be that bad," he said.

She said, "I'm not sure I can relive that car crash, the image of Hugo covered in blood. Dying, I guess."

"We'll have you prepped. You'll need the experience because you may have to take the stand if the case goes to trial."

"I don't want a trial, Buford. I've made myself clear. I'm sure you would like a big production, with plenty of bad guys sitting at the defense table, the jury in your pocket as always. Another big verdict."

Furr laughed. "That's what I live for, Lacy. Can you imagine hauling those crooks back from prison to sit through a trial? It's a lawyer's dream."

"Well, it's not mine. I can handle a deposition but not a trial. I really want to settle, Buford."

"We will, I promise. But right now we have to play the discovery game."

"I'm not sure I'm up to it."

"You want to dismiss our case?"

"No. I want it to go away after we settle. I still have nightmares and the lawsuit doesn't help."

"I understand, Lacy. Just trust me, okay? I've been down this road many times. You deserve a generous settlement and I promise I'll get one."

She nodded her gratitude.

21

Sergeant Faldo was re-indexing rape kits when the phone in his pocket rattled. It was his boss, **the** boss, the chief of all Pensacola police, and he was as blunt as usual. He said that Judge Ross Bannick needed to check an old file that afternoon. He would be in court until at least four but would meet with Faldo at precisely four thirty. Faldo was ordered to do whatever His Honor wanted. "Just kiss his ass, okay?"

"Yes sir," Faldo shot back. He did not need to be told how to handle his job.

He vaguely recalled that Bannick had been there before, years earlier. It was unusual for a circuit court judge, or any other judge for that matter, to stop by the evidence warehouse. Faldo's visitors were almost exclusively cops working on cases, bringing in evidence to be stored until trial, or digging through old files. But then Faldo had learned decades earlier that the treasure trove of old clues he guarded might attract just about anyone. He had logged in private investigators, reporters, novelists, desperate families looking for shreds of evidence, even a medium and at least one witch.

At four thirty, Judge Bannick appeared with a pleasant smile and said hello. He seemed genuinely pleased to meet the sergeant and asked about his distinguished career on the force. Always the politician, he thanked Faldo for his service and asked him to call if he ever needed anything.

At issue was an old file from way back, the year was 2001. A case in city court, a dismissal, a trivial matter that was of no consequence to anyone but a retired friend down in Tampa who needed a favor. And so the fiction went.

As they withdrew into the bowels of the warehouse, chatting about football, Faldo seemed to remember something about the file. He found April, May, then June, and pulled out an entire drawer. "Defendant's name is Verno," Bannick said as he watched Faldo thumb through the row of files.

"Here it is," Faldo said proudly as he removed it and handed it over.

Bannick adjusted his reading glasses and asked, "Anybody looked at this lately?"

Now he remembered. "Yes, sir. Guy came in a few weeks back, oddly enough. I copied his driver's license. Should be right there."

Bannick pulled out a sheet of paper and looked at the face of one Jeff Dunlap of Conyers, Georgia. "What did he want?"

"Don't know, other than the file. I copied it for him, a dollar a pop. Four bucks as I recall." And he further recalled that Dunlap dropped a $5 bill on the counter because Faldo used only credit cards, but decided not to mention this. It was a small theft, just a bit of graft by a veteran police officer who had always been grossly underpaid.

Bannick studied the pages, his reading glasses balanced intelligently at the very tip of his nose. "Who redacted the name of the complaining party?" he asked, not really expecting Faldo to have an answer.

Well, it was probably you, sir. According to my logbook up front, only two people have had any interest in that file in the past thirteen years. You, twenty-three months ago, and now this Dunlap fellow. But Faldo read the situation correctly and wanted no trouble. "I have no idea, sir."

"Okay. Can you run me a copy of this guy's driver's license?"

"Yes, sir."

Judge Bannick drove away in his Ford SUV, nothing flashy, nothing to attract attention. Never.

A private detective from Georgia traveled to Pensacola to dig through a useless old police file, some thirteen years after the case was closed. In doing so he found the scant records of the arrest and trial of Lanny Verno, may he rest in peace. Odd and hard to explain, other than the obvious explanation that someone was digging through his past.

Bannick's mind had been spinning for twenty-four hours, and he was eating ibuprofen to fight the headaches. It was crucial to think clearly, smartly, slowly, and to see around corners, but many images were blurred. He drove to the north side of Pensacola and stopped at a shopping center, one of two he owned. There was a Kroger on one end and a cinema fourplex at the other, and in between there were eight smaller businesses, all current with their rents. He parked near a popular gym, one that he used almost every day, and walked along a covered sidewalk like any other shopper. Between the gym and a yoga studio he turned in to a wide covered alley and stopped at an unmarked door where he scanned a key card and stared into the facial scanner. The door clicked and he quickly went inside. He turned off the alarms as the door closed behind him.

It was his other chamber, his sanctum, his refuge, his cave. No windows, only one entrance, heavily alarmed, and watched around the clock by hidden cameras. There was no record of its existence, no business permits, no utility bills, no access by anyone other than him. Electricity, water, sewer, Internet, and cable were siphoned from the gym, on the other side of a thick wall, and the rent was adjusted accordingly by a handshake deal with the lessee. It was technically in violation of a few petty ordinances and regulations, and as a judge he didn't like the fact that he was cheating a little. But no one would ever know. The privacy afforded by his other chamber far outweighed any nagging feelings of guilt.

He lived ten miles away in the town of Cullman, in a fine home with the usual busy man's office, one that could be easily raided by men with warrants. And his professional office was his rather somber chambers on the second floor of the Chavez County Courthouse, a space owned by the taxpayers and, though not exactly open to the public, clearly susceptible to being searched.

Let them come. Let them seize all the files and computers in his home and his official chambers, and they would not find one shred of evidence against him. They could stalk him online, dig through his computers and judicial data server files, trace every email he'd ever sent from those computers, and they would find nothing.

He had lived most of his adult life in fear of arrest, of warrants, of detectives, of getting caught. The fear had so thoroughly consumed him for so long that his daily routines included all manner of cautionary moves. And he remained, so far, ahead of the bloodhounds.

The fear of getting caught was not driven by the
fear of paying the price. Rather, it was the fear of
having to stop.

His passion for technology, security, surveillance, off-the-wall science, even espionage, was
rooted in a movie he had long since forgotten
the name of. He had watched it as a frightened
and damaged thirteen-year-old boy, alone in the
basement one night after his parents had gone to
bed. The protagonist was a scrawny misfit of a
kid who was the favorite target of neighborhood
bullies. Instead of lifting weights and learning
karate, he delved into the world of weird science,
spycraft, weaponry, ballistics, even chemical war-
fare. He bought the first computer in town and
taught himself how to program it. In due course,
he exacted revenge on the bullies and rode off
into the sunset. It wasn't much of a movie, but
it inspired young Ross Bannick to embrace science and technology. He begged his parents for
an Apple II computer for Christmas, and birthday
too. Plus, he tossed in $450 of his own savings.
Throughout high school and college, every paycheck and every spare dollar went for the latest
upgrade, the latest gadget. In his younger days, he
had secretly tapped phones, filmed frat brothers
having sex with their girlfriends, recorded lectures that were off-limits, disabled surveillance
cameras, picked locks, entered secured offices,
and taken a hundred other stupid chances that he

never regretted. He had never been caught, not even close.

The arrival of the Internet presented him with endless possibilities.

He took off his tie and jacket and tossed them on a leather sofa, a place he often slept. He had clothes in a closet in the rear, a small fridge with sodas and fruit drinks. There was a café a hundred yards away near the cinema and he often ate there, alone, when working late. He walked to a thick metal door, punched a code, waited for the lead bolts to release, then opened it and walked deeper inside his secret world. The Vault, as he proudly called it but only when talking to himself, was a fifteen-foot-square office that was soundproof, fireproof, waterproof, everything-proof. No one had ever seen it and no one ever would. There was a desk in the center with two thirty-inch computer screens. One wall was covered with IP cameras showing his home, office, courthouse, and the building he was in. On one wall there was a sixty-inch plasma screen television. The other two walls were bare—no ego puffery, no awards, commendations, diplomas. All that junk was preserved on walls that could be seen. Indeed, there was nothing anywhere in his other chamber that would indicate who owned the place. The name of Ross Bannick was nowhere to be found.

If he dropped dead tomorrow, his computers and phones would wait patiently for forty-eight hours, then wipe themselves clean.

He sat at his desk, flipped on his computer, and waited for the screen to come to life. He pulled the two letters out of his briefcase and placed them in front of him. The one in an envelope was postmarked PENSACOLA and informed him of the BJC investigation. The other, a silly poem, was in the envelope postmarked MONTGOMERY. Both sent by the same person at about the same time.

He went online, activated his VPN to blow past security walls, and passworded his way into the dark web, where Rafe was always waiting. As an employee of the state, Bannick had long ago hacked his way into the data networks of Florida's government. Using his customized spyware, called Maggotz, he had created his own data sleuth, a troll he christened Rafe, who roamed the systems and cloud with total anonymity. Because Rafe was not a criminal, was not stealing or holding data for ransom, but rather was only nosing around for esoteric information, his chances of being discovered were almost zero.

Rafe could, for example, observe internal memos between the seven members of the Florida Supreme Court and their clerks, and Bannick would know precisely how one of his cases on appeal would be decided. Since he couldn't do anything about the case, the information was basically useless, but it was certainly interesting to know which way the wind was blowing.

Rafe could also see sensitive correspondence between the Attorney General and the Governor. He could read comments made by prosecutors about sitting judges. He could dig deep into the files of the state police and report their progress, or lack of it.

And, most importantly at that moment, Rafe could watch the goings-on at the Board on Judicial Conduct. Bannick checked it for the second day in a row and found nothing with his name on it. This was confusing, and troublesome.

Hell, at that moment everything was troublesome. He swallowed more ibuprofen and thought about a shot of vodka. But he was not much of a drinker and planned to go to the gym. He needed two hours of pounding weights to break the stress.

It was amusing to read the complaints currently being investigated by BJC. He relished the allegations against his fellow members of the judiciary, a few of whom he knew well, a couple of whom he despised. Prolonged amusement, though, was out of the question.

Bannick reveled in his wrongdoing. The other complaints at BJC were chicken feed compared to his crimes. But now someone else knew his history. And, if a complaint had been filed against him, why was it being hidden?

This ramped up the head-spinning and he reached for the pills.

The person who sent the letter, and the poem, knew the truth. That person mentioned Kronke, Verno, and Dunwoody, and suggested others. How much did they know? If that person had filed the complaint with BJC, then he or she did so only with an agreement that there would be no record of it, at least not for the forty-five-day assessment period.

He went to a small room in the rear, undressed, took a long hot shower, and put on workout clothes. Back at his desk, he sent Rafe into the confidential files of the state police, files so sensitive and protected that Rafe had been waltzing through them for almost three years now. He found the Perry Kronke file from the town of Marathon, and was stunned to see a fresh entry by Detective Grimsley, the state's lead investigator. It read:

> call today from chief Turnbull in Marathon;
> he had a visit on March 31 from two lawyers
> with the Florida Board on Judicial Conduct—
> Lacy Stoltz and Darren Trope; they said they
> were curious about the murder of Kronke;
> said they might have a suspect but would not
> divulge anything; gave no names; they went
> to the approx site of where Kronke was found;
> revealed nothing; they left and promised to
> contact later; Turnbull was not too impressed,
> says he expects to hear nothing back, said no
> action needed on our part.

He had left nothing behind at the Kronke killing. He had even dipped himself into the ocean.

"Might have a suspect," he repeated to himself. After twenty-three years of remaining invisible, was it possible that someone finally considered him to be a "suspect"? If so, then who? It wasn't Lacy Stoltz or Darren Trope. They were simply low-level bureaucrats reacting to a complaint, one filed by the same person who was now sending him mail.

Deep breathing and meditation did nothing to break the stress.

He started for the vodka but left for the gym, locking his other chamber behind himself, always careful, always noticing everything, every person. As bewildered and frightened as he was, he told himself to relax and think clearly. He walked around the corner to the fitness center and joined a hot yoga class for twenty minutes of sweating before he hit the iron.

22

On Friday morning, April 11, Norris Ozment had just arrived at his desk off the main reception area at the Pelican Point resort when a call came through his landline from the hotel operator. "A Judge Bannick from over in Cullman."

Curious that he should hear the judge's name again so soon, Ozment took the call. They claimed to remember each other from Ozment's old days with the Pensacola police; then, with that door wide open, Bannick said, "I'm chasing a rabbit for an old friend down in Tampa and I'm looking for some info regarding a Lanny Verno, looks like a real lowlife, got himself murdered a few months back over in Biloxi. He had a case in city court years ago and you were the arresting officer. Any of this ring a bell?"

"Well, Judge, normally it would not ring any bell, but now it does. I remember the case."

"No kidding? It was thirteen years ago."

"Yes, sir, it was. You swore out a warrant and I arrested Verno."

"That's right," Bannick said with a loud fake laugh. "That guy pulled a gun on me in my own house and the judge let him go."

"A long time ago, Judge. I don't miss those days in city court and I've tried to forget them. I'm sure I wouldn't have remembered the case, but a private detective showed up last month asking questions about Verno."

"You don't say."

"Yes, sir."

"What did he want?"

"Just said he was curious."

"Well, if you don't mind my asking, what was he curious about?"

Actually, Ozment was bothered by his asking, but Bannick was a circuit judge with jurisdiction over criminal matters. He could probably subpoena the resort's records if he wanted to. He was also involved in the prosecution of Verno as the alleged victim. These thoughts rattled around as Ozment debated how much to say.

"He said Verno had been murdered and that he had been hired by his family in Georgia to chase down some gossip about a couple of stray children he might have left behind."

"Where was this guy from?"

"Said he was from Georgia, the Atlanta area, Conyers."

"Did you keep an ID?"

"No, sir. He never offered a business card. I never asked for one, didn't offer him one either. But our cameras got his car in the parking lot and we tracked the tags. It was a Hertz rental out of Mobile."

"Interesting."

"I guess. At the time I just figured he flew from Atlanta to Mobile and rented the car. To be honest, Judge, I didn't give it much thought. It was a petty criminal case in city court a hundred years ago and the defendant, Verno, was found not guilty. Now somebody killed him over in Mississippi. Not really much of my business."

"I see. Did you get a look at his car?"

"Yes, sir. It's on video."

"Mind emailing it to me?"

"Well, I'll have to check with our manager. We may have some security issues."

"I'm happy to speak with your manager." The statement had a slightly threatening tone to it. He was a judge and as such was accustomed to getting what he wanted.

A pause as Ozment glanced around his empty office. "Sure, Judge. Give me your email."

His Honor gave him a temporary address, one of many he used and discarded, and half an hour later he was looking at two photos: one a rear shot of a white Buick sedan with Louisiana license plates; the second from the same camera with Jeff Dunlap in the frame. Bannick sent an email back to Ozment saying thanks, and attached to it a useless brochure describing the mission and duties of the judges and officers of Florida's Twenty-Second Judicial District. When Ozment opened and downloaded it, Maggotz entered through the back door and Pelican Point's network was immediately infected. Not that Bannick would ever need to snoop, but he suddenly had access to the resort's guest lists, financial records, personnel files, tons of credit card and banking data. And not just Pelican Point. It was part of a small chain of twenty boutique resorts, and Rafe now had even more to explore if he ever wanted to.

But there were more pressing matters. Bannick called his office and spoke with his clerk. Other than an eleven o'clock attorney conference, there was nothing important on his schedule.

There were seven Jeff or Jeffrey Dunlaps in the Atlanta area, but only two in the town of Conyers. One was a schoolteacher whose wife sounded like a fifteen-year-old. The other was a retired city bus driver who said he had never been to Mobile. Both confirmed what Bannick suspected from the outset—Jeff Dunlap was a bogus front for the private detective. He would track down the other five later, just to be sure.

He called a Hertz office in Mobile and spoke to a young woman named Janet, who was quite helpful and zipped through the details of his weekend rental. She emailed the confirmation to one of Bannick's addresses, and he replied with: "Thanks Janet. The quote I received differs from your confirmation by $120. Please review the attached and address this discrepancy." As soon as Janet opened the attachment, Rafe sneaked through the back door of Hertz North America. Bannick hated hacking such large corporations because their security was much more sophisticated, but as long as Rafe just snooped and didn't try to steal or extort, he would probably go undetected. Bannick would wait a few hours and cancel the rental. In the meantime, he sent Rafe to the registration records for Hertz vehicles titled in Louisiana.

From prior experience, he knew that Hertz rented half a million vehicles in the U.S. and allocated their registrations to all fifty states. Enterprise, the largest car rental company, did the same with over 600,000 vehicles.

It proved to be a bit of a slog for Rafe, though he never complained, never stopped. He was programmed to work around the clock every day of the week if necessary. While he labored in the shadows, Bannick worked the phone to make sure all Jeff Dunlaps in the Atlanta area checked out.

—

At ten thirty, he straightened his tie, examined himself in the mirror, and thought he looked quite haggard and worried, with good reason. He had slept little and now the sky was falling. For the first time in his life he felt like he was on the run. He drove fifteen minutes to the Escambia County Courthouse in Pensacola for his meeting. The lawyers were all from downtown and he had scheduled around their convenience. He managed to flip a switch and appear as warm and personable as always. He listened to each side and promised a quick mediation. Then he hustled back to his other chamber and locked himself inside.

On March 11, the Buick was rented to one Rollie Tabor, a private investigator licensed by the State of Alabama. He used it for two days and returned it on March 12, traveling only 421 miles.

Tabor's online presence was quite meager, which was true of most private investigators. They tended to advertise only enough to attract business but not enough to reveal anything useful. His website claimed that he was a former detective, experienced, trustworthy, confidential. What was it supposed to say? He handled missing persons, divorce, child custody, background investigations, the usual. Downtown Mobile office address, office phone number, and email. There was no vanity photograph of Tabor.

Comparing the security camera shot taken at the resort to the bogus driver's license copied by Sergeant Faldo, it was clear that the same man, one who called himself Jeff Dunlap, had been to both places snooping around for information about Lanny Verno. The man was really Rollie Tabor, so why was he lying?

Bannick plotted and schemed for an hour, discarding one ruse after the other. When inspiration finally hit, he set up another email account and sent Tabor a note:

> Dear Mr. Tabor. I'm a physician in Birmingham and I need the services of a private investigator in the Mobile area. A possible domestic relations matter. You have been highly recommended. Are you available? And if so, what is your hourly rate? Dr. Albert Marbury.

Bannick sent the email, tracked it, and waited. Thirty-one minutes later, Tabor opened it and replied:

> Dr. Marbury. Thank you. I am available. My rate is $200 an hour. RT

Bannick scoffed at the $200 an hour. Obviously the Doctor's Rate. He sent back an email agreeing to the rate, and attached a link to a hotel website in Gulf Shores where he suspected his wife might be staying. When Tabor opened the email and looked at the attachment, Rafe slid through the back door and was on the prowl. He began by looking for current clients. Tabor's record-keeping was rudimentary at best, at least for the data he entered into his computer. Bannick knew full well that a lot of PIs kept two sets of books—one for the IRS, the other for themselves. Cash was still a popular lubricant. After an hour, he had found nothing. No mention of Lanny Verno, or Jeff Dunlap, or the trip to Pensacola and Seagrove Beach a month earlier. And certainly no clue as to the identity of the client behind the investigation.

He ate ibuprofen and took some Valium to settle his nerves. He realized he was weak with hunger but his systems were raging and he was afraid to tempt his stomach with more food. He was tired of the Vault, and at the moment he wanted to get behind the wheel and just drive, just go, hit the open road and get the hell out of town for the weekend. Maybe from a distant pier or beach or mountain he could look back with an unclouded eye and make sense of it.

Someone knew. And that someone knew a lot.

He walked out of the Vault and went to the small room in the rear where he stripped to his boxers and pulled on gym shorts and a T-shirt. He needed fresh air, a hike in the woods, but he couldn't leave. Not at this crucial moment. He found an orange in the fridge and ate it with black coffee.

Maggotz had been hiding in the shadows of the Harrison County Sheriff's Department since the killings of Lanny Verno and Mike Dunwoody. After they were found, Rafe came to life and began nosing around.

When the orange was finished, Bannick said hello to Rafe and sent him to the files of Detective Napier, the chief investigator in Biloxi. In a daily log, Napier had entered a note on March 25: Meeting today with Lacy Stoltz and Darren Trope of the Florida Board on Judicial Conduct, re the Verno/Dunwoody murders. Allowed them access to the file but nothing was taken or copied. They made a vague reference to a suspect but would provide no details. They know more than they are willing to say. Will follow up. ENapier.

Bannick cursed and walked away from his desk. He felt like a bleeding animal stumbling through the woods as the bloodhounds drew closer and louder.

Eileen was number four. Eileen Nickleberry. Age thirty-two at the time of her death. Divorced, according to her obituary.

He loved collecting his obits. They were all in the files.

He found her thirteen years later, thirteen years after she mocked him in his frat house bedroom, thirteen years after she had stumbled downstairs, drunk like all the rest, and broadcast to the rest of the party that Ross "couldn't get it up." Couldn't perform. She laughed and ran her big mouth, though by the next morning most of the hell-raisers had forgotten the incident. But she kept talking and word spread through their circles. Bannick has a problem. Bannick can't perform.

Six years later he found his first victim, the scoutmaster. His killing had gone as perfectly as planned. There was not one shred of remorse, not even a twinge of pity as he stepped back and looked at the body of Thad Leawood. It was euphoric, actually, and filled him with an indescribable sense of power, control, and—the best—revenge. From that moment on, he knew he would never stop.

Seven years after Leawood, and with three under his belt, he finally found Eileen. She was selling real estate north of Myrtle Beach, her pretty, smiling face splashed on every yard sign possible, as if she were running for city council. She had listings in a beachside development of forty condos. He rented one of the others for the summer of 1998, before he became a judge. On a Sunday morning, he lured her to an empty unit, one she was trying to sell, PRICE REDUCED!, and the very second when she froze as if she remembered him, he splintered her skull with Leddie. As the rope cut deep and she breathed her last, he hissed into her ear and reminded her of her mockery.

Five hours passed before there was a commotion. As things became frantic and people yelled, he sat with a beer on the balcony of his rental and watched across the courtyard as first responders scurried about. The sounds of sirens made him smile. He waited a week for the cops to come around knocking on doors and looking for witnesses, but they never showed. He paid his lease in full and never returned to the condo.

The crime occurred in the seaside town of Sunset Beach, in Brunswick County, North Carolina. Nine years passed before the county digitized its records, and when it happened Bannick was waiting with his first generation of spyware. As with all the other police departments, he updated his data often, always on the prowl for any movement, always watching with the latest hacker's toys.

The Eileen story had gone cold after a couple of years. There was never a serious suspect. The file reflected some occasional interest from crime writers, reporters, family members, and other police departments.

Late Friday afternoon, Bannick sent in Rafe to snoop around for the first time in months. Based on the latest digital time and date stamp, the file had not been touched in three years, not since a reporter, or someone claiming to be, wanted to have a look.

23

The orange stayed down. He tried to nap but was too wired. He grabbed his gym bag and walked around the corner where he spent two hours spinning, rowing, lifting, and pounding the treadmill. When he was beyond exhaustion, he stuck his head into the steam room. When he was certain he would be alone, he stripped and entered and stretched out on his towel.

It was a mistake to call Norris Ozment, but he'd had no choice. Ozment could now link him directly to Verno, the same way Tabor had linked him. But it was unlikely that the authorities in Mississippi would ever find Ozment, and even unlikelier that he would bother to go to them. Why should he?

The judge massaged his temples and tried to breathe slowly as the steam soothed his lungs. The person who filed the complaint with BJC did so anonymously and with the understanding that nothing would be entered into a digital file. Everything would be kept offline. The person who hired Rollie Tabor to pose as Jeff Dunlap and snoop through the old court case did so with the agreement that Tabor would store nothing online. The person who mailed the two anonymous letters went to great lengths to remove all possible clues.

The person knew about Eileen Nickleberry.

All these persons were the same. There was simply no other explanation. The evidence was far too coincidental. It was imperative to find this person.

And if he found him, what would the good judge do? He could certainly kill him, that would be easy enough. But was it too late? Did Ms. Stoltz at BJC have enough damning evidence to go to the police? He told himself the answer was no, and he believed it. Accusing and indicting were easy enough, but convicting would be impossible. He presided over murder trials, studied forensics and knew more about the science than the experts, and, most importantly, he knew how much evidence was needed to convict. A helluva lot! Beyond a reasonable doubt. Far more than any low-paid cop had been able to find along his graveyard trail.

There were a dozen on his list, give or take. More or less. Ten down, two to go. Maybe three. Dunwoody didn't count because he was never on the list. His timing was bad, and he was one victim that still troubled the judge. He didn't deserve to die, like the others. Troubled as he was, though, there was nothing he could do about it.

And now there were far more serious troubles.

A killer can't help but look over his shoulder, and for years he had feared this reckoning. In fact, he'd had so much time to think about it that he had pieced together several possible reactions. One was to simply go away, vanish, before being subjected to the humiliation of an indictment, arrest, and trial. He had plenty of money and there was a big world out there. He had traveled extensively and been to several places where he could easily blend in and never be found. He preferred those countries beyond the reach of U.S. extradition treaties.

Another strategy was to stay and fight. Declare innocence, even persecution, and lawyer up for a big trial. He knew precisely who to hire for his defense. No jury could convict him because no police department had the evidence. It was his firm belief that no prosecutor would ever indict, for the same reason. No sitting judge had ever been put on trial for murder in America, and to do so would cause a media circus of epic proportions. Even the most ambitious prosecutor would shy away from the horror of losing before such an audience.

Which of his murders would be the easiest to prove at trial? It was the great question that he toyed with almost every day. Because of his cunning and brilliance, he was of the lofty opinion that none of them could survive past the indictment phase. Staying and fighting was the most attractive option.

Staying would allow him to finish his list.

The last strategy was the easiest. He could simply end the game himself and take his crimes to his grave.

Judge Bannick allowed himself a martini late on Friday afternoons, usually with another judge or two, and there were several preferred bars in the area. One favorite was at a club on the oceanfront with the Gulf stretching in the distance. On this Friday, though, he was in no mood for socializing, but he did need the martini. He mixed it in the back room and sipped it in the Vault, and as he did so he asked himself the obvious question: "Who is this person?"

A cop would not bother with anonymous mail. Why waste the time? Why alert the suspect? Why play games? And the cops weren't looking. He had hacked his way into all the police departments and he knew how cold the files were. The sheriff in Biloxi and his detective Napier were still working the case every day, but that was only because there were two victims and one was local. They had nothing to show for their efforts and now, after six months, they were following the same pattern as the others.

A private investigator would cost too much money. Regardless of the hourly rate, there was simply too much labor involved to link the murder of Eileen in 1998, in North Carolina, to the murder of Perry Kronke in 2012, then to Verno and Dunwoody in Biloxi last fall. No one could afford such a project. He knew his victims and their families well. Perry Kronke was by far the wealthiest of the lot, but his widow was in poor health and probably reluctant to spend a fortune trying to find his killer. His two sons were Miami businessmen of modest success.

Bannick stepped to a corner and pulled back a rug. With a key he unlocked a safe hidden under the flooring and removed a thumb drive. He stuck it into his computer, pecked here and there, and within seconds a file labeled KRONKE appeared. Since he had researched and written everything in the file, he knew it by heart, but the constant review of his past was part of his life. Constant vigilance was just as important as meticulous planning.

Kronke's estate had been probated in Monroe County, Florida, four months after his murder. His older son, Roger, was named executor of his will and was so appointed by the court. Inventories of assets were filed on time. There were no mortgages and no debts other than routine credit card charges. At the time of his death,

Kronke and his wife jointly owned their retirement home, appraised at $800,000, two rental
homes at $200,000 each, a stock portfolio valued
at $2.6 million, a money market account with a
balance of $340,000, and various bank accounts
that totaled $90,000. With his cars and boat and
other smaller assets, the inventory added up to
$4.4 million.

The estate file was public record. Hacking
into the probate judge's office email had been
a breeze because of Maggotz and its familiarity
with the entire Florida court system. Rafe was
also spying on Mrs. Kronke and her finances as
a new widow. He watched her bank records and
knew that she drew a Social Security check of
$2,000 a month, a retirement check from the
law firm for $4,500 a month, and $3,800 from
a 401(k).

The bottom line was that she had plenty of cash
but there was no indication she was writing big
checks to private investigators. She didn't email
much, but there was correspondence between her
and the two sons. She was contemplating selling
the house and moving into an expensive retirement village. Emails between the sons indicated
the usual worries about Mom spending too much
and screwing up their inheritances.

There had been no chatter about devoting time
and money to search for the killer.

Bannick convinced himself that "the person"

was not stalking him on behalf of the Kronke family.

At the other end of the economic ladder was Lanny Verno. Having no estate, nothing had been probated. He left behind no assets, no children, no close family, nothing to hack, nothing but a live-in lady who'd come and gone and had shacked up with plenty. Verno was the last person on his list who might send in the investigators.

Bannick jumped to another file, labeled EILEEN NICKLEBERRY.

Her family was just as doubtful. She had died sixteen years earlier with no will and few assets. Her mother had been dragged into court to serve as administrator of her estate. Her condo and car were hocked and sold to satisfy the loans and pay off her credit cards. After all debtors were satisfied, her parents, who were divorced, and two siblings split about $4,000.

Interestingly enough, her father hired a lawyer to explore a wrongful death claim against the owner of the condo development where she was murdered. Rafe watched the emails for a year or so as the lawsuit fizzled. Bannick was intrigued by the idea of lawyers, not cops, digging through the murder. The police were baffled from the start, as were the lawyers, and the investigations went nowhere. Other than a handyman with no criminal record and a solid alibi, there had never been a suspect. Another perfect murder.

The last one mentioned by "the person" was
Mike Dunwoody. Bannick went to his file, certain
that his family had not hired private investigators.
His murder was only five months old, and Sheriff
Black and Detective Napier were doing and saying all the right things to convince the public they
were making progress. The family seemed content to mourn in private and trust the authorities.
Dunwoody's will left everything to his wife and
named her as executrix. Five months on, she had
yet to begin probate. According to their bank records, personal and business, the company fell in
line with most home contractors—up one year,
down the next, successful as a whole but no one
was getting rich. It was impossible to believe they
were in a position to spend tens of thousands on
their own investigation.

The person was not a cop and not a private eye.
However, he was clearly using people like Rollie
Tabor to snoop around. Who would hire an inves-
tigator from Mobile?

Someone looking for a story, a reporter, a free-
lancer, a writer, would not have the patience to
pursue such a project for so long. Money was their
motive, and who could survive decades without
a payoff?

He mixed another martini and took it to the
front room where he sat on the sofa in the dark.
He sipped it slowly and felt the gin work its way
into his muddled brain. For a few moments the

pain subsided. He was sick of the place but felt safe there. No one could see him. No one in the world knew where he was. For a man who had stalked his prey for most of his adult life, he found it terrifying that there was now someone out there watching him. His victims, though, never had a clue. He, on the other hand, knew the awful truth that someone was on to him.

He had lost track of time and his cell phone was in the Vault. He stretched out on the sofa and fell into a deep sleep.

As he slept, Rafe went about his work rummaging through the sparse and disjointed network of the Atlas Finders, otherwise known as the small office of Rollie Tabor, PI. He wormed his way into the computer of a part-time secretary named Susie, and there he found some photos. One was of her and her boss, Mr. Tabor.

Hours later, Bannick looked into the smiling face of Rollie and easily matched the photo with the one taken by Norris Ozment's security camera and also the one from Dunlap's fake driver's license. It confirmed what he already knew: Rollie Tabor, a run-of-the-mill private dick in Mobile, had been hired by someone to dig through Bannick's quite dirty laundry.

But Rafe could find no other clues with Atlas. It would be necessary to hack into Tabor's cell phone, a task Bannick was not quite up to. With diligent study and plenty of practice, he had become an accomplished amateur hacker of computers, but the smartphones were another story. He was still learning but wasn't quite there.

It was still dark when he finally ventured from his bunker at just minutes before 6:00 a.m. on Saturday morning. The twenty-four-hour gym was deserted, as was the parking lot. He was eager to get home and left in a hurry, the only car on the road. Turning onto the street, he caught himself glancing into the rearview, then he almost laughed at the absurdity.

Twenty minutes later he drove through the gates of his well-protected community in Cullman and parked in front of his garage as the sun peeked through the clouds in the east. He turned off the engine, took his smartphone, turned off the security system, and checked the surveillance cameras and recent footage. Assured that all was safe, he finally got out and went inside where he flipped on lights and made a pot of coffee. He watched it brew and tried to shake off the cobwebs from the martinis. He poured a cup and slowly walked through his den to the front door. He opened it, took a step onto his porch, looked up and down the street, then reached into the small mailbox mounted beside the door.

Another plain white envelope, no return address.

it seemed harmless enough
    another water park at the beach
bulldoze, burn, and build
    another pot of gold, just within reach
you tried to hide in the dark
    your good name nowhere to be seen
cowering behind your partners
    directing the little scheme

oh the beauty of a free press
    to find the truth, expose the lies
keep the crooks out of office
    keep the judges fair and wise
your loss to the old one hurt badly
    and killed your enormous pride
so you blamed me for your corruption
    and relished the day I died.

24

The lazy Saturday morning was interrupted twice before Lacy made it to the coffee pot. The first call awakened her at three minutes after eight. Caller unknown, potential spam. In other words, don't answer. But something said do it, and if it happened to be a robocall she could simply hang up, as always.

"Good morning, Lacy," Jeri said softly.

A flash of anger passed quickly as Lacy controlled herself. "Good morning, Jeri. What's the occasion?"

"Just thinking about you, a lot, these days. How are you?"

"Well, I was sleeping, Jeri, before you called. It's Saturday, a day off, and I'm not working today. I thought I had explained this."

"I'm sorry, Lacy," Jeri said, in a tone that conveyed anything but remorse. "Why does it have to be considered work? Why can't we talk as friends?"

"Because we're not friends yet, Jeri. We are acquaintances who met for the first time about a month ago. We may become friends one day, once the work that brought us together is finished, but we're not there yet."

"I see."

"The word 'friend' gets tossed around loosely, don't you think?"

"I suppose."

"And whatever the reason for this call, it's not about friendship. It's probably on the business side."

"It is, Lacy. And I'm sorry to bother you."

"It's Saturday morning, Jeri, and I was sleeping."

"Got it. Look, I'll hang up now, but first let me say what I want. Okay?"

"Sure."

"There is a good chance that Bannick knows about the complaint and knows that you're digging through his past. I can't prove this, but I have come to believe that he has some type of superpower, extrasensory, something. I don't know. But he is extremely bright and diligent, and well, I guess I might be a bit paranoid. I've been living with him for so long I just assume that he's everywhere. Be careful, Lacy. If he knows you're on his trail he might do anything."

"I've thought about that, Jeri."

"Okay. Goodbye."

She was gone, and Lacy immediately felt lousy for being so abrupt. The poor woman was a wreck and had been for many years, and Lacy should have been more patient.

But it was early Saturday morning.

She closed her eyes and was thinking about more sleep, but the dog was making noises. She was thinking about Allie and how nice it would be to have him beside her. And, wide awake now, she was thinking about Jeri Crosby and the sadness of her life.

What she wasn't thinking about was her older brother and only sibling. When Gunther called not ten minutes after Jeri, Lacy had a hunch that her carefree day would not go as planned. He said he had a new airplane he wanted to show off, and with the weather perfectly gorgeous on this spring day he had the urge to fly down and take his kid sister to lunch. "I'm on the runway, taking off now, landing in Tallahassee in eighty-four minutes. Meet me at the airport."

It was so typical of Gunther. The world revolved around him and everyone else was just an extra. She fed and let out the dog, threw on some jeans, brushed her teeth, and headed to the airport, her quiet Saturday shot to hell. But she wasn't really surprised. Nothing about her brother was surprising. He was an avid pilot who swapped airplanes almost as fast as he bought and sold sports cars.

He ran the women hard too, and the bankers and investors. When the markets were up he burned cash, and when things went flat he kept borrowing until he couldn't. Even when the demand was high for his strip malls and tract housing, he seemed to totter along the edge of financial disaster. Because he was known to embellish and outright fabricate, Lacy had lost count of the times he had filed for bankruptcy. She thought there were three, along with his two divorces, and one near-indictment.

But regardless of his problems, Gunther slept hard every night and attacked each day with enthusiasm and confidence. His zest for life was contagious, and if he found himself in the mood to fly in for lunch there was no way to stop him, regardless of what she had planned.

Waiting in the private terminal, watching the small planes come and go while sipping a cup of bad coffee, she both dreaded and looked forward to seeing Gunther. With both parents gone now, they needed each other. Both were single and childless and it certainly looked as if they would be the family's last generation. Trudy, their mother's sister, was trying to become the matriarch and getting too involved. Lacy and Gunther were united in their resistance.

But she wasn't exactly thrilled to see him, because he had too many opinions about almost everything. Since her car wreck, he'd had far too much to say about her lawsuit, her lawyer, their legal strategies. He thought she was wasting her time at BJC. He wasn't too keen on Allie Pacheco, though this was a reaction to Lacy's dislike of every girlfriend he had dared introduce her to. He thought Tallahassee was a hick town and she should move to Atlanta. He disapproved of her current car. And so on.

There he was, crawling out of a sleek little plane, bounding down from the wing with no luggage, no briefcase, a playboy out for a spin and a nice lunch. They hugged in the doorway and left the terminal.

As soon as he buckled up he said, "Still driving this cheap little thing?"

"Look, Gunther, it's great to see you, as always. But the last thing I want to hear today is a steady stream of bitching about my life. Car included. Got that?"

"Wow, Sis. You wake up on the wrong side?"

"I did."

"Did you see my airplane? Isn't it a beauty?"

"I did. It's lovely as far as airplanes go."

"Bought it last month from a guy whose wife caught him cheating. Sad."

Gunther was anything but sad. "What is it?" she asked, but only because she had to.

"A Socata TBM 700 turboprop, all the bells and whistles. Think of a Ferrari with wings. Three hundred miles an hour. Got a real deal."

A real deal for Gunther meant that he had

convinced yet another banker to make a loan. "Sounds exciting. Looks pretty small."

"Seats four, that's plenty for me. You wanna go for a spin?"

"I thought we were doing lunch." Lacy had been his passenger on two occasions and that was enough. Gunther was a serious pilot who didn't play around and take chances, but he was still Gunther.

"Right," he said, suddenly checking his phone. When he put it away he asked, "How's Allie? Still seeing him?"

"I am, hot and heavy. Who's your new squeeze?"

"Which one? Look, I think it's time for this guy to either make a move or move on. It's been, what, two years now?"

"Oh, so you've got marriage all figured out?"

Gunther burst out laughing and, after a beat, Lacy did too. The idea of him giving advice on the romantic front was indeed humorous.

"Okay, no more of that. You talked to Aunt Trudy lately? Where are we going?"

"Home, so I can shower and brush my teeth. Didn't have enough time earlier."

"How can you dawdle around so on such a gorgeous Saturday morning?"

"No, I have not talked to Trudy. I owe her a phone call. You?"

"No, I'm ducking her too. Poor thing. She's lost without Mom. They were best friends and now she's stuck with that husband of hers."

"Ronald's okay."

"He's a creep and you know it. They really don't like each other but I guess after fifty years they can't get out."

"Let's talk about something else. How's business these days?"

"I'd rather talk about Ronald."

"Pretty bad, huh?"

"No, actually I'm killing it. I need some help, Lacy, and I want you to come to Atlanta and work with me. Bright lights, big city, much more to do. We'll make a fortune and there are a dozen great guys I could introduce you to."

"I'm not sure I want to date your friends."

"Come on, Lacy. Trust me. These guys have money and they're going places. How much does Allie make a year with the FBI?"

"I have no idea and I don't care."

"Not much. He's working for the government."

"So am I."

"That's my point. You can do better. Most of these guys are already millionaires who own their own companies. They have everything."

"Yeah, including alimony and child support."

Gunther laughed and said, "Okay, some of that."

Of course his phone rang, and he was soon lost in a tense conversation about a line of credit. On Saturday morning?

He was still on the phone when she parked near

her apartment. They went inside and she left him in the den as she headed for her upstairs bedroom.

Lunch was outdoors on a shaded terrace at an upscale restaurant, far away from downtown. Lacy talked the reservationist into an early table, primarily because she was still hoping to salvage some of her afternoon, alone. They were seated at eleven thirty and the terrace was deserted.

They ordered iced tea for starters, with Lacy quickly going first. If Gunther ordered his usual bottle of wine, then he wouldn't be flying that afternoon. She was relieved when he ignored the wine list and commented on the menu. Usually, when dining in her town, he made some pithy comment on the lack of good food. Atlanta, again, was far superior. But he let it pass and settled on a crab salad. Lacy ordered grilled shrimp.

"You still eat like a bird," he said, admiring his sister. "And you're in great shape, Lacy."

"Thanks and let's not dwell on my weight. I know what you're getting at."

"Come on. You haven't gained a pound in twenty years."

"No, and I'm not starting now. What else would you like to talk about?"

"Of course, you were all skin and bones after your car wreck. I almost called it an 'accident,' but it wasn't that simple, was it?"

A nice lead into her lawsuit, which she was anticipating. She smiled and said, "Once all the plaster and gauze came off, I weighed a hundred pounds."

"I remember, and you've come a long way back. I'm proud of you, Lacy. Are you still in therapy?"

"Physical or otherwise?"

"Physical."

"Yes, twice a week, but it's about over. I've accepted the fact that I'll always have little aches and pains, some stiffness here and there, but I'm lucky, I guess."

Gunther mixed some lemon in his tea and looked away. "I wouldn't call it luck, but you came out of it better than Hugo. Poor guy. Are you still in touch with his widow, what's her name?"

"Verna, and yes we're still close friends."

"She has the same lawyer, right?"

"She does. We compare notes and lean on each other. Nobody wants a trial. I'm not sure she can handle it."

"It will never get near the courthouse. The goons will settle."

Gunther had far more experience with civil litigation, though his disputes dealt with broken contracts and defaulted loans. To her knowledge, he had no experience with personal injuries.

"I guess things are tied up in discovery," he said, trying to ease into the heart of the matter.

"Looks like it. My lawyer says I may have to give a deposition. I'm sure you've been there."

Gunther snorted in disgust and said, "Oh yeah. A lot of fun. Staring across the table at five lawyers, all scheming to pounce on every word, every syllable, salivating as they dream of getting more of your money. Why can't your lawyer get the case settled? It should've been over months ago."

"It's complicated. Sure, there's a big pile of money, but that only attracts more vultures, more hungry lawyers."

"I get that. But what would you settle for, Lacy? What's your figure?"

"I don't know. We're not there yet."

"You're entitled to millions, Sis. Those bastards deliberately set you up and crashed into your car. You—"

"Please. I know all this, Gunther, and we're not going over it again."

"Okay, sorry, but I just worry about you. I'm not sure you have the right lawyer."

"As I've said before, Gunther, I can take care of myself and my lawyer. You don't need to waste time worrying about it."

"I know. Sorry. I'm your big brother and I can't help it."

Their plates arrived and both seemed to welcome the interruption. They began eating and things went quiet. He was obviously preoccupied with ideas but couldn't manage to work them into the conversation.

Her biggest fear was that he would need an infusion of cash at the same time she settled her lawsuit. He would never ask for money outright, as a gift, but would use the ploy of an urgent loan. If it happened, she was determined to say no. She knew he borrowed from Peter to pay Paul, hocked everything he owned, and walked the fine line between prosperity and financial ruin. He wasn't about to touch her money, when and if she ever got it, and if her refusal created a rift, then so be it. She would rather keep the money and deal with an ugly fallout than fork it over, watch him lose it, and then deal with a future filled with empty promises.

He backed away from more discussion of her lawsuit, and proceeded to talk about his favorite subject: his latest project. It would be a planned community with mixed housing, a central town square with a faux courthouse in the center, churches and schools, lots of water and trails, and the obligatory golf course. A regular utopia. A $50 million development, with other investors, of course. Lacy forced herself to seem engaged.

The terrace began to fill and before long they were in a crowd. Gunther contemplated one glass of wine for dessert, but changed his mind when she ordered an espresso. He paid the check at one o'clock and said it was time to head to the airport. Another deal was hanging by a thread and he was needed in Atlanta.

She hugged him goodbye inside the private terminal and watched him taxi away. She loved him dearly, but took a deep breath and relaxed when he was gone.

25

From his well-stocked closet, Judge Bannick selected a designer suit from Zegna, light gray in color, worsted wool, a white shirt with French cuffs, and a solid navy tie. He admired himself in the mirror and thought the look was rather European. Late Saturday afternoon, he left his home in Cullman and drove into central Pensacola, into an historic district known as North Hills. The streets were shaded with the canopies of old oaks and their thick limbs were draped with Spanish moss. Many of the homes were two hundred years old and had weathered hurricanes and recessions. As a kid in Pensacola, Ross and his pals rode their bikes through North Hills and admired the fine homes. It never occurred to him that he would one day be welcome in the neighborhood.

He turned in to the cobblestone driveway of

a beautifully preserved Victorian and parked his SUV next to a shiny Mercedes sedan, then walked across the rear patio and tapped on a door. Melba, the ancient maid who kept Helen's life together, greeted him with her usual warm smile and said that the lady was getting dressed. Did he want a drink? He asked for a ginger ale and found his favorite seat in the billiard room.

Helen was a widow and a girlfriend of sorts, though he had no interest in romance. Nor did she. Her third or fourth husband had died of old age and left her rich, and she preferred to hang on to the money. All prospective men of an age were after her assets, she assumed. Thus, their relationship was nothing more than a convenience. She loved being escorted around town with a handsome younger man, and a judge at that. He liked her because she was witty and outrageous and never a threat.

She said she was sixty-four years old but this was doubted. Years of aggressive surgery had smoothed out some wrinkles, curved her chin, and brightened her eyes, but he suspected she was at least seventy. His harem, as he called it but only to himself, consisted of several women ranging in age from forty-one all the way up to Helen. To qualify, they had to be either rich or affluent, and happily single. He was not in the market for a wife, and over the years had discarded several who got complicated.

Melba brought his drink and left him in silence. Dinner was at seven thirty and there was no possible way they would arrive on time. For a judge who demanded punctuality in most matters, waiting for Helen demanded patience. So he waited, soaking up the fine worn-leather furniture, the Persian rugs, the paneled walls, the oak shelves laden with ancient books, the magnificent chandelier from another century. The house covered 10,000 square feet on four levels, and very little of it was used by Helen and Melba.

He closed his eyes and recited the latest poem. Its author had now linked him to Danny Cleveland, the former reporter for the **Ledger.** Disposed of in 2009, only five years ago. And before that, Eileen Nickleberry in 1998. And after, Perry Kronke in 2012, then Verno and Dunwoody less than a year ago. He felt like his victims were now crawling out of their graves and lining up, zombie-like, to come after him. He was living in a state of stunned disbelief, his thoughts a mush of rampant flashes, his debates raging over strategies that changed by the hour.

He closed his eyes and breathed deeply, then reached into a pocket, retrieved a loose capsule of Xanax, and chased it down with the ginger ale. He was taking too many of the pills. They were supposed to flatten his anxieties and relax him, but they weren't working anymore.

Could it be possible that he was about to lose

such a lofty and privileged place in life? Was he about to be exposed in some unimaginable way? The past that he had so brilliantly worked to conceal was now catching up with him. The present and all its status was at risk. The future was too horrible to dwell on.

"Hello dahling," she said as she entered the room. Bannick jumped to his feet, threw out his hands for a polite hug, and offered sexless air kisses while saying, "You look marvelous, Helen."

"Thank you, dear," she said, looking down at her red sleeveless dress. "You like it? Chanel."

"Beautiful, stunning."

"Thank you, dahling." She was from a small town in Georgia and fancied herself a real Southern belle. The "darling" came out **dahling.**

She leaned in closer, frowned, and said, "You do look tired, Judge. Dark circles around the eyes. Are you battling insomnia again?"

He had never been bothered with insomnia, but said, "I guess. A busy trial calendar." He was too polite to say, "Well, Helen, in that case, I notice an extra roll around the old waistline. Not looking as svelte as you think."

The good thing about Helen, and something he admired greatly, was that she never stopped trying. Always dieting, sweating, shopping for the latest fashions, studying the next surgical alternatives, buying the most expensive makeup and applying it with gusto. She claimed to be waiting

for the perfect female Viagra so she could hop in
the sack like a teenager. Both had laughed at this
because sex was a topic they avoided.

She worked so hard at looking good that
he could never say anything that might deflate her
considerable ego. He looked at her feet, never
a dull place, and smiled at her leopard skins.
"Love your hooker's heels," he said with a laugh.
"Jimmy Choo?"

"Always, dahling."

They said goodbye to Melba and left the
house. As usual, they would take her Mercedes
because, being a complete snob, Helen would be
humiliated to be seen arriving at the country club
in a Ford. Bannick opened the passenger door
for her and got behind the wheel. It was already
seven forty and the club was fifteen minutes away.
They chatted about his busy week, her grandkids
in Orlando—a rotten lot with problems that only
serious money could create—and after about ten
minutes in traffic she said, "You seem preoccupied,
Judge. What's the matter?"

"Nothing at all. Just looking forward to a fabu-
lous dinner of rubber chicken and cold peas."

"It's not that bad, really. But we can't seem to
keep a chef."

Both were members and knew the truth. Each
new head chef cooked for about six months before being fired. Each found it impossible to meet
the exacting wishes of a high-end crowd that

THE JUDGE'S LIST   263

had convinced themselves they knew great food and wine.

The Escambia Country Club was a hundred years old and had five hundred members, with another one hundred prospects on the waiting list. It was "the" country club in the Pensacola area and the place where every affluent family wanted to belong. The climbers too. It sat on a bay with water on three sides of the grand hall. Manicured fairways snaked away in several directions. The whole place, from the winding shaded drive to the two hundred acres of perfect greenery, reeked of old money and exclusivity.

The entrance was under a sweeping portico where the members arrived in German cars and were greeted by doormen in black tie. Only a red carpet was missing for the lucky ones. Helen loved saying, "Well good evening, Herbert," as he opened the door, took her hand, and got her out of the car, just as he had been doing for years. Once shed of old Herbert, she took the elbow of Judge Bannick and swept into the magnificent foyer where waiters circulated with trays of champagne. Helen practically assaulted one to get a drink, and not her first of the day. The judge took a glass of sparkling water. He was in for a long night and an even longer Sunday.

They were soon lost in a throng of well-heeled socialites, the men in the required suits and ties, the ladies in all manner of designer getup. The older ones favored clinging fabrics, dangerously plunging necklines, and no sleeves, as if determined to exhibit as much aging flesh as possible to prove they still could turn it on. The younger ladies, a small minority, seemed content with their figures and felt no need to flaunt things. Everyone talked and laughed at once as the crowd slowly inched along a wide hallway with thick carpets and large portraits on the walls. Inside the main banquet room, they weaved their way through large, round tables and eventually found their seating assignments. There was no speaker for the evening, no dais, no prime tables for sponsors. At the far end a band tuned up behind a dance floor.

The judge and Helen settled in with eight people they knew well, four other couples all properly married, but no one really cared about the arrangements. A doctor, an architect, a gravel entrepreneur, and their wives. And one man, the oldest at the table, who had dinner at the club every night with his wife and was reported to have inherited more money than all the others combined. The wine flowed and the conversations roared.

Judge Bannick flipped his switch, and flipped it again, and made himself laugh and smile and talk loudly about little that mattered. At times, though, he felt the weight of the future, the uncertainty of Monday's mail, the fear of being stripped naked and exposed, and he lapsed into moments of pensiveness. It was impossible not to look around the room at the friends and leaders and people he had always known and admired without asking: What will they say?

He, decked in Zegna and rubbing elbows with the rich, was a most respected judge, admired by important people, and he was also, at least in his opinion, the most brilliant killer in American history. He had studied the others. Thugs, all. Some downright ignorant.

He told himself to shake it off, and took a question about an oil spill in the Gulf. Some of the crude was inching toward Pensacola and the alarms were up. Yes, he surmised that there would be a great deal of litigation in the near future. You know the plaintiffs bar, he said, they'll sue the moment the oil slick is in sight, and probably before. The spill was front page and for a while the entire table quizzed His Honor on who might be able to sue whom. It passed; the women lost interest and pursued their own little chats as dinner was served.

The waitstaff was well trained and efficient and no one's wineglass was ignored, especially Helen's. As usual, she was pounding Chardonnay and getting louder. She'd be drunk by ten and he'd have to once again shovel her into the house with Melba's help.

He was happy to be quiet and listen to the others. He looked around the large room, smiled and nodded and acknowledged some friends. The mood was festive, even rowdy, and everyone

was wearing beautiful clothes. The women were
coiffured to perfection. Those over forty had the
same noses and chins, thanks to the handiwork of
a Dr. Rangle, the most sought-after face-lifter in
the Florida Panhandle. He was sitting two tables
away with his second wife, a gorgeous blonde of
indeterminate age, though she was rumored to be
in her early thirties. When Rangle wasn't carving
on women he was sleeping with them, they found
him irresistible, and his sexual escapades were the
source of endless salacious gossip in town.

Bannick loathed the man, as did many husbands, but he also secretly envied his libido. And
his current wife.

There were two in the room he'd like to kill.
Rangle was the second. The first was a banker who
had denied him a loan when he was thirty years
old and trying to buy his first office building. He
said Bannick's balance sheet was too light and his
chances of making good money as a lawyer were
too unlikely. The town was already saturated with
mediocre legal talent, and most ham-and-eggers
around the courthouse were barely paying their
bills. Typical banker, he thought he knew everything. Bannick bought another building, filled
it with tenants, then bought another. As his law
practice flourished, he joined the country club
and ignored the banker. When he was elevated
to the bench at the age of thirty-nine, the banker
suffered a stroke and had to retire.

Now he sat at a corner table, old and shriv-
eled and able only to mumble to his wife. He was
sad and deserved sympathy, an emotion foreign
to Bannick.

But killing him or Rangle would be too risky.
A local crime, in a small town. And, their trans-
gressions were too minor compared to the others.
He had never seriously considered putting them
on the list.

As dinner came to an end the band began playing softly, mostly old Motown hits that the crowd
loved. A few eager couples hit the floor during
dessert. Helen liked to dance and Bannick could
hold his own. They skipped the cake, made their
entrance, then jerked and gyrated through some
Stevie Wonder and Smokey Robinson. After a
few songs, though, she was parched and needed
a drink. He left her at the table with her friends
and went outside to the patio where the men were
smoking black cigars and sipping whiskey.

He was pleased to see Mack MacGregor standing alone near the edge, a glass in one hand, a
phone in the other. After ten years on the bench,
Bannick knew every lawyer between Pensacola and
Jacksonville, and many others too, and Mack had
always been one of his favorites. They had both
joined local firms about the same time, then spun
off into their own shops. Mack loved the courtroom and quickly became a skilled and sought-
after trial advocate. He was one of the few lawyers

in the area who could take a case from the beginning, the injury or death, and push it all the way
to a successful verdict. He was a pure trial lawyer,
not a mass tort chaser, and he handled criminal
cases as well. Bannick had seen his work firsthand,
but he had never allowed himself to believe that
one day he would need Mack's services.

In the past three days, he had caught himself
thinking about Mack far too much. If the sky fell,
and Bannick still believed it would not, Mack
would be his first call.

"Evenin' Judge," Mack said as he put away his
phone. "Lose your girl?"

"Ran 'em upstairs for a pee. Who's your
squeeze tonight?"

"A new one, a real cutie. My secretary fixed me
up." Mack had been divorced for ten or so years
and was known to prowl.

"Quite the looker."

"That's all, believe me."

"That's enough, right?"

"It'll do. Who's gonna get that tiki bar case in
Fort Walton?"

"Don't know yet. Judge Watson will decide.
You want it?"

"Maybe."

A month earlier, two bikers from Arizona
started a row in a low-end dive outside of Fort
Walton Beach, near the water. It went from fists
to knives to guns, and when the glass stopped

shattering, three people were dead. The bikers fled for a while but were caught near Panama City Beach.

On the principle that every person accused of a serious crime has a right to a good lawyer, Mack and his partner volunteered each year for at least one murder case. It kept them in the courtroom and sharp on the law. It also added some spice to their everyday practice. Mack enjoyed the gritty, often grisly details of a good murder case. He liked hanging around the jail. He enjoyed getting to know men who were capable of killing.

"Sounds like your kind of case."

"Life is pretty dull right now."

Well, Mack, that might change soon for both of us, Bannick thought to himself. "If you're volunteering, I can arrange things."

"Let me kick it around the office. I'll call you Monday. Probably not a capital case, right?"

"No. It was certainly not premeditated. Looks like a couple of idiots got drunk and started fighting. Are you signing up oil slick cases?"

"We'll get our share," Mack said with a laugh. "Half the bar's out in the Gulf right now in boats, looking for crude. It'll be a bonanza."

"As well as another environmental disaster."

They killed time swapping stories about lawyers they knew and the lawsuits they chased. Mack pulled out a leather cigar case and offered a Cohiba. Both men fired one up and found some whiskey. They aborted the lawyer talk and returned to the more pleasant topic of younger women. After a while, Judge Bannick knew his date would be looking for him. He said good-bye to Mack, and as he walked away he hoped he would not be seeing the lawyer anytime soon.

26

The handoff was rocky, as usual. Even in bare feet, Helen was unstable as they shuffled across the bricks of her rear patio. "Do come in for a drink, dahling," she cooed between breaths.

"No, Helen, it's past our bedtimes and I have a splitting headache."

"Wasn't it a great band? What a lovely evening."

Melba was waiting at the door and opened it for them. Bannick handed her the high heels, then handed her Helen, then turned and backed away. "Gotta run, dear, I'll call in the morning."

"But I want a drink."

Bannick shook his head, frowned at Melba, and hustled to his SUV. He drove to his shopping center and parked near other vehicles by the cinema. He walked to his other chamber, cleared himself through the scanners, and once inside stripped out of his suit and tie and put on gym clothes.

Half an hour after seeing the last of Helen, he was sipping espresso and again lost in the dark web, tracking Rafe's latest adventures.

The vigilance was time-consuming and usually not productive. Still using Maggotz and sending Rafe to troll here and there, he was watching the police files of his cases. So far, no department had managed to successfully firewall its data and network. Some were easier to hack than others, but none had been especially bothersome. He still marveled at the lax and weak security used by most county and city governments. Ninety percent of all data breaches could be prevented with modest effort. Standard passwords such as "Admin" and "Password" were routinely used.

The more tedious work was keeping up with the victims. There were ten groups of them, ten families he had destroyed. Mothers and fathers, husbands and wives, children, brothers and sisters, aunts and uncles. He had no pity for them. He simply wanted them to stay away.

The person stalking him was not a cop, not a private investigator, not some thrill-seeking true crime writer. The person was a victim, one who had been slithering back there in his shadows for many years, watching, gathering, trailing.

A new reality had arrived, and he in his brilliance would deal with it. He would find the victim and stop the letters. Stop the silly poems.

He had ruled out the families of Eileen Nickleberry, Perry Kronke, Lanny Verno, and Mike Dunwoody. He went back to the beginning, to his most satisfying triumph. He opened the file on Thad Leawood and looked at the photos: some old black-and-whites from his scouting days, one of the entire troop at a jamboree, one taken by his mother at an awards ceremony—Ross standing proudly in his smart uniform, merit badge sash filled with colorful circles, Leawood with an arm around him. He studied the faces of the other scouts, his closest friends, and wondered, as always, how many others were abused by Leawood. He had been too afraid to ask, to compare notes. Walt Sneed once remarked that Leawood liked to touch and hug a bit too much for a twelve-year-old's liking, called him "creepy," but Ross had been too afraid to pursue the conversation.

How could a seemingly normal young man rape a child, a boy? He still hated Leawood, so many years later. He'd had no idea a man could do those things.

He moved on, past the photos, always painful, and went to the family tree, such as it was. Leawood's brief obituary listed the names of his survivors: his parents, an older brother, no wife. His father died in 2004. His mother was ninety-eight and living without her marbles in a low-end nursing home in Niceville. He had often thought about rubbing her out just for the hell of it, just for the satisfaction of getting revenge against the woman who created Thad Leawood.

There were so many targets he had thought about over the years.

The brother, Jess Leawood, left the area not long after the abuse rumors surfaced and settled in Salem, Oregon, where he had lived for at least the last twenty-five years. He was seventy-eight, retired, a widower. Six years earlier, Bannick, using a disposable phone, called Jess and explained that he was a crime writer and was digging through some old police files in Pensacola. Did Thad's family know that he had a history of abusing kids? The line went dead, the call was over. It served no purpose other than to punish a Leawood.

As far as Bannick could tell, Jess had no contact with his hometown. And who could blame him?

The last poem was about Danny Cleveland, the former reporter for the **Pensacola Ledger.** He was forty-one when he died, divorced with two teenaged children. His family hauled him back to Akron for the funeral and burial. According to their social media, his daughter was now a junior at Western Kentucky and his son had joined the Army. It seemed impossible to believe that either would be old enough to put together an elaborate plan to track a brilliant serial killer. And it was safe to assume his ex-wife wouldn't care who killed him.

He scrolled through other files. Ashley Barasso, the only girl he had ever loved. They met in law school and had a delightful fling, one that ended abruptly when she ditched him for a football player. He was crushed and carried the wounds for six years until he caught her. When she was finally still, his pain suddenly vanished, his broken heart was healed. The score was even. Her husband gave interviews and put up $50,000 in reward money, but with time it went unclaimed and he moved on. He remarried four years later, had more children, and lived near DC.

Preston Dill had been one of his first clients. He and his wife wanted a no-fault divorce but couldn't manage to scrape together the $500 fee. The two hated each other and had future spouses already lined up, but Lawyer Bannick refused to take them to see the judge until he got paid. Preston then accused Bannick of sleeping with his wife and everything blew up. He filed a complaint with the state bar, one of many over the years. His game was to hire a lawyer, stiff him on the fee, then complain when the work didn't get finished. All of Dill's complaints were dismissed as frivolous. Four years later they found him in a landfill near Decatur, Alabama. His family was scattered, unremarkable, and probably not suspicious.

Professor Bryan Burke, dead at the age of sixty-two, his body found beside a narrow trail not far from his lovely little cabin near Gaffney, South

Carolina. The year was 1992. Looking at his photo from the law school yearbook, Bannick could almost hear his rich baritone as it wafted over the classroom. "Tell us about this case, Mr. . . ." and he always paused so they would squirm and pray someone else got the call. His students eventually came to admire Professor Burke, but Bannick didn't hang around long enough. After his nervous breakdown, one he blamed squarely on Burke, he transferred to Miami and began plotting his revenge.

Burke had two adult children. His son, Alfred, worked for a tech company in San Jose and was married with three kids. Or, that was where he had been during the last update, some eighteen months ago. Bannick dug around for a while and could not verify Alfred's current employment. Someone else now lived at his address. Obviously he had changed jobs and moved. Bannick cursed himself for not knowing this earlier. It took an hour to find Alfred living in Stockton, employment unknown.

Burke's daughter was Jeri Crosby, age forty-six, divorced, one child. The last update had her living in Mobile and teaching political science at South Alabama. He found the university's website and verified that she still taught there. Oddly enough, in the faculty directory there were photos of the professors in the Department of Political Science and Criminal Justice, but not of her. Evidently, she was very private.

An earlier file gave her undergraduate degree from Stetson, a master's from Howard in DC, and a PhD in political science from Texas. She married Roland Crosby in 1990, had a child within the first year, and divorced him six years later. In 2009, she joined the faculty at South Alabama.

The Mobile link was intriguing. The investigator the person had hired, Rollie Tabor, was based in Mobile.

Bannick sent Rafe back into the Hertz records and fell asleep on the sofa.

He was awakened by his alarm at 3:00 a.m., after two hours of sleep. He splashed water on his face, brushed his teeth, changed into jeans and sneakers, and locked the Vault and the outer door. He left town on Highway 90 along the beach, and stopped for gas at an all-night convenience store where cash was still welcome and there was only one security camera. After filling his tank, he parked in the darkness beside the store and changed license plates. Most toll roads in Florida now photographed every vehicle. He took an empty county road north, picked up Interstate 10, set his cruise on seventy-five, and settled in for a long day. He had six hundred miles to cover and plenty of time to think. He sipped strong coffee from a thermos, popped a benny, and tried to enjoy the solitude.

He had logged a million miles in the dark. Nine hours was nothing. Coffee, amphetamines, good music. Properly juiced, he could drive for days.

Dave Attison had been a fraternity brother at the University of Florida, a hard-partying frat boy who also finished near the top of his class. He and Ross had roomed together in the fraternity house for two years and shared many hangovers. They went their own ways after college, one to law school, the other to dental school. Dave studied endodontics and became a prominent dentist in the Boston area. Five years earlier, he had tired of the snow and long winters and returned to his home state, where he purchased a practice in Fort Lauderdale and was prospering doing nothing but root canals at a thousand bucks a pop.

He had not seen Ross since their twentieth reunion seven years earlier at a resort in Palm Beach. Most of the old Pikes were diligent with their emails and texts, others were not. Ross had never shown much interest in keeping up with the gang. Now, out of the blue, he was passing through and wanted a quick drink. On a Sunday afternoon. He was staying at the Ritz-Carlton and they agreed to meet at the bar by the pool.

Ross was waiting when Dave walked up. They embraced like the old roommates they were and immediately examined each other's graying hair and waistlines. Each agreed that the other one looked just fine. After a few insults, a waiter appeared and they ordered drinks.

"What brings you down here?" Dave asked.

"Looking at some apartment units out in East Sawgrass."

"You're buying apartments?"

"We. A group of investors. We buy stuff everywhere."

"I thought you were a judge."

"Duly elected from the Twenty-Second Judicial District. On the bench for ten years now. But in Florida a judge makes one hundred and forty-six thousand bucks a year, not exactly the road to riches. Twenty years ago I started buying rental properties. Our company has grown slowly and we're doing well. What about you?"

"Very well, thanks. There is a never-ending supply of sore teeth out there."

"Wife and kids?" Ross wanted to broach the family subject before Dave had the chance, in part to show that he was not afraid of it. Since their student days, he had suspected that his brothers had doubts about him. The incident with Eileen was legendary. Though he later lied and claimed he was active with other girls, he had always felt their suspicions. The fact that he had never married didn't help.

"All is well. My daughter is at Florida and my son is in high school. Roxie plays tennis five days a week and stays out of my hair."

According to another Pike, the marriage to Roxie had been anything but stable. They had taken turns moving out. When their son left home they would probably throw in the towel.

The cold beers arrived and they tapped glasses. A serious bikini sauntered by and they took the full measure of it.

"Those were the days," Ross said with admiration.

"We're almost fifty, you realize that?"

"Afraid so."

"You think we'll ever stop looking?"

"If I'm breathing I'm looking," Ross said, repeating the mantra. He sipped his beer slowly as it warmed. He wanted only one. The drive home was the same nine hours.

They batted some names back and forth, their old pals from the glory days. They laughed at the stupid things they had done, the pranks they had pulled, the near misses. It was the same aging frat boy talk every time.

Ross began his fiction with "I had a strange encounter last year. Remember Cora Laker, Phi Mu?"

"Sure, cute girl. Became a lawyer, right?"

"Right. I was at the state bar convention in Orlando and bumped into her. She's a partner in a big firm in Tampa, doing very well. Still lookin' good. We had a drink, then another. Somehow she brought up Eileen, I think they were close, and she got all choked up. She said the case will never be solved. Said an investigator of some sort tracked her down and wanted to talk about Eileen as a sorority girl. She hung up and that was it, but she was ticked off that somebody found her."

Dave snorted and looked away. "I got a call too."

Bannick swallowed hard. The quick trip, brutal as it was, might just pay off. He asked, "About Eileen?"

"Yep, probably three or four years ago. We were living here, could've been five years back. The lady said she was a crime writer and was asking about Eileen's college days. Said she was working on a book about cold cases. Women who were stalked, or something like that."

"A woman?"

"Yep. Said she had written several books, offered to send me one."

"Did she?"

"No, I got off the phone. That was another lifetime, Ross. It's really sad what happened to Eileen, but I can't do anything about it."

A woman. Digging through his cold cases. The long drive and its return leg were now worth the trouble.

"That's weird," Ross said. "Just the one conversation?"

"Yep. I got rid of her. And, really, I had nothing to offer. We raised so much hell back then I can't remember it all. Too much booze and pot."

"Those were the days."

"Why don't you come over for dinner? Roxie's still a lousy cook but we can do takeout."

"Thanks, Dave, but I'm meeting some investors for dinner later."

An hour later, Bannick was back on the road, fighting the traffic on Interstate 95, with six hundred miles to go.

27

Sadelle was ten minutes late for the Monday morning recap, and when she arrived on her little scooter she looked even closer to death. She apologized and said she was fine. Lacy had suggested several times that she take off a few days and get some rest. Sadelle was afraid of that. Work kept her alive.

Darren began with "We've done all we can do with the travel records. We finally heard from Delta, after another subpoena threat, and so all carriers are accounted for. Delta, Southwest, American, and Silver Air. We checked all flights originating from Pensacola, Mobile, Tallahassee, even Jacksonville, and going to Miami and Fort Lauderdale. The result is that for the month before the murder of Perry Kronke, no one by the name of Ross Bannick took a flight south."

Lacy said, "You're assuming he used his real name."

"Of course we are. We don't happen to know any of his aliases, now do we?"

She ignored him and returned to her coffee. He continued, "It's an eleven-hour drive from Pensacola to Marathon, and, needless to say, we would have no way of tracking him in his car."

"Toll records?"

"The state keeps them for only six months, then burns them. And, it's easy to avoid toll roads."

"What about hotels?"

Sadelle growled as she tried to fill her lungs, and said, "Another needle in another haystack. Do you know how many hotels there are in south Florida? Thousands. We picked a hundred of the likeliest mid-priced ones and found nothing. There are eleven in and around Marathon. Nothing."

Darren said, "We're wasting our time digging like this."

Lacy said, "It's called investigating. Some of the most infamous crimes were solved by tiny clues that at first seemed insignificant."

"What do you know about solving infamous crimes?"

"Not much, but I'm reading books about serial killers. Fascinating stuff."

Sadelle inhaled painfully and, somewhat oxygenized, asked, "Are we assuming he drove to Biloxi and back for the Verno murder?"

"And Dunwoody. Yes, that's our assumption. It's only, what, two hours?"

"Two's about right," Darren said. "That's what's fascinating. If you look at all eight murders, and I know we're not looking at all eight, but only three, they are all within driving distance from Pensacola. Danny Cleveland in Little Rock, eight hours away. Thad Leawood near Chattanooga, six hours. Bryan Burke in Gaffney, South Carolina, eight hours. Ashley Barasso in Columbus, Georgia, four hours. Perry Kronke in Marathon and Eileen Nickleberry near Wilmington are both twelve hours away. He didn't have to fly and rent cars and pay for hotel rooms. He could just drive."

"Those are just the ones we know about," Lacy said. "I'll bet there are more. And each crime scene was in a different state."

Sadelle said, "He knows more about killing than we do."

"I guess he's had more experience," Darren added. "And he's smarter."

Lacy said, "True, but we've got Betty and she's tracked him down. Think about it. If she's right, then she's identified the killer, something an army of homicide detectives couldn't do."

"And something we're not equipped to do, right?" Sadelle asked.

"No, but we've known that from the beginning. Let's keep plugging away."

Darren asked, "So, when do we go to the police?"

"Soon."

—

The two detectives from the state police pushed the doorbell at exactly 8:00 a.m., as requested. They wore dark suits, drove a dark car, had matching dark aviator sunglasses, and anyone watching from a hundred yards away would know immediately that they were cops of some variety.

They had been summoned to the home of a circuit court judge, an unusual occasion. They had met many judges, but always in their courtrooms, never in their homes.

Judge Bannick was all smiles as he led them into his spacious kitchen and poured two cups of coffee. On the table was a single white, legal-size envelope, addressed to the judge at the home where they were now standing. He pointed at it and said, "It arrived in the mail on Saturday, here at the house, the box by the front door. The third one in a week. Each contained a letter typewritten by an obviously deranged person. I'll keep the letters to myself for the time being. This third one is by far the most threatening. When I saw this one, after touching and opening the first two, I was more careful. I put on gloves and touched it and the letter as little as possible. I'm sure the postman touched all three of them."

Lieutenant Ohler said, "Probably so."

"Who knows what you'll find, but there will likely be prints from my mailman, none from me, and, if we're lucky, something left behind by this crazy person."

"Sure, Judge."

Lieutenant Dobbs pulled out a plastic bag and carefully shoved the envelope inside. He said, "We'll get right on this. Mind if we ask how urgent it is?"

"How serious is the threat?" Ohler asked.

"Well, I'm not going to pack a gun when I leave the house, but it would certainly be nice to know who's behind this."

"Anybody come to mind?" Dobbs asked.

"Not really. I mean, there are always a few crazies writing letters to every judge, but no one specific."

"Good. We'll drive it to the crime lab today. We'll know by tomorrow if there are any good prints. If so, then we'll try to match them."

"Thanks, gentlemen."

As they drove away, Ohler mused, "Do you wonder why he didn't show us the three letters?"

"That's what I'm wondering," Dobbs replied. "Obviously he doesn't want anyone to see the letters."

"And the other two envelopes?"

"He touched them and they're likely to have his prints."

"And we have his prints, right?"

"Sure. Every lawyer is printed before he gets a license."

Seconds passed as they left the gated community. On the highway, Ohler asked, "What are the chances of finding any useful prints on the envelope?"

"I'd say zero. Nuts who send anonymous mail are smart enough to use gloves and take other precautions. Not rocket science."

Ohler said, "I gotta hunch."

"Great. Another hunch. Let's hear it."

"He knows who it is."

"Based on what?"

"Based on nothing. It's a hunch. Hunches don't have to be based on anything."

"Especially yours."

An hour later, Judge Bannick parked in his reserved space beside the Chavez County Courthouse and walked through the rear doors. He spoke to Rusty and Rodney, the ancient twin janitors, as always attired in matching overalls, and he took the back staircase to the second floor where he had ruled supremely for the past ten years. He said good morning to his staff and asked Diana Zhang, his longtime secretary and only true confidant, to join him in his office. He closed the door, asked her to have a seat, then said, gravely, "Diana, I have some terrible news. I've been diagnosed with colon cancer, stage four, and it doesn't look good."

She was too stunned to respond. She gasped and immediately began wiping her eyes.

"I have a fighting chance, plus there are always miracles."

She managed to ask, "When did you find out?" She looked at him through the tears and once again realized how tired and gaunt he seemed.

"About a month ago. I've spent the past two weeks talking to doctors all over the country and I've decided to pursue an alternative treatment through a clinic in New Mexico. That's all I can tell you right now. I have informed Chief Judge Habberstam that I am taking a sixty-day leave of absence, beginning today. He will reassign my cases for the time being. You and the others will remain on full salary, without a lot to do." He managed a smile, but she was too shocked to return it.

"Things should be much quieter around here for the next two months. I'll check in all the time and make sure you're doing well."

Diana was at a loss. He had no wife, no children, no one she could run to with food and gifts and sympathy. She mumbled, "Will you be here or out there?"

"Back and forth. As I said, I'll be in touch and you can call me anytime. I'll pop in here to check on you. If I die it won't be for a few more months."

"Stop it!"

"Okay, okay. I'm not dying anytime soon, but

it might be a struggle for the next few months. I want you to contact all my lawyers and inform them that their cases will be taken up by other judges. If they ask why, just say it's an illness. After I leave in a few minutes, please inform the others. I'd rather not face them."

"I can't believe this."

"I can't either. But life isn't fair, is it?"

He left her sobbing and made a quick exit without another word. He drove to a GM dealership in Pensacola where he swapped vehicles and leased a new Chevrolet Tahoe. He signed the pile of paperwork, wrote a check for the balance, one from his many accounts, and waited as they screwed his old license plates onto his new SUV. He detested the silver color but, as always, wanted something that would blend in.

He settled into the soft leather seat and absorbed the rich new car smell. He fiddled with the GPS, ran through the apps, hooked up his phone, and drove away, heading west on Interstate 10. His phone pinged—a text from another judge. He read it on the large media screen: Judge Bannick. Sorry to hear the news. I'm here if you need me. Take care. TA.

Another ping, another message. Word was spreading quickly through the district's legal circles and by noon every lawyer, secretary, clerk, and fellow judge would know that he was ill and taking leave.

He had no patience for those who used bad health to their advantage. He hated the fiction of an illness to cover his tracks. As an elected official he would be on the ballot again in two years, but he would not allow himself to worry about politics. Being stricken with cancer might embolden a possible opponent to start making plans, but he could deal with that later. For now, it was imperative that he stay out of sight, go about the tasks at hand, get his pursuer off his back, and possibly dodge an investigation by the Board on Judicial Conduct. He chuckled at the idea of such a tiny agency trying to solve murders that veteran cops had all but abandoned years ago. Ms. Stoltz and her motley crew operated with a shrinking budget and a few toothless statutes.

From the tally of those he'd murdered, there were almost seventy victims, all related by blood or marriage. He had considered each one and eliminated all but five, with four of those considered unlikely. He was convinced he had found his tormentor. She was a woman with many secrets, an extremely private person who thought she was too smart for hackers.

Though Mobile was not far away, he had spent little time there and did not know the city. He had driven through it a hundred times but could not remember the last time he had stopped for any reason.

His new nav system worked to perfection and

he found the street where Jeri lived. He would scope out her neighborhood later. Her apartment was barely sixty minutes from his home in Cullman.

He had found her, practically under his nose.

28

The information was too important to exchange by email or phone. A face-to-face meeting would be better, Sheriff Black explained. He was four hours away in Biloxi and offered to split the difference. They agreed to meet at a fast-food restaurant beside Interstate 10 in the small town of DeFuniak Springs, Florida, at 3:00 p.m. on Wednesday, April 16.

Leaving Tallahassee, Darren asked Lacy to drive because he needed to finish editing a report. Evidently it was not well written and put him to sleep before they had traveled twenty miles. When he awoke after a solid thirty-minute nap, he apologized and admitted that he had stayed out a bit too late the night before.

"So what's this big news?" she asked. "Too important to whisper over the phone or put in an email."

"Don't ask me. You're the sleuth these days."

"Just because I'm reading books about serial killers doesn't mean I'm a sleuth."

"What does it mean?"

"I don't know. It's pretty frightening stuff, really. Some really sick puppies."

"Do you put Bannick in their category?"

"There is no category. Every case is so different, every killer demented in his own way. But I've yet to read about one as patient as Bannick or who's motivated purely by revenge."

"What's the normal motive?"

"There's no such thing, but sex is usually a factor. It's shocking how perverted some of these guys are."

"These books you're reading, do they have photographs?"

"Some do. Lots of blood and mutilation. Want to borrow them?"

"I don't think so."

His phone pinged and he read the text. "Interesting," he said. "It's Sadelle. She checked Bannick's docket today and everything has been canceled. Same yesterday, same tomorrow. She called his office and was told that His Honor is taking a leave of absence for health issues."

Lacy allowed this to sink in and said, "I like his timing. You think he's watching us?"

"What's to watch? Nothing is online and he has no idea what we're up to."

"Unless he's watching the police."

"I suppose that's possible." Darren scratched his jaw, deep in thought. "But even then, he wouldn't know anything because we don't know anything, right?"

They rode in silence for a few miles.

An unmarked sedan was the only other vehicle in the parking lot. Inside, Sheriff Black and Detective Napier were sipping coffee, watching and waiting, in plain clothes. They were seated as far away from the counter as possible. There were no other customers. Lacy and Darren got coffees and said hello. The four huddled around a small table and tried to give each other room. No one had bothered to bring a briefcase.

"This shouldn't take long," Black said. "But then again, it might." He nodded a go-ahead to Napier, who cleared his throat and glanced around as if some nonexistent person might be listening.

"As you know, there were two phones taken from the crime scene by the killer, who then dropped them off at a small post office an hour away."

"Addressed to your daughter in Biloxi, right?" Lacy asked.

"Right," Black said.

Napier continued, "Well, the FBI has had the two phones in its lab for the past month, running every possible test. They are now certain that there is a partial thumb print on Verno's phone. Several oddities, one of which is that there are no other prints, not even from Verno, so the killer was careful enough to wipe down the phones. Mike Dunwoody's has no prints at all. Again, the guy was being careful, which is not surprising given the crime scene. How much do you know about the fingerprint business?"

Lacy said, "Let's assume we know next to nothing."

Darren nodded, confirming his ignorance.

Expecting this, Napier said, "Okay. About twenty percent of the people in this country have been fingerprinted, and most prints are stored in a massive data bank kept by the FBI. As you might guess, they have the latest souped-up software with all manner of algorithms and such, stuff that's a bit over my head, and they can check a print from anywhere in a matter of minutes. In this case, they began in Florida."

The sheriff leaned in a bit and said, "We're assuming your suspect is from Florida."

Brilliant, thought Lacy, but she nodded and said, "Good assumption."

Darren, eager to speak, said, "You have to get fingerprinted before you're admitted to the bar. Same in every state."

Napier indulged him and replied, "Yes, we know that. So do the FBI analysts. Anyway, they found no match in Florida, or anywhere else for that matter. They've run every possible test on this print, and they've come to the conclusion that, well, it's been altered."

Napier paused and allowed this to sink in. Sheriff Black took the handoff and said, "So, the first question, the first of many, is whether or not your suspect is capable of altering his fingerprints?"

Lacy struggled for words, so Darren asked, "Fingerprints can be altered?"

"The short answer is yes, though it's almost impossible," Napier said. "Stonemasons and bricklayers sometimes lose their fingerprints through years of hard labor."

Lacy said, "Our guy is not a bricklayer."

"He's a judge, right?" asked Black.

"He is."

Napier continued, "Over time it's possible to wear down the skin on your fingertips, they're called friction ridges, but that's extremely rare. It would take years of constant scrubbing with sandpaper. Whatever. That's not what we have here. With this print, the ridges are well defined, but they do indicate the possibility of being surgically altered."

Lacy asked, "Could the print be from Verno's girlfriend or someone else he knew?"

"They checked. Not surprisingly, she has a few arrests and her prints are in the data bank. No match. We've spent hours with her and she knows of no one else who would have touched Verno's phone. She couldn't even remember the last time she touched it."

All four took a drink from their paper cups and avoided eye contact. After a moment, Darren said, "Surgically altered? How does one do that?"

Napier smiled and said, "Well, some experts say it's impossible, but there have been a few cases. A few years ago, the Dutch police got a tip and raided a small apartment in Amsterdam. The suspect was a real pro, a slick criminal who'd had quite a career stealing contemporary art, some of which was found hidden in his walls. Worth millions. His old fingerprints did not fully match his new ones. Since they caught him red-handed with the loot, he decided to cut a deal and talk. Said there was an unlicensed cosmetic surgeon in Argentina who was known in the underworld as the guy to go to if you needed a new face or a fresh set of scars. He also specialized in altering the friction ridges of fingertips. Just for fun, go online and type in 'Fingerprint alteration.' Keep typing and you'll find some ads for the work. Actually, it's not illegal to alter your fingerprints."

Lacy said, "I was just thinking of a face-lift."

"Why?" asked the sheriff with a smile.

Napier said, "At any rate, it's something that can be done, over time. How patient is your suspect?"

"Quite patient," Darren said.

Lacy added, "We suspect he's been active for over twenty years."

"Active?"

"Yes. Verno and Dunwoody are probably not the only two."

The two cops absorbed this with more coffee. Napier asked, "Would he have the money for surgery like this?"

Both nodded. Yes.

Lacy said, "I suppose that over a long period of time he could chip away at the project and eventually do all ten fingers."

"That's quite a commitment," Black said.

"Well, he's committed, determined, and very intelligent."

More coffee, more thoughts rattling around. Could this be their big break after so many dead ends?

The sheriff said, "It makes no sense, really. I mean, if this guy is so smart, why not pitch the phones in a lake or a river? Why get cute and drop them off in a postal box to be sent to my daughter's apartment? He had to know that we'd track them and find them within hours. This was a Friday. There was no way the two smartphones would sit undiscovered until Monday."

"I'm not sure we'll ever understand what makes him tick or what he thinks about," Lacy said.

"Pretty stupid if you ask me."

"He's making mistakes. He almost got caught by Mike Dunwoody. Later, his truck was spotted at the post office when he dropped off the phones. And, it looks like one of his gloves slipped or maybe tore a bit and now we have a thumb print."

"Yes we do," the sheriff said. "So now the question is what do we do with it. The next step is obvious—get some prints from your suspect. If there's a match, then we're in business."

Napier asked, "What are the chances of getting his prints?"

Lacy shot a blank look at Darren, who shook his head as if he had no idea.

"A search warrant?" asked the sheriff.

"Based on what?" Lacy asked. "There is no probable cause, as of right now. Our suspect is a judge who knows forensics as well as he knows criminal procedure. It would be impossible to convince another judge to issue a warrant."

"So they'll protect him?"

"No. But they'll want to see a lot more proof than we currently have."

"Are you going to give us his name?"

"Not yet. I will, and soon, but I can't say any more."

Sheriff Black folded his arms across his chest and glared at her. Napier looked away in frustration. She continued, "We're on the same team, I promise."

The cops barely kept their cool as they stewed for a moment. Napier finally said, "I'm afraid I don't understand."

Lacy smiled and said, "Look, we have an informant, a source, the person who brought us the case. This person knows far more than we do and is living in fear, has been for years. We made promises about how we will proceed. That's all I can say for now. We have to be extremely cautious."

Sheriff Black asked, "So, what are we supposed to do for now?"

"Wait. We'll wrap up our investigation and meet again."

"I want to get this straight. You have a solid suspect in a double murder, though you admit that you don't investigate murders, right? And this guy is a sitting judge in Florida who has committed other crimes, correct?"

"That's right, though I did not refer to him as a solid suspect. Before today, we had no physical proof of his involvement in any crime. There's still a chance, gentlemen, that our suspect is not the man. What if the partial thumb print doesn't match?"

"Let's find out."

"We will, but not right now."

The meeting ended with forced handshakes and smiles.

—

Lieutenant Ohler with the Florida state police called with the expected news that the envelope had produced nothing interesting. Two prints were lifted and traced to the man who delivered the mail each day around noon.

29

By Thursday he was weary of the well-wishers, their texts and voicemails, their concerns about his health. He waited until the mailman stopped by at noon. He put on gloves, retrieved his mail, and saw another plain envelope. Inside, there was another poem:

> greetings from the grave
> it's rather cold and dark down here
> whispers, voices, groans
> no shortage of things to fear
>
> your crimes took no courage
> the shock, the rope, the knot
> you're a coward in your sickness
> the worst of a loathsome lot.

a pathetic student of the law
the most pompous in the class
i had you pegged for failure
a cocky, bumbling ass

"She's writing about her father now," he said to himself as he stared at the sheet of paper on the kitchen table.

His bag was packed. He drove to Pensacola, to the shopping center, and parked in front of the gym. He went to his other chamber, opened the Vault, placed the latest letter in a folder, tidied things up a bit, checked his cameras and video footage, and when he was satisfied that his world was perfectly secure, he drove to the airport and waited three hours for a flight to Dallas. He changed planes there and landed in Santa Fe after dark. Reservations for the flight, the rental car, and the hotel were made in his real name and paid for with his credit card.

Dinner was room service. He tried to watch a baseball game on cable but switched to an hour of porn. He fell asleep and managed a few hours before his alarm clock went off at 2:00 a.m. He showered, popped a benny, put his tools in a small gym bag, and left the hotel. Houston was fifteen hours away.

At nine Eastern time, he called Diana Zhang and checked in by telling her he was at the cancer treatment facility in Santa Fe. He said he was feeling fine and mentally prepared to begin his fight against the disease. He sounded optimistic and promised to be back on the bench before he was missed. She passed along the usual sympathies and concerns and said everyone was so worried. Not for the first time, he explained that one reason he was being treated far away was because he didn't want all the fuss. It would be a long, solitary journey, one that he must face alone. Her voice was breaking when he hung up.

Such a devoted woman.

He turned off the smartphone and removed its battery.

At dawn, he stopped at a rest area near El Paso and changed license plates. He was now driving a four-door Kia registered to a Texan who did not exist. And he drove it carefully, the cruise control set precisely on the posted speed limit, every single rule of the road followed to perfection. A speeding ticket, or, heaven forbid, an accident, would quash the mission. As always, he wore a cap pulled low, one of many from his collection, and never took off his sunglasses. He bought gas and snacks with a valid credit card issued to one of his aliases. The monthly statements went to a post office box in Destin.

He rarely listened to music or books and couldn't stand the relentless chatter of talk radio. Instead, he had always used the solitude of the open road to plan his next move. He loved the details, the plotting, the what-ifs. He had become so proficient, so highly skilled, and so merciless, that for years now he had believed he would never be caught. Other times, he walked through his old crimes to keep them fresh and make sure he had missed nothing.

When you murder someone you make ten mistakes. If you can think of seven of them you're a genius. Where had he read this? Or perhaps it was a line from a movie.

What had been his mistake?

How had it happened? He had to know.

He had lived with the certainty that he would never be forced to plan the Exit.

In 1993, when he was barely two years out of law school, the Pensacola law firm where he was employed blew up when the partners argued over a large fee, the usual source of discontent. He found himself on the street with no office. He borrowed $5,000 from his father, opened up his own shop, and declared himself ready to sue. A new gunslinger in town. He didn't starve but business was slow. He stayed busy writing wills for people with few assets and hustling small-time criminals in city court. His big break came when a party boat loaded with bridesmaids sank in the Gulf and six young ladies drowned. The usual frenzied slugfest ensued as the local bar frothed and fought over the cases. One landed in his office, thanks in part to a $50 will he had prepared for a client.

A slick ambulance chaser named Mal Schnetzer roped in three of the families and filed the first lawsuit, practically before the funerals were over. Without the slightest reserve or concern about ethical niceties, he paid a visit to the home of Bannick's client and tried to steal the case. Bannick threatened him; they cursed each other and feelings were raw until Bannick agreed to join the lawsuit. He had no experience with death cases and Schnetzer talked a good game about going to trial.

The pot of gold soon turned out to be much smaller than the plaintiffs' lawyers were dreaming of. The company that owned the party barge had no other assets and filed for bankruptcy. Its insurance carrier at first denied any liability, but Schnetzer effectively threatened it and got some money on the table. He then went behind Bannick's back again and told his client that he could deliver a check for $400,000 immediately if the client agreed to ditch his lawyer and claim he never wanted him in the first place. Before Bannick could figure out his next move, Schnetzer had settled the cases and disbursed the money to the clients, to himself, and to the other lawyers, except, of course, the rookie who had just been thoroughly outmaneuvered. Bannick had neglected to negotiate a joint agreement with the tort team, and his deal with his ex-client had been verbal. They had agreed that he would receive one-third of any settlement.

One-third of $400,000 was a gigantic fee for a hungry young lawyer, but the money had vanished. Bannick complained to the judge, who was not sympathetic. He thought about suing Schnetzer but decided against it for three reasons. The first was that he was afraid to tangle with the crook. The second was that he doubted he would ever see a dime. And the third, and most important, was that he didn't want the embarrassment of a public lawsuit in which he played the role of a green lawyer who got duped by an ambulance chaser. There was enough humiliation already as the story made the rounds in the courthouses.

So he added Mal Schnetzer to his list.

To his delight, Mal eventually fleeced some more clients, got caught, indicted, convicted, disbarred, and sent to prison for two years. When he was released, he drifted to Jacksonville where he hustled cases for a gang of billboard lawyers. He made a few bucks and was brazen enough to set up a small law office at Jacksonville Beach, where he settled car wrecks without the benefit of any bar membership. When he was accused of practicing law without a license, he closed up shop and left the state.

Bannick watched him and tracked his movements. Years passed and he surfaced in Atlanta where he worked in the back room as a paralegal for some divorce lawyers. In 2009, Bannick found him in Houston working as a "consultant" for a well-known tort firm.

Two months earlier, Bannick had rented a furnished eighty-foot unit in a high-end trailer park just outside Sugar Land, half an hour from downtown Houston. It was a massive place with eight hundred identical white trailers parked in long neat rows with wide streets. The rules were strict and enforced: only two vehicles per trailer, no boats or motorcycles, no laundry hanging from lines, no yard signs, no excessive noise. The small neat lawns were maintained by management. All lawn chairs, bikes, and barbecue grills were stored in identical sheds behind the trailers. He had been there twice and, though he had never dreamed of living in a trailer, found it relaxing. No one within a thousand miles knew who he was or what he was doing.

After a quick nap, he drove down the street to a big-box discount store and paid $58 in cash for a Nokia burner phone with a prepaid SIM card good for seventy-five minutes. Since no contract was involved, the clerk didn't ask for personal information. If he had, there was an entire collection of fake driver's licenses ready in the wallet. Sometimes they wanted ID, but usually they didn't care. He had bought so many burners and tossed them all away.

Back at the trailer, he called the law firm late Friday afternoon and asked for Mal Schnetzer, who was gone for the day and the weekend. He explained to the secretary that it was urgent and he needed to speak with him. The secretary, obviously well trained by her bosses, pried a bit and was told that the case involved a young man who had been badly burned on an offshore oil rig, one owned by ExxonMobil. She offered to find another lawyer in the firm, but Mr. Butler said no, he had been referred by a friend and told that Mr. Schnetzer was the man to talk to.

Ten minutes later, his cheap phone buzzed and there was the voice he recognized. He raised his an octave and tried to sound somewhat squeakier. "My son is in the hospital in Lake Charles with burns over eighty percent of his body. It's just awful, Mr. Snitcher."

"It's Schnetzer, by the way." Still an ass. "And this happened on a rig, right?" Every injury on an offshore platform was covered by the Jones Act, a lawyer's bonanza.

"Yes, sir. Three days ago. I'm not sure he's gonna make it. I'm trying to get over there but I'm disabled and can't drive right now."

"And you're down in Sugar Land, right?"

"Yes, sir. And I got lawyers callin' right and left, buggin' the hell out of me."

"Not surprised to hear that."

"I just hung up on one."

"Don't talk to them. How old is your son?"

"Nineteen. He's a good boy, works hard, supports me and his mom. Still single. He's all we got, Mr. Schnetzer."

"I see. So you can't drive over here to the office."

"No, sir. If my wife was here she could drive me, but she's comin' in from Kansas. That's where we're from. We need to get to the hospital. I don't know what to do, sir. We need your help."

"Okay. Look, I can be there in about an hour, if that'll work."

"You can come here?"

"Yep, I think I can work in a quick trip over."

"That'd be great, Mr. Schnetzer. We gotta have someone to help us."

"Just sit tight, okay?"

"Can you get those other lawyers to leave us alone?"

"Sure, I'll take care of them, no problem. What's your address?"

Through the blinds, Bannick watched every car that passed as the minutes ticked by. Finally, a long, shiny Ford pickup with a club cab and oversized wheels slowed, stopped, backed up, and parked behind his rental.

The years had not been kind to Mal Schnetzer.

He was much heavier, with an impressive gut hanging over his belt and stretching his shirt, and he had a round face above a double chin. His thick gray hair was pulled back and bunched at the neck. He got out, looked around the neighborhood, sized up the trailer, and touched the automatic pistol in a holster on his hip.

Bannick had never encountered a victim with a weapon and it ramped up the excitement. He moved quickly, grabbed a walking cane off the sofa, opened the door, and stepped onto the small porch, hunched like a man in pain. "Hello there," he called out as Schnetzer walked past the rental car.

"Howdy," he said.

"I'm Bob Butler. Thanks for doin' this. I got a cold beer inside. You want one?"

"Sure." He seemed to relax as he took Butler in, bent at the waist and nonthreatening.

It had been twenty-one years since the two had been face-to-face, back in their days as lawyers in Pensacola. Bannick doubted he would be recognized, and with the cap pulled low and the cheap eyeglass frames he was confident Schnetzer would have no clue. He stepped inside, held the door open, and they entered the cramped den of the trailer. "Thanks for comin', Mr. Schnetzer."

"No problem."

Mal turned away, as if looking for a place to sit, and in that split second Bannick quickly removed

Leddie from his pocket, flicked it so that the telescopic sections doubled and tripled in length, and
whipped it at the back of Mal's head. The lead
ball sank hard, splintering his cranium. His hands
flew up as he grunted and tried to turn around.
Leddie landed against his left temple and he fell
across a cheap coffee table. Bannick quickly un-
snapped the holster, removed the pistol, and shut
the door. Schnetzer kicked as he floundered and
looked up with wild eyes and tried to say something. Bannick hit him again and again, shattering his skull into a hundred pieces.

"A hundred and thirty-three thousand dollars,"
Bannick said, almost spitting the words. "A nice
fat fee that you stole. Money I deserved and desperately needed. What a crook, Mal, what a slimy
little piece of shit you were as a lawyer. I was so
happy when you went to prison."

Mal grunted and Bannick hit him again. More
blood spattered on the sofa and against a wall.

He took a deep breath and watched him try
to breathe. He pulled on the plastic gloves, got
the rope, wrapped it twice around his neck, and
stared at his bloodshot eyes as he pulled it tight.
He put a foot on his chest and tried to crush it as
he tightened the rope and watched it cut into the
skin. A minute passed, then another. Sometimes
they died with their eyes open, and those were his
favorite ones. He tied off the rope and stood to
admire his work.

"One hundred and thirty-three thousand dollars, taken from a kid, stolen from another lawyer. You piece of shit."

When Mal breathed his last, his bloodshot eyes stayed open, as if something in there wanted to watch the cleanup. Blood was covering his face and neck and puddling on the cheap carpet. What a mess.

Bannick paused and took a breath. He listened for voices from the outside, for any unusual sound, and heard nothing. He walked to the front bedroom and looked out the window. Two kids rode by on bicycles.

Lingering was a luxury he'd rarely enjoyed, but with this one he was in no hurry. He fished through the pockets of Mal's pants and found his keys. From a rear pocket he removed his cell phone and placed it on his stomach, where he would leave it. In a closet he found the cheap vacuum cleaner he had bought a month earlier, for cash at a discount store, and cleaned the floors of the kitchen and den, careful not to touch the blood. When he finished, he removed the bag and replaced it with a fresh one. He took a pack of kitchen wipes and wiped down Leddie and the pistol. He changed plastic gloves and put the old pair in an empty grocery sack. He wiped the doorknobs, the kitchen counter, the walls, every surface in the bathroom, though he had touched almost nothing. He flushed the toilet and turned off the water to it. He stripped down to his boxers and put his clothes in the small washing machine. As the cycle ran he took a can of diet soda from the empty fridge and sat in the kitchen, his old pal Mal just a few feet away.

A raw, nagging burden he had carried for twenty years had now been lifted, and he was at peace.

When the cycle finished, he put his clothes in the dryer and waited some more. Mal's phone was buzzing. Someone wanted to know where he was. It was almost seven, at least an hour to go before darkness.

Knowing Mal, he figured the crook had not told anyone at the office what he was up to. He had left behind no notes, no phone number, no address of his potential new client. There was an excellent chance Mal had not even gone by the office but had hustled over to Sugar Land to sign up a lucrative case, one that he would try to keep to himself and steal another fee.

But there was a chance he had said something to the secretary. The lingering became monotonous, and as the clock ticked the risks grew.

When his clothes were dry, he put them on and packed his stuff in the grocery sack—Leddie, the used wipes, the bag from the vacuum cleaner, the pistol. After dark, he stepped outside and walked to the Ford pickup. Some kids were kicking a soccer ball down the street. Still wearing gloves, he got in the truck, started the engine, and drove away. Three blocks over he parked it in the lot of a central market, one with a gas station, a convenience store, some cheap shops, and the management's office. He left the keys in the ignition and disappeared into the darkness. Ten minutes later he was back at his trailer. He went inside to get the grocery sack and take one last, satisfied look at Mal, still quite dead.

He switched off his burner and removed its battery, then drove away.

An hour later, he pulled into a truck stop on Interstate 45 south of Huntsville and parked behind some rigs. He changed the license plates and put the fake ones in his grocery bag, then tossed it into a large, dirty dumpster. Getting caught with Mal's Glock was unthinkable.

Suddenly famished, he went inside and enjoyed eggs and biscuits with the truckers. Santa Fe was twelve hours away and he looked forward to the drive.

30

Jeri's flight landed at Detroit International at 2:40 Friday afternoon. As she walked through the busy terminal she felt a sense of freedom, of relief at being so far away from Mobile and Florida and her worries there. On the plane she had convinced herself that her nightmare was finally coming to an end, that she had taken the first bold steps in finding justice for her father, and that no one was watching her. She found her rental car and drove away, headed for Ann Arbor.

Denise, her only child, was in her second year of graduate studies in physics at Michigan. She had grown up in Athens, Georgia, where Jeri had been on the faculty. Denise had breezed through the university there in three years and landed a hefty scholarship to Michigan. Her father, Jeri's ex, worked for the State Department in Washington. He had remarried and Jeri had little contact with him, but he kept close tabs on his daughter.

Jeri had not seen her since the Christmas holidays when the two of them spent a week on a beach in Cabo. She had been to Ann Arbor twice and enjoyed the town. She had lived alone for many years now and envied her daughter's busy social life and wide circle of friends. When she parked on the street in front of her apartment building in Kerrytown, Denise was waiting. They hugged and looked each other over and seemed satisfied with their appearances. Both were staying in shape and knew how to dress, though Denise had the advantage. She looked great in anything, including the jeans and sneakers she was wearing. They hauled the bags into her small apartment, where she lived alone. The building was filled with graduate and law students and there was usually loud music and a gathering of some sort. Especially on a Friday in late April. There was a keg by the pool and they made their way into the courtyard. Denise delighted in introducing her mom to her friends, and occasionally referred to her as Dr. Crosby. Jeri was content to sip a beer from a plastic cup and listen to the chatter and laughter of those twenty years younger.

A law student drifted closer and seemed more interested than the others. Denise had hinted on the phone that there might be a guy in the picture, and Jeri's radar was on high alert. His name was Link, a handsome kid from Flint, and it didn't take long to realize he was more than a casual friend. Jeri was secretly delighted that he was African American. Denise had dated all types and Jeri was fine with that, but deep inside she was like most folks. She wanted her grandchildren to look like her.

Without asking Jeri, Denise invited Link to join them for drinks. The three left the apartment complex and took a leisurely walk through Kerrytown. They snagged a table outdoors at the Grotto Watering Hole and enjoyed watching the endless parade of students going nowhere. Jeri fought the temptation to grill Link about his family, his studies, his interests, his plans for the future. To do so would rankle her daughter and she had vowed to avoid all drama for the weekend. She and Denise ordered wine, and Link asked for a draft beer. A check in the positive column. Jeri knew enough about students, especially the males, to raise an eyebrow at the ones who began the evening with hard liquor.

Link was a schmoozer who laughed easily and seemed deeply interested in Dr. Crosby's curriculum. Jeri knew he was gaming her but she enjoyed him nonetheless. More than once, she caught the two lovebirds looking at each other with pure adoration. Or maybe it was lust.

After an hour with Link, Jeri thought she might be falling for him too.

At some point Denise gave the signal, one that Jeri didn't catch, and Link said he had to go. His law school softball team had a night game in the intramural league and, of course, he was the star. Jeri wanted him to join them for dinner, but he begged off. Maybe tomorrow night.

As soon as he was gone, Jeri zeroed in and asked, "Okay, how serious is it?"

"Come on, Mom, let's not go there."

"I'm not blind, girl. How serious?"

"It's not serious enough to talk about as of now."

"Are you sleeping with him?"

"Of course. Wouldn't you?"

"Don't ask that question."

"And who are you sleeping with?"

"No one, and that's the problem." Both laughed, but somewhat nervously.

Denise said, "Now, changing the subject, Alfred called two days ago. He checks in occasionally."

"How nice of him. I'm glad he's calling some-one." Alfred was Jeri's older brother, Denise's uncle, and Jeri had not seen him in at least three years. They had been close until their father's murder, after which they had tried to support one another. But Jeri's obsession with finding the killer had eventually driven them apart. In her opinion, Alfred had given up too soon. Once he became convinced the crime would never be solved, he stopped talking about it. Since she talked of little else, in those days anyway, he shut her out. To get away, and to start over, he moved to California and he wasn't coming back. He had a wife Jeri detested and three kids she adored, BUT SHE WAS TOO FAR AWAY TO BE INVOLVED IN their lives.

They sipped their wine for a few minutes and watched the students. Jeri finally said, "I'm sure your father checks in from time to time."

"Look, Mom, let's get the family stuff out of the way and be done with it, okay? Dad sends me a hundred dollars a month and calls every other week. We text and email and stay in touch. I wish he wouldn't send money. I don't need it. I have a scholarship and a job and I'm on my own."

"It's guilt, Denise. He left us when you were a toddler."

"I know, Mom, and we are now finished with the family discussion. Let's go to dinner."

"Have I told you I'm proud of you?"

"At least once a week. I'm proud of you too."

Dinner was at Café Zola, a popular restaurant in a handsome old redbrick building just around the corner. Denise had reserved a table near the front, and they settled in for a long dinner and lots of catching up. They ordered another glass of wine and then salads and fish. At Jeri's prompting, Denise talked about her studies and lab work, and used scientific terms that were over her mother's head. She got the science and math gene from her father, the one for history and literature from her mother.

Halfway through the meal, Jeri got serious and said, "I have something important to tell you."

"You're pregnant?"

"In more ways than one, that's biologically impossible."

"Just kidding, Mom." Denise suspected the big news had something to do with the murder, a subject they rarely broached.

"I know." Jeri put down her fork and took her glass, as if she needed fortification. "I, uh, I know who killed my father."

Denise stopped chewing and glared at her in disbelief.

Jeri went on, "That's right. After twenty years of research, I've found the man."

Still speechless, Denise swallowed and took a sip. She nodded, go on.

"I've notified the authorities, and, well, maybe this nightmare is coming to an end."

Denise exhaled and kept nodding but struggled for words. "Am I supposed to be thrilled by this? I'm sorry, but I don't know how to react. Is there a chance he'll be arrested?"

"I think so. Let's hope and pray."

"Uh, where is he?"

"Pensacola."

"That's awfully close to Mobile."

"Close enough."

"Don't tell me his name, okay? I'm not sure I'm ready for it."

"I've told no one, except the authorities."

"You've gone to the police?"

"No. There are other investigative authorities in Florida. They have the case now. I'm assuming the police will be notified by them in the near future."

"Do you have proof? Is the case ironclad, as they say?"

"No. I'm afraid it will be hard to prove, and of course that worries me greatly."

Denise took another sip, emptying her glass. The waitress happened by and she asked for another. She glanced around and lowered her voice. "Okay, Mom, but if there's no proof how will they nail this guy?"

"I don't have all the answers, Denise. That will be up to the police and prosecutors."

"So, there will be a big trial and all of that?"

"Again, I hope so. I won't be able to sleep until he's convicted and put away."

Denise often worried about her mother's obsession. Alfred seemed to think that his sister teetered on the edge of delusion. A fierce obsession with anything, and especially something as traumatic as a murder, was not healthy. Denise and Alfred had discussed it over the years, but not recently. They worried about Jeri, though they could do nothing to change her.

For the rest of the family, the murder was a subject to be avoided.

"Will you have to testify in court?" The idea clearly troubled her.

"I suppose. A family member of the deceased is usually one of the first witnesses called by the State."

"And you're ready for that?"

"Yes, I'm fully prepared to meet the killer in court. I won't miss a word of his trial."

"I'm not going to ask how you found this guy."

"It's a long and complicated story, Denise, and one day I'll talk about it. But not now. Let's enjoy the moment and dwell on happier thoughts. I just thought you would want to know."

"Have you told Alfred?"

"No, not yet. But I will soon."

"I guess I should be satisfied. This is good news, right?"

"Only if he's convicted."

Saturday morning began late with yogurt on the sofa, Jeri's bed for the weekend, and they stayed in their pajamas until past noon. They eventually showered and ventured out, first to a coffee bar on Huron Street. It was a perfect spring day and they sat in the sun talking about life, the future, fashion, television shows, movies, boys, whatever came to mind. Jeri savored the time with

Denise and knew the moments were precious. She was maturing into a smart and ambitious young woman with a promising future, one that would probably take her far away from Mobile, a place she had never lived anyway.

Denise worried that her mother was watching life slip away with no one to share it with. At forty-six, she was still beautiful and sexy and had so much to offer, but she had chosen to commit herself to finding justice for her father. Her obsession had precluded any thoughts of serious romance, even friendships. It was a subject they avoided throughout the day.

The law school was engaged in an all-day softball tournament, with a dozen teams playing double elimination. With Denise behind the wheel of her little Mazda, they found the sports complex, unloaded chairs and a cooler, and made a place under a tree beyond the left-field fence. Link found them immediately and took a seat on a quilt. He drank a pregame beer—most of the players seemed to be enjoying a beverage, even on the field—and Jeri quizzed him about his future. His dream job was with the Department of Justice in Washington as a starter, then perhaps something in private practice. He was wary of the big firm grind and wanted to litigate civil rights for the disabled. His father had been injured on the job and was confined to a wheelchair.

The more Jeri watched him around her

daughter, the more convinced she became that Link was the future. And she was fine with that. He was engaging, smart, quick-witted, and obviously enamored with Denise.

After he left to play, Denise said, "Okay, Mom, I want to know how you found this guy."

"Which guy?"

"The killer."

Jeri smiled, shook her head, and finally said, "The whole story?"

"Yes. I want to know."

"This might take some time."

"What else are we doing for the next few hours?"

"Okay."

31

Late Saturday morning, Lacy and her boyfriend left Tallahassee for a three-hour drive to Ocala, north of Orlando. Allie did the driving as Lacy handled the entertainment. They began with an audiobook by Elmore Leonard, but she soon decided she'd had enough of crime and dead bodies and switched to a podcast on politics. It, too, quickly became depressing so she found NPR and they laughed through an episode of **Wait Wait . . . Don't Tell Me!** Their appointment with Herman Gray was at 2:00 p.m.

Mr. Gray was an FBI legend who had overseen the Behavioral Analysis Unit at Quantico for two decades. Now pushing eighty, he had retired to Florida and lived behind a gate with his wife and three dogs. Allie had been referred to him by a supervisor and had made the necessary calls. Herman said he was bored and had plenty of time, especially if the conversation was about serial killers. He had tracked and studied them throughout his career, and, according to the legend, knew more about the breed than anyone. He had published two books on the subject, neither of which was particularly helpful. Both were more or less collections of his war stories, complete with gory photographs and a bit too much self-congratulation.

He greeted them warmly and seemed genuinely pleased to have guests. His wife offered lunch, which they declined. She served them iced tea without sugar, and they talked for the first half hour on the patio with the spaniels licking their ankles. When he began talking about his career, Lacy interrupted politely with "We've read both of your books, so we know something about your work."

He liked that and tried to defer with "Most of that stuff is accurate. Maybe a bit of embellishment here and there."

"It's fascinating," she said.

Allie said, "As I explained on the phone, Lacy would like to walk through each of the victims and get your thoughts."

"The afternoon belongs to you," Herman said with a smile.

Lacy said, "It's extremely confidential and we won't use any real names."

"I understand discretion, Ms. Stoltz. Believe me, I do."

"Can we go with Lacy and Allie?"

"Sure, and I'm Herman. I see you've brought a briefcase, so I assume there's paperwork, maybe some photos."

"Yes."

"Perhaps we should go to the kitchen and use the table."

They followed him inside, as did the dogs, and Mrs. Gray refilled their glasses. Herman sat on one side of the table and faced Lacy and Allie. She took a deep breath and began, "There are eight murders that we know about. The first was in 1991, the most recent less than a year ago. The first seven were by strangulation, same type of rope, same method, but for the last one no rope was used. Just a few blows to the head."

"Twenty-three years."

"Yes, sir."

"Could we drop the 'sirs'?"

"Yep."

"Thank you. I'll be eighty in two months but I am refusing to let the old man in." Thin as a weed, he looked like he could walk ten miles in the hot sun.

"Obviously, we believe our suspect killed all eight people. Six men, two women."

"There are probably more, you know?"

"Yes, but we have no knowledge of them."

Herman took out his pen and found a note-pad. "Let's talk about Number One."

Allie opened the briefcase and handed Lacy a file. She said, "Number One was a forty-one-year-old white male—all but one were white—who was found beside a walking trail in Signal Mountain, Tennessee." She handed Herman a sheet of paper she had prepared with the words **Number One** typed in bold letters at the top. Date, place, age of victim, cause of death, and a color photo of Thad Leawood lying in the bushes.

Herman studied the summary and the photo and took notes. They watched him carefully and said nothing. When he had reviewed it, he asked, "Other than the body, was there anything from the crime scene?"

"The police found nothing. No prints, fibers, hair, no blood other than the victim's. Same for all the crime scenes."

"A strange knot, something like a clove hitch."

"A double clove hitch, not very common."

"Rare indeed. If he used it every time, then it's obviously his calling card. How many blows to the head?"

"Two, with what appears to be the same weapon."

"Autopsy?"

"The skull splintered, numerous cracks radiating from the contact point. The police in Wilmington, North Carolina, at another crime scene, thought it was something like a hammer or small round metal ball."

"Works every time, though it does make a messy scene. The blood spatters to such a degree that the suspect probably had some on his clothing."

"Which, of course, was never found."

"Of course not. Motive?"

"The theory is that Number One sexually abused the killer when he was a young boy."

"That's a lot of motive. Any proof of this?"

"Not really."

"Okay. How about Number Two."

Lacy handed him the sheet for Bryan Burke and said, "The following year, 1992."

Herman looked at it and said, "South Carolina."

"Yes, each was in a different state."

He smiled and made notes. "Motive?"

"Their paths crossed in college when the killer was a student. Number Two was one of his professors." Lacy was careful not to use the words "law school." That would come later. Allie had not told Herman much about her and had not revealed where she worked or who she investigated. Again, that would be discussed later in the afternoon.

Number Three was Ashley Barasso. Lacy said, "Four years later, in Columbus, Georgia. We know nothing of motive, only that they were in school together."

"College?"

"Yes."

"Was she sexually abused in any way?"

"No. She was fully clothed, nothing was disturbed, no sign of molestation."

"That's unusual. Sex is a factor in about eighty percent of serial crimes."

Number Four was Eileen Nickleberry, in 1998.

With Number Five, Danny Cleveland, Lacy said, "Our man took a break for eleven years, at least as far as we know."

"That's quite a gap," Herman said, studying the photo. "Same knot. He doesn't want to get caught, too smart for that, but he wants someone to know that he's out there. Not at all uncommon." He scribbled more notes as his wife appeared and offered them cookies. She did not stay in the kitchen but Lacy got the impression she was close by, probably listening.

Number Six was Perry Kronke down in Marathon. Herman studied the photos and asked, "Where did you get these?"

"They were given to us by a source who's been working on this for many years. Freedom of Information Act, FBI clearinghouse, the usual. We have photos from the first six crime scenes but not the last."

"Too recent, I suppose. Poor guy was out fishing, just minding his own business. In broad daylight."

"I've been to the scene and it was pretty remote."

"Okay. Motive?"

"They crossed paths in the workplace, probably a disagreement over a job offer that didn't materialize."

"So he knew him too?"

"He knew all of them."

Herman just thought he'd seen it all and was visibly impressed. "Okay, let's see the last one."

Lacy handed over **Number Seven** and **Number Eight,** and explained their theory that the first victim was the target and the second arrived on the scene at the wrong time. Herman studied the summaries and photos for a long time, then said with a grin, "Well, is that all?"

"That's all we know about."

"You can bet there's more, and you can bet he's not finished."

They nodded and both took a bite of a cookie.

Herman said, "So, now you want a profile, right?"

Allie said, "Sure, that's one reason we're here."

Herman put down his pen, stood and stretched his back, and scratched his chin as he thought. "White male, age fifty, started his mischief when he was mid-twenties. Single, probably never married. Except for the first two, he kills on Fridays and weekends, clear indication that he has an important job. You mentioned college, and it's obvious he's bright, even brilliant, and patient. No sex angle, so he's probably impotent. You know the motive, driven by a sick need for revenge. Kills without remorse, which is usually the case.

Sociopathic to say the least. Antisocial but, being educated, probably manages to put up a front and maintain what appears to be a normal life. Seven crime scenes in seven states over a twenty-three-year period. Very unusual. He knows the police won't dig deep enough to link the crimes. And the FBI is not involved?"

"Not yet," Allie said. "That's another reason we're here."

"He knows forensics, police procedure, and the law," Lacy said.

Herman slowly sat down and looked at his notes. "Quite unusual. Even unique. I'm impressed with this guy. What do you know about him?"

Lacy said, "Well, he certainly fits your profile. He's a judge."

Herman exhaled as if somewhat overwhelmed. He shook his head and thought for a long time. Finally he said, "A sitting judge?"

"Duly elected by the voters."

"Wow. Quite unusual. Narcissistic, split personality, able to live in one world as a respected, productive member of society while spending his off-hours plotting the next kill. It'll be hard to nail this guy. Unless."

Allie said, "Unless he makes a mistake, right?"

"Right."

Lacy said, "We think he's made one, at his last stop. You asked about the FBI. They're not involved in the investigation but they have found a clue. He left a partial thumb print on a cell phone. The lab in Quantico has spent months with it, run all the tests. The problem is there is no match anywhere. The FBI thinks he's probably altered his prints."

Herman shook his head in disbelief. "Well, I'm not a print guy, but I know that's virtually impossible, without extensive surgery."

Lacy said, "He can afford it, and he's had plenty of time."

Allie said, "I've checked around, talked to some of our experts. There have been a handful of cases where the prints were altered."

"If you say so. I have my doubts."

Lacy said, "So do we. If we can't get a match, then the case looks hopeless. There's no other proof, other than motive, and that's not enough. Right?"

"I don't know. I suppose there's no way to get his prints, his current ones?"

"Not without a warrant," Lacy said. "We have suspicion, but that's not enough to convince a judge to issue one."

"We need advice, Herman," Allie said. "What's our next step?"

"Where does the guy live?"

"Pensacola."

"And the print is in Mississippi, right?"

"Correct."

"Will the authorities there call in the Bureau?"

"I'm sure they will. They're desperate to solve the murders."

"Then you have to start there. Once our boys are involved, it'll be easier to convince a federal magistrate to issue a search warrant."

"And search what?" Lacy asked.

"His home, his office, anyplace there might be prints."

Allie said, "There might be a couple of problems with that. The first is that this guy is capable of leaving no prints anywhere. The second is that he might disappear at the first whiff of trouble."

"Let our boys worry about the prints. They'll find 'em. No one is capable of wiping clean their home or office. As for the disappearing act, that's a chance you take. You can't arrest him until there is a match with the prints, right? No other proof?"

"So far, none," Lacy said.

"There might be another problem," Allie said. "Is there a chance the Bureau will decline to get involved?"

"Why?"

"The slim chance of success. The first six crime scenes yielded zero evidence. Those cases are ice cold and have been for years. You know the politics at Quantico. And you know how perpetually understaffed the BAU is. Is it possible they could take a hard look at this and pass?"

Herman waved off the idea. "No, I don't see

it. We've tracked serial killers for years and never found them. Some of the cases I worked on thirty years ago are still unsolved, always will be. That will not deter the BAU. This is their meat and potatoes. And, keep in mind, they don't have to solve all of the murders. You just need one to put this guy away."

Herman put down his pen and folded his arms across his chest. "You have no choice but to bring in the Bureau. I sense some hesitation."

Lacy told the story of Betty Roe and her twenty-year quest to find her father's murderer. Herman interrupted with "Is she looking for a job? I think the Bureau needs her."

"She has a career," Lacy said after a laugh. "She filed a complaint with the Board on Judicial Conduct. That's where I work. She's very fragile, and frightened, and I promised we would not bring in the police until we finished our initial investigation."

Herman didn't like this and said, "Too bad. She's no longer a factor. You have a very sophisticated killer still at work, and it's time to bring in the Bureau. The longer you wait, the more bodies they'll find. This guy will not stop."

32

On Tuesday, the **Pensacola Ledger** ran a brief story on page 5 of its news section. Mal Schnetzer, a local lawyer from years past, had been murdered the previous Saturday in a trailer in Sugar Land, Texas, west of Houston, where he had been living. The police gave the barest of details, saying only that he had been strangled in a trailer rented by a person who had yet to be found. The story recalled his days as a well-known plaintiff's lawyer in the Panhandle, before he was disbarred and sent to prison for robbing his clients. There was a small photo of Mal in his better days.

Jeri saw the story online and read it with her morning coffee. She immediately pulled together the other stories: Danny Cleveland, the former **Ledger** reporter, who had been strangled in his apartment in Little Rock in 2009; Thad Leawood, strangled in 1991 near Signal Mountain, Tennessee; and

Lanny Verno, murdered in Biloxi the previous year. Schnetzer, Cleveland, and Leawood had been known in Pensacola and the **Ledger** reported their deaths. Verno had been passing through and was not known; thus, there was no local coverage. She found the stories of the murders from the local newspapers in Little Rock, Chattanooga, Houston, and Biloxi, and arranged them all neatly in a file that she sent through a new email account to a reporter named Kemper, the woman who had written about the Schnetzer murder. She attached a cryptic note: Four unsolved strangulations of people with close ties to Pensacola. Verno lived here in 2001. Do your homework!!

She had not heard of the Schnetzer murder and wasn't about to start digging. She was exhausted, and virtually broke, and simply couldn't muster the energy for another investigation. As always, she suspected Bannick, but someone else would have to worry about the case.

The following morning, on the front page beneath the fold, was a sensational story about the four Pensacola men who had been murdered in other states. The local police wouldn't comment and deflected all questions because they knew nothing. The killings were not in their jurisdiction. Likewise, the state police wouldn't comment.

Jeri read it gleefully and immediately sent it, encrypted as always, to Lacy Stoltz. Minutes later she texted her the encryption key.

Lacy was at her desk reading assessments of other complaints when she saw the email and opened the file. There was no message. Who else would send her a private email, and then the key? Who else would have the old stories from the **Ledger** and the other newspapers? Once again she marveled at Jeri's research and tenaciousness, and managed a chuckle at Herman Gray's comment about her being needed by the FBI.

She closed her door and for a long time re-read the reports of the old murders, and the new ones. She tried to gauge the impact of the morning's story and finally concluded there was no way to predict what might happen. There was little doubt, though, that it would change the land-scape. Bannick would see it, probably already had. Who in the world could guess his next move?

Judge Bannick was in a hotel room in Santa Fe when he saw it. As always, he scanned the **Ledger** online for all the news from home, and when he saw it he began cursing.

The only other person who could possibly link Lanny Verno to Pensacola was Jeri Burke. Maybe the ex-cop, Norris Ozment, but he was not in the loop.

A few of the older lawyers could link him to Schnetzer and their fee dispute, back in 1993.

Perhaps a reporter at the **Ledger** might remember Danny Cleveland and his muckraking article about Bannick when he first ran for office, though this was doubtful. Cleveland had gone after several shady developers. No one to his knowledge was still around to link him to Thad Leawood. There had been no criminal charges and the frightened victims hid behind their parents, who had no idea what to do.

He was thirteen years old and had achieved the rank Life, with eighteen merit badges, including all the required ones. His goal was to make Eagle by his fourteenth birthday, something his father encouraged because after that the high school years arrived and scouting would become less important. He led the Shark Patrol, the finest in the troop. He loved every part of it—the weekends in the woods, the training for the mile swim, the jamborees, the challenge of making Eagle, the search for more merit badges, the awards ceremonies, the community service.

After the assault, he missed a meeting, something that never happened. When he missed the second one, his parents were curious. He could not carry the burden alone, and so he told them. They were horrified and devastated, and had no clue about where to go for help. His father finally met with the police and was distressed to learn that there had been another complaint, from a boy unwilling to be identified.

He suspected it was Jason Wright, a friend who had abruptly quit the troop two months earlier.

The police wanted to meet with Ross, but the idea terrified him. He was sleeping at the foot of his parents' bed and hated to leave the house. They decided that protecting their child was more important than demanding punishment. The nightmare went from bad to worse when the **Ledger** ran a story about a police investigation into "allegations of sexual misconduct" by Thad Leawood, age twenty-eight. It was obviously leaked by the police, in Dr. Bannick's opinion, and sent the town into orbit.

Leawood slinked away and was not seen again. Fourteen years passed before he paid for his crimes.

Late Wednesday afternoon, Lacy was out of excuses and weary of procrastinating. She closed and locked her office door and called the first of several phone numbers for Betty Roe. None were answered, which was not unusual. Minutes later, her smartphone pinged with a text from an unknown number. Betty wrote: "Go to the green line." Code for **Use your burner.** Lacy picked up her disposable phone and waited another minute for the call.

Betty began cheerfully with "How about that story in the **Ledger**?"

"Interesting to say the least. I wonder how they put all the murders together so fast."

"Oh, I don't know. I'm sure it was an anonymous email from someone who's familiar with the murders, wouldn't you say?"

"I would indeed."

"I wonder how our boy reacted."

"I'm sure it ruined his day."

"I hope he had a massive stroke and gagged to death on his vomit. They say he's in bad health anyway. Rumor of colon cancer, but I doubt it. More like a good reason to get out of town."

"You sound feisty."

"I'm in pretty good spirits, Lacy. I went to Michigan and spent last weekend with my daughter, had a great visit."

"Good, because I have some news that you may not want. We've finished our assessment of your complaint and we believe it has merit. We are referring it to the state police and the FBI. Our decision is final."

Silence on the other end. Lacy plowed on. "You shouldn't be surprised, Betty. This is what you've always wanted. You used us to start the investigation and give it credibility while you hid in the dark. Nothing wrong with that, and I assure you your name has not been used. We will continue to protect your identity, to the extent possible."

"What does that mean? 'To the extent possible'?"

"It means I'm not sure how the investigation will go. I don't know if the FBI will want your input, but if they do I'm sure they know how to protect a key witness."

"I won't sleep until he's arrested and locked up. You should be worried too, Lacy. I've warned you about this."

"You have and I'm being careful."

"He's smarter than we are, Lacy, and he's always watching."

"You think he knows about our involvement?"

"Assume he does, okay? Just assume the worst. He's back there, Lacy."

Lacy closed her eyes and was ready to end the call. Betty's paranoia was at times irksome.

33

The computer and phone networks of the Harrison County Sheriff's Department had been turned over to Nic Constantine, a twenty-year-old part-time student at a community college down the road. He enjoyed the work and loved hanging around the deputies and other law enforcement types, most of whom needed plenty of help with technology. He had serious talent for it and could design and fix anything. He was constantly urging them to upgrade here and there, but there were always budget problems.

Nic knew the Verno/Dunwoody case was top secret. The vultures from the press were still circling, and Sheriff Black had put a lid on all communications, most of which were kept offline. To his great delight, Nic had been at the murder scene, and, later, led the sheriff and Deputy Mancuso to the two cell phones in the tiny town of Neely, Mississippi. An easy job any twelve-year-old could handle.

Nic routinely swept the network for viruses, but had been unable to detect Rafe and his evil pals from Maggotz. They were dormant for the vast majority of the time. The mistake was made by Detective Napier, who sent a naked email to the sheriff confirming a meeting with the FBI on Friday, April 25, at the Bureau's office in Pensacola. Napier referred to the FBI as "Hoovies," said a team from Washington would fly in, with an expert, the cell phone, and the PTP. Napier immediately realized his mistake, deleted the email, found Nic, and asked him to wipe it clean from the network. He tracked it through the department's internal server and was confident everything had been erased.

Napier and Nic then found the sheriff and explained what had happened. Nic dreamed of working for the FBI and was thrilled at the news of the meeting. He offered to be there, with the warning that he might be needed in case of more mistakes. Sheriff Black was not impressed.

Rafe, dormant but ever present, saw the email. Thirty minutes later, Judge Bannick saw it too and was stricken with panic. He knew how much the FBI loved acronyms. He knew the lingo as well as the agents in the field. PTP—partial thumb print.

Quickly, he checked the surveillance cameras and security systems at his home, courthouse office, and vault. There had been no entries. He booked the earliest flight out of Santa Fe, checked out of his hotel room, and headed home.

The trip was interminable but gave him plenty of time to think. He was certain he had left no prints behind, but what if he had? Any print taken from one of the cell phones would never find a match these days. After years of altering, the only match would have to be from a current print, something he had touched in the last decade.

He arrived home at three in the morning and needed rest, but the bennies were working too well. He kept the overhead lights off so the neighbors wouldn't know he was home, and worked in the semidarkness. He put on plastic gloves and filled the dishwasher with the first load. Some of the cups and glasses went into a large garbage liner.

Wiping almost any surface at least smears the latent prints and renders them useless. Smearing, though, was not the plan. He mixed a solution of water, distilled alcohol, and lemon juice and wiped the counters and appliances with a microfiber cloth. Light switches, walls, pantry shelves. From the refrigerator he removed jars, cans, bottles, and plastic wrappers and dumped the contents into the disposal. The containers went into the garbage sack. He didn't cook much and the fridge was never full.

Latent prints can last for years. As he cursed to himself he kept mumbling, "PTP."

In the bathroom he scrubbed the surfaces, walls, toilet, shower knobs, and floor. He emptied the cabinet, leaving behind only a toothbrush, a disposable razor, shaving cream, and a half-empty tube of Colgate. Prints were virtually impossible to lift from cloth, but he filled the washing machine anyway, with bath and hand towels.

In the den he threw away the TV remote and wiped the LED screen. He threw away all magazines and a couple of old newspapers. He scrubbed the walls and the leather chairs.

In his office, he wiped the keyboard, an old laptop, two outdated cell phones, and a pile of stationery and envelopes. He stared at a cabinet filled with files and decided to get them later.

The cleansing would take hours if not days, and he knew this was only the first pass through. There would be a second, hopefully a third. At dawn, before the neighbors began moving about, he hauled three large black garbage liners to his SUV and sat down for a nap.

Sleep was impossible. At eight, he showered and changed, throwing away the towels and clothes. He stared into his closet and realized how much stuff had to be tossed. He filled the washing machine with underwear and clothing and doubled the detergent.

He dressed casually and left. He called Diana

Zhang, said he was back in town, felt good, and wanted to run by the courthouse to say hello. When he arrived at nine, his staff greeted him like a returning hero. He chatted with them for a while, assuring them that his first round of chemo had gone well and his doctors were encouraged. He would be home for a few days before heading back to Santa Fe.

They thought he looked tired, even haggard.

He sat at his desk and dictated to his secretary a list of things to do. He needed to make some calls and asked her to leave. He locked the door and looked around his office. The desk, leather chairs, worktable, file cabinets, shelves lined with books and treatises. Thankfully, he hadn't touched most of them in years. The task seemed impossible, but he had no choice. He opened his briefcase, put on plastic gloves, removed three packs of alcohol wipes, and went to work.

After two hours, he told his staff he was going home to rest. Please don't call. He drove instead to his hidden office in Pensacola. He doubted any-one sniffing for fingerprints would ever find the place, but he could take no chances. He had de-signed it with extreme caution, careful to leave no clues in case of an emergency. Everything was digitized—no books, files, bills, nothing to leave a trail.

He stretched out on the sofa and managed to sleep for two hours.

—

According to Jeri's class schedule, posted officially online, she taught a class in comparative politics at 2:00 p.m. in the Humanities Building. He drove an hour to Mobile and found the building from a campus map he had memorized.

Her car, a white 2009 Toyota Camry, was parked with a hundred others in a lot for faculty and students, authorized stickers required. He left, drove to a car wash several blocks away, ran his new Tahoe through the self-wash, then parked by the vacuums and opened all four doors. As he toiled away, he swapped license plates and was now registered in Alabama. When things were shiny and spotless, he drove back to the Humanities Building and found a spot as close to the Camry as possible. He popped the hatch on his Tahoe, removed the jack and spare, and got busy pretending to change a rear tire that wasn't flat.

A campus security guard in an old Bronco eased between the row of parked cars and stopped behind the Tahoe. "Need a hand?" he asked helpfully, without making a move to get out.

"No thanks," Bannick said. "I got it."

"I don't see a parking sticker."

"No, sir. Had a flat out there," he said, nodding to the street. "I'll be gone in a minute."

The guard drove away without a word.

Shit! A mistake that couldn't be avoided.

With the Tahoe jacked up, and without touching a lug nut, he removed a BlueCloud TS-180 GPS tracker with a magnetic mount. It weighed fourteen ounces and was about the size of a thick paperback. He walked nonchalantly to the Camry, watching anything that moved from behind his sunglasses, noticed three students entering the building but certainly not concerned with him, then quickly ducked and stuck the device to the side of the gas tank. Its battery lasted 180 hours and was motion-activated; thus, it took a nap when the car wasn't moving. He walked back to his Tahoe, jacked it down, put away the spare and the jack, closed the hatch, and left the parking lot. The security guard was nowhere to be seen.

Two hours later, the Camry began moving. He tracked it with his smartphone and soon had it in sight. Jeri stopped at a dry-cleaners, did her business, then drove to her condo.

The tracker worked beautifully.

He returned to Cullman, waited until five thirty when the courthouse was closed, and entered through a rear door with his own key. He had been coming and going as he pleased for ten years and rarely saw anyone after hours. He was committing no crime, just tidying up his office.

He wiped it again and left after dark with two thick briefcases filled with files and notepads. A hardworking judge.

34

On Friday morning Lacy and Darren arrived at a downtown office building at 9:45 for a ten o'clock meeting, a summit of sorts. The FBI office was on the sixth floor, and they were met at the elevator there by Special Agent Dagner, of Pensacola.

From a third-story hotel room two blocks away, Judge Bannick monitored the parking lot through a handheld monocular telescope. He watched Lacy and Darren disappear into the building. Ten minutes later, he saw an unmarked sedan with Mississippi tags park and two men get out. They were in street clothes, even wearing coats and ties for the big meeting. Next was a black SUV. All four doors opened at the same time and the Feds, three men and one woman, in nicer dark suits, spilled out and hustled inside. The last two arrived in a car with Florida license plates. More dark suits.

When the traffic stopped at ten after ten, Bannick sat on the edge of the bed and rubbed his temples. The FBI had arrived, the Hoovies from the big office in Washington, along with the state police and the boys from Mississippi.

He could not know what was being said over there. Rafe had failed to penetrate the network.

But the judge had a pretty good idea of what was going on, and he knew how to find out.

They gathered around a long table in the suite's largest room while two secretaries brought in coffee and pastries. After a round of introductions, so many names that Darren tried to write them all down, the boss called the meeting to order. He was Clay Vidovich, the Special Agent in Charge (SAC), and he assumed the chair at the head of the table. To his right were Special Agents Suarez, Neff, and Murray. To his left were Sheriff Dale Black and Detective Napier from Biloxi. Next to them were two investigators from the Florida state police, Harris and Wendel. Lacy and Darren sat at the far end of the table, as if they really didn't belong with real cops.

Noticeably absent were the Pensacola police. The suspect was a local guy with plenty of contacts. Loose lips sink ships and all that. The city boys would only get in the way.

Vidovich began with "Now, the paperwork has been completed, all protocols have been cleared, and the FBI is officially engaged in this case. This is now a joint task force with all of us cooperating fully. Sheriff, what about the Mississippi state police?"

"Well, they've certainly been kept up to date, but I was asked to not mention this initial meeting. I assume they're ready if we need them."

"Not now, maybe later. Lieutenant Harris, have you notified the police down in Marathon?"

"No sir, but I will if we need them."

"Good. Let's proceed without them. Now, we've all read the summaries and I think we're up to speed. Ms. Stoltz, since you got all this started, why don't you take a few minutes and go over the basics."

"Sure," she said, flashing a smile. The only other woman in the room was Agent Agnes Neff, a tough-looking veteran who had yet to smile.

Lacy stood and pushed back her chair. "This began with a complaint against Judge Bannick, filed by one Betty Roe, an alias."

"When do we get her real name?"

"Well, it's now your case, so I guess anytime you want. But I prefer to keep her out of it as long as possible."

"Very well. And why is she involved?"

"Her father was murdered in 1992 near Gaffney, South Carolina. The case went cold, almost immediately, and she became determined to find his killer. She's been obsessed with the case for years."

"And we're talking about eight murders, right?"

"Eight that she knows of. There could be more."

"I think we can assume there are more. And all she has is motive, right?"

"And method."

Vidovich looked at Suarez, who shook his head and said, "It's the same guy. Same type of rope and the knot is his trademark. We got the crime scene photos from Schnetzer in Texas, same rope and knot. We've studied the autopsies, same type of blow to the head, same instrument. Something like a claw hammer that shatters the skull in one defined point of impact and radiates rupture lines in all directions."

Vidovich looked at Lieutenant Harris and asked, "And the killer knew him in another life, right?"

Harris said, "That's right. They were both lawyers here in town many years ago."

"And you don't know this judge—right, Ms. Stoltz?"

"No, I've not had the pleasure. He's never had a complaint filed against him. A clean record, and a good reputation."

"This is remarkable," Vidovich said to the table and everyone frowned in agreement.

He continued, "Ms. Stoltz, what do you think he would do if we simply asked him to stop by for a few questions? He is a well-known judge, an officer of the court. He doesn't know about the PTP. Why wouldn't he want to cooperate?"

"Well, if he's guilty, why would he cooperate? In my opinion he would either disappear or lawyer up. But he will not make himself available."

"And he's a flight risk?"

"Yes, in my opinion. He's smart and he has assets. He's done a superb job of avoiding detection for the past twenty years. I think this guy could vanish in a split second."

"Thank you."

Lacy sat down and looked at the faces around the table.

Vidovich said, "It's obvious that we need his prints, his current ones. Agnes, talk to us about a search warrant."

Still unsmiling, she cleared her throat and looked at her notepad. "I met with Legal yesterday in Washington, and they think we can do it. A prime suspect in a murder, two of them actually, the Biloxi case, and a mysterious partial print there that matches nothing. Legal says we can push hard for a warrant. The U.S. Attorney in Mississippi has been briefed and has a magistrate on standby."

Lacy said, "May I ask what you plan to search?"

"His home and office," Vidovich said. "They're covered with his prints. We get a match, game over. No match, and we apologize and leave town. Betty Roe can go back to her Sherlock Holmes routine."

"Okay, but he's a fanatic about security and surveillance. He'll know the instant someone kicks in a door or somehow gets inside. Then he's gone."

"Do we know where he is at this moment?"

A unified shaking of heads. Vidovich glared at Harris who said, "No, we haven't been watching him. No reason to. There's no case, no file. He's not a suspect, yet."

Lacy said, "He's also on leave for medical reasons, claims he's in treatment for cancer, according to a source we have here in Pensacola. His office told one of our contacts that he would not sit on the bench for at least the next two months. The district court's web page confirms this."

Vidovich frowned and rubbed his jaw as everyone else waited. He said, "Okay, let's start with surveillance and find the guy. In the meantime let's get a search warrant from the magistrate in Mississippi, bring it to the magistrate here, and sit on it until we find him. At that time, he can't disappear and we'll execute the warrant."

They discussed surveillance for an hour: Who, where, how. Lacy and Darren grew bored, their initial excitement dissipated, and they finally asked to be excused.

Vidovich promised to keep them in the loop, but it was obvious their work was over.

Leaving town, Darren asked, "Are you going to report this to Betty?"

"No. She doesn't need to know what's going on."

"Are we done with her? Can we close the case?"

"I'm not sure."

"Well, aren't you the boss?"

"Certainly."

"Then why can't you say that BJC is no longer involved?"

"Tired of it?"

"We're lawyers, Lacy, not cops."

The three-hour drive back to Tallahassee was a relief. It was almost noon on a Friday, on an oddly cool spring day, and they decided to forget about the office.

As they discussed his fate, Judge Bannick drove ten minutes to his shopping center and disappeared into his other chamber and his Vault. He wiped his computers clean, removed the hard drives, gathered the thumb drives from the hidden safes, and scrubbed the place again. Leaving, he reset the security cameras and sensors, and left for Mobile.

He spent the afternoon roaming a mall, drinking espressos in a Starbucks, drinking club soda in a dark bar, loitering along the harbor, and driving around until dark.

35

The plain, white, legal-size envelope contained copies of her three little poems. It was sealed and addressed in heavy black ink—**Jeri Crosby.** No postal address was given, but then none was needed. The words **Hand Delivered** were scrawled under her name. He waited until 9:00 p.m. and parked at the curb two short blocks away.

Jeri was idling away another Friday night, flipping stations on TV and resisting the temptation to go online and look for more murders. Lacy had called after lunch with the news that the FBI was in town and assuming control of the investigation. Jeri should be in a better mood now that her work was over and Bannick was being pursued by the pros. She was learning, though, that obsessions die hard and it was impossible to simply flip a switch and move on. She had lived in his life for so long, she couldn't force him out of her being. She had no other purpose, other than her neglected work and her lovely daughter. And she was terrified, still. She asked herself how long the fear would last. Would she ever go a full hour without glancing over her shoulder?

The doorbell jolted her. She fumbled with the remote, got the TV muted, grabbed the nearest pistol from a table by the door, and peeked through the blinds. A streetlamp lit the front lawns of the four condos in her row, and revealed nothing. She wasn't about to open the door, not at 9:00 p.m. on a Friday night, and could think of no one who would be stopping by without calling first. Not even the political candidates worked such hours. She waited for it to ring again, gripping her pistol and resisting the urge to look into the peephole. Long minutes passed, and the fact that whoever was out there did not ring again, and did not really want to see her, made the situation worse. Could it be some kids pulling pranks? That had never happened before, not on her quiet little street. She realized she was sweating and her stomach was in knots. She tried to breathe deeply but her heart was racing.

Slowly, she stepped to the door and said loud enough to be heard on the stoop, "Who is it?"

Of course there was no answer. She found the courage to look through the peephole, half expecting to see some bloodshot eyeball leering back at her, but there was nothing. She took a step back, breathed deep again, kept the pistol in her right hand, and unlocked the deadbolt with her left. With the chain latched, she looked out through the storm door but saw no one. Was she hearing things again? Had the doorbell really been punched by someone?

The camera, you idiot! Her doorbell was used so infrequently she forgot about the camera. She walked to the kitchen, picked up her smartphone, and with badly shaking hands managed to find the app. She gawked at the video. The doorbell camera was motion-activated, and from five feet away, as the person seemed to come out of the bushes, the video began. He bounded up the stoop, stuck an envelope in the storm door, and disappeared. She watched it again and again and felt sick to her stomach.

Male, with long sandy hair that touched his shoulders. A cap with no logo pulled low. Thick-framed glasses, and under them was a skin-colored mask with pockmarks and scars, something from a horror film.

She turned on lights and sat on the sofa with her gun and phone. She watched the video again. It ran for six seconds, though he was visible for only half of it. Three seconds were enough. She caught herself crying, something she hated, but the tears had nothing to do with sorrow. They were tears of sheer terror. Her stomach flipped and she wanted to throw up. Her body shook to her toes as her heart raced away.

And matters would soon get worse.

Eventually, she forced herself to stand and walk to the door. She unlocked and cracked it again, then unlocked the storm door. The envelope fell to the threshold. She grabbed it, relocked everything, and returned to the sofa where she stared at it for ten minutes.

When she opened it, and saw her silly poems, her hands instinctively flew up to her mouth and muffled her scream.

The police were irritated by such a frivolous call. It took them twenty minutes to arrive, thankfully without the benefit of all those blue lights, and she met them on the stoop.

"A prowler?" the first one asked.

For her benefit, the second one poked around the flower bed with a flashlight, seeing nothing.

Jeri showed them the video. "It's just a prank, ma'am," the first one said, shaking his head at such a nuisance. "Somebody just tryin' to scare the hell out of you." It was Friday night in a big city, and they had far more pressing matters with violent crimes, drug dealers, and drunk teenagers.

"Well, the prank certainly worked," she said.

Mr. Brammer from next door walked over and

the cops quizzed him. Jeri hadn't spoken to him in weeks; same for all of her neighbors. She was known as a recluse and not that friendly.

He told her to call if it happened again. The police were ready to leave and promised to patrol the area for the next few hours. After they were gone, she refortified her condo and sat on the sofa, all lights on. Thinking the unthinkable.

Bannick knew it was her. He had been to her house, rang her doorbell, left behind her poems. And he would be back.

She thought about calling Denise, but why frighten her? She was a thousand miles away and could do nothing to help. She thought about calling Lacy, just so someone would know. But she was three hours away and probably wouldn't take the call at such an hour.

At midnight she turned off all the lights and sat in the dark, waiting.

An hour later, she packed a small bag and, pistol in hand, left through her back door and got in the car. She drove away, eyes glued to the rearview mirror, and saw nothing suspicious. She zigzagged through quiet neighborhoods, turned east on Interstate 10, and when the downtown lights were behind her she relaxed, relieved to be out of the city. She took an exit and went south toward the Gulf on Highway 59. The road was deserted at that hour and she was certain no one was following. Through the towns of Robertsdale and Foley.

She parked at an all-night convenience store and watched the road behind her. A car passed every ten minutes. The highway stopped at the beach in Gulf Shores. East or west were the choices. Bannick was probably still lurking around Mobile, so she turned left and drove through the beach-side towns in Alabama, then crossed into Florida. For an hour she drifted along Highway 98 until a traffic light stopped her in Fort Walton Beach. A car had been behind her for a few miles and it was odd because there was virtually no other traffic. On a whim, she turned north on Highway 85, but the car did not follow. Half an hour later she crossed Interstate 10 and saw signs for fast food, gas, and lodging.

She needed to rest and was attracted to the bright lights and half-empty parking lot of the Bayview Motel. She parked, put her pistol in her bag, and went in to get a room.

Twenty minutes later, Bannick turned in to the parking lot. He sat with his laptop in his SUV, again with Alabama tags, and reserved a room online. When the confirmation email landed he waited ten minutes and replied that there had been a problem with the reservation. Please look at his attachment. When the clerk did so, Rafe eased through the rather lame security system and began fishing around the network.

Since 9:28 the previous evening, only one guest had checked in, a Margie Frazier, who evidently used a prepaid credit card.

How cute, thought the judge. She likes to use different names.

Rafe found her in room 232. Across the hall, 233 appeared to be vacant. Down the hall was an exit door and stairwell, for emergencies only.

The motel used a typical electronic keycard system with a master switch for fire evacuations. Rafe found the lighting smart panel, and for fun the judge flipped off the lights in the lobby, left the place in the dark for a few seconds, then turned them back on. Not a soul was stirring.

He entered the empty lobby and tapped the bell at the reception desk. Eventually, a sleepy-eyed young man appeared and said hello. They went through the quick paperwork for a single for one night only, with the judge chatting away. He asked for room 233, said he stayed in it six months earlier and slept for nine hours, a recent record. Wanted to try his luck again. Superstition and all that. The kid didn't care.

He took the elevator to the second floor, eased into room 233 without a sound, and inspected the door. For added security, it had the square bar lock as well as the electronic dead bolt. Nothing fancy, but then it was a tourist motel renting rooms for $99 a night. He pulled on a pair of flesh-colored plastic gloves, opened his laptop, hooked up with Rafe, and looked at the security and lighting systems.

Margie was across the hall in 232. Next door, 234 was vacant. For practice, he instructed Rafe to unlock all room doors, then he stepped over to 234 and opened it by simply turning the knob. Back in his room he relocked all the doors, then arranged his tools on the cheap credenza, carefully laying out a small bottle of ether, a microfiber cloth, a small flashlight, and a latch bypass blade. He put these in the front pockets of a vest he'd worn on several of these special occasions. Beside the tool bag he gently arranged a hypodermic needle and a small bottle of ketamine, a strong barbiturate used for anesthesia.

He stretched his back, took some deep breaths, and reminded himself of two important truths: first—he had no choice; second—failure was not an option.

It was eighteen minutes past 3:00 a.m., Saturday, April 26.

With his laptop, he instructed Rafe to first unlock all doors, then kill the electricity. Everything was instantly black. With the flashlight between his teeth, he opened his door, stepped across the hall, quietly turned the knob to 232, slid the latch bypass blade through the crack, pushed back the square bar lock, opened the door two feet wide, got on his knees, turned off the flashlight, and crawled into the room. As far as he knew at that moment, he had not made a sound.

She was sleeping. He listened to her heavy breathing, smiled, and knew that the rest would be easy. Feeling his way, he inched beside her bed, removed a microfiber cloth soaked with ether from his vest pocket, clicked on the flashlight, and attacked. Jeri was sleeping on her side, under the sheets, and knew nothing was wrong until a heavy hand slapped her mouth and pressed so hard she couldn't breathe. Groggy, bewildered, terrified, she tried to wiggle free but her assailant was strong and had every advantage. The last thing she remembered was the sweet taste of something on a cloth pad.

He checked the hallway—pitch blackness, no voices anywhere. He dragged her into his room and situated her on the bed, then went to the laptop and turned on the electricity.

He had never seen her before. Average height, slender, sort of pretty though hard to tell with her eyes closed. She had gone to bed in black yoga pants and a faded blue T-shirt, probably ready to run again at a moment's notice. He drew 500 milligrams of ketamine and shot her in her left arm. The drug should keep her out for three to four hours. He hurried back to her room, got her sneakers and a light jacket, noticed the pistol on the nightstand, a 9-millimeter automatic, for a split second considered himself lucky she didn't use it, left the room, and closed the door.

His SUV was parked as close to the exterior stairwell as possible. He tossed his bag inside, opened the hatch, looked around the parking lot and saw nothing, then returned to his room. He went to his laptop, switched off the electricity, double-checked to make sure all security cameras were off, then lifted Jeri from the bed, flung her over his shoulder, grunted, and hurried down the hallway and down the stairs. He stopped at the edge of the building for another look, again saw nothing moving, no headlights anywhere, and hurried through the dark shadows to his SUV.

Breathing heavily now, and sweating, he returned to his room to gather his laptop, her sneakers and jacket, and to make sure nothing was left behind. At 3:38, he left the parking lot of the Bayview Motel and headed east along the coast.

36

She awoke in complete blackness with a heavy cloth over her head that made breathing difficult. Her wrists were locked behind her and her hands and arms ached from being twisted like a pretzel. Her ankles too were stuck together. She was lying on a quilt. She could feel what seemed to be leather behind her, like a sofa. The air was warm, even smoky.

She was alive, at least for now. As her head slowly cleared and she put together two thoughts, she became aware of the soft popping noises of a fire. A man coughed, not far away. She dared not move. But her shoulders were screaming and she couldn't help but squirm.

"It's probably time for you to come around," he said. The voice was familiar.

She jerked and struggled and managed to sit up. "My arms are killing me," she said. "Who are you?"

"I think you know."

The sudden movement made her nauseous and she was afraid she would vomit. "I'm sick," she mumbled as acid filled her mouth.

"Lean forward and puke all you want."

She swallowed hard and quick and choked it back. The heavy breathing made her sweat. "I need some air, please. I'm suffocating."

"That's one of my favorite words."

He stepped over, leaned down to her face, and yanked off the hood. Jeri gawked at the pale mask with the pockmarks and scars, and screamed. Then she gagged and retched and vomited on the floor. When she finished, he gently reached behind her and unlocked the handcuffs. She pulled her hands free and shook her arms as if to get the blood moving. "Thanks, asshole," she said.

He walked to the fireplace, to a stack of office files, which he slowly tossed one by one into the flames.

"Can I have some water?" she asked.

He nodded to a bottle next to a lamp. She grabbed it and took a drink, trying not to look at him. He ignored her as he burned the files.

The room was dark, shades pulled down, quilts over the two windows, not a shred of sunlight anywhere. The ceiling was low, the walls were perfect logs with white plaster between them. On a coffee table there was a coil of nylon rope, yards of it, blue and white in color, with two strands cut off, all on display for her to gawk at.

"Where are we?" she asked.

"And you think I'll answer that?"

"No. Take the mask off, Bannick. I know who you are. I recognize your voice."

"Have we met?"

"No, thank God, not until now. I saw you on-stage, **Death of a Salesman.**"

"How long have you stalked me?"

"Twenty years."

"How did you find me?"

"How did you find me?"

"You made some stupid mistakes."

"So did you. My ankles and legs are numb."

"Too bad. You're lucky to be alive."

"So are you. I thought about killing you years ago."

He was amused by this and sat on the stool in front of her. She couldn't bear to look at his mask and instead stared at the fire. Her breathing was still heavy and her heart felt like a jackhammer. Had she not been so terrified she would have cursed herself for being stupid enough to get caught by the man she had hated for decades. She needed to vomit again.

"Why didn't you kill me?" he asked.

"Because you're not worth prison and I'm not a killer."

"It's an art, when done properly."

"You should know."

"Oh, I do."

"Am I next?"

"I don't know." He slowly stood, peeled off the mask, and tossed it in the fire, then added some more office files to it. He returned to the stool in front of her, their knees almost touching.

"Why haven't you killed me yet, Bannick? I would be, what, number nine, ten, eleven?"

"At least. Why should I tell you?"

"So I missed a couple." A wave rolled through her and she grimaced as she choked it down. She closed her eyes to avoid his stare.

He walked back to the stack of files on the firewood rack, took several, and slowly tossed them into the flames. She wanted to ask what he was burning but it didn't concern her. Nothing mattered but staying alive, though that looked doubtful. Her thoughts flashed to Denise, the only person on the planet who would miss her.

He returned to the stool and stared at her. "I have a couple of choices, Ms. Crosby—"

"Oh, please, don't show me any respect. I don't want yours. Let's stick with Jeri and Bannick, okay?"

"The more you talk the better your chances, because I want to know what you know, and, more importantly, I want to know what the cops know. I can leave, Jeri, vanish into thin air and never be seen again. How much have you told Lacy Stoltz?"

"Leave her out of it."

"Oh really? That's an odd thing to say. You went to her with your complaint, mentioned Verno, Dunwoody, and Kronke, hinted at others, got her involved in whatever the hell she's doing, and now you say leave her out of it. Not only that, you sent me an anonymous letter with the news that she was formally investigating me for the murders. One of your mistakes, Jeri. You knew she would have no choice but to go to the police, something you were afraid of doing. Why were you afraid of the police?"

"Maybe I don't trust the police."

"That's smart. So you dump me on Lacy because she has no choice but to investigate the judiciary. You knew she would go to the cops. You hid behind her, and now you want me to leave her alone. Right?"

"I don't know."

"How much does Lacy know?"

"How am I supposed to know? She's in charge of her own investigation."

"So what did you tell her, or I guess the question is—how much do you know?"

"Why does it matter? You'll kill me anyway. Guess what, Bannick? I caught you."

He didn't respond but returned to the files, took several, and methodically tossed them onto the fire, waiting for one to enflame before adding the next. The room was warm and smelled of smoke. The only light came from the fireplace, and shadows darkened the walls and whatever was behind her. He walked away and returned with a cup and asked, "Would you like some coffee?"

"No. Look, my ankles are breaking and my legs are numb. Cut me some slack here so we can talk, okay?"

"No. And just so you'll know, there's only one door over there and it's locked. This little cabin is deep in the woods, far from anyone else, so if you feel like it you can scream until you're hoarse. If you manage to get outside, good luck. Watch out for rattlesnakes, copperheads, bears, and coyotes, not to mention some heavily armed Bubbas who don't care for people of color."

"And I'm supposed to feel safer in here with you?"

"You have no phone, wallet, money, or shoes. I left your pistol in your hotel room, but I have two hidden just over there. I prefer not to use them."

"Please don't."

"How much does Lacy know?"

Jeri stared at the fire and tried to think clearly. If she told the truth, she might endanger Lacy. But, if she told the truth and convinced him that Lacy, and now the FBI, knew everything, he might indeed disappear. He had the means, the money, the contacts, the brains to vanish.

He asked slowly, "How much does Lacy know?"

"She knows what I've told her about Verno, Dunwoody, and Kronke. Beyond that, I have no idea."

"That's a lie. You obviously know about your own father, Eileen, Danny Cleveland. And you expect me to believe you haven't told Lacy."

"I can't prove them."

"You can't prove anything. Nobody can!"

He reached and grabbed one strand of rope and quickly looped it around her neck. He held both ends with his hands and applied a little pressure. Jeri recoiled but couldn't get away. He was practically on top of her, his face two feet from hers.

He hissed, "Listen to me. I want them in order, one name after the other, beginning with your father."

"Please get off me."

He pulled tighter. "Don't make me."

"Okay, okay. My father was not the first, was he?"

"No."

"Thad Leawood was the first, then my father." She closed her eyes and began sobbing, loud, anguished, uncontrolled. He backed away and let the rope dangle from her neck. She buried her face in her hands and bawled until she finally caught her breath. "I hate you," she mumbled. "You have no idea."

"Who was next?"

She wiped her face with her forearm and closed her eyes. "Ashley Barasso, 1996."

"I didn't kill Ashley."

"That's hard to believe. Same rope, same knot, the double clove hitch you probably learned in scouts, right Bannick? Did Thad Leawood teach you the double clove hitch?"

"I didn't kill Ashley."

"I'm in no position to argue with you."

"And you missed one."

"Good."

He stood and walked to the fireplace where he tossed in some more files. When he turned his back, she yanked the rope off her neck and flung it across the room. He picked it up and returned to the stool in front of her, fiddling with the rope.

"Go on," he said. "Who was next?"

"Who did I miss?"

"Why should I tell you?"

"Good point. I don't care anymore, Bannick."

"Go on."

"Eileen Nickleberry, 1998."

"How'd you find her?"

"By digging through your past, same for all of them. A victim is found strangled with the same rope, tied tight with a weird knot, and eventually the information gets into the FBI clearinghouse on violent crime. I know how to access it. I have some contacts. I've done it for twenty years,

Bannick, and I've learned a lot. With a name, I start the research, most of which leads to dead ends. But persistence pays off."

"I can't believe you found me."

"Am I talking enough?"

"Go on. Next?"

"You took off a few years, a little hiatus, not unusual in your sick world, and tried to go straight. Couldn't do it. Danny Cleveland was found strangled in his home in Little Rock in 2009."

"He had it coming."

"Of course he did. Exposing corruption by good reporting should always be a capital offense. Got him. Another notch in the old belt."

"Go on. Next."

"Two years ago, Perry Kronke was found dead in his boat, roasting in the hot summer sun, blood everywhere. He pissed you off when you were twenty-four and he didn't offer you a job, like every other summer clerk. Another capital offense."

"You missed another."

"Forgive me."

"Go on."

"Verno and Dunwoody last year in Biloxi. Verno beat you in court when you were a hot-shot young lawyer, so of course he deserved to die. Dunwoody showed up at the wrong time. No remorse for his family? Wife, three kids, three grandkids, a wonderful man with lots of friends. Nothing whatsoever, Bannick?"

"Anybody else?"

"Well, that story in the **Ledger** included Mal Schnetzer, rather recent vintage. Killed only a week ago somewhere near Houston. Seems as though your paths crossed, same as all your victims. I haven't had time to look at the Schnetzer murder. You're killing so fast these days that I can't keep up." She paused and looked at him. He was listening to her, as if amused.

Keep talking, she told herself. "Why is it, Bannick, that serial killers often get busy at the end? Do you read about them, the others? Are you ever curious about how they operate? Ever pick up pointers or strategies from their stories, most written after they're caught or dead, I might add. Well, I've read them all, and often, but certainly not always because God knows there's no real method to this madness, they feel trapped and lash out by speeding up. Kronke, then Verno and Dunwoody, now Schnetzer. That's four in just two years."

"Just three in my book."

"Of course. Dunwoody doesn't count because he never insulted you, or pulled a gun, or embarrassed you in class."

"Shut up."

"You told me to keep talking."

"Now I'm telling you to shut up."

"I don't want to, Bannick. I've lived in your miserable life for so long and I never dreamed I would one day be able to have a chat like this and tell you what a miserable scumbag I think you are. You're a coward. Your crimes took no courage."

"You said that in one of your silly poems."

"I thought they were rather clever."

"And quite stupid. Why did you bother with them?"

"Good question, Bannick. Not sure I have the answer. I just wanted to lash out myself, I guess. Maybe as a way to torment you. I want you to suffer. And now that the end is near I can't believe that it's you who's on the run, hiding here in the woods, planning to kill one last time. Your game is over, Bannick; so is your life. Why don't you surrender like a man and take your punishment?"

"I said shut up."

"There are so many things I want to say."

"Don't say them. I'm tired of your voice. If you want to talk next week, then shut up now."

He abruptly stood, walked to her, sat on the stool, again with their knees almost touching. She pulled back as far as possible, certain he was about to strike. He reached for his pocket and pulled out two burner phones. "I'm going to get Lacy. I want her here with you. We'll have us a nice long conversation and I'll find out how much she knows."

"Leave her alone. She's done nothing but her job."

"Oh really? She's called in the FBI."

"Leave her alone. Blame me, not her. She had never heard of you until I entered her life."

He showed her both phones and said, "These

are yours. Not sure which one will work, but I want you to call Lacy and arrange a meeting. Tell her you have a piece of evidence that will prove beyond all doubt that I'm the killer, but you can't discuss it over the phone. It's urgent and she must meet with you now."

"Just go ahead and kill me."

"Listen to me, you stupid woman. I'm not going to kill you, not now anyway, maybe never. I want Lacy here. We'll talk, and once I know everything there's a good chance I'll simply disappear, go to some exotic village by the sea or in the mountains, someplace where no one speaks English. They'll never find me. I've already been there, you know? It's all planned."

She breathed deeply as her heart raced.

"Which phone?" he asked.

She took one of them without looking at it. From nowhere, he produced a pistol, a rather large one, and set it beside him on the stool. "You tell her to meet you at the Bayview Motel near Crestview, just off the interstate. Has she ever seen your car?"

"Yes."

"Good. It's still there in the parking lot. Tell her to park beside it. Your room was 232. I've reserved it for another night, in the same name of Margie Frazier, so when she checks she'll see you're staying there. I told the manager not to clean the room. Maybe your stuff is still there."

"I don't care."

"Do you care about your 9 millimeter? It was on the nightstand."

"I wish I'd grabbed it in time."

"So do I."

There was a long pause as she stared at the fire and he stared at the floor. Slowly, he picked up the gun but did not point it at her. "Make the call. You will meet her tonight at nine at the Bayview Motel. And sell it, okay?"

"I'm not a very good liar."

"Bullshit. You're a gifted liar, just a lousy poet."

"Promise me you won't hurt her."

"No promises, except that if I return here without Lacy, I'll use this." He grabbed a strand of rope and tossed it on her. She shrieked and tried to slap it away.

37

The game began at nine, an awful hour to expect ten-year-old boys to be in uniform, properly stretched, warmed-up, and ready to play. The Royals took the field in the top of the first, and a handful of parents clapped politely from the bleachers. A few shouted words of encouragement that the players didn't hear. The coaches clapped their hands and tried to create excitement.

Diana Zhang sat alone in a lawn chair on the first-base side, a quilt tucked over her legs, a tall coffee in hand. The morning air was crisp and surprisingly cool for late April in the Panhandle. Across the way, down the third-base line, her ex-husband leaned on the fence and watched their child jog out to center field. Their divorce was too recent for any effort at civility.

From behind her, a female voice said quietly, "Excuse me, Ms. Zhang."

She glanced to her right and confronted an officious-looking badge in a black leather wallet. A woman held it and said, "Agent Agnes Neff, FBI. Got a minute for a quick word?"

Startled, like anyone would be, Diana said, "Well, I was planning to watch my son play."

"So are we. Let's just move down the fence line there and have a word. Won't take ten minutes."

Diana stood and looked at the bleachers to make sure no one was watching. She turned around and saw what could only be another agent. He led the way and they stopped near the foul pole.

Neff said, "This is Special Agent Drew Suarez."

She shot him a look of irritation and he nodded in return.

Neff continued, "We'll be brief. We're looking for your boss and can't find him. Any idea where Judge Bannick might be right now?"

"Well, uh, no. I assume he's at home on a Saturday morning."

"He's not."

"Well, then, I don't know. What's going on?"

"When did you last see him?"

"He stopped by the office Thursday morning, two days ago. Haven't talked to him since."

"We understand he's undergoing treatment."

"He is. Cancer. Is he in trouble or something?"

"No, not at all. We just have some routine questions regarding allegations from another investigation."

That was vague enough to mean nothing, cop-speak at its best, but Diana decided this was no time to push. She nodded as if she understood completely. Neff said, "So, no idea where he might be?"

"I'm sure you've checked the courthouse. He has a key and comes and goes at all hours."

"We're watching it. He's not there. He's not at home. Any idea where else he might be?"

Diana watched the game for a few seconds, not sure how much to say. "He has a bungalow at Seaside, though he rarely goes there."

"We're watching it too. He's not there."

"Okay. You say he's not in trouble, so why are you watching everywhere?"

"We need to talk to him."

"Obviously."

Suarez took a step closer, gave her a hard look, and said, "Ms. Zhang, you are talking to the FBI. May I remind you it's against the law to be untruthful?"

"Are you calling me a liar?"

"No."

Neff shook her head. No. She said, "It's important that we find him as soon as possible."

Diana glared at Suarez, then looked at Neff. "There's a chance he went back to Santa Fe. He's undergoing treatment there for colon cancer. Look, he's very private and makes his own travel arrangements. He's taken leave and he doesn't discuss things with anyone." She looked at Suarez and said plainly, "Honestly. I have no idea where he is."

Neff said, "He's booked no flights in the past forty-eight hours."

"As I said, I don't handle his travel."

"Do you know the name of the treatment center in Santa Fe?"

"No."

Neff and Suarez looked at each other and nodded as if they believed her. Neff said, "I'd like to keep this conversation between us, okay, off the record."

Suarez chimed in with, "In other words, don't mention it to the judge should you hear from him. Okay?"

"Sure."

"If you tell him about us you might be held for aiding and abetting."

"I thought you said he's done nothing wrong."

"Not yet. Just keep it quiet."

"Got it."

She knew only that Allie was somewhere in the Caribbean, watching, stalking, intercepting. He had let it slip that it was a joint effort with the DEA. Something big was happening, but then she'd heard that for almost three years now. All that mattered was his safety, but he had been gone for eight days with hardly a word. She was growing tired of his job, as was he, and she couldn't imagine being married to a man who was constantly disappearing. Their summit was growing closer, weeks now instead of months. The big conversation in which nothing would be held back. Complicated, yet simple. Either we commit ourselves to each other and a different future, or we call it quits and stop wasting time.

She was in pain, stretching in some form of mixed yoga and physical therapy, a thirty-minute routine she was supposed to check off twice a day, when the phone rang at 10:04. Probably Jeri, looking for an update.

Instead, it was the not too pleasant voice of Clay Vidovich, her new pal from yesterday at the FBI meeting in Pensacola. Sorry to bother on a Saturday morning, he went on, but didn't really seem concerned with the interruption.

"We can't find this guy, Lacy," he said. "You have any ideas?"

"Well, no, Mr. Vidovich—"

"It's Clay, okay? I thought we dropped the formalities yesterday."

"Right, Clay. I don't know this guy, never met him, so I have no idea where he hangs out. Sorry."

"Does he know you're involved, that BJC is investigating?"

"We haven't contacted him directly, we're not

required to until after our initial assessment, but he probably knows about us."

"How would he?"

"Well, Betty Roe, our source, believes Bannick can see around corners and hears everything. So far, she's been right most of the time. Anytime you investigate a judge, the gossip seems to leak out. People love to talk, especially lawyers and court clerks. So, yes, there's a decent chance Bannick knows we're investigating."

"But he would not know that you've gone to the state police and the FBI."

"Clay, I have no idea what Bannick knows."

"Good point. Look, I'm not trying to ruin your Saturday morning or anything, but are you somewhere safe?"

Lacy looked around her condo. Looked at her dog. Looked at her front door, certain that it was locked. "Sure. I'm at home. Why?"

"Are you alone?"

"Now you're prying."

"Okay, I'm prying. But I'd be remiss if I didn't say that we'd feel better if you were not alone, at least until we find him."

"You're serious?"

"Dead serious, Lacy. This guy, a sitting judge, has simply vanished in the past thirty-six hours. He could be anywhere, and he could be dangerous. We'll find him, but until then I think you should take precautions."

"I'll be okay."

"Sure you will. Please call if you hear anything."

"Will do."

She stared at her phone as she walked to the door and checked the lock. It was a gorgeous spring morning, cool with no clouds, and she had planned to shop at her favorite nursery and plant some azaleas in her flower beds. She scolded herself for being frightened on such a perfect day.

Allie was off playing cop. Darren had taken a new girlfriend to the beach for a getaway. She walked around the condo, checking doors and windows, still scolding. To relax, she lowered herself to her yoga mat and folded into a child's pose. After two deep breaths, her phone buzzed again, startling her. Why was she so jumpy?

It was the third man in her life, and she was not unhappy to hear Gunther's voice. He apologized for missing her weekly call the previous Tuesday; of course it was all because of a critical development meeting with his new team of architects.

She stretched out on the sofa and they chatted for a long time. Both admitted to being bored. Gunther's current girl, if indeed he had a serious one, was away too. Once he realized that Lacy had nothing planned for the afternoon, he was even more animated and finally mentioned lunch.

It had been only two weeks since their last one, and the fact that he was so eager to fly down again this soon was disheartening. More than likely, he was one step away from the bankers and they were closing in fast.

He said, "I'm an hour from the airport and the flight takes about eighty minutes. Wanna say two p.m.?"

"Sure."

As troublesome as he was, it would be comforting to have him around, at least for the next twenty-four hours. She would convince him to stay for dinner, then sleep over, and at some point they would have no choice but to talk about her lawsuit.

It might be a relief to get that conversation out of the way.

38

The first two calls went unanswered, which was not unusual, especially on a Saturday. He nodded, said try again.

"Could you please put the gun down?" she asked.

"No."

He just sat there, five feet away, his back to the fire, with the thirty-inch section of nylon rope draped around his collar and falling harmlessly to his chest. "Try again."

She had lost all feeling in her ankles and feet, and maybe that was a good thing. They were numb, so if they were broken the pain could not be felt. But the numbness was radiating up her legs and she felt paralyzed. She had asked to use the restroom. He said no. She had not moved in hours, and had no idea of the time.

On the third call, Lacy answered.

"Lacy, hi, it's Jeri, how are you dear?" she sang as cheerily as humanly possible with a six-inch barrel watching every move. He raised the gun a few inches.

They went back and forth with the weather, the beautiful spring day, then got down to business with the FBI's futile search for Bannick.

"They'll never find him," Jeri said, staring into Bannick's soulless eyes.

She closed her own and launched into the fiction: an anonymous informant had given her clear physical proof that would nail Bannick. She couldn't discuss it on the phone—they needed to meet and it was urgent. She was hiding in a motel two hours away and she didn't care what was planned for the evening. Cancel it.

She said, "My car is in the lot on the south side of the motel. Park next to it, I'll be watching. And Lacy, please come alone. Is that possible?"

"Sure—there's no danger, right?"

"No more than usual."

The conversation was brief, and when she hung up Bannick actually smiled. "See, you are a gifted liar."

She handed him the burner and said, "Please, give me the dignity of going to the bathroom."

He put away the gun and the phone and reached to unlock her ankle chains and cuffs. He tried to help her stand but she pushed him away, her first contact made in anger. "Just give me a minute, okay?"

She stood for a moment as the blood rushed to her feet and lower legs, and the pain returned in hot bolts. He handed her a walking cane, which she took to steady herself. She was tempted to crack him with it, to strike at least one blow for all the victims, but she wasn't balanced enough. Besides, he would easily subdue her and the aftermath wouldn't be pretty. She shuffled into a small bedroom where he waited, with the pistol, as she managed to lock the door to a closet-style bathroom with no tub or shower. And no window. The dim light barely worked. She relieved herself and sat on the toilet for a long time, so content to be locked away from him.

Content? She was a dead woman and she knew it. Now, what had she done to Lacy?

She flushed again, though it wasn't necessary. Anything to stall. He finally tapped on the door and said, "Let's go. Time's up."

In the bedroom, he nodded at the bed and said, "You can rest in here. I'll be right in there. That window is locked and it won't open anyway. Do anything stupid and you know what will happen."

She almost thanked him, but caught herself and stretched out on the bed. It was the perfect time and place for a sexual assault, but she wasn't worried. Evidently, it never crossed his mind.

Though the cabin was warm, she pulled a dusty blanket over herself anyway and was soon sleepy. It was the fatigue, the fear, and probably the remnants of his drugs still racing through her body.

When she was asleep, he popped a benny and tried to stay awake.

Always eager to show off for a pretty girl, even for his sister, Gunther had the idea of flying off to lunch and dining on great seafood. He claimed that all small aircraft pilots in that part of the world were familiar with Beau Willie's Oysters on a bayou near Houma, Louisiana. A 4,000-foot airstrip was surrounded by water on three sides and made for white-knuckle landings. Once on the ground, the restaurant was a ten-minute walk. During the day, most of the customers were pilots out looking for fun and good food.

When they landed and got out of the plane, Lacy checked her phone. Jeri had called twice. Seconds later, she called again and they chatted as she followed her brother to Beau Willie's. Though the call was somewhat mysterious, the news was breathtaking. Clear proof that would nail Bannick.

Her appetite vanished but she managed to choke down half a dozen raw oysters as she watched Gunther gorge on a dozen for starters and then attack a fried oyster po'boy. They talked about Aunt Trudy and got that out of the way. He quizzed her about any news on the Allie front and again

THE JUDGE'S LIST   395

offered too much advice. It was time for her to find a husband and start a family and forget the notion of going through life alone. She reminded him that he was perhaps the last person she would listen to when the subject was long-term commitments. That was always good for a laugh and Gunther was a sport about it. She asked about his current flame and he seemed as disinterested as he'd been two weeks earlier.

"Got a question," she said as she sipped iced tea. Gunther had toyed with the idea of a cold beer, even said he had never eaten oysters without one, but he was, after all, flying an airplane.

"Anything."

"I just got a call that sort of changes my plans. There's a town called Crestview about an hour east of Pensacola, population twenty thousand. I need to meet an important witness there at nine tonight. Would it be possible to land there and rent a car?"

"Probably. Any town of that size will have an airport. What's going on?"

"It's big." She glanced around. They were on a deck at the edge of the water and the other tables were empty. It was almost 5:00 p.m., on a Saturday, too late for lunch and too early for dinner. The bar was crowded with locals drinking beer.

"Last time I mentioned that we're investigating a judge who might be involved in a murder."

"Sure. Not one of your run-of-the-mill cases."

"Hardly. Well, the call came from our star witness and she says she has some important information. I need to see her."

"In Crestview?"

"Yes. It's on the way home. Could we stop there?"

"I guess I'm not going back to Atlanta tonight."

"Please. It would be a big favor, plus I'd like to have someone with me."

Gunther pulled out his smartphone and went online. "No problem. They say they have rentals. This could be dangerous?"

"I doubt it. But a little caution might be in order."

"I love it."

"And this is strictly confidential, Gunther."

He laughed and looked around. "And who might I tell?"

"Just keep it between us."

He stood in the dark room beside her bed and listened to her heavy breathing. His instincts told him to take the rope dangling from his left hand and finish her off. It would be the easiest one of all. He could do it quickly, effortlessly, then wipe down the cabin and drive away. It would be days before she was found.

On the one hand, he hated her for what she had done to him. She had brought down his world and his life would never be the same. She and she alone had stalked him, tracked him, and now his game was over. But on the other hand, he couldn't help but admire her pluck, brains, and doggedness. This woman had done better work than a hundred cops in several states, and now he was on the run.

He tossed the rope onto the bed, took a microfiber cloth wet with ether, and held it onto her face. As she jerked, he clasped one arm around her neck and held the cloth as tightly as possible with his hand. She fought and kicked but was no match. A minute passed and she began to go limp. When she was still, he released his grip and put away the cloth. Slowly, methodically, he took a hypodermic needle and poked it into her arm. Five hundred milligrams of ketamine, enough to keep her out several hours. He toyed with the idea of another dose, but it was risky. Too much and she might never wake up. If he had to kill her, he preferred doing it the proper way.

He walked into the other room, tossed some more files onto the fire, picked up the handcuffs and ankle chains, and took them to the bed where he pinned her wrists tightly behind her back and locked the cuffs. He secured her ankles with the chains, and for fun wrapped the nylon rope lightly around her neck. As always, he was wearing plastic gloves, but for good measure he wiped down the surfaces anyway. He checked the windows, again, and could not open them. It was an old cabin, and in bad repair, and the windows had been locked by dried paint and disuse. He burned the last of the files, and when he was certain the fire was safe he locked the cabin's only door, stepped onto the porch, and checked his watch. 7:10. He was about an hour north of Crestview, near Gantt Lake, in Alabama.

The dirt trail wound through the woods with only an occasional glimpse of the lake. It passed a drive here and there but the other cabins were not visible. He turned onto a gravel road and waved at two scruffy teenagers on ATVs. They stopped to watch him go by.

He preferred not to be seen by anyone and debated returning to the cabin, just to make sure the kids were not curious. He let it pass, called it paranoia. The gravel eventually yielded to a paved county road and he was soon on a state highway, headed south.

39

It was dark when Lacy spotted the white Camry in the motel's lot. As instructed by Jeri, she parked her rental next to it and got out. Gunther did not.

She entered the lobby a few minutes early and loitered in the gift shop looking at postcards for sale. At 9:01, Gunther entered from a side door and said hello to the receptionist. Lacy took the elevator to the second floor. Gunther took the stairs. The hallway was short, about ten rooms on each side, and a red EXIT sign glowed at the far end. She stopped at the door to room 232 and took a deep breath. She knocked three times, and at that moment all the lights went out.

Across the hall, Bannick used his laptop to turn off the lights and security cameras. He tossed it on the bed, grabbed a cloth with ether, and opened his door. Lacy heard him and turned around just as he lunged for her in the darkness. She managed to yell, "Hey!" before her brother charged from nowhere in the pitch blackness and bulled over them. All three fell into a pile. Lacy screamed and scrambled to her feet while Bannick flailed away at his attacker. He landed a kick somewhere near his ribs and Gunther grunted. Both men punched and grappled violently at each other as Lacy ran to the end of the hall, screaming. Someone opened a door and yelled, "Hey, what's going on!"

"Call the police!" Lacy said.

Bannick landed a kick in the face and Gunther was stunned. He crawled away, grabbing at anything, finding nothing. Bannick ducked into his room, got his laptop, and disappeared toward the exit.

Lacy and Gunther found the stairs and hustled down one flight to the dark lobby. The receptionist had a flashlight and was saying to some guests, "I don't know, I don't know. Same thing happened last night."

"Call the police," Lacy said. "We were attacked on the second floor."

"Who attacked you?"

That's a long story, Lacy thought, but said, "Hell if I know. Hurry, he's getting away." More flashlights appeared from behind the desk as more guests stumbled down in the dark.

Gunther found a chair and took a seat to nurse his wounds. "Son of a bitch can kick like a mule," he said, still dazed. "I think my ribs are broken." Lacy sat next to him as things settled down and they waited for the police. She said, "I have to call Jeri. I think she's in trouble."

"Who's Jeri?"

"Betty Roe. Our girl. The source. I'll explain later."

Jeri did not answer her phone, which was not at all unusual. Lacy scrolled through her recent calls and punched the number for Clay Vidovich. He answered after the second ring and she told him where she was, what had happened, and said she was certain they had been set up by Ross Bannick. She could not positively identify him but everything added up. He was in the process of fleeing the area. No, she did not see what he was driving. Vidovich was having dinner with his team in downtown Pensacola, an hour away. He would notify the Florida state police and get the authorities in Mobile to check on Jeri. Lacy was certain they would not find her there. Vidovich was headed her way and told Lacy to inform the motel not to touch the two rooms.

Moments later, the local police arrived with blue lights flashing. They found the lobby in chaos as guests milled about in the semidarkness. The motel's lighting smart panel and security grid had been hacked and no one on the skeletal staff knew what to do. Lacy explained as much as she could and gave a general description of Bannick. No, she had no idea what he was driving. They, too, called the state police, but with no description of the vehicle they were not sure where to begin.

A clerk appeared with two small bags of ice, one for Gunther's ribs, the other for his jaw, which was swollen but probably not broken. He was still a bit groggy and breathing was painful, but he refused to complain and wanted to get back to his airplane. A janitor rigged up a portable gas generator and, suddenly, the lobby was lit. There was not enough voltage for air-conditioning and the temperature rose fast. Several of the guests spilled into the parking lot and loitered around their vehicles.

He fought the urge to race down the state highway and kept his speed close to the limit. Overreacting would only cause more trouble, and he willed himself to drive reasonably while he thought through what had just happened. He had been ambushed for the first time in his career and he was certain he'd made mistakes. But he still wore plastic gloves and knew he'd left behind no prints, no evidence. He had entered the room with only a smartphone and a laptop and both were now at the bottom of a pond outside of Crestview.

His right shoulder ached from the fight, or whatever it could be called. He never saw the man, never heard him coming. He had his hands on Lacy for only a second before being tackled and knocked down. Then she started screaming.

It was probably Darren Trope, her colleague. Son of a bitch.

He soon crossed into Alabama, took a detour, and drove through the Conecuh National Forest. As he approached the town of Andalusia, population 9,000, he decided to circle around it. It was almost ten thirty on a Saturday night and the cops would be out in force. He didn't need a GPS because he had memorized the highways and roads. He saw the signs for Gantt Lake and zigzagged his way in its direction. He drove through the quiet village of Antioch without seeing another human, and the roads narrowed. Less than two miles from his next turn onto a gravel road, he was shocked to see blue lights bearing down from behind. His speedometer was at fifty, the limit, and he knew he had not been speeding. There were no traffic lights to run through. He slowed even more and gawked at the county patrol car as it flew past. Saturday night, probably a brawl in a honky-tonk. The blue lights disappeared in front of him.

He would kill her quickly and be on his way. The cabin was clean, no clues as always. He would decorate the job with a perfect knot, only fitting since she was so curious about it.

The gravel road ran deeper into the woods, into the darkness where the cabin waited. Suddenly there were more blue lights, another county boy hot on his trail. He slowed almost to a stop and got out of the way. The car slid past, missing his by inches, a boiling cloud of dust in its wake. Something wasn't right.

He turned onto the dirt trail that ended at the cabin's front door, so deep in the woods it could not be seen by anyone passing by. He saw a clearing with a gap in the fence and pulled off the road. He backed into some undergrowth, got out, and jogged toward the cabin. Around a bend, he saw a terrible sight. The cabin was a scene, with cops and blue lights everywhere.

The two boys, ages fifteen and sixteen, had arrived on ATVs before dark. They noticed the smoke from the chimney and knew someone was there for the weekend, but the silver Tahoe had just left. They watched the cabin, watched the road, and waited until long after dark before kicking in the front door. They were looking for guns, fishing gear, anything of value. They found nothing but a dead black woman lying on the bed, her wrists cuffed behind her, her ankles chained together.

They panicked, fled, and didn't stop until they

wheeled into a country store, closed for the evening. They called 911 from a pay phone and reported a dead woman in the old Sutton cabin off Crab Hill Road. When the dispatcher asked their names, they hung up and hurried home.

Jeri was taken by ambulance to a regional hospital in Enterprise, Alabama. She was awake, severely nauseated, dehydrated, and still not lucid, but recovering quickly. At midnight, she was talking to the state police and filling in the gaps. She had been drugged so much by Bannick that she had not seen his vehicle, so there was no description. A quick search, though, gave the police his make, model, and license plates.

At 1:00 a.m., a detective called Lacy's number. She was at home in Tallahassee, safe, and tending to her brother, who had been X-rayed and given painkillers. The detective smiled, handed his phone to Jeri, and when they heard each other's voices, they burst into tears.

By then he was cruising into Birmingham, with fake Texas tags on his Tahoe. He parked in the long-term lot at the international airport and, carrying his overnight bag, entered the main terminal. He sipped an espresso at a coffee bar and killed time. He found a row of seats with a view of the runways and tried to nap, just another weary traveler. When the Avis counter opened at six, he ambled over and chatted with the clerk. Using a fake driver's license and a prepaid credit card issued to an alias, he rented a Honda, one with California tags, and left the airport, headed west. Far west. For the next twenty hours he would drive virtually nonstop, pay cash for gas, pop bennies, and slug endless cups of black coffee.

40

At seven thirty Sunday morning two teams of FBI agents and technicians, backed up by locals, crashed into Bannick's world. The first entered his home with a crowbar and disarmed his security systems, but not before arousing the neighbors. The second entered the Chavez County Courthouse, with the assistance of Diana Zhang and a janitor, and began combing through his desk, file cabinets, bookshelves, anything he might have touched. They quickly realized the file cabinets were empty, as were his desk drawers. Diana was surprised to see so many of his personal items missing. Framed photos and awards and certificates, letter openers, pens, writing pads, paperweights. She went to her desk to look for files he had dealt with, and found the drawers empty. His desktop computer could not be accessed and its hard drive was missing. It was taken to a van to be shipped to a lab.

In his home, the technicians found a refrigerator that was virtually empty, as were all garbage cans. Piles of clothing and towels had been washed and tossed on the bed. In the small office, they found no phones or laptops. This desktop, too, could not be accessed and was hauled out. Its hard drive was gone.

The searches would take hours if not days, but it was soon apparent that his home and his office in the courthouse had been thoroughly wiped. After two hours of powdering the obvious surfaces, not a single latent print had been identified. But the technicians labored on, methodically, and confident that they would find prints. It was impossible to live and work in an area for years and not leave something behind.

Jeri was discharged at noon. She was still suffering from nausea and couldn't eat, but there was nothing else the doctors could do but ply her with meds. Her head ached and the ibuprofen did little to ease the throbbing. Her wrists and ankles were numb but slowly growing more sensitive. She had talked to Denise twice and assured her that she was safe and healthy and there was no need for her to rush down. She set off with two escorts, both young and rather cute FBI agents, one the driver, the other in the back seat doing most of the talking. However, she was not in a glib mood and after a few miles they left her alone. She stared through the passenger window, reliving the past forty-eight hours, still in disbelief that she was alive.

And Bannick had not been found. She had believed for a long time that the man was capable of anything, especially moving in the shadows without being detected. He had boasted of vanishing to some faraway place. As the miles clicked by and the hours passed, a horrible reality began to consume her. What if he walked away? And was never brought to justice? And his monstrous crimes were never solved? What if her lonely quest to find her father's killer was for nothing?

Mobile was out of the question. He had been to her home, rang her doorbell, knew exactly where she lived. He had tracked her to the motel and abducted her without being seen or leaving behind a clue. As always. She wondered if she could ever go home.

Two hours later they entered Tallahassee and were soon winding through downtown. When they stopped at the renovated warehouse, Lacy was waiting on her stoop. She and Jeri hugged and cried and eventually went inside.

Allie had returned a few hours earlier and had been debriefed by Lacy. And by Gunther, who relished his role as the hero. Lacy had little doubt that as the story was told and retold, his fearless attack of a serial killer would only be embellished and become legendary.

Lacy asked one of the agents to go fetch a pizza. The other sat by the door, guarding the place. Inside, the four lounged in the den and swapped stories. Eventually they found humor, especially when Gunther, always animated, stopped mid-sentence to clutch his ribs. His swollen jaw did not throttle his narratives.

For her own benefit, Jeri recounted her conversations with Bannick. He had not explicitly admitted to any of the murders, but had grudgingly acquiesced to parts of her narrative. He denied killing Ashley Barasso, though that seemed hardly credible. More troubling were his assertions that he had killed others that Jeri had missed.

At five, they arrived at the FBI office in the federal building. Clay Vidovich welcomed them and they settled around a table in the main conference room. The big news was that they had recovered two latent prints from Bannick's garage. The bad news was that they were not from his thumb. He was confident, though, that they would find more prints, but admitted they were taken aback by Bannick's efforts to wipe everything clean. His cell phone had stopped working in Crestview. He'd probably tossed it. No one named Ross Bannick had booked a flight in the past seventy-two hours. His secretary had not heard a word. He had no family in the area, only a sister who lived far away and had had no contact.

Nonetheless, Vidovich was certain they would

find him. A nationwide manhunt was in full swing and it was only a matter of time.

Jeri wasn't so sure but kept her thoughts to herself. When she finally relaxed, she began talking about the past two days. She was not feeling well, though, and promised a longer debriefing on Monday.

Thank God someone broke into the cabin.

41

He stopped in Amarillo long enough to leave an overnight FedEx envelope in a drop box. He was the "Sender" and used his office address at the Chavez County Courthouse. The "Recipient" was Diana Zhang at the same address. If everything went as planned, it would be picked up by five Monday afternoon and delivered to her by ten thirty Tuesday morning.

At 8:00 a.m. Monday, he parked the rental outside Pecos Mountain Lodge and took a moment to admire the beautiful mountains in the distance. The high-end rehab facility was tucked into a hillside and hardly visible from the winding county road. He changed gloves and wiped down the steering wheel, door handles, console, and media screen. He had worn gloves for the past twenty hours and knew the car was clean, but he took no chances. With his small bag, he walked inside the plush lobby and said good morning to the receptionist.

"I have an appointment with Dr. Joseph Kassabian," he said politely.

"And your name please?"

"Bannick, Ross Bannick."

"Please have a seat and I'll get him."

He sat on a sleek leather sofa and admired the contemporary art on the walls. At $50,000 a month the wealthy drunks certainly deserved pleasant surroundings. Pecos was kept busy by rock stars, Hollywood types, and jet-setters, and, in spite of being so well known, it prided itself on keeping a low profile. Its challenge with confidentiality was that so many of its former patients couldn't wait to sing its praises.

Dr. Kassabian soon appeared and they retired to his office down the hall. He was about fifty, a former addict. "Aren't we all?" he'd said on the phone. They sat at a small table and sipped designer water.

"Tell me your story," he said with a warm, welcoming smile. **Your nightmare is over. You've come to the right place.**

Bannick wiped his face with his hands and seemed ready to cry. "It's all booze, no drugs. Vodka, at least a quart a day, for many years now. I can function okay. I'm a judge and the job is demanding, but I gotta quit the stuff."

"That's a lot of vodka."

"It's never enough, and it's getting worse. That's why I'm here."

"When was your last drink?"

"Three days ago. I've always managed to quit for short periods, but I can't kick the stuff. It's killing me."

"So you probably don't need detox."

"I don't think so. I've done this before, Doctor. This is my third rehab in the past five years. I'd like to stay for a month."

"How long were your other rehabs?"

"A month."

"Thirty days won't do it, Mr. Bannick. Trust me on this. Thirty days will get you dried out and feeling great, but you need at least sixty. Ninety is our recommended stay."

I guess so. At $50,000 a month.

"Maybe. Right now I'm just praying for thirty days. Just get me sober. Please."

"We'll do that. We're very good at what we do. Trust us."

"Thank you."

"I'll introduce you to our admissions director who'll do the paperwork and such. Do you have insurance or will it be private pay?"

"Private. I have assets, Doctor."

"Even better."

"Okay. Look, I'm an elected official, so confidentiality is a prime concern. No one can know

I'm here. I'm single, no family, a few friends, but I've told no one. Not even my secretary."

Dr. Kassabian smiled because he heard it all the time. "Believe me, Mr. Bannick, we understand confidentiality. What's in the bag?"

"A few items, clothing, a toothbrush. I brought no phone, no laptop, no devices."

"Good. In about a week you can use the phone. Nothing until then."

"I know. Not my first rodeo."

"I understand. But I'll need to take the bag and inventory it. We provide nice linen gowns, Ralph Lauren, for the first two weeks."

"Sure."

"You bring a car?"

"It's a rental. I flew in."

"Okay. After the paperwork, we'll do a complete physical. That'll take most of the morning. You and I will have lunch together, just the two of us, and talk about the past, and the future. Then I'll introduce you to your counselor."

Bannick nodded as if thoroughly defeated.

Dr. Kassabian said, "I'm glad you came in sober, it's a good start. You wouldn't believe some of the poor folks who stagger in here."

"I don't feel sober, Doctor. Anything but."

"You're in the right place."

They walked next door and met the director of admissions. Bannick paid the first $10,000 with a credit card and signed a promissory note for the other $40,000. Dr. Kassabian kept his bag. When the admission was complete he was shown to his rather spacious room on the second floor. Dr. Kassabian excused himself and said he was looking forward to lunch. When Bannick was finally alone, he quickly took off his stylish nylon tactical travel belt and removed small plastic bags from its hidden pockets. The bags contained two sets of pills that would be needed later. He hid them under a chest of drawers.

A steward knocked on his door and handed him a stack of gowns and towels. He waited until Bannick undressed in the bathroom, then left with his clothing, including the belt and his shoes.

He showered, put on one of the soft linen gowns, stretched out on the bed, and fell asleep.

Lacy, Jeri, and Allie dropped Gunther off at the airport and watched him taxi out and take off. When he was in the air, they felt like celebrating. They returned to the FBI office and met with Clay Vidovich and two other agents. Jeri signed an affidavit that recited the facts of her weekend encounter with Bannick. A warrant for kidnapping was issued and circulated nationally, everywhere but the Pensacola area. They were certain Bannick was not hanging around the Panhandle and did not want to alert his friends and acquaintances.

Vidovich gave them an update on the searches of his office and home and was bothered by the fact that no more prints had been found. The FBI was searching his real estate holdings, but so far had found nothing useful.

The room began to fill as other agents joined them. All ties were loosened, all sleeves rolled up, all collars unbuttoned. As a group they gave every indication of having worked through the weekend. Lacy called Darren and told him to join them. Trays of coffee, water, and pastries were brought in by secretaries.

At ten, Vidovich called things to order and made sure the two video cameras were working. He said, "This is for informational purposes only. Since you're not a suspect, Jeri, we don't need to deal with Miranda."

"I should hope not," she said and got a laugh.

"At the outset, I want to say that we would not be here if not for you. Your detective work over the past twenty years is nothing short of brilliant. It's a miracle, actually, and I've never encountered anything like it. So, on behalf of the families, and all of law enforcement, I say thanks."

She nodded, embarrassed, and glanced at Lacy.

"He hasn't been caught yet," Jeri said.

"We'll get him."

"Soon, I hope."

"I'd like to start at the beginning. A lot of this will be repetitious, but please indulge us."

She began with the death of her father and
its aftermath, the lack of clues, the months that
dragged by with little contact with the police, and
absolutely nothing in the way of progress. And
what could possibly have been the motive. She
spent years trying to answer that question. Who in
Bryan Burke's world had ever said anything nega-
tive about him? No relatives, colleagues, maybe a
student or two. He had no business deals, no partners, no lovers, no jealous husbands along the way.
She eventually settled on Ross Bannick but knew
from the beginning that she was only guessing.
He was a long shot. She had no proof, nothing
but her hyperactive imagination. She dug through
his past, kept up with his career as a young lawyer in Pensacola, and slowly became obsessed. She
knew where he lived, worked, grew up, went to
church, and played golf on the weekends.

She stumbled across an old story in the **Ledger**
about the murder of Thad Leawood, a local who'd
moved away under suspicious circumstances. She
tied him to Bannick through Boy Scout records
obtained from the national headquarters. When
she eventually saw the crime scene photos, a big
piece of the puzzle fell into place.

She couldn't stop rubbing her wrists. She said,
"According to my research, the next one was
Ashley Barasso, in 1996. However, Bannick said,
last Saturday, that he didn't kill her."

Vidovich was shaking his head. He looked at

Agent Murray, who was also in disagreement. Murray said, "He's lying. We have the file. Same rope, same knot, same method. Plus he knew her in law school at Miami."

"That's what I told him," Jeri said.

"Why would he deny it?" Vidovich asked the table.

"I have a theory," Jeri said, sipping coffee.

Vidovich smiled and said, "I'm sure you do. Let's hear it."

"Ashley was thirty years old, his youngest victim, and she had two small kids, ages three and eighteen months. They were in the house when she was murdered. Perhaps he saw them. Maybe for once in his life he felt remorse. Maybe it's the one murder he couldn't shake off."

"Makes sense, I guess," Vidovich said. "If any of it makes sense."

"It's all rational in his sick mind. He never admitted to any of the murders, but he did say I missed a couple."

Murray shuffled some paperwork and said, "We may have found one that you missed. In 1995 a man named Preston Dill was murdered near Decatur, Alabama. The crime scene looks familiar. No witnesses, no forensics, same rope and knot. We're still digging, but it looks as though Dill once lived in the Pensacola area."

Jeri shook her head and said, "I'm glad I missed one."

Agent Neff said, "That's at least five victims who had ties to the area, though none of them lived there when they were murdered."

Vidovich said, "With the exception of Leawood, they were just passing through, lived there long enough to cross paths with our man."

Neff said, "And over a twenty-three-year period. I wonder if anyone, anyone other than you, Jeri, would have ever connected the murders."

She didn't respond and no one else ventured a guess. The answer was obvious.

42

For his last meal he dined alone. The kitchen opened at seven and he arrived a few minutes later, ordered wheat toast and scrambled eggs, poured a glass of grapefruit juice, and took his tray outside to a patio where he sat under an umbrella and watched a magnificent sunrise over the distant mountains. The morning was quiet and still. The other patients, none of whom he had made an effort to meet, were waking to another glorious, sober morning, all clear-eyed and clean.

He was at peace with his world, a serenity aided by a couple of pre-breakfast Valium tablets. He took his time and enjoyed the food. When he finished, he returned his tray and went to his room. On his door, a steward had tacked his schedule for the day. A group hike at nine, counseling at ten thirty, lunch, and so on.

He arranged his paperwork, then got down

to business. He put on plastic gloves and wiped down all surfaces in the room and bathroom. He removed the small packets of pills from under the chest of drawers, returned to the bathroom, and closed the door. He stopped the sink and ran three inches of water, then dumped in two packets of hydrochloric acid tablets. Upon touching the water, they immediately reacted with pop and fizzle and within seconds the water seemed to be boiling. From two other packets, he shook out forty tablets of oxycodone, 30 milligrams each, ate them and washed them down with water in a paper cup. He flushed the packets, the paper cup, and the gloves down the toilet. He took a small hand towel, crammed it in his mouth to muffle any anguished reactions, then plunged all eight fingers and both thumbs into the bubbling superacid. The pain was immediate and fierce. He groaned and grimaced but kept pressing as the acid burned through the first layer of skin and began corroding the second. His hands felt as though they were on fire and he began to feel weak. When his knees buckled, he grabbed the sink, unstopped it, and opened the door. He fell onto his bed, spat out the hand towel, and stuffed his hands under the sheets. The pain vanished as he lost consciousness.

—

Diana was in the reception area when the FedEx envelope arrived at 10:35. She took one look at the **Sender**'s name and address and took it to her office, closing the door behind her. For the third day in a row, their office suite was besieged by a team of brusque, even rude, FBI technicians, and she needed the privacy.

Her hands were shaking as she ripped off the tab and removed one of his office envelopes. Inside were four sheets of letter-sized paper. The first was a letter to her. It read:

> **Dear Diana. When you read this I'll be dead. Sorry to do this to you but there's no one else. Please call Dr. Joseph Kassabian at the Pecos Mountain Lodge near Santa Fe and inform him that you are my secretary, my executrix, and my sole heir. As directed in the attached Last Will and Testament, you are directed to have my body cremated immediately and my ashes scattered over the Pecos Mountains here in New Mexico. Do not, under any circumstances, have my body returned to the State of Florida, and do not permit an autopsy. Tomorrow, send the Press Release to Jane Kemper at the Pensacola Ledger. Please delay notifying the police as long as possible. Ross.**

She gasped, muffled a shriek, and dropped the papers. She was crying when she picked them up. The second sheet was a "Press Release," and it read:

Circuit Court Judge Ross Bannick died this morning at a facility near Santa Fe, New Mexico, where he was undergoing treatment for colon cancer. He was 49. Judge Bannick proudly served the people of the Twenty-Second Judicial District for the past ten years. A native of Pensacola, he resided in the town of Cullman. A graduate of the University of Florida and the University of Miami Law School, he was in private practice in Pensacola for almost fifteen years before being elected to the bench in 2004. A lifelong bachelor, he was predeceased by his parents, Dr. and Mrs. Herbert Bannick, and is survived by a sister, Ms. Katherine LaMott of Savannah, Georgia. In lieu of flowers, the family requests donations to the American Cancer Society. There will be no memorial service.

The third sheet of paper was titled: "Last Will and Testament of Ross L. Bannick." It read:

I, Ross L. Bannick, being of sound and disposing mind and memory, do hereby make and declare this to be my last will and testament, expressly revoking all

prior wills. This instrument is prepared solely by me and for all intents and purposes is to be considered my final, holographic will.

1. I appoint my faithful friend, Diana Zhang, as my executrix and direct her to probate this will as soon as possible. I waive bond and accounting.

2. I instruct my executrix to immediately have my remains cremated and my ashes scattered over the Pecos Mountains outside of Santa Fe.

3. I give, devise, and bequeath all of my assets to Diana Zhang.

4. Other than the usual monthly bills, there are no liabilities. Attached hereto is a list of assets.

Signed, Ross L. Bannick.

Stapled to the will was the fourth sheet. It listed eight bank accounts with their approximate balances; his home in Cullman, valued at $700,000; a beach bungalow worth $550,000; two shopping centers owned by corporations; and a stock portfolio valued at $240,000.

For a long time she was too stunned to move or to think clearly. Any interest in his assets was negated by the horror of the moment.

She managed to go online and found the website for the Pecos Mountain Lodge. An addiction facility? Nothing made sense. She called the number and was informed that Dr. Kassabian was not available. She would not take no for an answer and pressed on with the urgent matter. When he finally took her call, she explained who she was and so on. He confirmed the death, said it appeared to be an overdose, and could she call back later? No, she could not. He settled down and they had a conversation, one that ended with the arrival of the coroner.

She found the business card for Special Agent Neff, and called the FBI.

The lodge was a pleasant getaway where damaged people began their new lives, not a place where people went to die. Dr. Kassabian had never dealt with the death of a patient, and he wasn't sure what to do. The last thing he wanted was for such a traumatic event to rattle the other patients. In his second conversation with Ms. Zhang, she mentioned the request for cremation and explained that she had clear directions from the deceased about what to do with his remains. Common sense, though, dictated the preservation of the corpse and the room until higher authorities were on the scene. When two FBI agents from the Santa Fe office arrived, he was not happy about their presence, but he was relieved that someone else would make the next few decisions. When they informed him that Judge Bannick was wanted on kidnapping charges, he quipped, "Well, I think you're too late."

They stepped into the room and stared at Bannick.

The first agent said, "We have technicians on the way and we need to fingerprint him."

"That might be a problem." Dr. Kassabian slowly reached down, took a corner of a sheet, and pulled it back. Bannick's hands were swollen grotesquely, his fingers were black from corrosion, and his nails had melted and popped off. A rust-colored liquid stained his gown and the sheets under him.

"Looks like he knew you were coming," Dr. Kassabian said.

"Okay," said the second agent. "Don't touch anything."

"Don't worry."

43

They were finishing lunch at a downtown café when an urgent call came from Clay Vidovich. They hurried to the FBI office in the federal building and waited in the conference room. Vidovich and Agents Neff and Suarez entered in a rush and it was obvious they had news.

Without sitting, Vidovich announced, "Ross Bannick is dead. An apparent overdose at a rehab clinic near Santa Fe."

Jeri collapsed and buried her face in her hands. Lacy was too stunned to say anything.

Vidovich went on, "He checked himself in early yesterday morning and they found him dead in his room about three hours ago. Our agents there have confirmed everything."

Allie asked, "What about prints?"

"Not so sure. I just got a video from one of our agents there. Do you want to see it?"

"Of what?" Lacy asked.

"Our man in rehab. There's one part that's pretty graphic."

Jeri wiped her eyes, bit a lip, said, "I want to see it."

Agent Murray pressed some buttons on a tablet and the video began on a big screen behind Vidovich. He moved out of the way as they gawked at the image taken with a smartphone. Bannick had not been moved and was lying face-up, eyes closed, unshaven, mouth half open, a white liquid leaking from one corner, dead as a doornail. The camera moved slowly down his body and stopped at his hands, which had been placed next to each other over his crotch.

Vidovich narrated, "Probably dipped his fingers in an acid right before he died."

Allie mumbled just loud enough to be heard, "That sonofabitch."

The camera zoomed in close on the fingers and Lacy looked away.

Vidovich said, "You asked about prints. We may have a problem. The damage is obviously substantial and the wounds will not heal, not now anyway. Looks like he knew exactly what he was doing."

Lacy asked, "Can you stop it right there?"

Agent Suarez froze the video. Lacy said, "So, let's go slow here. He apparently tried to mutilate his fingers to avoid getting printed, which I assume is possible even after death."

Agent Neff said, "Yes, it happens all the time, assuming the hands and fingers are in decent shape."

"Okay. So, assuming he wanted to destroy his prints, and assuming that he had already altered them in some way—wouldn't it be reasonable to assume he knew about the partial thumb print?"

Vidovich smiled and said, "Exactly. Somehow Bannick knew we had a print."

They looked at Jeri and she shook her head. "No idea."

Allie asked, "Why would he care? If he's planning a suicide anyway, why would he worry about getting caught?"

Jeri replied, "Now you're trying to think like Bannick. He had a death wish, which is not unusual for serial killers. They can't stop what they're doing on their own volition, so they want someone else to stop them. The ruined reputation. The disgrace to the memory of his parents. The loss of everything he had worked for."

Vidovich said, "Some of the more famous killers had strong death wishes. Bundy, Gacy. It's not at all unusual."

The video ended. Jeri asked, "Could you please go back to the beginning?" Suarez pressed buttons and there was Bannick's ghostly face again. Jeri said, "Just freeze it right there. I want to see him dead. I've waited a long time."

Vidovich glanced at Lacy and Allie. After a pause, he continued. "We could have a messy situation brewing here. Evidently he left a new will and some specific instructions, wants to be cremated immediately and his ashes scattered over the mountains out there. How nice. We, of course, want to preserve the body so we can try like hell to get a thumb print. The problem is that he's not exactly in our custody. You can't arrest a corpse. Our warrant expired the moment he died. I just spoke with Legal in Washington and they're scratching their heads."

"You can't allow him to be cremated," Lacy said. "Get a court order."

"Evidently it's not that simple. Which court? Florida, New Mexico? There's no law requiring a dead person to be transported back home for a burial. This guy planned everything and ordered his executor to cremate him out there with no autopsy."

Jeri stared at the still shot of the corpse, shook her head, and said, "Even from the grave, he's disrupting our lives."

"But it's over, Jeri," Lacy said, touching her on the arm.

"It'll never be over now. Bannick will never be brought to justice. He got away with it, Lacy."

"No. He's dead and he won't kill again."

Jeri snorted and looked away. "Let's get out of here."

—

Allie dropped them off at Lacy's apartment and went to his. He had been summoned to Orlando for work but, in a rather testy conversation, had informed his supervisor that he needed a couple of days at home.

The women sat in the den and tried to absorb even more drama. What could be next? What could top the news of Bannick's death?

If there was never a match for the partial thumb print, then there would never be physical evidence linking him to the murders of Verno and Dunwoody.

As for the other murders, they had only motive and method. Convicting him with such flimsy evidence would be impossible. And, now that he was dead, no police—local, state, or federal—would waste time pursuing him. Their cases had been cold for decades anyway. Why get excited now? Jeri was certain they would welcome the news of Bannick's probable guilt, inform the families, and happily close the files.

His comments, denials, deflections, and assertions the previous Saturday in a dark cabin deep in the Alabama countryside were of little help to the police. None of what he said could ever be admitted in court, and he had been careful not to expressly admit any wrongdoing. He was, after all, a trial judge.

At times Jeri was emotional, and at times inconsolable. Her life's work had come to an abrupt and unsatisfactory end. Dead as he was, Bannick was walking away practically unscathed. The kidnapping charge, if and when it was ever reported, would only add confusion and prove nothing. The details behind it would never be made known. He had not been arrested for anything. His name would never be linked to his victims.

But there were also moments of visible relief. The monster was no longer on her trail. She would no longer inhabit the same world as Ross Bannick, a man she had loathed for so long that he had become a part of her life. She would never miss him, but how would she fill the vacancy?

She had read somewhere that we often grow to admire, even love, the very thing we so obsessively hate. It can become a part of our life, and we grow to rely on it, to need it. It defines us.

At two thirty, an FBI agent knocked on the door and informed Lacy that her little security detail had been called back to the office. The danger was now gone, the coast was clear. She thanked him and said goodbye.

Jeri asked to spend one more night. It might take some time to completely relax, and she wanted to go for a long walk, alone, through the neighborhood, the campus, and downtown. She wanted to taste the freedom of moving about without glancing around, without worrying, without even thinking of him. And when Lacy came home from the office, she, Jeri, wanted to get in the kitchen and cook dinner together. She had stopped cooking years earlier, even decades ago, when her evenings became consumed with her pursuit.

Lacy said of course. After she left, Jeri sat on the sofa and kept repeating to herself that Bannick was dead.

The world was a better place.

44

Diana Zhang had never given a thought to serving as the executrix of someone's will and estate. In fact, as the secretary to a judge, she knew enough about probate to know it should be avoided when possible. Now that she had been victimized by her former boss, and saddled with an unwanted task that gave every indication, at least initially, of being complicated and burdensome, if not impossible, she struggled to find a good attitude toward her new role.

The fourth page, the one with the list of assets, kept her in the game. She had never thought about Judge Bannick's death—he was so young—and she had certainly never thought about being included in his estate plans. Not long after the shock of his death began to wear off, she couldn't help but think about her windfall.

Frankly, she didn't care if he was cremated

or where he was buried, especially with the FBI
breathing down her neck. They asked her to hold
off on any burial plans, and everything else for
that matter. There was no hurry. He was being
iced in the county morgue far away, and if the FBI
wanted her to take things slow, then she had no
qualms with that. They had agreed not to tamper
with the body as long as she agreed to allow them
to extensively photograph the hands and fingers.

She was quoted at length in Wednesday's edition of the **Ledger.** After some glowing comments
about her old boss, she said that he had been ill
for some time but was too private to discuss his
health. The entire office was "shocked and saddened," as were his colleagues and members of the
bar. The story covered the entire bottom half of
the front page, with a fine photo of a younger
Bannick. There was no mention of the arrest warrant for kidnapping.

By noon Wednesday, the FBI had seized and
searched the SUV he left behind in the long-term
lot of the Birmingham airport, as well as the Avis
rental they tracked to Pecos Mountain Lodge. Not
surprisingly, both had been thoroughly wiped and
there were no prints. The FedEx envelope sent to
Diana was covered with prints, but none matched
the partial found on Verno's phone. The cabin
at Gantt Lake was combed through and yielded

nothing useful. Every square inch of his room at the lodge, and every surface he could have possibly touched, had been examined twice over, without success. A steward said he had seen him several times, always with gloves.

A team of the Bureau's top fingerprint experts hurried down and examined the fingers and thumbs. All were cooked and corroded to the point of being thoroughly destroyed. Since the body was to be cremated, Vidovich made the decision to remove the hands and take them to the lab. He mentioned this to Diana Zhang, who was at first horrified. However, as Vidovich leaned on her and made it plain that the hands and fingers, along with the entire body, were about to be ashes anyway, what was the harm? When she still hesitated, he threatened to haul her before a federal magistrate.

Diana was already tired of her new job. The longer he was in the morgue, the more problems he was creating. She would never see his body, with or without the hands. It was a thousand miles away and that wasn't far enough. She finally said yes to the amputations, and the hands were removed and rushed to the forensics lab in Clarksburg, West Virginia.

What was left of Judge Ross Bannick was hauled to a crematorium in Santa Fe, properly reduced to ashes, and stuffed in a plastic urn that the mortician put in storage until further orders.

—

Lacy spoke to Vidovich throughout the day and relayed the developments to Jeri, who was suddenly eager to gather her things and get home.

The FBI had searched her car and found no useful prints, but did find the GPS monitor next to the gas tank. They sent it to Clarksburg for examination.

Somehow, somewhere in the horror and chaos of the kidnapping, Bannick had taken her pistol and small carry-on bag, but had left behind her phone and laptop. She assumed he did not want to risk being tracked with her devices. He also left behind her purse and keys. He didn't need the small amount of cash, nor her credit cards, and he was driving his own vehicle, though Jeri never saw it.

The same two handsome agents who had driven her away from the hospital on Sunday now appeared in Tallahassee with her Camry and belongings. They had been ordered to follow her back to Mobile and arrange for her door locks to be changed. She said no thanks, and they reluctantly left.

After an early dinner with Lacy and Allie, Jeri hugged them both, offered her heartfelt thanks, promised to see them again soon, and left for Mobile, four hours away. As she left town, she turned the rearview mirror sideways so she wouldn't keep glancing at it. Some habits would be hard to break.

Her thoughts were scrambled and her moods swung radically. She was lucky to be alive and her sore wrists were a constant reminder of the close call. However, that episode, as terrifying as it was, had a clear end to it. Luck intervened and she escaped a certain death. She was destined to keep living, but for what purpose? She felt as though her project was incomplete, but where was the finish line? She smiled at the pleasant thought of not living in the same world with Bannick, but then she almost cursed at the reality that he got away with his murders. He would never face his victims, never be hauled into a courtroom, perhaps even his own, in an orange jumpsuit with shackles around his ankles. He would never suffer the immeasurable humiliation of seeing his mug shot on the front page, of being scorned by his friends, removed from the bench, convicted of his heinous crimes, and locked away. He would not make history as the first American judge to be convicted of murder, nor would he be remembered as a legendary serial killer. He would never rot in the prison cell he so deserved.

Without further proof of his guilt, the families of his victims would never know of his probable guilt. She knew their names, all of them. The parents and siblings of Eileen Nickleberry; the two children of Ashley Barasso, now both in their early twenties; the widow and two sons of Perry Kronke; the family of Mike Dunwoody, the only accidental victim she knew of; the children of Danny Cleveland; the families of Lanny Verno and Mal Schnetzer.

And what would she tell her own family—her older brother, Alfred, in California, and Denise at Michigan? Would she upset their worlds with the hard-to-believe story that she found the killer but he escaped justice?

Why bother? The only time they discussed the murder of Bryan Burke was when she, Jeri, brought up the subject.

She managed to lighten up by reminding herself that the case was not closed. The FBI was fully involved and they were due a break. Bannick might yet get implicated in one or more of his murders. If one could be proven, then surely the FBI could inform the local police departments, who could in turn meet with the families. Justice would remain permanently elusive, but perhaps some of the families could find closure if they knew the truth.

For Jeri, closure seemed impossible.

45

Late Thursday morning, Lacy and her task force met for the last time and were happily retiring the Bannick matter into the "Dismissal" drawer when Felicity interrupted with an urgent call. Sadelle was savoring her oxygen and Darren was debating what size latte to run and fetch.

"It's Betty Roe and she says it's important," Felicity announced through the speaker.

Lacy rolled her eyes and sighed with frustration. She had hoped that she might be able to go a few days without hearing Jeri's voice, but wasn't really surprised. Darren bolted for the door on his coffee run. Sadelle closed her eyes as if ready for another nap.

"Good morning, Betty," Lacy said.

"We can drop the Betty routine, can't we now, Lacy?"

"Sure. And how are you this morning, Jeri?"

"Marvelous. I feel fifty pounds lighter and I can't stop smiling. The fact that he's gone is such a burden off my brain and body. I can't tell you how wonderful it feels."

"That's great to hear, Jeri. It's been a long time."

"It's been a lifetime, Lacy. I've lived with that creep for decades. Anyway, though, I couldn't sleep. I was up all night because I thought of one more little adventure and I need your help. Preferably with Allie in tow."

"Allie left this morning, for parts unknown."

"Then bring Darren. I suppose he's the next available white boy."

"I guess. Bring him where?"

"To Pensacola."

"I'm listening but I'm already skeptical."

"Don't be. Trust me. Surely I've earned your trust by now."

"You have."

"Good. Please drop what you're doing and come to Pensacola."

"Okay, I'm struggling but still listening. It's not exactly right around the corner."

"I know, I know. One hour for me, three for you, but it could be crucial. It could put the final nail in his coffin."

"So to speak. He didn't want a coffin."

"Right. Look, Lacy, I've found the truck."

"Which truck?"

"The truck Bannick was driving the day he killed Verno and Dunwoody in Biloxi. The truck that was spotted by the old man sitting on his porch in downtown Neely, Mississippi, when Bannick dropped the phones in the mailbox. That truck."

Lacy slowly said, "So?"

"So, it hasn't been checked for prints."

"Wait. I believe Darren tracked it down."

"Yes, sort of. It's a 2009 half-ton pickup, light gray in color, purchased by Bannick in 2012. He owned it for two years, used it in the Biloxi murders, then traded it in a month later. A man named Trager bought it from a used car lot, drove it two months until he was hit by a drunk driver. State Farm totaled the truck and gave a check to Trager, who signed over the title. State Farm sold it for scrap. This is all according to what you told me three weeks ago."

"Right, I remember now. Darren said it was a dead end."

"Well, not exactly. The truck was not sold for scrap, but for parts. I think I've found it in a salvage yard outside of Milton, just north of Pensacola. Do you have Google Maps?"

"Sure."

"Okay, I'll send you the link for Dusty's Salvage outside of Milton. It buys wrecks from insurance companies, sells off the parts. Ninety acres of nothing but banged-up cars and trucks. I tracked down the adjuster who handled the Trager claim and he's pretty sure the truck went to Dusty's."

Expecting the worst, Lacy asked, "And what am I supposed to do?"

"Right. The three of us—you, me, Darren—are going to find the truck and have a look. If Bannick owned it for two years then there might be prints. He wouldn't wipe it down because he didn't know about his wayward thumb on Verno's phone. He sold it months before that."

"Ninety acres?"

"Come on, Lacy, this might be our big break. Sure, it's a needle in a haystack, but the needle is there."

"How long do prints last?"

"Years, depending on a bunch of factors— surface, weather, imprint, etc."

Lacy was not surprised that Jeri knew the ins and outs of fingerprints. "Let's just call the FBI."

"Gee, I've never heard that before. We'll call them later. Let's find the truck first, then decide what to do."

The impulse was to tell Jeri how swamped she was, how chaotic the office had become in her absence, and so on, but she knew any and all excuses would be blown off, completely ignored. Jeri had tracked down a serial killer the police had never heard of, and she had done so by being tenacious. Lacy simply wasn't up to an argument.

She frowned at Sadelle, who was dozing, and said, "We can't be there until four."

"Dusty closes at five. Hustle up. Don't wear a dress."

Ernie worked one end of the long front counter, and when they entered the parts department he was the only one of four "associates" who was not on the phone. Without a smile, he waved them over to his turf. The decor was dented hubcaps and old steering wheels, and behind the counter were tall rows of bins filled with used auto parts. One wall was an impressive rack of used car batteries. The place reeked of stale oil, and all four associates had at least two grease stains on their shirts. Ernie had his share, plus an oil rag hanging from a rear pocket. An unlit cigar was screwed into one side of his mouth. "Help you?" he growled. They were obviously out of place.

Lacy turned on the megawatt smile and said, "Yes, thank you. We're looking for a 2009 Chevrolet pickup truck."

"Got thousands here. Need to narrow it down, honey."

At another time, the "honey" would have sent her into orbit, but the moment was not right to set him straight.

"You lookin' for parts?"

"No, not exactly," she said, still all smiles.

"Look, ma'am, we sell parts, used parts, nothin' but parts. We got over a hundred thousand wrecks out there, more comin' in ever' day."

Lacy realized they were getting nowhere. She slid across a business card and said, "We're investigating allegations of wrongdoing. We work for the State of Florida."

"You a cop?" he asked, recoiling. Dusty's gave every indication of being the type of place where cash was king, taxes were routinely avoided, and all manner of criminal activity was just below the surface. Two other associates, both still on the phone, glanced over.

"No," Lacy said quickly. Jeri was admiring some hubcaps as Darren checked his phone. "Not at all. We just need to find this truck." She slid across a copy of the title Jeri had found online.

Ernie took it and gazed at the screen of his bulky, 1970s-style computer. It, too, with oil stains. He finger-pecked and frowned and shook his old keyboard. He finally mumbled, "Came in back in January. South lot, row eighty-four." He looked at Lacy and said, "Got it? Look, lady, we sell parts here. We don't give free tours, you know?"

A bit louder, she said, "Sure. I can always come back with a warrant."

It was apparent, from his startled reaction, that warrants were not welcome around Dusty's. Ernie nodded toward the back and said, "Follow me." He led them through a rear door. To one side was a long metal building with bays filled with cars and trucks in various stages of demolition. To the other side was a grand view of acres and acres of nothing but wrecked vehicles. He waved to his right and said, "Cars over there." He waved to his left and said, "Trucks and vans over there. South lot is that way, 'bout half a mile. Look for row eighty-four. With some luck you'll find it. We close at five and you don't want to get locked in here at night."

Darren pointed to a kid in a golf cart and asked Ernie, "Can we borrow that?"

"Ever'thang's for sale around here, boss. Ask Herman."

Without another word, Ernie turned and walked away. For $5, Herman would take them to row 84. They piled in the cart and were soon zipping past thousands of wrecked and gutted vehicles, most missing their hoods, all without tires, some with weeds growing through the windows. He stopped in front of a gray truck and they got out.

Lacy handed him another $5 bill and said, "Look, Herman, can you come back and get us at closing time?"

He grinned, took the money, grunted a response, and wheeled away.

The truck had been T-boned at the passenger's door and was well demolished, but the engine was intact and had already been scavenged. As they gawked at it, Lacy asked, "So what do we do now?"

"Let's take out some pistons," Darren said like a real smart-ass.

"Not exactly," Jeri said, "but you're on the right track. Think of things Bannick wouldn't touch, and the engine comes first. Now think of the things he would have touched. Steering wheel, dash, signal switch, gear shift, all the switches and buttons."

"And you brought your dusting powder?" Lacy said.

"No, but I do know how to find prints. Our backup plan is to get the FBI out here for a proper search. Right now I just want to look around."

"The glove box," Darren said.

"Yes, and under the seat, behind the seat. Think about your own car and all the crap that falls through the cracks. Gloves anyone?" She reached into her purse and removed plastic gloves. They dutifully put them on.

"I'm going in," Jeri said. "Darren, you check the back. Lacy, see if you can look behind the seat on the other side."

"Watch for snakes," Darren said, and the women almost shrieked.

Half the bench seat was crushed and mangled, and the passenger door was hanging by a thread. Lacy stepped through weeds and managed to get it open. Its side pocket was empty. She saw nothing of interest on the passenger's side. Jeri gently scraped glass from the driver's seat and sat at the wheel. She reached over and tried to open the glove box, but it was jammed tight.

Their first pass produced nothing. Jeri said, "We need to open the glove box. If we're in luck there's an owner's manual and assorted paperwork, same as in every car, right?"

Lacy asked, "What's an owner's manual?"

"Typical," mumbled Darren.

Lacy was suddenly hit with a memory and her knees went weak. She gasped and bent over, hands on knees, trying to breathe.

"Are you okay?" Jeri asked, touching her shoulder.

"No. Sorry. Just give me a moment."

Darren looked at Jeri and said, "It's her car wreck, the one where Hugo was killed. Not that long ago."

Jeri said, "I'm so sorry, Lacy. I just wasn't thinking."

She stood and took a deep breath.

"We should've brought some water," Jeri said. "I'm sorry."

"It's okay. I'm fine now. Let's get out of here

and report this to the FBI. They can handle the search."

Jeri said, "Okay, but first I want to see what's in that glove box."

Parked five feet away was a large Ford with a crushed roof. Darren poked around it and found a torn piece of the left door rocker panel. He twisted it free and eased into the seat of the gray Chevy truck. He jammed his new tool into the damaged glove box but it would not open. He pried, shoved, dug, jammed again and again, but its door would not open. The glove box was partially crushed and locked tight.

"I thought you were stronger than that," Lacy observed as she and Jeri watched every move.

Darren glared at her, took a deep breath, wiped his forehead, and attacked the glove box again. He finally pried open a narrow gap and managed to snap off the door.

He grinned at Lacy and Jeri and tossed his tool into the weeds. He pulled his gloves tight, then slowly removed a plastic bifold; a brochure for tire warranties; a receipt for an oil change, charged to a Mr. Robert Trager; a AAA solicitation of some variety; and two rusted screwdrivers.

He handed the bifold to Jeri and got out of the truck. The three of them stared at their loot. "Should we open it?" Lacy asked.

Jeri held it with both hands and said, "Odds are Bannick touched this at some time. Odds are he didn't wipe it down, couldn't have really, at least not in the past month when he was scrubbing everything else."

Lacy said, "Let's play it safe and take it to the FBI."

"Yes, absolutely. But let's have a peek first." She slowly opened the bifold and removed the owner's manual. Stuffed inside it were extended warranty papers, an old Florida registration card issued to Robert Trager, and two receipts from an auto parts store.

A card fell out and floated to the ground. Lacy picked it up, read it, smiled, and said, "Bingo."

It was a State Farm insurance card issued to Waveland Shores, one of Bannick's fronts. It covered the six-month period from January to July of 2013, and listed the policy number, limits of coverage, VIN, and agent's name. On the back side were instructions on what to do in case of an accident. She showed it to Jeri and Darren, who were afraid to touch it, then placed it back in the owner's manual.

Jeri said, "I like our odds right now."

"I'm calling Clay Vidovich," Lacy said as she pulled out her phone.

They hiked for ten minutes until they saw Herman in his golf cart. He drove them to the front where they checked in with Ernie, who, of course, wanted $10 for the owner's manual. Lacy bargained him down to $5, to be covered by the taxpayers of Florida, and they left Dusty's.

An hour later, they were in downtown Pensacola having a soda in the conference room with Vidovich and Agents Neff and Suarez. As they detailed their adventure, two technicians were poring over the manual, insurance card, and other items from the glove box.

Vidovich was saying, "Yes, we're heading out in the morning, flight's at eight. We'll get back to Washington in the afternoon. Thanks to you, Jeri, it's been a rather productive trip, wouldn't you say?"

"It's a mixed bag," she said without a smile. "We found our man, but he got away, on his own terms."

"The killings have stopped, and that's not always the case. We can close this one, but we have others."

"How many, if I may be so bold to inquire?" Darren asked.

Vidovich looked at Neff, who shrugged as if she couldn't say.

"About a dozen, of all varieties."

"Anyone like Bannick?" Lacy asked.

He smiled and shook his head. "Not that we know of, and we don't pretend to know them all. Most of these guys kill at random and never know their victims. Bannick was certainly different. He had a list and he stalked them for years. We would have never found him, Jeri, without you."

The door opened; a technician walked in and said, "We have two very good thumb prints, both from the insurance card. I just sent them to the lab at Clarksburg."

He left and Vidovich followed him out.

Suarez said, "They'll give them priority and ram them through the data banks. We can check millions of prints in a matter of minutes."

"Pretty amazing," Darren said.

"It is."

Lacy asked, "So, if there's a match, what happens?"

"Not much," Neff said. "We'll know for sure that Bannick killed Verno and Dunwoody, but it will be impossible to pursue the case."

"If he were alive?"

"Still a tough one. I wouldn't want to be the prosecutor."

"What about the other murders?" Jeri asked.

Suarez said, "Not much we can do, really. I'm sure we'll meet with the local police and pass along the news. They'll meet with the families, if the families are up to it. Some will want to talk, others will not. What about your family?"

Jeri said, "Oh, I'm sure I'll tell them at some point."

The conversation waned as they waited. Darren went to the men's room. Lacy freshened the soft drinks.

Vidovich returned with a smile and said, "We have a clear match. Congratulations. It can now be

proven that Judge Bannick did indeed kill Lanny
Verno and Mike Dunwoody. At this point, folks,
that's the best we can hope for."

Lacy said, "I need a drink."

Vidovich said, "Well, I was thinking about
a drink followed by a long, celebratory dinner.
Courtesy of the FBI."

Jeri nodded her approval as she wiped tears.

46

Two weeks later, Lacy and Allie flew to Miami, rented a car, and made a leisurely drive down Highway 1, south through Key Largo to Islamorada, where they stopped for a long lunch on a patio at the water's edge. They continued on, passed through Marathon, then stopped when the highway ended in Key West. They checked into the Pier House Resort and got a room on the ocean. They splashed in the water, walked through the sand, lounged on the beach, and had a cocktail watching a beautiful sunset.

The following day, a Saturday, they left Key West, drove an hour to Marathon, and found the Kronke home in Grassy Key, a plush, gated community on the water. Their appointment was for 10:00 a.m. and they arrived a few minutes early. Jane Kronke greeted them warmly and led them to the patio where her two sons, Roger and Guff, were waiting. They had driven down from Miami the day before. Minutes later, Chief Turnbull of the Marathon Police arrived. Allie excused himself and took his coffee to the front of the house.

After the obligatory round of chitchat, Lacy said, "This won't take long. As I said on the phone, I'm the interim director of the Board on Judicial Conduct and it is our duty to investigate complaints of misconduct filed against state court judges. Back in March, we met with a woman whose father was murdered in 1992, and she claimed she had learned the identity of his killer. She filed a formal complaint and we were required by state law to get involved. She alleged that the suspect, a sitting judge, was responsible for the murders of Mr. Kronke, as well as two men in Biloxi, Mississippi. We don't normally investigate murders, but we had no choice. A colleague and I came here to Marathon in March and met with the chief, who was most cooperative. We got nowhere, really, because, as you well know, evidence has been hard to come by. We eventually contacted the FBI and welcomed its Behavioral Analysis Unit, the elite team that goes after serial killers."

She paused and took a sip of lemonade. They were hanging on every word and seemed thoroughly overwhelmed. She almost felt sorry for them.

"The judge in question is Ross Bannick, from the Pensacola district. We suspect he was responsible for at least ten murders over the past twenty years, including Mr. Kronke. Three weeks ago, he committed suicide in an addiction treatment facility near Santa Fe. A thumb print links him to the two killings in Biloxi, but there is still no evidence that he killed Mr. Kronke. All we have is motive and method."

Jane Kronke wiped her eyes as Guff patted her arm.

"What's the motive?" Roger asked.

"It goes back to 1989 when Bannick worked in your father's firm as a summer intern. For reasons unknown, he was not offered an associate's position upon graduation. Your father supervised the interns that year and wrote Bannick the letter denying him a job. Evidently, he took it hard."

"And he waited twenty-three years to kill him?" Guff asked.

"He did. He was very patient, very calculating. He knew all of his victims, and he stalked them until the right moment. We'll never know the details because Bannick destroyed everything before he killed himself. Records, notes, hard drives, everything. He knew the FBI was finally closing in. He was extremely thorough, quite brilliant actually. The FBI is impressed."

They absorbed this in disbelief and said nothing. After a long pause, Chief Turnbull said, "You mentioned method."

"They were all the same, with one exception. A

blow to the head, then strangulation with a rope. The same type of rope every time, secured with a seldom-used tie-off called the double clove hitch. It's sometimes used by sailors."

"His calling card."

"Yes, his calling card, which is not unusual. The FBI profilers believe he had no desire to get caught but wanted someone to know of his work. They also believe he had some type of a death wish, thus the suicide."

"How'd he kill himself?" Roger asked.

"Drug overdose. We're not sure of the drug because there was no autopsy, at his instructions. One was not really needed. The FBI examined his thumbs and fingers, but they were too damaged to yield any prints."

"My father was killed by a judge?" Guff asked.

"That's what we believe, yes, but it will never be proven."

"And he will never be exposed?"

"The thumb print was left behind in the Biloxi murders. The sheriff there plans to meet with the victims' families and decide what to do. There is a chance they will release the information that the murders have been solved and that Bannick was the killer."

"I certainly hope so," Roger said.

"But no prosecution?" Guff asked.

"No. He's dead and I seriously doubt they will

try to convict him in absentia. The sheriff believes the families, at least one of them, will not want to pursue the matter. Any prosecution will be complicated, if not impossible, because Bannick will not be around to confront his accusers."

Jane Kronke gritted her teeth and said, "I don't know what to say. Are we supposed to be relieved, or angry, or what?"

Lacy shrugged and said, "I'm afraid I can't answer that."

Guff said, "But there will be no report, no news, nothing to let the public know that our father was killed by this guy. Right?"

"I can't control what you might say to a reporter, but, without more evidence, I'm not sure anything can be printed. It might be problematic to accuse a dead man with insufficient proof."

Another long pause as they struggled to make sense of it. Roger finally asked, "These other victims, who were they?"

"People from his past, people who had aggrieved him in some way. A law school professor, a lawyer who screwed him out of a fee, a couple of old girlfriends, a former client who filed a complaint, a reporter who exposed a shady land deal. A scoutmaster. We believe that Bannick was sexually abused by his scoutmaster when he was twelve or so. Maybe that's where it all started. We'll never know."

Guff shook his head in exasperation, stood, stuffed his hands in his pockets, and walked around the deck.

Jane asked, "If he was so brilliant, how did you catch him?"

"We didn't. The police didn't. Chief here can attest to the fact that there was almost no evidence left behind."

"So how?"

"Well, it's a long story, and an unbelievable one at that. I'll skip the details and cut to the chase. His second victim, or at least the man who we think was number two, was Bannick's professor at law school. He has a daughter who became obsessed with her father's murder. Eventually she became suspicious of Bannick, and she stalked him for twenty years. When she became convinced, and when she mustered the courage, she brought the case to us. We didn't want it, but we had no choice. It didn't take long to get the FBI involved."

"Please tell her we say thanks," Jane said.

"I will. She's quite remarkable."

"We'd like to meet her one day," Roger said.

"Maybe, who knows. But she is quite timid."

The chief said, "Well, she solved the case that we couldn't. Sounds like the FBI should hire her."

"They would love to. Look, I'm sorry to deliver this news, but I thought you would want to know. You have my phone number if you have any questions."

Guff said, "Oh, I'm sure we'll have a thousand questions."

"Anytime, but I can't promise all the answers."

Lacy was ready to go. They thanked her again and again, and walked her to the car where Allie was waiting.

Late in the afternoon, the resort was hopping with music from the bars, a rowdy volleyball game in the sand, kids splashing in the pool. A reggae band tuned up under some palm trees. Sailboats crisscrossed the crystal blue water in the distance.

Lacy had enough of the sun and wanted to go for a walk. At the point, they happened upon a wedding being organized around a small chapel on the sand. Guests were arriving and sipping champagne.

"What a lovely chapel," she said. "Not a bad place for a wedding."

"It's nice," Allie said.

"I have it reserved for September the twenty-seventh. Are you busy that day?"

"Uh, well, I don't know. Why?"

"You can be so slow at times. That's the day we're getting married. Right here. I've already paid the deposit."

He took her hand and pulled her closer. "What about the proposal and all that?"

"I just proposed. Evidently, you couldn't do it. And I'll take that ring now."

He laughed and kissed her. "Why don't you just go ahead and buy one yourself since you're taking charge?"

"I've thought about it, but that's left for you. And I like oval diamonds."

"Okay. I'll get right on it. Anything else I should know?"

"Yes. I picked that date because it gives us four months to wrap up our careers and begin our new life. I'm quitting. You're quitting. It's either me or the FBI."

"Do I have a choice?"

"No."

He laughed, kissed her again, and then laughed some more. "I'll stick with you."

"Good answer."

"And I'm sure the honeymoon is planned."

"It is. We're leaving for a month. We'll start on the Amalfi Coast in Italy, bum around there, take trains to Portofino, Nice, southern France, maybe end up in Paris. We'll play it by ear and decide as we go."

"I like it. And when we come back?"

"If we come back, then we'll figure out the next chapter."

A barefoot groomsman in Bermuda shorts, pink shirt, and bow tie walked over with two glasses of champagne and said, "Join the party. We need more guests."

They took the champagne, found seats in the back row, and felt right at home watching two complete strangers exchange vows.

Lacy was already taking notes on how she would do things differently.

AUTHOR'S NOTE

When last seen in **The Whistler,** Lacy Stoltz was recovering from injuries and struggling with her future. I've thought a lot about her since then and always wanted to bring her back for one more adventure. I could not, however, find a story that would equal such a dramatic success as her first, until I found a judge who's also a murderer.

You gotta love fiction.

As I point out in one of the few accurate parts of the book, every state has its own way of dealing with complaints against judges. In Florida, the Judicial Qualifications Commission has been doing a fine job since 1968. The Board on Judicial Conduct does not exist.

Many thanks to Mike Linden, Jim Lamb, Tim Heaphy, Lauren Powlovich, Neal Kassell, Mike Holleman, Nicholas Daniel, Bobby Moak, Wes Blank, and Talmage Boston.

John Grisham

ABOUT THE AUTHOR

JOHN GRISHAM is the author of thirty-seven novels, one work of nonfiction, a collection of stories, and seven novels for young readers.

jgrisham.com
Facebook: @JohnGrisham
Twitter: @JohnGrisham
Instagram: @johngrisham

LIKE WHAT YOU'VE READ?

Try these titles by John Grisham,
also available in large print:

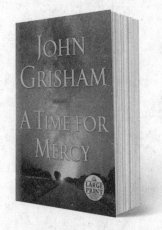

A Time for Mercy
ISBN 978-0-593-16859-2

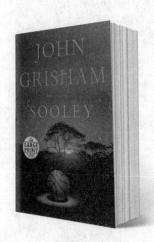

Sooley
ISBN 978-0-593-45931-7

Camino Winds
ISBN 978-0-593-16861-5

For more information on large print titles, visit
www.penguinrandomhouse.com/large-print-format-books